lena's eyes were not serene when Stefan shut the door to his room behind him. They were shining with a light that nearly stopped him in the doorway.

He hurt *you.*

"Damon hurts everyone. He doesn't seem to be able to help it. But there was something weird about him today."

He's . . . Elena paused. She didn't know the right words. *Something inside him. Growing inside him. Like . . . cold fire, dark light,* she said finally. *But hidden. Fire that burns from the inside out.*

Stefan tried to match this up with anything he'd heard of and came up blank. He was still humiliated that Elena had seen what had happened. "All *I* know that's inside him is my blood. Along with that of half the girls in town."

Books by L. J. Smith

L. J. SMITH

THE VAMPIRE DIARIES

THE RETURN:
VOL. 1
NIGHTFALL

HARPER TEEN

An Imprint of HarperCollinsPublishers

HarperTeen is an imprint of HarperCollins Publishers.

The Vampire Diaries: The Return: Nightfall
www.harperteen.com

Produced by Alloy Entertainment
151 West 26th Street, New York, NY 10001
www.alloyentertainment.com

Library of Congress Cataloging-in-Publication Data
Smith, L. J. (Lisa J.)
    Nightfall / L.J. Smith. — 1st ed.
        p. cm. — (Vampire diaries: the return)
    Summary: After returning from the afterlife, Elena is forced to battle
an ancient evil when Stefan, her vampire boyfriend, goes missing.
    ISBN 978-0-06-172080-2
    [1. Supernatural—Fiction.   2. Interpersonal   relations—Fiction.
3. Vampires—Fiction.]   I. Title.
PZ7.S6537Nm   2009   2008055606
[Fic]—dc22   CIP
                                                    AC

Typography by Jennifer Heuer
            14   CG/RRDC   10

❖

First paperback edition, 2010

For Kathryn Jane Smith, my late mother, with much love

te-fan?

Elena was frustrated. She couldn't make the mind-word come out the way she wanted.

"Stefan," he coaxed, leaning on an elbow and looking at her with those eyes that always made her almost forget what she was trying to say. They shone like green spring leaves in the sunlight. "Stefan," he repeated. "Can *you* say it, lovely love?"

Elena looked back at him solemnly. He was so handsome that he broke her heart, with his pale, chiseled features and his dark hair falling carelessly across his forehead. She wanted to put into words all the feelings that were piled behind her clumsy tongue and stubborn mind. There was so much she needed to ask him . . . and to tell him. But the sounds wouldn't come yet. They tangled on her tongue. She couldn't even send it telepathically to him—it all came as fragmented images.

After all, it was only the seventh day of her new life.

Stefan told her that when she'd first woken up, first come back from the Other Side after her death as a vampire, she'd been able to walk and talk and do all sorts of things that she seemed to have forgotten now. He didn't know why she'd forgotten—he'd never known anyone who'd come back from death except vampires—which Elena had been, but certainly was no longer.

Stefan had also told her excitedly that she was learning like wildfire every day. New pictures, new thought-words. Even though sometimes it was easier to communicate than others, Stefan was sure she would be herself again someday soon. Then she would act like the teenager she really was. She would no longer be a young adult with a childlike mind, the way the spirits had clearly wanted her to be: growing, seeing the world with new eyes, the eyes of a child.

Elena thought that the spirits had been a little unfair. What if Stefan found someone in the meantime who could walk and talk—and write, even? Elena worried over this.

That was why, some nights ago, Stefan had woken up to find her gone from her bed. He had found her in the bathroom, poring anxiously over a newspaper, trying to make sense of the little squiggles that she knew were words she once recognized. The paper was dotted with the marks of her tears. The squiggles meant nothing to her.

"But why, love? You'll learn to read again. Why rush?"

That was before he saw the bits of pencil, broken from too hard a grip, and the carefully hoarded paper napkins. She had been using them to try to imitate the words. Maybe if she could write like other people, Stefan would stop sleeping in his chair and would hold her on the big bed. He wouldn't go looking for someone older or smarter. He would *know* she was a grown-up.

She saw Stefan put this together slowly in his mind, and she saw the tears come to his eyes. He had been brought up to think he was never allowed to cry no matter what happened. But he had turned his back on her and breathed slowly and deeply for what seemed like a very long time.

And then he had picked her up, taken her to the bed in his room, and looked into her eyes and said, "Elena, tell me what you want me to do. Even if it's impossible, I'll do it. I swear it. Tell me."

All the words she wanted to think to him were still jammed up inside her. Her own eyes spilled tears, which Stefan dabbed off with his fingers, as if he could ruin a priceless painting by touching it too roughly.

Then Elena turned her face up, and shut her eyes, and pursed her lips slightly. She wanted a kiss. But . . .

"You're just a child in your mind now," Stefan agonized. "How can I take advantage of you?"

There was a sign language they had had, back in her old life, which Elena still remembered. She would tap under her chin, just where it was softest: once, twice, three times.

It meant she felt uncomfortable, inside. As if she were too full in her throat. It meant she wanted . . .

Stefan groaned.

"I *can't*. . . ."

Tap, tap, tap . . .

"You're not back to your old self yet. . . ."

Tap, tap, tap . . .

"Listen to me, love. . . ."

TAP! TAP! TAP! She gazed at him with pleading eyes. If she could have spoken, she would have said, *Please, give me some credit—I'm not totally stupid. Please,* listen *to what I can't say to you.*

"You hurt. You're really hurting," Stefan had interpreted, with something like dazed resignation. "I—if I—if I only take a little . . ."

And then suddenly Stefan's fingers had been cool and sure, moving her head, lifting it, turning it at just *this* angle, and then she had felt the twin bites, which convinced her more than anything she was alive and not a spirit anymore.

And *then* she had been very sure that Stefan loved her and no one else, and she could tell Stefan some of the things she wanted to. But she had to tell them in little exclamations—not of pain—with stars and comets and streaks of light falling around her. And Stefan had been the one who had not been able to think a single word to her. Stefan was the one struck mute.

Elena felt that was only fair. After that, he held her at night and she was always happy.

amon Salvatore was lounging in midair, nominally supported by one branch of a . . . who knew the names of trees anyway? Who gave a damn? It was tall, it allowed him to peep into Caroline Forbes's third-story bedroom, and it made a comfy backrest. He lay back in the convenient tree fork, hands clasped together behind his head, one neatly booted leg dangling over thirty feet of empty space. He was comfortable as a cat, eyes half-closed as he watched.

He was waiting for the magic moment of 4:44 A.M. to arrive, when Caroline would perform her bizarre ritual. He'd already seen it twice and he was enthralled.

Then he got a mosquito bite.

Which was ridiculous because mosquitoes didn't prey on vampires. Their blood wasn't nutritious like human blood. But it certainly felt like a tiny mosquito bite on the back of his neck.

He swiveled to see behind him, feeling the balmy summer night all around him—and saw nothing.

The needles of some conifer. Nothing flying about. Nothing crawling on them.

All right then. It must have been a conifer needle. But it certainly did hurt. And the pain got worse with time, not better.

A suicidal bee? Damon felt the back of his neck carefully. No venom sack, no stinger. Just a tiny squishy lump that hurt.

A moment later his attention was called back to the window.

He wasn't sure exactly what was going on but he could feel the sudden buzzing of Power around the sleeping Caroline, like a high-tension wire. Several days ago, it had drawn him to this place, but once he'd arrived he couldn't seem to find the source.

The clock ticked 4:40 and beeped an alarm. Caroline woke and swatted it across the room.

Lucky girl, Damon thought, with wicked appreciation. If I were a rogue human instead of a vampire, then your virtue—presuming you've any left—might be in danger. Fortunately for you, I had to give up all that sort of thing nearly half a millennium ago.

Damon flashed a smile at nothing in particular, held it for a twentieth of a second, and then turned it off, his black eyes going cold. He looked back into the open window.

Yes . . . he'd always felt that his idiot younger brother Stefan didn't appreciate Caroline Forbes enough. There was no doubt that the girl was worth looking at: long, golden-brown limbs, a shapely body, and bronze-colored hair that fell around her face in waves. And then there was her mind. Naturally skewed, vengeful, spiteful. Delicious. For instance, if he wasn't mistaken, she was working with little voodoo dolls on her desk in there.

Terrific.

Damon liked to see the creative arts at work.

The alien Power still buzzed, and still he couldn't get a fix on it. Was it inside—in the *girl*? Surely not.

Caroline was hastily grabbing for what looked like a handful of silken green cobwebs. She stripped her T-shirt off and—almost too fast for the vampire eye to see—had herself dressed in lingerie that made her look like a jungle princess. She stared intently at her own reflection in a stand-alone full-length mirror.

Now, what *can* you be waiting for, little girl? Damon wondered.

Well—he might as well keep a low profile. There was a dark flutter, one ebony feather fell to the ground, and then there was nothing but an exceptionally large crow sitting in the tree.

Damon watched intently from one bright bird-eye as Caroline moved forward suddenly as if she'd gotten an electric jolt, lips parted, her gaze on what seemed to be her own reflection.

Then she smiled at it in greeting.

Damon could pinpoint the source of Power now. It was inside the mirror. Not in the same *dimension* as the mirror, certainly, but contained inside it.

Caroline was behaving—oddly. She tossed back her long bronze hair so that it fell in magnificent disarray down her back; she wet her lips and smiled as if at a lover. When she spoke, Damon could hear her quite clearly.

"Thank you. But you're late today."

There was still no one but her in the bedroom, and Damon could hear no answer. But the lips of the Caroline in the mirror were not moving in synch with the real girl's lips.

Bravo! he thought, always willing to appreciate a new trick on humans. Well done, whoever you are!

Lip-reading the mirror girl's words, he caught something about *sorry*. And *lovely*.

Damon cocked his head.

Caroline's reflection was saying, ". . . you don't *have* to . . . after today."

The real Caroline answered huskily. "But what if I can't fool them?"

And the reflection: ". . . have help. Don't worry, rest easy . . ."

"Okay. And nobody will get, like, *fatally* hurt, right? I mean, we're not talking about death—for *humans*."

The reflection: "Why should we . . . ?"

Damon smiled inwardly. How many times had he heard exchanges like *that* before? As a spider himself, he knew: First you got your fly into the parlor; then you reassured her; and before she knew it, you could have anything from her, until you didn't *need* her any longer.

And then—his black eyes glittered—it was time for a new fly.

Now Caroline's hands were writhing in her lap. "Just as long as you really—you know. What you promised. You really mean it about loving me?"

". . . trust me. I'll take care of you—and your enemies, too. I've already begun . . ."

Suddenly Caroline stretched, and it was a stretch that boys at Robert E. Lee High School would have paid to watch. "That's what I want to see," she said. "I'm just *so* sick of hearing about Elena this, Stefan that . . . and now it's going to start all over."

Caroline broke off abruptly, as if someone had hung up on her on the phone and she'd only just realized it. For a moment her eyes narrowed and her lips thinned. Then, slowly, she relaxed. Her eyes remained on the mirror, and one hand lifted until it was resting lightly on her stomach. She stared at it and slowly her features seemed to soften, to melt into an expression of apprehension and anxiety.

But Damon hadn't taken his eyes off the mirror for an instant. Normal mirror, normal mirror, normal mirror—*là era*! Just at the last moment, as Caroline turned away, a flash of red.

Flames?

Now, what *could* be going on? he thought lazily, fluttering as he transformed from a sleek crow back into a drop-dead gorgeous young man lounging in a high branch of the tree. Certainly the mirror-creature wasn't from around Fell's Church. But it sounded as if it meant to make trouble for his brother, and a fragile, beautiful smile touched Damon's lips for a second.

There was nothing he loved more than to watch self-righteous, sanctimonious, *I'm-better-than-you-cos-I-don't-drink-human-blood* Stefan get in trouble.

The teenagers of Fell's Church—and some of the adults—regarded the tale of Stefan Salvatore and their local beauty Elena Gilbert as a modern Romeo-and-Juliet story. She had given her life to save his when they'd both been captured by a maniac, and afterward he had died of a broken heart. There were even whispers that Stefan had been not *quite* human . . . but something else. A demon lover that Elena had died to redeem.

Damon knew the truth. Stefan was dead all right—but he had been dead for hundreds of years. And it was true that he was a vampire, but calling him a demon was like calling Tinkerbell armed and dangerous.

Meanwhile Caroline couldn't seem to stop talking to an empty room.

"Just you wait," she whispered, walking over to the piles of untidy papers and books that littered her desk.

She rummaged through the papers until she found a miniature video camera that had a green light shining at her like a single unblinking eye. Delicately, she connected the camera to her computer and began typing a password.

Damon's eyesight was much better than a human's, and he could clearly see the tanned fingers with the long shining bronze nails: CFRULES. Caroline Forbes rules, he thought. Pitiful.

Then she turned around, and Damon saw tears well up in her eyes. The next moment, unexpectedly, she was sobbing.

She sat heavily on the bed, weeping and rocking herself back and forth, occasionally striking the mattress with a clenched fist. But mainly she just sobbed and sobbed.

Damon was startled. But then custom took over and he

murmured, "Caroline? Caroline, may I come in?"

"What? Who?" She looked around frantically.

"It's Damon. May I come in?" he asked, his voice dripping with mock sympathy, simultaneously using mind control on her.

All vampires had such powers of control over mortals. How great the Power was depended on many things: the vampire's diet (human blood was by far the most potent), the strength of the victim's will, the relationship between the vampire and the victim, the fluctuation of day and night—and so many other things that even Damon didn't begin to understand. He only knew when he felt his own Power quicken, as it was quickening now.

And Caroline was waiting.

"I can come in?" he said in his most musical, most beguiling voice, at the same time crushing Caroline's strong will under one much stronger.

"Yes," she answered, wiping her eyes quickly, apparently seeing nothing unusual in his entrance by a third-story window. Their eyes locked. "Come in, Damon."

She had issued the necessary invitation for a vampire. With one graceful motion he swung himself over the sill. The interior of her room smelled like perfumes—and not subtle ones. He felt really quite savage now—it was surprising the way the bloodfever had come on so suddenly, so irresistibly. His upper canines had extended to about half again their size, and their edges were razor-sharp.

This was no time for conversation, for loitering around as he usually did. For a gourmet, half the pleasure was in the anticipation, sure, but right now he was in *need*. He drew strongly on his Power to control the human brain and gave Caroline a dazzling smile.

That was all it took.

Caroline had been moving toward him; now she stopped. Her lips, partly open to ask a question, remained parted; and her pupils suddenly widened as if she were in a dark room, and then contracted and remained contracted.

"I . . . I . . ." she managed. "Ohhh . . ."

There. She was his. And so easily, too.

His fangs were throbbing with a kind of pleasurable pain, a tender soreness beckoning him to strike as quickly as the lunge of a cobra, to sink his teeth to the hilt in an artery. He was hungry—no, *starving*—and his whole body was burning with the urge to drink as deeply as he liked. After all, there were others to choose from if he drained this vessel dry.

Carefully, never taking his eyes from hers, he lifted Caroline's head to expose her throat, with the sweet pulse throbbing in its hollow. It filled all his senses: the beating of her heart, the smell of the exotic blood just under the surface, dense and ripe and sweet. His head was spinning. He'd never been so excited, so eager—

So eager that it gave him pause. After all, one girl was as good as another, right? What was different about this time? What was *wrong* with him?

And then he knew.

I'll have my own mind back, thank you.

Suddenly Damon's intellect was icy cold; the sensual aura in which he'd been trapped frozen over instantly. He dropped Caroline's chin and stood very still.

He had almost fallen under the influence of the thing that was using Caroline. It had been trying to snare him into breaking his word to Elena.

And again, he could just barely sense a whisk of red in the mirror.

It was one of those creatures drawn to the nova of Power that Fell's Church had become—he knew that. It had been using him, spurring him on, trying to get him to drain Caroline dry. To take all her blood, to kill a human, something he hadn't done since meeting Elena.

Why?

Coldly furious, he centered himself, and then probed in all directions with his mind to find the parasite. It should still be here; the mirror was only a portal for it to travel small distances. And it had been controlling him— *him, Damon Salvatore*—so it had to be very close indeed.

Still, he could find nothing. That made him even angrier than before. Absently fingering the back of his neck, he sent a dark message:

I will warn you once, and once only. Stay away from ME!

He sent the thought out with a blast of Power that flashed like sheet lightning in his own senses. It ought to have knocked something dead nearby—from the roof, from the air, from a branch . . . maybe even from next door. From *somewhere*, a creature should have plummeted to the ground, and he should have been able to sense it.

But although Damon could feel clouds darkening above him in response to his mood, and the wind rubbing branches together outside, there was no falling body, no attempt at dying retaliation.

He could find nothing close enough to have entered his thoughts, and nothing at a distance could be that strong. Damon might amuse himself sometimes by pretending to be vain, but underneath he had a cool and logical ability to analyze himself. He was strong. He knew that. As long as he kept himself well nourished and free of weakening sentiment, there were few creatures that could stand against him—at least in this plane.

Two were right here in Fell's Church, a little mocking counterpoint in his mind said, but Damon shrugged that off disdainfully. Surely there could be no other vampire Elders nearby, or he would sense them. Ordinary vampires, yes, they were already flocking. But they were all too weak to enter *his* mind.

He was equally certain there was no creature within

range that could challenge him. He would have sensed it as he sensed the blazing ley lines of uncanny magical power that formed a nexus under Fell's Church.

He looked at Caroline again, still held motionless by the trance he'd put on her. She would come out of it gradually, none the worse for the experience—for what *he'd* done to her, at least.

He turned and, as gracefully as a panther, swung out of the window, onto the tree—and then dropped easily thirty feet to the ground.

2

Damon had to wait some hours for another opportunity to feed—there were too many girls in deep sleep—and he was furious. The hunger that the manipulative creature had roused in him was real, even if it hadn't succeeded in making him its puppet. He needed blood; and he needed it *soon*.

Only then would he think over the implications of Caroline's strange mirror-guest: that truly *demonic* demon lover who had handed her over to Damon to be killed, even while pretending to make a deal with her.

Nine A.M. saw him driving down the main street of the town, past an antique store, eateries, a shop for greeting cards.

Wait. There it was. A new store that sold sunglasses. He parked and got out of the car with an elegance of motion born of centuries of careless movement that wasted not

an erg of energy. Once again, Damon flashed the instantaneous smile, and then he turned it off, admiring himself in
the dark glass of the window. Yes, no matter how you look
at it, I am gorgeous, he thought absently.

The door had a bell that made a tinkling sound as he
entered. Inside was a plump and very pretty girl with
brown hair tied back and large blue eyes.

She had seen Damon and she was smiling shyly.

"Hi." And though he hadn't asked, she added, in a
voice that quavered, "I'm Page."

Damon gave her a long, unhurried look that ended in a
smile, slow and brilliant and complicit. "Hello, Page," he
said, drawing it out.

Page swallowed. "Can I help you?"

"Oh, yes," Damon said, holding her with his eyes, "I
think so."

He turned serious. "Did you know," he said, "that
you really belong as a chatelaine in a castle in the Middle
Ages?"

Page went white, then blushed furiously—and looked
all the better for it. "I—I always wished that I'd been born
back then. But how could you know that?"

Damon just smiled.

Elena looked at Stefan with wide eyes that were the dark
blue of lapis lazuli with a scattering of gold. He'd just told
her that she was going to have Visitors! In all the seven

days of her life, since she had returned from the afterlife, she had never—ever—had a Visitor.

First thing, right away, was to find out what a Visitor was.

Fifteen minutes after entering the sunglasses shop, Damon was walking down the sidewalk, wearing a brand-new pair of Ray-Bans and whistling.

Page was taking a little nap on the floor. Later, her boss would threaten to make her pay for the Ray-Bans herself. But right now she felt warm and deliriously happy—and she had a memory of ecstasy that she would never entirely forget.

Damon window-shopped, although not exactly the way a human would. A sweet old woman behind the counter of the greeting cards shop . . . no. A guy at the electronics shop . . . no.

But . . . something drew him back to the electronics shop. Such clever devices they were inventing these days. He had a strong urge to acquire a palm-sized video camera. Damon was used to following his urges and was not picky about donors in an emergency. Blood was blood, whatever vessel it came in. A few minutes after he'd been shown how to work the little toy, he was walking down the sidewalk with it in his pocket.

He was enjoying just walking, although his fangs were

aching again. Strange, he should be sated—but then, he'd had almost nothing yesterday. That must be why he still felt hungry; that and the Power he'd used on the damnable parasite in Caroline's room. But meanwhile he took pleasure in the way his muscles were working together smoothly and without effort, like a well-oiled machine, making every movement a delight.

He stretched once, for the pure animal enjoyment of it, and then stopped again to examine himself in the window of the antiques store. Slightly more disheveled, but otherwise as beautiful as ever. And he'd been right; the Ray-Bans looked wicked on him. The antiques store was owned, he knew, by a widow with a very pretty, very young niece.

It was dim and air-conditioned inside.

"Do you know," he asked the niece when she came to wait on him, "that you strike me as someone who would like to see a lot of foreign countries?"

Some time after Stefan explained to Elena that Visitors were her friends, her *good* friends, he wanted her to get dressed. Elena didn't understand why. It was hot. She had given in to wearing a Night Gown (for at least most of the night), but the daytime was even warmer, and she didn't have a Day Gown.

Besides, the clothes he was offering her—a pair of his

jeans rolled up at the hems and a polo shirt that would be much too big—were . . . wrong somehow. When she touched the shirt she got pictures of hundreds of women in small rooms, all using sewing machines in bad light, all working frantically.

"From a sweat shop?" Stefan said, startled, when she showed him the picture in her mind. *"These?"* He dropped the clothes on the floor of the closet hastily.

"What about this one?" Stefan handed her a different shirt.

Elena studied it soberly, held it to her cheek. No sweating, frantically sewing women.

"Okay?" Stefan said. But Elena had frozen. She went to the window and peered out.

"What's wrong?"

This time, she sent him only one picture. He recognized it immediately.

Damon.

Stefan felt a tightening in his chest. His older brother had been making Stefan's existence as miserable as possible for nearly half a millennium. Every time that Stefan had managed to get away from him, Damon had tracked him down, looking for . . . what? Revenge? Some final satisfaction? They had killed each other at the same instant, back in Renaissance Italy. Their fencing swords had pierced each other's hearts almost simultaneously, in a duel over a vampire girl. Things had only gone downhill from there.

But he's saved your life a few times, too, Stefan thought, suddenly discomfited. And you promised you'd watch out for each other, take care of each other. . . .

Stefan looked sharply at Elena. *She* was the one who'd made both of them take the same oath—when she was dying. Elena looked back with eyes that were limpid, deep blue pools of innocence.

In any case, he had to deal with Damon, who was now parking his Ferrari beside Stefan's Porsche in front of the boardinghouse.

"Stay in here and—and keep away from the window. *Please*," Stefan hastily told Elena. He dashed out of the room, shut the door, and almost ran down the steps.

He found Damon standing by the Ferrari, examining the dilapidated boardinghouse's exterior—first with sunglasses on, then with them off. Damon's expression said that it didn't make a great deal of difference whichever way you looked at it.

But that wasn't Stefan's first concern. It was Damon's aura and the variety of different scents lingering on him—which no human nose would ever be able to detect, much less untangle.

"What have you been *doing*?" Stefan said, too shocked for even a perfunctory greeting.

Damon gave him a 250-watt smile. "Antiquing," he said, and sighed. "Oh, and I did some shopping." He fingered a new leather belt, touched the pocket with the video camera, and pushed back his Ray-Bans. "Would you believe it, this little dust speck of a town has some pretty decent shopping. I like shopping."

"You like stealing, you mean. And that doesn't account for half of what I can smell on you. Are you dying or have you just gone crazy?" Sometimes, when a vampire had been poisoned or had succumbed to one of the few mysterious curses or illnesses that afflict their kind, they would feed feverishly, uncontrollably, on whatever—whomever—was at hand.

"Just hungry," Damon replied urbanely, still surveying the boardinghouse. "And what happened to basic civility, by the way? I drive all the way out here and do I get a 'Hello, Damon,' or 'Nice to see you, Damon'? No. Instead I hear 'What have you been doing, Damon?'" He gave the imitation a whining, mocking twist. "I wonder what Signore Marino would think of that, little brother?"

"Signore Marino," Stefan said through his teeth, wondering how Damon was able to get under his skin every time—today with a reference to their old tutor of etiquette and dancing—"has been dust for hundreds of years by now—as we should be, too. Which has nothing to do with this conversation, *brother*. I asked you what you were doing, and you know what I meant by it—you must have bled half the girls in town."

"Girls and women," Damon reproved, holding up a finger facetiously. "We must be politically correct, after all. And maybe you should be taking a closer look at your own diet. If you drank more, you might begin to fill out. Who knows?"

"If I drank more—?" There were a number of ways to finish this sentence, but no good ones. "What a pity," he said instead to the short, slim, and compact Damon, "that *you'll* never grow another millimeter taller however long you live. And now, why don't you tell me what you're doing here, after leaving so many messes in town for me to clean up—if I know you."

"I'm here because I want my leather jacket back," Damon said flatly.

"Why not just steal anoth—?" Stefan broke off as he suddenly found himself flying briefly backward and then pinned against the groaning boards of the boardinghouse wall, with Damon right in his face.

"I didn't steal these things, *boy*. I paid for them—in my own coin. Dreams, fantasies, and pleasure from beyond this world." Damon said the last words with emphasis, since he knew they would infuriate Stefan the most.

Stefan *was* infuriated—and in a dilemma. He knew Damon was curious about Elena. That was bad enough.

But right now he could also see a strange gleam in Damon's eyes. As if the pupils had, for a moment, reflected a flame. And whatever Damon had been doing today was abnormal. Stefan didn't know what was going on, but he knew just how Damon was going to finish this off.

"But a real vampire shouldn't pay," Damon was saying in his most taunting tones. "After all, we're so wicked that we ought to be dust. Isn't that right, little brother?" He held up the hand with the finger on which he wore the lapis lazuli ring that kept him from crumbling to dust in the golden afternoon sunlight. And then, as Stefan made a movement, Damon used that hand to pin Stefan's wrist to the wall.

Stefan feinted to the left and then lunged right to break Damon's hold on him. But Damon was fast as a snake— no, faster. Much faster than usual. Fast and strong with all the energy of the life force he'd absorbed.

"Damon, you . . ." Stefan was so angry that he briefly lost his hold on rational thought and tried to swipe Damon's legs out from under him.

"Yes, it's me, Damon," Damon said with jubilant venom. "And I don't pay if I don't feel like it; I just take. I *take* what I want, and I give nothing in return."

Stefan stared into those heated black-on-black eyes and again saw the tiny flicker of flame. He tried to think. Damon was always quick to attack, to take offense. But *not like this*. Stefan had known him long enough to know something was off; something was wrong. Damon seemed almost feverish. Stefan sent a small surge of Power toward his brother, like a radar sweep, trying to put his finger on what was different.

"Yes, I see you've got the idea, but you'll never get anywhere that way," Damon said wryly, and then suddenly Stefan's insides, his entire body was on fire, was in agony, as Damon lashed out with a violent whip of his own Power.

And now, however bad the pain was, Stefan had to be coldly rational; he had to keep *thinking*, not just reacting. He made a small movement, twisting his neck to the side, looking toward the door of the boardinghouse. If only Elena would stay inside . . .

But it was hard to think with Damon still whiplashing him. He was breathing fast and hard.

"That's right," Damon said. "We vampires *take*—a lesson you need to learn."

"Damon, we're supposed to take care of each other— we promised—"

"Yes, and I'm going to take care of *you* right now."

Then Damon bit him.

And Damon bled him.

It was even more painful than the lashings of Power, and Stefan held himself carefully still for it, refusing to put up a struggle. The razor-sharp teeth shouldn't have hurt as they plunged into his carotid, but Damon was holding him at an angle—now by his hair—deliberately so that they did.

Then came the real pain. The agony of having blood drawn out against your will, against your resistance. That was a torture that humans compared with having their souls ripped out from their living bodies. They would do anything to avoid it. All Stefan knew was that it was one of the greatest *physical* anguishes that he had ever had to endure, and that at last tears formed in his eyes and rolled down his temples and down into his wavy dark hair.

Worse, for a vampire, was the humiliation of having another vampire treat you like a human, treat you like *meat*. Stefan's heart was pounding in his ears as he writhed under the double carving knives of Damon's canines, trying to bear the mortification of being used this way. At least—thank God—Elena had listened to him and stayed in his room.

He was beginning to wonder if Damon had truly gone insane and meant to kill him when—at last—with a shove that sent him off balance, Damon released him. Stefan tripped and fell, rolled, and looked up, only to find Damon standing over him again. He pressed his fingers to the torn flesh on his neck.

"And now," Damon said coldly, "you will go up and get me my jacket."

Stefan got up slowly. He knew Damon must be savoring this: Stefan's humiliation, Stefan's neat clothes wrinkled and covered with torn blades of grass and mud from Mrs. Flowers' scraggly flower bed. He did his best to brush them off with one hand, the other still pressed to his neck.

"You're quiet," Damon remarked, standing by his Ferrari, running his tongue over his lips and gums, his eyes narrow with pleasure. "No snappy back talk? Not even a word? I think this is a lesson I should teach you more often."

Stefan was having trouble making his legs move. Well, that went about as well as could be expected, he thought as he turned back toward the boardinghouse. Then he stopped.

Elena was leaning out of the unshuttered window in his room, holding Damon's jacket. Her expression was very sober, suggesting she'd seen everything.

It was a shock for Stefan, but he suspected it was an even greater shock for Damon.

And then Elena whirled the jacket around once and threw it so that it made a direct landing at Damon's feet, wrapping around them.

To Stefan's astonishment, Damon went pale. He picked up the jacket as if he didn't really want to touch it. His eyes were on Elena the whole time. He got in his car.

"Good-bye, Damon. I can't say it's been a pleasure—"

Without a word, looking for all the world like a naughty

child who'd been whipped, Damon turned on the ignition.

"Just leave me alone," he said expressionlessly in a low voice.

He drove off in a cloud of dust and gravel.

Elena's eyes were not serene when Stefan shut the door to his room behind him. They were shining with a light that nearly stopped him in the doorway.

He hurt *you*.

"He hurts everyone. He doesn't seem to be able to help it. But there was something weird about him today. I don't know what. Right now, I don't care. But look at you, making sentences!"

He's . . . Elena paused, and for the first time since she'd first opened her eyes back in the glade where she had been resurrected, there was a frown-wrinkle on her forehead. She couldn't make a picture. She didn't know the right words. *Something inside him. Growing inside him. Like . . . cold fire, dark light,* she said finally. *But hidden. Fire that burns from the inside out.*

Stefan tried to match this up with anything he'd heard of and came up blank. He was still humiliated that Elena had seen what had happened. "All *I* know that's inside him is my blood. Along with that of half the girls in town."

Elena shut her eyes and shook her head slowly. Then, as if deciding not to go any further down that path, she patted the bed beside her.

Come, she ordered confidently, looking up. The gold in her eyes seemed especially lustrous. *Let me . . . unhurt . . . the pain.*

When Stefan didn't come immediately, she held out her arms. Stefan knew he shouldn't go to them, but he *was* hurt—especially in his pride.

He went to her and bent down to kiss her hair.

Later that day Caroline was sitting with Matt Honeycutt, Meredith Sulez, and Bonnie McCullough, all listening to Stefan on Bonnie's mobile phone.

"Late afternoon would be better," Stefan told Bonnie. "She takes a little nap after lunch—and anyway, it'll be cooler in a couple hours. I told Elena you'd be coming by, and she's excited to see you. But remember two things. First, it's only been seven days since she came back, and she's not quite . . . herself yet. I think she'll get over her—symptoms—in just a few days, but meanwhile don't be surprised by anything. And second, don't *say* anything about what you see here. Not to anyone."

"Stefan Salvatore!" Bonnie was scandalized and

offended. "After all we've been through together, you think we'd blab?"

"Not blab," Stefan's voice came back over the mobile, gently. But Bonnie was going on.

"We've stuck together through rogue vampires and the town's ghost, and werewolves, and Old Ones, and secret crypts, and serial killings and—and—*Damon*—and have we ever told people about them?" Bonnie said.

"I'm sorry," Stefan said. "I just meant that Elena won't be safe if any of you tells even one person. It would be all over the newspapers right away: GIRL RETURNS TO LIFE. And *then* what do we do?"

"I understand about that," Meredith said briefly, leaning in so that Stefan could see her. "You don't need to worry. Every one of us will vow not to tell *anyone*." Her dark eyes flicked momentarily toward Caroline and then away again.

"I *have* to ask you"—Stefan was making use of all his Renaissance training in politeness and chivalry, particularly considering that three of the four people watching him on the phone were female—"do you really have any way to enforce a vow?"

"Oh, I think so," Meredith said pleasantly, this time looking Caroline directly in the eyes. Caroline flushed, her bronzed cheeks and throat turning scarlet. "Let us work it out, and in the afternoon, we'll come over."

Bonnie, who was holding the phone, said, "Anybody have anything else to say?"

Matt had remained silent during most of the conversation. Now he shook his head, making his shock of fair hair fly. Then, as if he couldn't hold it back, he blurted, "Can we talk to Elena? Just to say hi? I mean—it's been a whole *week*." His tanned skin burned with a sunset glow almost as brightly as Caroline's had.

"I think you'd better just come over. You'll see why when you get here." Stefan hung up.

They were at Meredith's house, sitting around an old patio table in the backyard. "Well, we can at least take them some food," Bonnie suggested, rocketing up from her seat. "God knows what Mrs. Flowers makes for them to eat—or *if* she does." She made waving motions to the others as if to raise them from their chairs by levitation.

Matt started to obey, but Meredith remained seated. She said quietly, "We just made a promise to Stefan. There's the matter of the vow first. And the consequences."

"I know you're thinking about me," Caroline said. "Why don't you just say so?"

"All right," Meredith said, "I'm thinking about you. Why are you suddenly interested in Elena again? How can we be sure that you won't go spreading the news of this all around Fell's Church?"

"Why would I want to?"

"Attention. You'd love to be at the center of a crowd, giving them every juicy detail."

"Or revenge," Bonnie added, suddenly sitting down again. "Or jealousy. Or boredom. Or—"

"Okay," Matt interrupted. "I think that's enough with the reasons."

"Just one more thing," Meredith said quietly. "Why do you *care* so much about seeing her, Caroline? The two of you haven't gotten along in almost a year, ever since Stefan came to Fell's Church. We let you in on the call to Stefan, but after what he said—"

"If you really need a reason why I should care, after everything that happened a week ago, well . . . well, I would think you'd understand without being told!" Caroline fixed shining cat-green eyes on Meredith.

Meredith looked back with her best no-expression expression.

"All right!" Caroline said. "She killed him for me. Or had him called to Judgment, or whatever. That vampire, Klaus. And after being kidnapped and—and—and— *used*—like a toy—whenever Klaus wanted blood—or—" Her face twisted and her breathing hitched.

Bonnie felt sympathy, but she also was wary. Her intuition was aching, warning her. And she noticed that although Caroline spoke about Klaus, the vampire, she was strangely silent about her other kidnapper, Tyler

Smallwood, the werewolf. Maybe because Tyler had been her boyfriend until he and Klaus had held her hostage.

"I'm sorry," Meredith said in a quiet voice that *did* sound sorry. "So you want to thank Elena."

"*Yes*. I want to thank her." Caroline was breathing hard. "And I want to make sure that she's okay."

"Okay. But this oath covers quite a bit of time," Meredith continued calmly. "You may change your mind tomorrow, next week, a month from now . . . we haven't even thought about consequences."

"Look, we can't *threaten* Caroline," Matt said. "Not physically."

"Or get other people to threaten her," Bonnie said wistfully.

"No, we can't," Meredith said. "But for the short term—you're a sorority pledge this coming fall, aren't you, Caroline? I can always tell your prospective sorority sisters that you broke your solemn vow about somebody who is helpless to hurt you—who I'm sure doesn't *want* to hurt you. Somehow I don't think they'd care for you much after that."

Caroline's face flushed deeply again. "You wouldn't. You wouldn't go interfering with my college—"

Meredith cut her off with two words. "Try me."

Caroline seemed to wilt. "I never said I wouldn't take the vow, and I never said I wouldn't keep it. Just *try* me, why don't you? I—I've learned a few things this summer."

I should hope so. The words, although nobody said them aloud, seemed to hover over all of them. Caroline's hobby for the entire last year had been trying to find ways to hurt Stefan and Elena.

Bonnie shifted position. There was something—shadowed—behind what Caroline was saying. She didn't know how she knew; it was the sixth sense that she'd been born with. But maybe it just had to do with how much Caroline had changed, with what she had learned, Bonnie told herself.

Look how many times she'd asked Bonnie in the last week about Elena. Was she really all right? Could Caroline send flowers? Could Elena have visitors yet? When *would* she be all right? Caroline really had been a nuisance, although Bonnie didn't have the heart to tell her that. Everyone else was waiting just as anxiously to see how Elena was . . . after returning from the afterlife.

Meredith, who always had a pen and paper, was scribbling some words. Now she said, "How about this?" and they all leaned forward to look at the pad.

I swear not to tell <u>anyone</u> about any supernatu-
ral events relating to Stefan or Elena, unless given
specific permission to do so by Stefan or Elena. I

*will also help in the punishment of anyone who
breaks this vow, in a way to be determined by the
rest of the group. This vow is made in perpetuity,
with my blood as my witness.*

Matt was nodding his head. "'In perpetuity'—
perfect," he said. "It sounds just like what an attorney
would write."

What followed was not particularly attorney-like. Each
of the individuals around the table took the piece of paper,
read it aloud, and then solemnly signed it. Then they each
pricked a finger with a safety pin that Meredith had in her
purse and added a drop of blood beside their signatures,
with Bonnie shutting her eyes as she pricked herself.

"Now it's really binding," she said grimly, as one who
knows. "I wouldn't try to break this."

"I've had enough of blood for a long time," Matt said,
squeezing his finger and looking at it gloomily.

That was when it happened. Meredith's contract was
sitting in the center of the table so all could admire it
when, from a tall oak where the backyard met the forest,
a crow came swooping down. It landed on the table with a
raw-throated scream, causing Bonnie to scream, too. The
crow cocked an eye at the four humans, who were hastily pulling back their chairs to get out of its way. Then
it cocked its head the other way. It was the biggest crow
any of them had ever seen, and the sun stroked iridescent

rainbows from its plumage.

The crow seemed, for all the world, to be examining the contract. And then it did something so quickly that it made Bonnie dart behind Meredith, stumbling over her chair. It opened its wings, leaned forward, and pecked violently at the paper, seeming to aim at two specific spots.

And then it was gone, first fluttering, and then soaring off until it was a tiny black speck in the sun.

"It's ruined all our work," Bonnie cried, still safely behind Meredith.

"I don't think so," said Matt, who was closer to the table.

When they dared to move forward and look at the paper, Bonnie felt as if someone had thrown a blanket of ice around her back. Her heart began to pound.

Impossible as it seemed, the violent pecking was all red, as if the crow had retched up blood to color it. And the red marks, surprisingly delicate, looked exactly like an ornate letter:

And under that:

Elena is mine.

4

With the signed contract safely tucked in Bonnie's purse, they pulled up to the boardinghouse in which Stefan had taken up residence again. They looked for Mrs. Flowers but couldn't find her, as usual. So they walked up the narrowing steps with the worn carpet and splintering balustrade, hallooing as they came.

"Stefan! Elena! It's us!"

The door at the very top opened and Stefan's head came out. He looked—different somehow.

"Happier," Bonnie whispered wisely to Meredith.

"Is he?"

"*Of course.*" Bonnie was shocked. "He's got Elena back."

"Yes, he does. Just the way she was when they met,

I bet. You saw her in the woods." Meredith's voice was heavy with significance.

"But . . . that's . . . oh, no! She's *human* again!"

Matt looked down the stairs and hissed, "Will you two quit it? They're gonna hear us."

Bonnie was confused. Of course Stefan could hear them, but if you were going to worry about what Stefan heard you'd have to worry about what you *thought*, too— Stefan could always catch the shape of what you were thinking, if not the actual words.

"Boys!" hissed Bonnie. "I mean I know they're totally necessary and all, but sometimes they Just Don't Get It."

"Just wait till you try men," whispered Meredith, and Bonnie thought of Alaric Saltzman, the college student that Meredith was more or less engaged to.

"I could tell you a thing or two," Caroline added, examining her long, manicured nails with a world-weary look.

"But Bonnie doesn't need to know even one yet. She has plenty of time to learn," Meredith said, firmly in mothering mode. "Let's go inside."

"Sit down, sit down," Stefan was encouraging them as they entered, the perfect host. But nobody could sit down. All eyes were fixed on Elena.

She was sitting in lotus position in front of the room's only open window, with the fresh wind making her white nightgown billow. Her hair was true gold again, not the perilous white-gold it had become when Stefan had unintentionally turned into a vampire. She looked exactly the way Bonnie remembered her.

Except that she was floating three feet off the floor.

Stefan saw them all gawking.

"It's just something she does," he said almost apologetically. "She woke up the day after our fight with Klaus and started floating. I think gravity hasn't quite got a hold on her yet."

He turned back to Elena. "Look who's come to see you," he said enticingly.

Elena was looking. Her gold-flecked blue eyes were curious, and she was smiling, but there was no recognition as she looked from one visitor to another.

Bonnie had been holding her arms out.

"Elena?" she said. "It's *me*, Bonnie, remember? I was there when you came back. *I'm* sure glad to see *you*."

Stefan tried again. "Elena, remember? These are your friends, your good friends. This tall, dark-haired beauty is Meredith, and this fiery little pixie is Bonnie, and this guy with the all-American looks is Matt."

Something flickered in Elena's face, and Stefan repeated, "Matt."

"And what about me? Or am I invisible?" Caroline said from the doorway. She sounded good-humored enough, but Bonnie knew that it made Caroline grind her teeth just to see Stefan and Elena together and out of danger.

"You're right. I'm sorry," Stefan said, and he did something that no ordinary eighteen-year-old could have pulled off without looking like an idiot. He took Caroline's hand and kissed it as gracefully and unthinkingly as if he were some count from nearly half a millennium ago. Which, of course, was pretty much what he was, Bonnie thought.

Caroline looked slightly smug—Stefan had taken his time with the hand kiss. Now he said, "And last but not least, this tanned beauty here is Caroline." Then, very gently, in a voice that Bonnie had heard him use only a few times since she'd known him, he said, "Don't you remember them, love? They nearly died for you—and for me." Elena was floating easily, in a standing position now, bobbing like a swimmer trying to keep still.

"We did it because we care," Bonnie said, and she put her arms out again for a hug. "But we never expected to get you back, Elena." Her eyes filled. "You came back to us. Don't you *know* us?"

Elena floated down until she was directly in front of Bonnie.

There was still no sign of recognition on her face, but there was something else. There was a kind of limitless benediction and tranquility. Elena radiated a calming peace and an unconditional love that made Bonnie breathe in deeply and shut her eyes. She could feel it like sunshine on her face, like the ocean in her ears. After a moment Bonnie realized she was in danger of crying at the sheer feeling of *goodness*—a word that was almost never used these days. Some things still could be simply, untouchably *good*.

Elena was good.

And then, with a gentle touch on Bonnie's shoulder, Elena floated toward Caroline. She held out her arms.

Caroline looked flustered. A wave of scarlet swept up her neck. Bonnie saw it, but didn't understand it. They'd all had a chance to pick up on Elena's vibes. And Caroline and Elena *had* been close friends—until Stefan, their rivalry had been friendly. It was *good* of Elena to pick Caroline to hug first.

And then Elena went into the circle of Caroline's hastily raised arms and just as Caroline began to say "I've—" she kissed her full on the mouth. It wasn't just a peck, either. Elena wrapped her arms around Caroline's neck and hung on. For long moments Caroline stood deathly still as if in shock. Then she reared back and struggled, at first feebly, and then so violently that Elena was catapulted backward in the air, her eyes wide.

Stefan caught her like an infielder going for a pop fly.

"What the *hell*—?" Caroline was scrubbing at her mouth.

"Caroline!" Stefan's voice was filled with fierce protectiveness. "It doesn't mean anything like what you're thinking. It's got nothing to do with sex at all. She's just identifying you, learning who you are. She can do that now that she's come back to us."

"Prairie dogs," Meredith said in the cool, slightly distant voice she often used to bring down the temperature of a room. "Prairie dogs kiss when they meet. It does exactly what you said, Stefan, helps them identify specific individuals. . . ."

Caroline was far beyond Meredith's abilities to cool down, however. Scrubbing her mouth had been a bad idea; she had smeared scarlet lipstick all around it, so that she looked like something out of a *Bride of Dracula* movie. "Are you crazy? What do you think I am? Because some hamsters do it, that makes it okay?" She had flushed a mottled red, from her throat to the roots of her hair.

"Prairie dogs. Not hamsters."

"Oh, who gives a—" Caroline broke off, frantically fumbling in her purse until Stefan offered her a box of tissues. He had already dabbed the scarlet smears off Elena's mouth. Caroline rushed into the small bathroom attached to Stefan's attic bedroom and slammed the door hard.

Bonnie and Meredith caught each other's eye and let out their breaths simultaneously, convulsing with laughter. Bonnie did a lightning-quick imitation of Caroline's expression and frantic scrubbing, miming someone using handful after handful of tissues. Meredith gave a reproving shake of her head, but she and Stefan and Matt all had a case of the *mustn't-laugh* snickers. A lot of it was simply the release of tension—they had seen Elena alive again, after six long months without her—but they couldn't stop laughing.

Or at least they couldn't until a tissue box sailed out of the bathroom, nearly hitting Bonnie in the head—and they all realized that the slammed door had rebounded—and that there was a mirror in the bathroom. Bonnie caught Caroline's expression in the mirror and then met her full-on glare.

Yep, she'd seen them laughing at her.

The door closed again—this time, as if it had been kicked. Bonnie ducked her head and clutched at her short strawberry curls, wishing the floor would open up and swallow her.

"I'll apologize," she said after a gulp, trying to be adult about the situation. Then she looked up and realized that everyone else was more concerned about Elena, who was clearly upset by this rejection.

It's a good thing we made Caroline sign that oath in blood, Bonnie thought. And it's a good thing that you-know-who signed it, too. If there was one thing Damon would know about, it was consequences.

Even as she was thinking this, she joined the huddle around Elena. Stefan was trying to hold Elena; Elena was trying to go after Caroline; and Matt and Meredith were helping Stefan and telling Elena that it was okay.

When Bonnie joined them, Elena gave up trying to get to the bathroom. Her face was distressed, her blue eyes swimming with tears. Elena's serenity had been broken by hurt and regret—and underneath that, a surprisingly deep apprehension. Bonnie's intuition gave a twinge.

But she patted Elena's elbow, the only part of her that she could reach, and added her voice to the chorus: "You didn't know she'd get so upset. You didn't hurt her."

Crystal tears spilled down Elena's cheeks, and Stefan caught them with a tissue as if each one was priceless.

"She thinks that Caroline *is* hurt," Stefan said, "and she's worried about her—for some reason I don't get."

Bonnie realized that Elena could communicate after all—by mind-link. "I felt that, too," she said. "The hurt. But tell her—I mean—Elena, I *promise* I'll apologize. I'll grovel."

"It may take some groveling from all of us," Meredith said. "But meanwhile I want to make sure that this 'angel unaware' recognizes *me*."

With an expression of tranquil sophistication, she took Elena out of Stefan's arms and into her own, and then she kissed her.

Unfortunately, this coincided with Caroline stalking out of the bathroom. The bottom of her face was paler than the top, having been denuded of all makeup: lipstick, bronzer, blush, the works. She stopped dead and stared.

"I don't believe it," she said in scathing tones. "You're *still* doing it! It's dis—"

"Caroline." Stefan's voice was a warning.

"I came here to see Elena." Caroline—beautiful, lithe, bronze-limbed Caroline—was twisting her hands together as if in terrible conflict. "The *old* Elena. And what do I see? She's like a baby—she can't talk. She's like some smirking guru floating in the air. And now she's like some kind of perverted—"

"Don't finish that," Stefan said quietly but firmly. "I told you, she ought to be over the first symptoms in just a few days, to judge by her progress so far," he added.

And he *was* different, somehow, Bonnie thought. Not just happier to have gotten Elena back. He was . . . stronger somehow at the core of himself. Stefan had always been quiet inside; her powers sensed him as a pool of clear water. Now she saw that same clear water built up like a tsunami.

What could have changed Stefan so much?

The answer came to her immediately, although in the form of a wondering question. Elena was still part spirit— Bonnie's intuition told her that. What did it do if you drank the blood of someone who was in that state?

"Caroline, let's just drop it," she said. "I'm sorry, I'm really, really sorry for—you know. I was wrong, and I'm sorry."

"Oh, you're *sorry*. Oh, that makes everything all right

then, doesn't it?" Caroline's voice was pure acid, and she turned her back on Bonnie with finality. Bonnie was surprised to feel the sting of tears behind her eyes.

Elena and Meredith still had their arms around each other, their cheeks wet with the other's tears. They were looking at each other and Elena was beaming.

"Now she'll know you anywhere," Stefan told Meredith. "Not just your face, but—well, the inside of you, too, or the shape of it, at least. I should have mentioned that before this started, but I'm the only one she's 'met,' and I didn't realize—"

"*You should have realized!*" Caroline was pacing like a tiger.

"So you kissed a girl, so *what*?" Bonnie exploded. "What do you think, you're going to grow a beard now?"

As if powered by the conflict around her, Elena suddenly took off. All at once she was zipping around the room as if she'd been shot from a cannon; her hair crackled with electricity when she made sudden stops or turns. She soared around the room twice, and as she was silhouetted against the dusty old window, Bonnie thought, *Oh, my God! We've got to get her some* clothes! She looked at Meredith and saw that Meredith had shared her realization. Yes, they had to get Elena clothes—and most especially underclothes.

As Bonnie moved toward Elena, as shyly as if she'd never been kissed before, Caroline exploded.

"You just keep doing it and doing it and doing it!" She was practically screeching by now, Bonnie thought. "What's *wrong* with you? Don't you have any morals at all?"

This, unfortunately, caused another case of the *don't-laugh-don't-laugh* choked giggles in Bonnie and Meredith. Even Stefan turned away sharply, his gallantry toward a guest clearly fighting a losing battle.

Not just a guest, Bonnie thought, but a girl he'd gone *pret-ty* darn far with, as Caroline hadn't been shy about letting people know when she'd gotten her hands on him. About as far as vampires *could* go, Bonnie remembered, which was not the whole way. Something about the blood-sharing substituting for—well, for Doing It. But he wasn't the only one Caroline had bragged about. Caroline was infamous.

Bonnie glanced at Elena, saw that Elena was watching Caroline with a strange expression. Not as if Elena were afraid of her, but rather as if Elena were deeply worried *about* her.

"Are you all right?" Bonnie whispered. To her surprise, Elena nodded, then looked at Caroline and shook her head. She carefully looked Caroline up and down and her expression was that of a puzzled doctor examining a very sick patient.

Then she floated toward Caroline, one hand extended.

Caroline shied away, as if she were disgusted to have Elena touch her. No, not disgusted, Bonnie thought, but *frightened*.

"How do I know what she'll do next?" Caroline snapped, but Bonnie knew that wasn't the real reason for her fear. What do we have going on here? she wondered. Elena afraid *for* Caroline, and Caroline afraid *of* Elena. What does that equal?

Bonnie's psychic senses were giving her gooseflesh. There was something *wrong* with Caroline, she felt, something she'd never encountered before. And the air . . . it was thickening somehow, as if it were building up to a thunderstorm.

Caroline made a sharp turn to keep her face averted from Elena's. She moved behind a chair.

"Just keep her freakin' *away* from me, all right? I won't let her touch me again—" she began, when Meredith changed the whole situation with two quiet words.

"*What* did you say to me?" Caroline said, staring.

5

Damon was driving aimlessly when he saw the girl.

She was alone, walking down the side of the street, her titian hair blowing in the wind, her arms weighted down by packages.

Damon immediately did the chivalrous thing. He let the car glide to a stop, waited for the girl to take a few striding paces to catch up with him—*che gambe!*—and then jumped out and hastened to open the passenger side door for her.

Her name, as it turned out, was Damaris.

In moments the Ferrari was back on the road, going so fast that Damaris's titian hair was flowing behind her like a banner. She was a young woman who fully merited the kind of trance-inducing compliments he'd been handing out freely all day—which was a good thing, he thought laconically, because his imagination was very nearly drained dry.

But flattering this lovely creature, with her nimbus of red-gold hair and her pure, milky skin, wouldn't take any imagination at all. He didn't expect any trouble from her, and he planned to keep her overnight.

Veni, vidi, vici, Damon thought, and flashed a wicked smile into the middle distance. And then he amended— Well, perhaps I haven't conquered *yet*, but I'd bet my Ferrari on it.

They stopped by a "scenic view roundabout" and when Damaris had dropped her purse and bent to pick it up, he'd seen the nape of her neck, where those fine titian hairs were startlingly delicate against the whiteness of her skin.

He'd kissed it immediately, impulsively, finding it as soft as a baby's skin—and warm against his lips. He'd allowed her complete freedom of action, interested to see whether she would slap him, but instead she had just straightened up and taken a few shaky breaths before allowing him to take her in his arms to be kissed into a trembling, heated, uncertain creature, her dark blue eyes entreating and trying to resist at the same time.

"I—shouldn't have let you do that. I won't let you again. I want to go home now."

Damon smiled. His Ferrari was safe.

Her ultimate yielding would be particularly pleasant, he thought as they continued their drive. If she shaped up as well as she seemed to be doing, he might even keep her a few days, might even Change her.

Now, though, he was bothered by an inexplicable disquiet inside. It was Elena, of course. Being so close to her at the boardinghouse and not daring to demand to go to her, because of what he might do. Oh, hell, what I *should* have done already, he thought with a sudden vehemence. Stefan was right—there was something wrong with him today.

He was frustrated to a degree that he wouldn't have imagined possible. What he *should* have done was to have ground his little brother's face in the dirt, wrung his neck like a fowl, and then gone up those narrow tacky stairs to *take* Elena, willing or no. He hadn't done it before because of some syrupy nonsense, caring about her screaming and carrying on as he lifted that incomparable chin and buried his swollen, aching fangs in her lily-white throat.

There was a noise going on in the car. "—don't you think?" Damaris was saying.

Annoyed and too busy with his fantasy to go over what his mind might have heard of her speech, he shut her off, and she was instantly quiet. Damaris was lovely but *una stomata*—a ditz. Now she sat with her titian hair whipping in the wind, but with blank eyes, the pupils contracted, absolutely still.

And all for nothing. Damon made a hissing sound of exasperation. He couldn't get back into his daydream; even in silence, the imagined sounds of Elena's sobbing prevented him.

But there would be no more sobbing once he'd made her into a vampire, a little voice in his mind suggested. Damon cocked his head and leaned back, three fingers on the steering wheel. He'd once sought to make her his princess of darkness—why not again? She would belong to him utterly, and if he had to give up her mortal blood . . . well, he wasn't exactly getting any of that right now, was he? the insinuating voice said. Elena, pale and glowing with a vampire's aura of Power, her hair almost white-blond, a black gown against her satiny skin. Now there was a picture to make any vampire's heart beat faster.

He wanted her more than ever now that she had been a spirit. Even as a vampire she would retain most of her own nature, and he could just picture it: her light for his darkness, her soft whiteness in his hard, black-jacketed arms. He would stop that exquisite mouth with kisses, smother her with them—

What was he *thinking* about? Vampires didn't kiss like that for enjoyment—especially not other vampires. The blood, the hunt was all. Kissing beyond whatever was necessary to conquer their victim was pointless; it could lead nowhere. Only sentimental idiots like his brother bothered with such foolishness. A mated vampire pair might share the blood of a mortal victim, both striking at once, both controlling the victim's mind—and joined together in mind-link, too. That was how they found their pleasure.

Still, Damon found himself excited by the idea of kissing Elena, of forcing kisses on her, of feeling her desperation to get away from him suddenly pause—with the little hesitation that came just before response, before yielding herself completely to him.

Maybe I'm going crazy, Damon thought, intrigued. He had never gone crazy before that he could recall, and there was some appeal in the idea. It had been centuries since he'd felt this kind of excitement.

All the better for you, Damaris, he thought. He had reached the point where Sycamore Street cut briefly into the Old Wood, and the road there was winding and dangerous. Regardless, he found himself turning to Damaris to wake her again, noting with approval that her lips were naturally that soft cherry color, without lipstick. He kissed her lightly, then waited to gauge her response.

Pleasure. He could see her mind go soft and rosy with it.

He glanced at the road ahead and then tried it again,

this time holding the kiss. He was elated with her response, with both of their responses. This was amazing. It must have to do with the amount of blood he'd had, more than ever before in one day, or the combination—

He suddenly had to wrench his attention from Damaris to driving. Some small russet animal had appeared as if by magic on the road in front of him. Damon normally didn't go out of his way to run over rabbits, porcupines, and the like, but this one had annoyed him at a crucial moment. He grasped the steering wheel with both hands, his eyes black and cold as glacial ice in the depths of a cave, and headed straight for the russet thing.

Not all *that* small—there would be a bit of a bump.

"Hang on," he murmured to Damaris.

At the last instant, the reddish thing dodged. Damon wrenched the wheel round to follow it, and then found himself faced with a ditch. Only the superhuman reflexes of a vampire—and the finely tuned response of a very expensive vehicle—could have kept them out of the ditch. Fortunately Damon had both, swinging them in a tight circle, tires squealing and smoking in protest.

And no bump.

Damon leaped over the car door in one fluid motion and looked around. But whatever it was, had vanished completely, as mysteriously as it had appeared.

Sconosciuto. Weird.

He wished he wasn't heading into the sun; the bright afternoon light cut down his visual acuity severely. But he'd had a glimpse of the thing as it got close, and it had looked deformed. Pointed at one end and fan-like at the other.

Oh, well.

He turned back to the car, where Damaris was having hysterics. He wasn't in the mood to coddle anyone, so he simply put her back to sleep. She slumped back into the seat, tears left to dry on her cheeks unheeded.

Damon got back into the car feeling frustrated. But he knew now what he wanted to do today. He wanted to find a bar—either seedy and sleazy or immaculate and expensive—and he wanted to find another vampire. With Fell's Church being such a hot spot on the ley-line map, that shouldn't be difficult in the surrounding areas. Vampires and other creatures of darkness were drawn to hot spots like bumblebees to honeysuckle.

And then he wanted a fight. It would be completely unfair—Damon was the strongest vampire left that he knew of, plus he was tick-full of a cocktail of the blood of Fell's Church's finest maidens. He didn't care. He felt like taking his frustrations out on something, and—he flashed that inimitable, incandescent smile at nothing—some werewolf or vampire or ghoul was about to meet its *quietus*. Maybe more than one, if he were only lucky enough to find them. After which—delicious Damaris for dessert.

Life was good, after all. And unlife, thought Damon, his eyes glinting dangerously behind the sunglasses, was even better. He wasn't just going to sit and sulk because he couldn't have Elena immediately. He was going to go out and enjoy himself and get stronger—and then some-time soon, he was going to go over to his pathetic milksop of a younger brother's place and *take* her.

He happened to glance in the car's rearview mirror for a moment. By some freak of light or inversion of the atmo-sphere, it seemed that he could see his eyes behind his sunglasses—burning red.

6

"I said, *get out*," Meredith repeated to Caroline, still quietly. "You've said things that never should have been said in any civilized place. This happens to be Stefan's place—and, yes, it's his *place* to order you out, too. I'm doing it for him, though, because he never would ask a girl—and a former girlfriend, I might add—to get the hell out of his room."

Matt cleared his throat. He'd stepped back into a corner and everyone had forgotten about him. Now he said, "Caroline, I've known you way too long to be formal, and Meredith's right. You want to say the kind of things you've been saying about Elena, you do it somewhere far *away* from Elena. But, look, there's one thing I know. No matter what Elena did when she was—was down *here* before"— his voice dropped a little in wonder, and Bonnie knew that he meant, when Elena was here on Earth before—"she's as close to an angel *now* as you can get. Right now she's . . . she's . . . completely . . ." He hesitated, stumbling for the right words.

"Pure," Meredith said easily, filling in the blank for him.

"Yeah," Matt agreed. "Yeah, pure. Everything she does is pure. And it's not like any of your nasty words could stain her, anyway, but the rest of us just don't like hearing you try."

There was a low "Thank you" from Stefan.

"I was already going," Caroline said, now through her teeth. "And don't you *dare* preach at *me* about *purity*! Here, with all this going on! You probably just want to watch it going on yourself, two girls kissing. You probably—"

"Enough." Stefan said it almost expressionlessly, but Caroline was swept off her feet, up and out of the door, and deposited there by invisible hands. Her purse trailed after her.

Then the door quietly shut.

Fine hairs rose on the back of Bonnie's neck. This was Power, in such amounts that her psychic senses were stunned and temporarily paralyzed. Moving Caroline— and she wasn't a small girl—now that took *Power*.

Maybe Stefan had changed just as much as Elena had. Bonnie glanced at Elena, whose pool of serenity was rippling because of Caroline.

Might as well take her mind off it, and maybe make herself worthy of a *thank you* from Stefan, Bonnie thought.

She tapped Elena's knee, and when Elena turned, Bonnie kissed her.

Elena broke the kiss very quickly, as if afraid to set off some holocaust again. But Bonnie saw at once what Meredith had said about it not being sexual. It was . . . more like being examined by someone who used all her senses to the fullest. When Elena moved away from Bonnie she beamed at her just as she had at Meredith, all the distress washed away by—yes, the *purity* of the kiss. And Bonnie felt as if some of Elena's tranquility had soaked into her.

". . . should have known better than to bring Caroline," Matt was saying to Stefan. "Sorry about butting in. But I *know* Caroline, and she could have gone on ranting for another half hour, never actually leaving."

"Stefan took care of that," Meredith said, "or was that Elena, too?"

"It was me," Stefan said. "Matt had it right: she could keep on talking forever without actually leaving. And I'd just as lief nobody run Elena down like that in my hearing."

Why are they talking about those things? Bonnie wondered. Of all people, Meredith and Stefan were least inclined to chatter, but here they were, saying things that didn't really need to be said. Then she realized it was for Matt, who was moving slowly but with determination toward Elena.

Bonnie got up as quickly and as lithely as if she could fly, and managed to pass Matt without looking at him. And then she was joining Meredith and Stefan in small talk—well, medium-small talk—about what had just happened. Caroline made a bad enemy, everyone agreed, and nothing seemed to teach her that her schemes against Elena always backfired. Bonnie would bet that she was hatching a new scheme right now against all of them.

"She feels lonely all the time," Stefan said, as if trying to make excuses for her. "She wants to be accepted, by anyone, on any terms—but she feels—apart. As if nobody who really got to know her would trust her."

"She's defensive," Meredith agreed. "But you'd think she'd show *some* gratitude. After all, we did rescue her and save her life just over a week ago."

There was more to it than that, Bonnie thought. Her intuition was trying to tell her something—something about what might have happened *before* they had been able to rescue Caroline—but she was so angry on Elena's behalf that she ignored it.

"Why should anybody trust her?" she said to Stefan. She sneaked a peek behind her. Elena was definitely going to know Matt anywhere, and Matt looked as if he were fainting. "Caroline's beautiful, sure, but that's it. She never has a good word to say about anybody. She plays games all the time—and—and I *know* we used to do some of that, too . . . but hers are always meant to make other people look bad. Sure, she can take most *guys* in"—a sudden anxiety swept over her, and she spoke more loudly to try to push it away—"but if you're a girl she's just a pair of long legs and big—"

Bonnie stopped because Meredith and Stefan had frozen, with identical *Oh-God-not-again* expressions on their faces.

"And she also has very decent hearing," said a shaking, threatening voice from somewhere behind Bonnie. Bonnie's heart leaped into her throat.

That was what you got for ignoring premonitions.

"Caroline—" Meredith and Stefan were both trying for damage control, but it was too late. Caroline stalked in on her long legs as if she didn't want her feet to touch Stefan's floorboards. Oddly, though, she was carrying her high heels.

"I came back in to get my sunglasses," she said, still in that trembling voice. "And I heard enough to know now what my so-called 'friends' think of me."

"No, you didn't," Meredith said, as rapidly eloquent as Bonnie was stunned mute. "You heard some very angry people letting off steam after you'd just insulted them."

"Besides," Bonnie said, suddenly able to speak again, "admit it, Caroline—you *hoped* you'd hear something. That's why you took off your shoes. You were right behind the door, listening, weren't you?"

Stefan shut his eyes. "This is my fault. I should have—"

"No, you shouldn't," Meredith said to him, and to Caroline she added, "And if you can tell me one word we said that isn't true, or was exaggerated—except maybe for what Bonnie said, and Bonnie is . . . just being Bonnie. Anyway, if you can point to one word of what the rest of us said that isn't true, *I'll* beg your pardon."

Caroline wasn't listening. Caroline was twitching. She had a facial tic, and her lovely face was convulsed, dark red, with fury.

"Oh, you're *going* to beg my pardon all right," she said, wheeling to point her long-nailed forefinger at each of them. "You're *all* going to be sorry. And if you try that—that witchcraft-vampire type thing on me again," she said to Stefan, "I have friends—real friends—who'd like to know about it."

"Caroline, just this afternoon you signed a contract—"

"Oh, who gives a damn?"

Stefan stood up. It was dark now inside the small room with its dusty window, and Stefan's shadow was thrown before him by the bedside lamp. Bonnie looked at it and then poked Meredith, as the hairs tingled on her arms and neck. The shadow was surprisingly dark and surprisingly tall. Caroline's shadow was weak, transparent, and short—an imitation shadow beside Stefan's very real one.

The thunderstorm feeling was back. Bonnie was shaking now; trying not to, but unable to stop the shivering that had come on as if she had been thrown into icy water. It was a cold that had gotten directly into her bones and was ripping layer after layer of heat off them like some greedy giant, and now she was beginning to shake *hard*. . . .

Something was happening to Caroline in the darkness—something was coming from her—or coming *for* her—or maybe both. In any case, it was all around her now, and all around Bonnie, too, and the tension was so thick that Bonnie felt choked, her heart pounding. Beside her, Meredith—practical, level-headed Meredith—stirred uneasily.

"What—?" Meredith began in a whisper.

Suddenly, as if it had all been exquisitely choreographed by the things in the dark—the door to Stefan's room slammed shut . . . the lamp, an ordinary electric one, went off . . . the ancient rolled-up shutter over the window came rattling down, dropping the room into sudden and complete darkness.

And Caroline screamed. It was an awful sound—raw, as if it had been stripped like meat from Caroline's backbone and yanked out of her throat.

Bonnie screamed, too. She couldn't help it, although her scream sounded too faint and too breathless, like an echo, not the coloratura job that Caroline had done. Thank God that at least Caroline wasn't screaming any longer. Bonnie was able to stop the new scream building in her own throat, even though her shaking was worse than ever. Meredith had an arm around her tightly, but then, as the darkness and the silence went on and Bonnie's shaking only continued, Meredith got up and heartlessly passed her to Matt, who seemed astonished and embarrassed, but tried awkwardly to hold her.

"It's not as dark once your eyes get used to it," he said. His voice was creaky, as if he needed a drink of water. But it was the best thing that he could have said, because of all things in the world to fear, Bonnie was most afraid of the dark. There were *things* in it, things that only she saw. She managed, despite the terrible shaking, to stand with his support—and then she gasped, and heard Matt gasp, too.

Elena was glowing. Not only that, but the glow extended out behind her and far to either side of her in a pair of what were beautifully defined, and undeniably *there* . . . wings.

"She h-has wings," Bonnie whispered, the stutter caused by her shaking rather than by awe or fear. Matt was clinging to *her* now, like a child; he obviously couldn't answer.

The wings moved with Elena's breathing. She was sitting on thin air, steady now, one hand held out with her fingers all spread in a gesture of denial.

Elena spoke. It wasn't any language that Bonnie had heard before; she doubted it was any language people on Earth used. The words were sharp, thin-edged, like the splintering of myriad shards of crystal that had fallen from somewhere very high and very far away.

The shape of the words *almost* made sense in Bonnie's head as her own psychic abilities were sparked by Elena's tremendous Power. It was a Power that stood tall against the darkness and now was sweeping it aside . . . making the things in the dark scamper away before it, their claws scritching in all directions. Ice-sharp words followed them all the way, dismissive now. . . .

And Elena . . . Elena was as heartbreakingly beautiful as when she'd been a vampire, and seemed almost as pale as one.

But Caroline was shouting, too. She was using powerful words of Black Magic, and to Bonnie it was as if the shadows of all sorts of dark and horrible things were coming from her mouth: lizards and snakes and many-legged spiders.

It was a duel, a face-off of magic. Only how had Caroline learned so much dark magic? She wasn't even a witch by lineage, like Bonnie.

Outside Stefan's room, surrounding it, was a strange sound, almost like a helicopter. *Whipwhipwhipwhipwhip* ... It terrified Bonnie.

But she had to do something. She was Celtic by heritage and psychic because she couldn't avoid it, and she had to help Elena. Slowly, as if making her way against gale-force winds, Bonnie stumbled to put her hand on Elena's hand, to offer Elena her power.

When Elena clasped hands with her, Bonnie realized that Meredith was on her other side. The light grew. The scrabbling lizard things ran from it, screaming and tearing at each other to get away.

The next thing Bonnie knew, Elena had slumped over. The wings were gone. The dark scrabbling things were gone, too. Elena had sent them away, using tremendous amounts of energy to overwhelm them with White Power.

"She'll fall," Bonnie whispered, looking at Stefan. "She's been using magic so strong—"

Just then, as Stefan started to turn to Elena, several things happened very fast, as if the room was caught in the flashes of a strobe light.

Flash. The window shade rolled back up, rattling furiously.

Flash. The lamp went back on, revealing it was in Stefan's hands. He must have been trying to fix it.

Flash. The door to Stefan's room opened slowly, creaking, as if to make up for slamming shut before.

Flash. Caroline was now on the floor, on all fours, groveling, breathing hard. Elena had won. . . .

Elena fell.

Only inhumanly fast reflexes could have caught her, especially from across the room. But Stefan had tossed the lamp to Meredith and was across the distance faster than Bonnie's eyes could follow. Then he was holding Elena, encircling her protectively.

"Oh, *hell*," said Caroline. Black trails of mascara ran down her face, making her look like something not quite human. She looked at Stefan with unconcealed hatred. He looked back soberly—no, *sternly*.

"Don't call on Hell," he said in a very low voice. "Not here. Not now. Because Hell might hear and call back."

"As if it already hadn't," Caroline said, and in that moment, she was pitiful—broken and pathetic. As if she had started something she didn't know how to stop.

"Caroline, what are you saying?" Stefan knelt. "Are you saying that you've already—made some bargain—?"

"Ouch," Bonnie said, suddenly and involuntarily, shattering the ominous mood in Stefan's room. One of Caroline's broken nails had left a trail of blood on the floor. Caroline had knelt in it, too, making things pretty messy. Bonnie felt a sympathetic throb of pain in her own fingers until Caroline waved her bloody hand at Stefan. Then Bonnie's sympathy turned to nausea.

"Want a lick?" she said. Her voice and face had changed entirely, and she wasn't even trying to hide it. "Oh, come on, Stefan," she went on mockingly, "you *do* drink human blood these days, don't you? Human or—whatever she is, whatever she's become. You two fly like bats together now, do you?"

"Caroline," Bonnie whispered, "didn't you *see* them? Her wings—"

"Just like a bat—or another vampire already. Stefan's made her—"

"I saw them too," Matt said flatly, behind Bonnie. "They weren't bat wings."

"Doesn't anybody have eyes?" Meredith said from where she stood by the lamp. "Look here." She bent. When she stood again she was holding a long white feather. It shone in the light.

"Maybe she's a white crow, then," Caroline said. "That would be appropriate. And I can't believe how you're all—all—fawning on her as if she were some sort of princess. Always everybody's little darling, aren't you, Elena?"

"Stop it," Stefan said.

"*Everybody's*, that's the key word," Caroline spat.

"Stop it."

"The way you were kissing people one after another."

She gave a theatrical shudder. "Everyone seems to have forgotten, but that was more like—"

"Stop, Caroline."

"The *real* Elena." Caroline's voice had become pretend-prissy, but she couldn't keep the venom out, Bonnie thought. "Because anyone who knows you knows what you *really* were before Stefan *blessed* us with his *irresistible* presence. You were—"

"Caroline, stop right there—"

"A slut! That's all! Just a cheap, anybody's *slut*!"

7

There was a sort of universal gasp. Stefan went white, his compressed lips showing in a tight line. Bonnie felt as if she were choking on words, on explanations, on recriminations about Caroline's own behavior. Elena may have had as many boyfriends as the stars in the sky, but in the end she had given all that up—because she fell in love—not that Caroline would know anything about *that*.

"Don't have anything to say now?" Caroline was taunting. "Can't find any cute answer? Bat got your tongue?" She began to laugh, but it was forced, glassy laughter, and then words were spilling out of her almost as if uncontrollably, all words that weren't supposed to be spoken in public. Bonnie had said most of them at one time or another, but *here*, and *now*, they formed a stream of venomous power.

Caroline's words were building up to some kind of crescendo—something was going to happen—this kind of force couldn't be contained—

Reverberations, Bonnie thought as the sound waves began building up. . . .

Glass, her intuition told her. *Get away from glass.*

Stefan just had time to whirl to Meredith and shout, *"Get rid of the lamp."*

And Meredith, who was not only quick on the uptake but also a baseball pitcher with a 1.75 ERA, snatched it up and threw it at—no, through—

—an explosion as the porcelain lamp shattered—

—the open window.

There was a similar shattering in the bathroom. The mirror had exploded behind the closed door.

Then Caroline slapped Elena across the face.

It left a bloody smear, which Elena patted tentatively. It also left a white handprint, turning to red. Elena's expression was one to wring tears from a stone.

And then Stefan did what Bonnie considered the most astonishing thing of all. He very gently put Elena down on the floor, kissed her upturned face, and turned to Caroline.

He put his hands on her shoulders, not shaking, only holding her still, forcing her to look at him.

"Caroline," he said, "stop it. *Come back*. For the sake of your old friends who care for you, come back. For the sake of the family that loves you, come back. For the sake of your own immortal soul, *come back. Come back to us!*"

Caroline just eyed him belligerently.

Stefan half turned aside, toward Meredith, grimacing. "I'm not really cut out to do this," he said wryly. "It's not any vampire's forte."

Then he turned toward Elena, his voice tender. "Love, can you help? Can you help your old friend again?"

Already Elena was trying to help, trying to get to Stefan. She had pulled herself up very shakily, first by the rocking chair and then by Bonnie, who tried to help her under the burden of gravity. Elena was as wobbly as a newborn giraffe in roller skates, and Bonnie—almost half a head shorter—was finding her hard to handle.

Stefan made a motion as if to help, but Matt was already there, steadying Elena on the other side.

Then Stefan had Caroline turned around, and he was holding her, not letting her dart away, forcing her to face Elena fully.

Elena, while being held at the waist so that her hands were free, made some curious motions, seeming to draw designs more and more quickly in the air in front of Caroline's face, at the same time clasping and unclasping her hands with the fingers in different positions. She seemed to know exactly what she was doing. Caroline's eyes followed the movements of Elena's hands as if compelled, but it was clear from her snarling that she hated it.

Magic, Bonnie thought, fascinated. White Magic. She's calling on angels, just as surely as Caroline was calling demons. But is she strong enough to pull Caroline out of the darkness?

And at last, as if to complete the ceremony, Elena leaned forward and kissed Caroline chastely on the lips.

All hell broke loose. Caroline somehow squirmed out of Stefan's grip and tried to claw Elena's face with her nails. Objects in the room went sailing through the air, propelled by no human force. Matt tried to grab Caroline's arm and got a punch in the stomach that doubled him over, followed by a chop to the back of the neck.

Stefan let go of Caroline to scoop up Elena and get her and Bonnie out of harm's way. He seemed to assume that Meredith could take care of herself—and he was right. Caroline swung at Meredith, but Meredith was ready. She grabbed Caroline's fist and helped her in the direction of the swing. Caroline landed on the bed, twisted, and then rushed Meredith again, this time getting a grip on her hair. Meredith pulled free, leaving a tuft of hair in Caroline's fingers. Then Meredith got under Caroline's guard and hit her squarely on the jaw. Caroline collapsed.

Bonnie cheered and refused to feel guilty about it. Then, for the first time, as Caroline lay still, Bonnie noticed that Caroline's fingernails were all there again—long, strong, curved, and perfect, not one of them chipped or broken.

Elena's Power? It must be. What else could have done it? With just a few motions and a kiss, Elena had healed Caroline's hand.

Meredith was massaging her own hand. "I never realized it *hurt* so much to knock people out," she said. "They never show it in movies. Is it the same for guys?"

Matt flushed. "I . . . uh, I've never actually . . ."

"It's the same for everyone, even vampires," Stefan said briefly. "Are you all right, Meredith? I mean, Elena could . . ."

"No, I'm fine. And Bonnie and I have a job to do." She nodded at Bonnie, who nodded weakly back. "Caroline's our responsibility, and we should have realized why she *really* had to come back this last time. *She doesn't have a car.* I'll bet she used that downstairs telephone and tried to get somebody to pick her up, but couldn't, and then she came upstairs again. So now we have to take her home. Stefan, I'm sorry. It hasn't been much of a visit."

Stefan looked grim. "It's probably as much as Elena could take, anyway," he said. "More than I thought she could take, honestly."

Matt said, "Well, I'm the one with the car, and Caroline is my responsibility, too," he said. "I may not be a girl, but I'm a human."

"Maybe we could come back tomorrow?" Bonnie said.

"Yes, I suppose that would be best," Stefan said. "I almost hate to let her go at all," he added, staring at the unconscious Caroline, his face shadowed. "I'm afraid for her. Very much afraid."

Bonnie pounced on this. "Why?"

"I think—well, it may be too early to say, but she seems to be almost possessed by something—but I have no idea what. I think I have to do some serious research."

And there it was again, the ice water dripping down Bonnie's back. The feeling of how close the frigid ocean of fear was, ready to topple down on her and take her on a swift trip to the bottom.

Stefan added, "But what's certain is that she was behaving strangely—even for Caroline. And I don't know what *you* heard when she was cursing, but I heard another voice behind it, prompting her." He turned to Bonnie. "Did you?"

Bonnie was thinking back. Had there been something—just a whisper—and just a beat before Caroline's voice came? Less than a beat, and just the faintest of sibilant whispers?

"And what happened here may have made it worse. She called on Hell at a moment when this room was saturated with Power. And Fell's Church itself is at the crossing of so many ley lines, it isn't funny. With all that going on—well, I just wish we had a good parapsychologist around."

Bonnie knew they were all thinking of Alaric.

"I'll try to get him to come," Meredith said. "But usually he's off in Tibet or Timbuktu doing research these days. It'll take a while even to get a message to him."

"Thank you." Stefan looked relieved.

"Like I said, she's our responsibility," Meredith said quietly.

"We're sorry to have brought her," Bonnie said loudly, rather hoping that something inside Caroline could hear her.

They said their good-byes separately to Elena, not sure of what might happen. But she simply smiled at each of them and touched their hands.

By good luck or by the grace of something far beyond their understanding, Caroline woke up. She even seemed mostly rational, if a little fuzzy, when the car reached her driveway. Matt helped her out of the car and walked her to the door on his arm, where Caroline's mother answered the doorbell. She was a mousy, timid, tired-looking woman who did not seem surprised to be receiving her daughter in this state on a late summer afternoon.

Matt dropped the girls off at Bonnie's house, where they spent a night in worried speculation. Bonnie fell asleep with the sound of Caroline's curses echoing in her head.

> *Dear Diary,*
>
> *Something is going to happen tonight.*
>
> *I can't talk or write, and I don't remember how to type on a keyboard very well, but I can send thoughts to Stefan and he can write them down. We don't have any secrets from each other.*
>
> *So this is my diary now. And . . .*

*This morning I woke up again. I woke up
again! It was still summer outside, and everything
was green. The daffodils in the garden are all in
bloom. And I had visitors. I didn't know exactly
who they were, but three of them are strong, clear
colors. I kissed them so I won't forget them again.*

*The fourth one was different. I could only see
a shattered color, laced with black. I had to use
strong words of White Power to keep that one from
bringing dark things into Stefan's room.*

*I'm getting sleepy. I want to be with Stefan and
feel him holding me. I love Stefan. I would give up
anything to stay with him. He asks me, Even flying?
Even flying, to be with him and keep him safe. Even
anything, to keep him safe. Even my life.*

Now I want to go to him.

Elena

(And Stefan is sorry about writing in
Elena's new diary, but he has to say some
things, because someday maybe she will
want to read them, to remember. I've written
down her thoughts in sentences, but they
don't come that way. They come as thought-
fragments, I guess. Vampires are used to
translating people's everyday thoughts into

coherent sentences, but Elena's thoughts need more translation than most. Usually she thinks in bright pictures, with a scattered word or two.

The "fourth one" that she talks about is Caroline Forbes. Elena has known Caroline almost since babyhood, I think. What bewilders me is that today Caroline attacked her in almost every way imaginable, and yet when I search Elena's mind I can't find any feelings of anger or even any pain. It's almost frightening to scan a mind like that.

The question I'd really like to answer is: What happened to Caroline during the short time she was kidnapped by Klaus and Tyler? And did she do what she did today of her own free will? Does some remnant of Klaus's hatred still linger like miasma, tainting the air? Or do we have another enemy in Fell's Church?

And most importantly, what do we do about it?

Stefan, who is being pulled from the compu

8

The clock's old-fashioned hands showed three A.M. when Meredith was suddenly roused from a fitful sleep.

And then she bit her lip, stifling a scream. A face was bending over hers, upside down. The last thing she remembered was lying on her back in a sleeping bag, talking about Alaric with Bonnie.

Now Bonnie was bending over her, but with her face inverted and her eyes shut. She was kneeling at the head of Meredith's pillow and her upside-down nose almost touched Meredith's. Add to that an odd pallor in Bonnie's cheeks and rapid warm breath that tickled Meredith's forehead, and anyone—*anyone*, Meredith insisted to herself—would be entitled to a half-scream.

She waited for Bonnie to speak, staring in the gloom at

those eerily closed eyes.

But instead, Bonnie sat up, stood, walked backward flawlessly to Meredith's desk, where Meredith's mobile lay charging, and picked it up. She must have turned it on for a video recording for she opened her mouth and began to gesture and speak.

It was terrifying. The sounds that came out of Bonnie's mouth were all too identifiable: backward speech. The tangled, guttural or high-pitched noises all carried the cadence that horror movies had made so popular. But to be able to speak that way on purpose . . . it wasn't possible for a normal human or a normal human mind. Meredith had an eerie sense of something trying to stretch its mind toward them, trying to reach them through unimaginable dimensions.

Maybe it lives backward, Meredith thought, trying to distract herself as the frightening sounds went on. Maybe it thinks we do. Maybe we just don't—intersect. . . .

Meredith didn't think she could stand much more. She was beginning to imagine that she heard words, even phrases in the backward sounds, and none of them were pleasant. Please let it stop—now.

A wailing and mumbling . . .

Bonnie's mouth shut with a clash of teeth. The sounds stopped instantly. And then, like a video being rolled back in slow motion, she walked backward to her sleeping bag, knelt, and back-crawled into it, lying down with her head on the pillow—all without opening her eyes to look where she was going.

It was one of the scariest things Meredith had ever seen or heard, and Meredith had seen and heard a fair amount of scary things.

And Meredith could no more have left that recording until morning than she could have flown—without assistance.

She got up, tiptoed to the desk, and took the mobile phone to the other room. There she attached it to her computer, where she could run the backward message forward.

When she'd listened to the message in reverse once or twice she decided that Bonnie must never hear it. It would frighten her out of her senses, and there would be no more contact with the paranormal for Elena's friends.

There *were* animal sounds in there, mixed up with the twisted, backward voice . . . that wasn't Bonnie's voice in any way. It wasn't any normal person's voice. It almost sounded worse going forward than backward—which maybe meant that whatever being had spoken the words normally spoke the other way.

Meredith could make out human voices over the groaning and distorted laughter and the animal noises straight from the veldt. Though they made the hairs on her body stand up and tingle, she tried to put together the words in between the nonsense. Putting them together she got:

"Aaahhh . . . waggge . . . n . . . ing wuh illlillll . . . *be* . . . sud-ud-ud . . . den . . . *AND* shhhh . . . ohhh . . . ging. *YOOOOU* . . . hand-and-nd . . . Iiii . . . mmmust . . . *BE* therefore . . . herrr . . . aaahhh waggge . . . ning . . . Wewone . . . *BE* therefor-or-or-or-r"—(was there a "herrr" next, or was it just part of the growling?)—"*LADE* . . . errrrrrrrrrr . . . ahhn. *Thaaass . . . FORRRRR* . . . oththth . . . *ERRR* . . . handandnd . . . ssssssssss . . . t-t-todo. . . ."

Meredith, working with pad and pen, eventually got these words on paper:

> *Awakening will be sudden and shocking.*
> *You and I must be there for her Awakening. We*
> *won't be there for (her?) later on. That's for other*
> *hands to do.*

Meredith put the pen very precisely beside the deciphered message on the pad.

And after that Meredith went and lay hunched in her sleeping bag watching the unmoving Bonnie like a cat at a mouse hole, until, finally, blessed tiredness took her into the dark.

"I said *what?*" Bonnie was honestly bewildered the next morning, squeezing grapefruit juice and pouring cereal, like a model host, even if it was Meredith who was scrambling eggs at the stove.

"I've told you three times now. The words are not going to change, I promise."

"Well," Bonnie said, suddenly switching sides, "it's clear that the Awakening is going to happen to Elena. Because, for one thing, you and I have to be there for it, and for another thing, she's the one who needs to *wake up*."

"Exactly," said Meredith.

"She needs to remember who she really was."

"Precisely," said Meredith.

"And we've got to help her remember!"

"*No!*" said Meredith, taking out her anger on the eggs with a plastic spatula. "No, Bonnie, that's not what you said, and I don't think we *could* do it anyway. We can teach her little things, maybe, the way Stefan has. How to tie her shoes. How to brush her hair. But from what you said, the Awakening is going to be shocking and sudden—and you didn't say anything about us doing it. You only said that we have to be there for her, because after that, somehow we *won't* be there."

Bonnie contemplated that in gloomy silence. "Won't be there?" she said finally. "Like, won't be with Elena? Or won't be there, like . . . won't be anywhere?"

Meredith eyed a breakfast that she suddenly didn't want to eat. "I don't know."

"Stefan said we could come over again today," Bonnie urged.

"Stefan would be polite while he was being staked to death."

"I know," Bonnie said suddenly. "Let's call Matt. We can go see Caroline . . . if she *will* see us, I mean. We can see if she's any different today. Then we can wait until it's afternoon, and *then* we can call Stefan and ask if we can come over again to see Elena."

At Caroline's house, her mother said she was sick today and was going to stay in bed. The three of them—Matt, Meredith, and Bonnie—went back to Meredith's house without her, but Bonnie kept chewing her lip, looking back occasionally toward Caroline's street. Caroline's mother had looked sick herself, with shadows under her eyes. And the thunderstorm feeling, the feeling of pressure, had been squashing Caroline's house almost flat.

At Meredith's, Matt tinkered with his car, which perpetually needed work, while Bonnie and Meredith went through Meredith's wardrobe for clothes that Elena could wear. They would be big, but that was better than Bonnie's, which would be much too small.

At four P.M. they called Stefan. Yes, they were welcome. They went downstairs and picked up Matt.

At the boardinghouse, Elena didn't repeat the kissing ritual of the previous day—to Matt's obvious disappointment. But she was delighted with the new clothes, although not for any reason that the old Elena would have been. Floating three feet off the floor, she kept holding them to her face and taking deep, happy sniffs, and then beaming at Meredith, although when Bonnie picked up a T-shirt, she couldn't smell anything but the fabric softener they'd used. Not even Meredith's Beach cologne.

"I'm sorry," Stefan said helplessly as Elena went into a sudden sneezing fit, cuddling a sky-blue top in her arms as if it were a kitten. But his face was tender, and Meredith, while looking slightly embarrassed, reassured him that it was nice to be so appreciated.

"She can tell where they come from," Stefan explained. "She won't wear anything that's come from a sweatshop."

"I only buy from places listed on the Sweatshop-Free Clothing website," Meredith said simply. "Bonnie and I have something to tell you," she added. While she recounted Bonnie's late-night prophecy, Bonnie took Elena into the bathroom and helped her change into the shorts, which fit, and the sky-blue top, which almost fit, being just a little long.

The color set off Elena's tangled but still glorious hair perfectly, but when Bonnie tried to get her to look in the hand mirror that she had brought—the old mirror's shards had all been cleared away—Elena seemed as confused as a puppy held up to see its own reflection. Bonnie kept holding the mirror in front of her face, and Elena kept popping out on one side or another from behind it, like a baby playing peek-a-boo. Bonnie had to be satisfied with a good brushing out of the tangles in that golden mass, which Stefan clearly didn't know how to handle. When Elena's hair was finally silky and smooth, Bonnie proudly took her out to be shown off.

And was promptly sorry. The other three were in deep, and it looked like grim, conversation. Reluctantly, Bonnie let go of Elena who immediately flew—literally—into Stefan's lap, and joined them herself.

"Of course we understand," Meredith was saying. "Even before Caroline went off her rocker, what other choice was there, ultimately? But—"

"What 'what other choice is there'?" Bonnie said, as she sat down on Stefan's bed beside him. "What are you guys talking about?"

There was a long pause, and then Meredith got up to put an arm around Bonnie. "We were talking about why Stefan and Elena need to leave Fell's Church—need to go far away."

At first Bonnie didn't react—she knew she should be feeling something, but she was too deep in shock to access what it was. When words came to her, the only thing she could hear herself saying stupidly was, "Go *away? Why?*"

"You saw why—here, yesterday," Meredith said, her dark eyes filled with pain, her face for once showing the uncontrollable anguish she must be feeling. But for the moment, no anguish meant anything to Bonnie but her own.

And it was coming now, like an avalanche burying her in red-hot snow. In ice that burned. Somehow she struggled out of it long enough to say, "Caroline won't do anything. She signed a vow. She knows that to break it—especially when—when you-know-who signed it, too . . ."

Meredith must have told Stefan about the crow, because he sighed and shook his head, gently fending off Elena, who was trying to look up into his face. Clearly she sensed the unhappiness in the group, but just as clearly she couldn't really understand what was causing it.

"The last person I want around Caroline is my brother." Stefan pushed his dark hair out of his eyes irritably, as if he had been reminded of how much they looked alike. "And I don't think Meredith's threat about the sorority sisters is going to work, either. She's too far gone into the darkness."

Bonnie shivered inside. She didn't like the thoughts that those words summoned up: *into the darkness*.

"But . . ." Matt began, and Bonnie realized that he felt the same way she did—stunned and sick, as if they were getting off some cheap carnival ride.

"Listen," Stefan said, "there's another reason why we can't stay here."

"What other reason?" Matt said slowly. Bonnie was too upset to speak. She had thought about this, somewhere deep in her unconscious. But she'd pushed the thoughts away every time they came.

"Bonnie understands it already, I think." Stefan looked at her. She looked back with eyes that were misting over with tears.

"Fell's Church," Stefan explained gently and sadly, "was built at a meeting of the ley lines. The lines of raw Power in the ground, remember? I don't know if it was deliberate. Does anybody know if the Smallwoods had anything to do with the location?"

No one did. There was nothing in Honoria Fell's old diary about the werewolf family having a choice in the founding of the town.

"Well, if it was an accident, it was a pretty unlucky one. The town—I should say, the town cemetery—was built directly over a place where a lot of ley lines cross. That's what made it a beacon for supernatural creatures, bad or—or not quite so bad." He looked embarrassed, and Bonnie realized that he was talking about himself. "I was drawn here. So were other vampires, as you know. And with every person who had the Power who came here, the beacon became stronger. Brighter. More attractive to other people with the Power. It's a vicious cycle."

"Eventually, some of them are going to see Elena," Meredith said. "Remember, these are people like Stefan, Bonnie, but not people with his moral sense. When they see her . . ."

Bonnie almost burst into tears at the thought. She seemed to see a flurry of white feathers, each tumbling in slow motion to the ground.

"But—she wasn't this way when she first woke up," Matt said slowly and stubbornly. "She talked. She was rational. She didn't *float*."

"Talking or not talking, walking or floating, she has the *Power*," Stefan said. "Enough to drive ordinary vampires crazy. Crazy enough to hurt her to get it. And she doesn't kill—or wound. At least, I can't imagine her doing that. What I'm hoping," he said, and his face darkened, "is that I can take her somewhere where she'll be . . . protected."

"But you can't take her," Bonnie said, and she could hear the wail in her own voice without being able to control it. "Didn't Meredith tell you what I said? She's going to wake up. And Meredith and I need to be with her for that."

Because we won't be with her later. Suddenly it made sense. And while it wasn't quite as bad as thinking that they would be not-anywhere-at-all, it was more than bad enough.

"I wasn't thinking of taking her until she can at least walk properly," Stefan said, and he surprised Bonnie with a quick arm around her shoulders. It felt like Meredith's hug, sibling-ish, but stronger and briefer. "And you don't know how glad I am that she's going to wake up. Or that you'll be there to support her."

"But . . ." But the ghoulies are still going to come to Fell's Church? Bonnie thought. And we won't have you to protect us?

She glanced up and saw that Meredith knew exactly what she'd been thinking. "I would say," Meredith said, in her most careful, measured tones, "that Stefan and Elena have been through enough for the town's sake."

Well. There was no arguing with *that*. And there was no arguing with Stefan, either, it seemed. His mind was made up.

They talked until after dark anyway, discussing different options and scenarios, pondering over Bonnie's prediction. They didn't get anything decided, but at least they had thrashed out some possible plans. Bonnie insisted that there be some means of communication with Stefan, and she was just about to demand some of his blood and hair for the summoning spell when he gently pointed out that he did have a mobile phone now.

At last it was time to leave. The humans were starving, and Bonnie guessed that Stefan probably was, too. He looked unusually white as he sat with Elena on his lap.

When they said good-bye at the top of the stairs, Bonnie had to keep reminding herself that Stefan had promised that Elena would be there for her and Meredith to support. He would never take her away without telling them.

It wasn't a *real* good-bye.

So why did it feel so much like one?

9

When Matt, Meredith, and Bonnie were all on their way, Stefan was left with Elena, now decently attired by Bonnie in her "Night Gown." The darkness outside was comforting to his sore eyes—not sore from daylight, but from telling good friends the sad news. Worse than the sore eyes was the slightly breathless feeling of a vampire who hasn't fed. But he'd remedy that soon, he told himself. Once Elena was asleep, he'd slip out into the woods and find a white-tailed deer. No one could stalk like a vampire; no one could compete with Stefan at hunting. And even if it took several deer to assuage the hunger inside him, not one of *them* would be permanently injured.

But Elena had other plans. She wasn't sleepy, and she was never bored being alone with him. As soon as the sounds of their visitors' car were decently out of hearing, she did what she always did in this mood. She floated to him and tipped her face up, eyes closed, lips just slightly pursed. Then she waited.

Stefan hurried to the one unshuttered window, pulled the shade down against unwanted peeping crows, and returned. Elena was in exactly the same position, blushing slightly, eyes still shut. Stefan sometimes thought that she would wait forever that way, if she wanted a kiss.

"I'm really taking advantage of you, love," he said, and sighed. He leaned over and kissed her gently, chastely.

Elena made a noise of disappointment that sounded exactly like a *purruping* kitten, ending on a note of inquiry. She bumped his chin with her nose.

"Lovely love," Stefan said, stroking her hair. "Bonnie got all the knots out without pulling?" But he was leaning into her warmth now, helpless. A distant ache in his upper jaw was already beginning.

Elena bumped again, demanding. He kissed her for slightly longer. Logically, he knew she was a grown-up. She was older and vastly more experienced than she had been nine months ago, when they'd lost themselves in adoration kissing. But guilt was never far from his thoughts, and he couldn't help but worry about having her competent consent.

This time the *purrup* was one of exasperation. Elena

had had enough. All at once, she gave her weight to him, forcing him to suddenly support a warm, substantial bundle of femininity in his arms, and at the same time, her *Please?* chiming clear as a finger swirling on a crystal glass.

It was one of the first words she had learned to think to him when she'd woken up mute and weightless. And, angel or no, she knew exactly what it did to him—inside.

Please?

"Oh, little love," he groaned. "Little lovely love . . ."

Please?

He kissed her.

There was a long time of silence, while he felt his heart beat faster and faster. Elena, his Elena, who had once given her very life for him, was warm and drowsily heavy in his arms. She was his alone, and they belonged just like this, and he never wanted anything to change from this moment. Even the quickly growing ache in his upper jaw was something to be enjoyed. The pain of it changed to pleasure with Elena's warm mouth under his, her lips forming little butterfly kisses, teasing him.

He sometimes thought she was most awake when she seemed half-asleep like this. She was always the instigator, but he followed helplessly wherever she wanted him to go. The one time he had refused, had stopped in mid-kiss, she had broken off speaking to him with her mind and floated to a corner, where she then sat among the dust and spiderwebs . . . and *wept*. Nothing he could do would console her, although he knelt on the hard wooden floorboards and begged and coaxed and almost wept himself—until he took her back into his arms.

He had promised himself never to make that mistake again. But still, his guilt nagged at him, although it was growing more and more distant—and more confused as Elena changed the pressure of her lips suddenly and the world rocked and he had to back up until they were sitting on his bed. His thoughts fragmented. He could only think that Elena was back with him, sitting on his lap, so excited, so vibrant, until there was a sort of silken explosion inside him and he didn't need to be forced anymore.

He knew that she was enjoying the pleasure-pain of his aching jaw as much as he was.

There was no more time or reason to think. Elena was melting into his arms, her hair under his stroking fingers a liquid softness. Mentally, they had already melted together. The aching in his canines had finally produced the inevitable result, his teeth lengthening, sharpening; the touch of them against Elena's lower lip causing a bright flicker of pleasure-pain that almost made him gasp.

And then Elena did something she never had done before. Delicately, carefully, she took one of Stefan's fangs and captured it between her upper and lower lips. And then, delicately, deliberately, she just held on.

The whole world reeled around Stefan.

It was only by the grace of his love for her, and their connected minds, that he didn't bite down and pierce her lip. Ancient vampire urges that could never be tamed out of his blood were screaming at him to do just that.

But he loved her, and they were one—and besides, *he couldn't move an inch*. He was frozen in pleasure. His fangs had never extended so far or become quite as sharp, and without him doing a thing the razor edge of his tooth had cut into Elena's full lower lip. Blood was trickling very slowly down his throat. Elena's blood, which had changed since she had come back from the spirit world. It had once been wonderful, full of youthful vitality and the essence of Elena's living self.

Now . . . it was simply in a class of its own. Indescribable. He'd never experienced anything like the blood of a returned spirit. It was charged with a Power that was as different from human blood as human was from animal blood.

To a vampire, blood flowing down the throat was a pleasure as sharp as anything imaginable to a human.

Stefan's heart was pounding out of his chest.

Elena daintily worried the fang she had captured.

He could *feel* her satisfaction as the tiny sacrificial pain turned to pleasure, because she was linked to him, and because she was one of the rarest of all breeds of humans:

one who actually enjoyed nurturing a vampire, loved the feeling of feeding him, of him needing her. She was one of the elite.

Hot shivers traveled down his spine, Elena's blood still making the world spin.

Elena let go of his fang, sucking on her lower lip. She let her head drop back, exposing her neck.

The head-drop was really too much to resist, even for him. He knew the traceries of Elena's veins as well as he knew her face. And yet . . .

All's right. All's well . . . Elena chimed telepathically.

He sank twin aching fangs into a small vein. His canines were so razor-sharp by then that there was nearly no pain for Elena, who was used to the snakebite sensation. And for him, for both of them, there was the feeding at last, as the indescribable sweetness of Elena's new blood filled Stefan's mouth, and an outpouring of giving swept Elena into incoherency.

There was always a danger of taking too much, or of not giving her enough of his own blood to keep her—well, frankly, to keep her from dying. Not that he needed more than a small amount, but there would always be that danger in trafficking with vampires. In the end, though, dark thoughts swam away in the sheer bliss that had overcome them both.

* * *

Matt fished for keys as he and Bonnie and Meredith all crowded into the wide front seat of his rattletrap car. Embarrassing to have to park that next to Stefan's Porsche. The upholstery in back was in shreds that tended to stick to the derriere of whoever sat on it, and Bonnie easily fit on the jump seat, which had a jerry-rigged seat belt, between Matt and Meredith. Matt kept an eye on her, since when she was excited she tended not to use the belt. The road back through the Old Wood had too many difficult turns to be taken lightly, even if they were going to be the only travelers on it.

No more deaths, Matt thought as he pulled away from the boardinghouse. No more miraculous resurrections, even. Matt had seen enough of the supernatural to last him the rest of his life. He was just like Bonnie; he wanted things to settle down to normal so he could get on with living the plain old ordinary way.

Without Elena, something inside him whispered mockingly. Giving up without even a fight?

Hey, I couldn't beat Stefan in any kind of fight if he had both arms tied behind his back and a bag over his head. Forget it. That's finished, however she kissed me. She's a friend, now.

But he could still feel Elena's warm lips on his mouth from yesterday, the light touches that she didn't know yet weren't socially acceptable between just-friends. And he could feel the warmth and the swaying, dancing slenderness of her body.

Damn, she came back perfect—physically, at least, he thought.

Bonnie's plaintive voice cut into his pleasant reminiscences.

"Just when I thought everything was going to be all right," she was wailing, almost weeping. "Just when I thought it's all going to work out after all. It's going to be the way it was *supposed* to be."

Meredith said, very gently, "It's difficult, I know. We seem to keep on losing her. But we can't be selfish."

"*I* can," Bonnie said flatly.

I can, too, Matt's inner voice whispered. At least inside, where nobody can see my selfishness. Good old Matt; Matt won't mind—what a good sport Matt is. Well, this is one time when good old Matt does mind. But she chose the other guy, and what can I do? Kidnap her? Keep her locked up? Try to take her by force?

The thought was like a dash of cold water, and Matt woke up and paid more attention to his driving. Somehow he'd already automatically navigated several curves of the pitted, one-lane road that ran through the Old Wood.

"We were supposed to go to college together," Bonnie persisted. "And then we were supposed to come back here to Fell's Church. Back *home*. We had it all planned out—since kindergarten, practically—and now Elena's human again, and I thought that meant that everything was going to go back to the way it was *supposed* to be. And it's *never* going to be the same again, *ever*, is it?" She finished more quietly and with a little gulping sigh, "Is it?" It wasn't even really a question.

Matt and Meredith found themselves glancing at each other, surprised by the sharpness of their pity, and helpless to comfort Bonnie, who now had her arms folded around herself, shrugging off Meredith's touch.

It's Bonnie—just Bonnie being theatrical, Matt thought, but his own native honesty rose to mock him.

"I guess," he said slowly, "that's what we were all sort of thinking, really, when she first came back." When we were dancing around in the woods like crazy people, he thought. "I guess we sort of thought that they could live quietly somewhere near Fell's Church, and that things would go back to the way they were before. Before Stefan—"

Meredith shook her head, looking off into the distance beyond the windshield. "Not Stefan."

Matt realized what she meant. Stefan had come to Fell's Church to rejoin humanity, not to take a human girl away from it into the unknown.

"You're right," Matt said. "I was just thinking about something like that. She and Stefan could have probably worked out some way to live here quietly. Or at least to stay close to us, you know. It was Damon. He came to take Elena against her will, and that changed everything."

"And now Elena and Stefan are leaving. And once they leave, they'll never come back," Bonnie wailed. "Why? Why did Damon start all this?"

"He likes to change things out of sheer boredom, Stefan once told me. This time it probably started out of hatred for Stefan," Meredith said. "But I wish that for once he could have just left us alone."

"What difference does it make?" Bonnie *was* crying now. "So it was Damon's fault. I don't even care anymore. What I don't understand is why things have to change!"

"'You can never cross the same river twice.' Or even once if you're a strong enough vampire," Meredith said wryly. Nobody laughed. And then, very gently: "Maybe you're asking the wrong person. Maybe Elena's the one who could tell you why things have to change, if she remembers what happened to her—in the Other Place."

"I didn't *mean* that they *do* have to change—"

"But they do," Meredith said, even more gently and wistfully. "Don't you see? It's not supernatural; it's—life. Everybody has to grow up—"

"I know! Matt has a football scholarship and you're going away to college and then you're going to get *married*! And probably have babies!" Bonnie managed to make this sound like some indecent activity. "I'm going to be stuck in junior college *forever*. And you'll both be all grown up and you'll forget about Elena and Stefan . . . and me," Bonnie finished in a very small voice.

"Hey." Matt had always been very protective of the injured and ignored. Right now, even with Elena so recently on his mind—he wondered if he would *ever* get rid of the feeling of that kiss—he was drawn to Bonnie, who seemed so small and fragile. "What are you talking about? I'm coming back after college to live. I'll probably die right here in Fell's Church. *I'll* be thinking about you. I mean, if you want me to."

He patted Bonnie's arm, and she didn't shy away from his touch as she had from Meredith's. She leaned into him, her forehead against his shoulder. When she shivered once, slightly, he put his arm around her without even thinking.

"I'm not cold," Bonnie said, although she didn't try to shrug off his arm. "It's warm tonight. I just—I don't like it when you say things like 'I'll probably die right'—*watch out!*"

"*Matt, look out!*"

"*Whoa—!*" Matt pumped the brakes, cursing, both hands wrestling with the steering wheel as Bonnie ducked and Meredith braced herself. Matt's replacement for the first beat-up old car he'd lost was just about as old and didn't have airbags. It was a miscellany of junkyard cars pieced together.

"*Hang on!*" Matt yelled as the car skidded, tires

screaming, and then they were all flung around as the back end swerved into a ditch and the front bumper hit a tree.

When everything stopped moving, Matt let out his breath, easing his death-grip on the steering wheel. He started to turn toward the girls and then froze. He scrabbled to switch on the map light, and what he saw held him frozen again.

Bonnie had turned, as always in moments of deepest distress, to Meredith. She was lying with her head on Meredith's lap, hands locked onto her friend's arm and shirt. Meredith herself was sitting, braced, leaning as far as possible backward, her feet stretched to push against the floor beneath the dashboard; her body bowed back in the seat, head flung backward, arms holding Bonnie down tightly.

Thrusting straight through the open window—like a knobby, shaggy green spear or the grasping arm of some savage earthen giant—was the branch of a tree. It just cleared the base of Meredith's arched neck, and its lower branches passed over Bonnie's small body. If Bonnie's seat belt hadn't let her turn; if Bonnie hadn't flung herself down like that; if Meredith hadn't held onto her . . .

Matt found himself staring directly into the splintered but very sharp end of the lance. If his own seat belt hadn't kept him from leaning that way . . .

Matt could hear his own hard breathing. The smell of evergreen was overpowering within the car. He could even smell the places where smaller branches had broken off and were oozing sap.

Very slowly, Meredith reached out to break off one of the twigs that was pointed at her throat like an arrow. It wouldn't break. Numb, Matt reached over to try it himself. But although the wood wasn't much thicker than his finger, it was tough and wouldn't even bend.

As if it's been fire-hardened, he thought dazedly. But that's ridiculous. It's a living tree; I can feel the splinters.

"Ow."

"Can I please get up now?" Bonnie said quietly, her voice muffled against Meredith's leg. "Please. Before it grabs me. It wants to."

Matt glanced at her, startled, and scratched his cheek against the splintered end of the big branch.

"It's not going to grab you." But his stomach was churning as he fumbled blindly for his seat belt fastening. Why should Bonnie have the same thought as he had: that the thing was like a huge, crooked, shaggy arm? She couldn't even see it.

"You know it wants to," Bonnie whispered, and now the slight shivering seemed to be taking over her whole body. She reached backward to undo her seat belt.

"Matt, we need to slide," Meredith said. She had carefully maintained her painful-looking bowed-backward position, but Matt could hear her breathing harder. "We need to slide toward you. It's trying to get around my throat."

"That's impossible. . . ." But he could see it, too. The freshly splintered ends of the smaller branch had moved only infinitesimally, but there was a curve to them now, and the splinters were pressing into Meredith's throat.

"It's probably just that nobody can stay bent backward like that forever," he said, knowing that this was nonsense. "There's a flashlight in the glove compartment. . . ."

"The glove compartment is completely blocked by branches. Bonnie, can you reach to unfasten my seat belt?"

"I'll try." Bonnie slid forward without raising her head, fumbling to find the release button.

To Matt it looked as if the shaggy, aromatic evergreen branches were engulfing her. Pulling her into their needles.

"We've got a whole freakin' Christmas tree in here." He looked away, out through the glass of the window on his side. Cupping his hands to see better into the darkness, he leaned his forehead against the surprisingly cool glass.

There was a touch on the back of his neck. He jumped, then froze. It was neither cool nor warm, like a girl's fingernail.

"Damn it, Meredith—"

"Matt—"

Matt was furious with himself for jumping. But the touch was . . . scratchy.

"Meredith?" He slowly moved his hands away until he could see in the dark window's reflection. Meredith wasn't touching him.

"Don't . . . move . . . left, Matt. There's a long sharp bit there." Meredith's voice, normally cool and a bit remote, usually made Matt think of those calendar pictures of blue lakes surrounded by snow. Now it just sounded choked and strained.

"Meredith!" Bonnie said before Matt could speak. Bonnie's voice sounded as if it were coming from underneath a featherbed.

"It's all right. I just have to . . . hold it away," Meredith said. "Don't worry. I won't let go of you, either."

Matt felt a sharper prickle of splinters. Something touched his neck on the right side, delicately. "Bonnie, stop it! You're pulling the tree *in*! You're pulling it on Meredith and me!"

"Matt, *shut up*!"

Matt shut up. His heart was pounding. The last thing he felt like doing was reaching behind him. But that's stupid, he thought, because if Bonnie really is moving the tree, I can at least hold it still for her.

He reached behind him, flinching, trying to watch what he was doing in the window's reflection. His hand closed over a thick knot of bark and splinters.

He thought, I don't remember seeing a knot when it was pointed at my throat. . . .

"Got it!" a muffled voice said, and there was the click of a seat belt coming undone. Then, much more shakily, the voice said, "Meredith? There are needles shoved all into my back."

"Okay, Bonnie. Matt," Meredith was speaking with effort, but great patience, the way they'd all been talking to Elena. "Matt, you have to open your door now."

Bonnie said in a voice of terror, "It isn't just needles. It's little branches. Sort of like barbed wire. I'm . . . stuck. . . ."

"Matt! You need to open your door *now*—"

"*I can't.*"

Silence.

"Matt?"

Matt was bracing himself, pushing with his feet, both hands locked around the scaly bark now. He thrust backward with all his strength.

"Matt!" Meredith almost screamed. "It's cutting into my throat!"

"I can't get my door open! There's a tree on that side, too!"

"How can there be a tree there? *That's the road!*"

"How can there be a tree *growing* in here?"

Another silence. Matt could feel the splinters—the slivers of broken branch—biting deeper into the back of his neck. If he didn't move soon, he would never be able to.

10

Elena was serenely happy. Now it was her turn.

Stefan used a sharp wooden letter opener from his desk to cut himself. Elena always hated to see him do this, use the most efficient implement that would penetrate vampire skin; so she shut her eyes tightly and only looked again when red blood was trickling from a little cut on his neck.

"You don't need to take a lot—and you shouldn't," Stefan whispered, and she knew he was saying these things while he *could* say them. "I'm not holding you too hard or hurting you?"

He was always so worried. This time, *she* kissed *him*.

And she could see how strange he thought it was, that he wanted kisses more than he wanted her to take his blood. Laughing, Elena pushed him flat and hovered over him and went for the general area of the wound again, knowing that he thought she was going to tease him. But instead she fastened herself on the wound like a limpet and sucked hard, *hard*, until she had made him say *please* with his mind. But she wasn't satisfied until she made him say *please* out loud as well.

In the car, in the dimness, Matt and Meredith thought of the idea at the same time. She was faster, but they spoke almost together.

"I'm an idiot! Matt, where's the seatback release?"

"Bonnie, you have to unfold her seat backward! There's a little handle, you should be able to reach it and pull up!"

Bonnie's voice was hitching now, hiccupping. "My arms—they're sort of poking into—my arms—"

"Bonnie," Meredith said thickly. "I know you can do it. Matt—is the handle right—under—the front seat or—"

"Yes. At the edge. One—no, two o'clock." Matt didn't have breath for more. Once he had grabbed the tree, he found that if he loosened pressure for an instant, it pushed harder on his neck.

There's no choice, he thought. He took as much of a deep breath as he could, pushed back on the branch, hearing a cry from Meredith, and *twisted*, feeling jagged splinters like thin wooden knives tear his throat and ear and scalp. Now he was free of the pressure on the back of his neck, although he was appalled by how much more tree there was in the car than the last time he had seen it.

His lap was filled with branches; evergreen needles were thickly piled everywhere.

No wonder Meredith was so mad, he thought dizzily, turning toward her. She was almost buried in branches, one hand wrestling with something at her throat, but she saw him.

"Matt . . . get . . . your own seat! Quick! Bonnie, I *know* you can."

Matt dug and tore into the branches, then groped for the handle that would collapse the backrest of his seat. The handle wouldn't move. Thin, tough tendrils were wrapped around it, springy and hard to break. He twisted and snapped them savagely.

His seatback dropped away. He ducked under the huge arm-branch—if it still deserved the name, since the car was full of similar huge branches now. Then, just as he reached to help Meredith, her seat abruptly folded back, too.

She fell with it, away from the evergreen, gasping for air. For an instant she just lay still. Then she finished scrambling into the backseat proper, dragging a needle-shrouded figure with her. When she spoke, her voice was hoarse and her speech was still slow.

"Matt. Bless you . . . for having . . . this jigsaw puzzle . . . of a car." She kicked the front seat back into position, and Matt did likewise.

"Bonnie," Matt said numbly.

Bonnie didn't move. Many tiny branches were still entwining her, caught in the fabric of her shirt, wound into her hair.

Meredith and Matt both started pulling. Where the branches let go, they left welts or tiny puncture wounds.

"It's almost as if they were trying to grow into her," Matt said, as a long, thin branch pulled away, leaving bloody pinpricks behind.

"Bonnie?" Meredith said. She was the one disentangling the twigs from Bonnie's hair. "Bonnie? Come on, up. Look at me."

The shaking began again in Bonnie's body, but she let Meredith turn her face up. "I didn't think I could do it."

"You saved my life."

"I was so scared. . . ."

Bonnie went on crying quietly against Meredith's shoulder.

Matt looked at Meredith just as the map light flickered and went out. The last thing he saw was her dark eyes, which held an expression that made him suddenly feel even sicker to his stomach. He looked out the three windows he could now see from the backseat.

It should have been hard to see anything at all. But what he was looking for was pressed right up against the glass. Needles. Branches. Solid against every inch of the windows.

Nevertheless, he and Meredith, without needing to say anything, each reached for a backseat door handle. The doors clicked, opened a fraction of an inch; then they slammed back hard with a very definitive *wham*.

Meredith and Matt looked at each other. Meredith looked down again and began to pluck more twigs off Bonnie.

"Does that hurt?"

"No. A little . . ."

"You're shaking."

"It's cold."

It was cold now. Outside the car, rather than through the once-open window that was now completely plugged with evergreen, Matt could hear the wind. It whistled, as if through many branches. There was also the sound of wood creaking, startlingly loud and ridiculously high above. It sounded like a storm.

"What the *hell* was it, anyway?" he exploded, kicking the front seat viciously. "The thing I swerved for on the road?"

Meredith's dark head lifted slowly. "I don't know; I was about to roll up the window. I only got a glimpse."

"It just appeared right in the middle of the road."

"A wolf?"

"It wasn't there and then it *was* there."

"Wolves aren't that color. It was red," Bonnie said

flatly, lifting her head from Meredith's shoulder.

"Red?" Meredith shook her head. "It was much too big to be a fox."

"It *was* red, I think," Matt said.

"Wolves aren't red . . . what about werewolves? Does Tyler Smallwood have any relatives with red hair?"

"It wasn't a wolf," Bonnie said. "It was . . . backward."

"Backward?"

"Its head was on the wrong side. Or maybe it had heads on both ends."

"Bonnie, you are *really* scaring me," Meredith said.

Matt wouldn't say it, but she was really scaring him, too. Because his glimpse of the animal had seemed to show him the same kind of deformed shape that Bonnie was describing.

"Maybe we just saw it at a weird angle," he said, while Meredith said, "It may just have been some animal scared out by—"

"By what?"

Meredith looked up at the top of the car. Matt followed her gaze. Very slowly, and with a groan of metal, the roof dented. And again. As if something very heavy was leaning on it.

Matt cursed himself. "While I was in the front seat, why didn't I just floor it—?" He stared hungrily through branches, trying to make out the accelerator, the ignition.

"Are the keys still there?"

"Matt, we ended up half in a ditch. And besides, if it would have done any good, I'd have told you to floor it."

"That branch would've taken your head off!"

"Yes," Meredith said simply.

"It would have *killed* you!"

"If it would have gotten you two out, I'd have suggested it. But you were trapped looking sideways; I could *see* straight ahead. They were already here; the trees. In every direction."

"That . . . isn't . . . possible!" Matt pounded the seat in front of him to emphasize each word.

"Is *this* possible?"

The roof creaked again.

"Both of you—stop fighting!" Bonnie said, and her voice broke on a sob.

There was an explosion like a gunshot and the car sank suddenly back and left.

Bonnie started. "What was that?"

Silence.

". . . a tire blowing," Matt said at last. He didn't trust his own voice. He looked at Meredith.

So did Bonnie. "Meredith—the branches are filling up the front seat. I can hardly see the moonlight. It's getting dark."

"I know."

"What are we going to *do*?"

Matt could see the tremendous tension and frustration in Meredith's face, as if everything she said should come out through gritted teeth. But Meredith's voice was quiet.

"I don't know."

With Stefan still shuddering, Elena curled herself like a cat over the bed. She smiled at him, a smile drugged with pleasure and love. He thought of grasping her by the arms, pulling her down, and starting all over again.

That was how insane she'd made him. Because he knew—all too well, from experience—the danger they were flirting with. Much more of this and Elena would be the first spirit-vampire, as she'd been the first vampire-spirit he'd known.

But look at her! He slipped out from beneath her as he sometimes did and just gazed, feeling his heart pound just at the sight of her. Her hair, true gold, fell like silk down to the bed and pooled there. Her body, in the light of the one small lamp in the room, seemed to be outlined in gold. She truly seemed to float and move and sleep in a golden haze. It was terrifying. For a vampire, it was as if he'd brought a living sun into his bed.

He found himself suppressing a yawn. She did that to him, too, like an unwitting Delilah taking Samson's strength away. Hyper-charged as he might be by her blood, he was also delightfully sleepy. He would spend a warm night in—or below—her arms.

In Matt's car it only got darker as the trees continued to cut out the moonlight. For a while they tried yelling for help. That did no good, and besides, as Meredith pointed out, they needed to conserve the oxygen in the car. So they sat still again.

Finally, Meredith reached into her jeans pocket and produced a set of keys with a tiny keychain flashlight. Its light was blue. She pressed it and they all leaned forward. Such a tiny thing to mean so much, Matt thought.

There was pressure against the front seats now.

"Bonnie?" Meredith said. "No one will hear us out here yelling. If anyone could hear us, they would have heard the tire and thought it was a gunshot."

Bonnie shook her head as if she didn't want to listen. She was still picking pine needles out of her skin.

She's right. We're miles away from anybody, Matt thought.

"There is something very bad here," Bonnie said. She said it quietly, but as if every word was being forced out one by one, like pebbles thrown into a pond.

Matt suddenly felt grayer. "How . . . bad?"

"It's so bad that it's . . . I've *never* felt anything like this before. Not when Elena got killed, not from Klaus, not from *anything*. I've *never* felt *anything* as bad as this. It's *so* bad, and it's so *strong*. I didn't think anything could be so strong. It's *pushing* on me, and I'm *afraid*—"

Meredith cut her off. "Bonnie, I know we can both only think of one way out of this—"

"There's *no* way out of this!"

"—I know you're afraid—"

"Who is there to call? I could do it . . . if there were someone to call. I can stare at your little flashlight and try to pretend it's a flame and do it—"

"Trancing?" Matt looked at Meredith sharply. "She's not supposed to do that anymore."

"Klaus is dead."

"But—"

"There's nobody to hear me!" Bonnie shrieked and then she broke down into huge sobs at last. "Elena and Stefan are too far away, and they're probably asleep by now! And there isn't anyone else!"

The three of them were being pushed together now, as branches pressed the seats back onto them. Matt and Meredith were close enough to look at each other right over Bonnie's head.

"Uh," Matt said, startled. "Um . . . are we sure?"

"No," Meredith said. She sounded both grim and hopeful. "Remember this morning? We are not at all sure.

In fact *I'm* sure he's still around somewhere."

Now Matt felt sick, and Meredith and Bonnie looked ill in the already strange-looking blue light. "And—right before this happened, we were talking about how a lot of stuff—"

"—basically everything that happened to change Elena—"

"—was all his fault."

"In the woods."

"With an open window."

Bonnie sobbed on.

Matt and Meredith, however, had made a silent agreement by eye contact. Meredith said, very gently, "Bonnie, what you said you would do; well, you're going to have to do it. Try to get through to Stefan, or waken Elena or—or apologize to . . . Damon. Probably the last, I'm afraid. But he's never seemed to want us all dead, and he must know that it won't help him with Elena if he kills her friends."

Matt grunted, skeptical. "He may not want us all dead, but he may wait until some of us are dead to save the others. I've never trus—"

"You've never wished him any harm," Meredith over-rode him in a louder voice.

Matt blinked at her and then shut up. He felt like an idiot.

"So, here, the flashlight's on," Meredith said, and even

in this crisis, her voice was steady, rhythmic, hypnotic. The pathetic little light was so precious, too. It was all they had to keep the darkness from becoming absolute.

But when the darkness became absolute, Matt thought, it would be because all light, all air, everything from the outside had been shut out, pushed out of the way by the pressure of the trees. And by then the pressure would have broken their skeletons.

"Bonnie?" Meredith's voice was the voice of every big sister who ever had come to her younger sibling's rescue. That gentle. That controlled. "Can you try to pretend it's a candle flame . . . a candle flame . . . a candle flame . . . and then try to trance?"

"I'm in trance already." Bonnie's voice was somehow distant—far away and almost echoing.

"Then ask for help," Meredith said softly.

Bonnie was whispering, over and over, clearly oblivious to the world around her: "Please, come help us. Damon, if you can hear me, please accept our apologies and come. You gave us a terrible scare, and I'm sure we deserved it, but please, please help. It hurts, Damon. It hurts so bad I could scream. But instead I'm putting all that energy into Calling you. Please, please, please help . . ."

For five, ten, fifteen minutes she kept it up, as the branches grew, enclosing them with their sweet, resinous scent. She kept it up far longer than Matt had ever thought she could endure.

Then the light went out. After that there was no sound but the whisper of the pines.

You had to admire the technique.

Damon was once again lounging in midair, even higher this time than when he'd entered Caroline's third-story window. He still had no idea of the names of trees, but that didn't stop him. This branch was like having a box seat over the drama unfolding below. He was starting to get a little bored, since nothing new was happening on the ground. He'd abandoned Damaris earlier this evening when *she* had gotten boring, talking about marriage and other subjects he wished to avoid. Like her current husband. Bo-ring. He'd left without really checking to see if she'd become a vampire—he tended to think so, and wouldn't that be a surprise when hubby got home? His lips trembled on the edge of a smile.

Below him, the play had almost reached its climax.

And you really had to admire the technique. Pack hunting. He had no idea what sort of nasty little creatures were manipulating the trees, but like wolves or lionesses, they seemed to have gotten it down to an art. Working together to capture prey that was too quick and too heavily armored for one of them alone to manage. In this case, a car.

The fine art of cooperation. Pity vampires were so

solitary, he thought. If we could cooperate, we'd own the world.

He blinked sleepily and then flashed a dazzling smile at nothing at all. Of course, if we could do that—say, take a city and divvy up the inhabitants—we'd finish it off by divvying up one another. Tooth and nail and Power would be wielded like the blade of a sword, until there was nothing left but shreds of quivering flesh and gutters running with blood.

Nice imagery, though, he thought, and let his eyelids droop to appreciate it. Artistic. Blood in scarlet pools, magically still liquid enough to run down white marble steps of—oh, say, the Kallimarmaron in Athens. An entire city gone quiet, purged of noisy, chaotic, hypocritical humans, with only their necessary bits left behind: a few arteries to pump the sweet red stuff out in quantity. The vampire version of the land of milk and honey.

He opened his eyes again in annoyance. Now things were getting loud down there. Humans yelling. Why? What was the point? The rabbit always squeals in the jaws of the fox, but when has another rabbit ever rushed up to save it?

There, a new proverb, *and* proof that humans are as stupid as rabbits, he thought, but his mood was ruined. His mind slid away from the fact, but it wasn't just the noise below that was disturbing him. Milk and honey, that had been . . . a mistake. Thinking about that had been a blunder. Elena's skin had been like milk that night a week ago, warm-white, not cool, even in the moonlight. Her bright hair in shadow had been like spilled honey. Elena wouldn't be happy to see the results of this night's pack hunting. She would cry tears like crystal dewdrops, and they would smell like salt.

Suddenly Damon stiffened. He sent one stealthy query of Power around him, a circle of radar.

But nothing bounced back, except the mindless trees at his feet. Whatever was orchestrating this, it was invisible.

Right, then. Let's try *this*, he thought: Concentrating on all the blood he'd drunk in the last few days, he blasted out a wash of pure Power, like Vesuvius erupting with a deadly pyroclastic explosion. It encircled him completely in every direction, a fifty-mile-per-hour bubble of Power like superheated gas.

Because it was back. Unbelievably, the parasite was trying to do it again, to get into his mind. It had to be.

Lulling him, he supposed, rubbing the back of his neck with absentminded fury, while its packmates finished off their prey in the car. Whispering things into his mind to keep him still, taking his own dark thoughts and echoing them back a shade or two darker, in a cycle that might have ended in him flying off to kill and kill again for the pure black velvet enjoyment of it.

Now Damon's mind was cold and dark with fury. He

stood, stretching his aching arms and shoulders, and then searched carefully, not with a simple radar ring, but with a blast of Power behind each stab, probing with his mind to find the parasite. It had to be out there; the trees were still going about their business. But he could find nothing, even though he'd used the fastest and most efficient method of scanning he knew: a thousand random stabs per second in a Drunkard's Walk search pattern. He should have found a dead body immediately. Instead he'd found *nothing*.

That made him even angrier than before, but there was a tinge of excitement to his fury. He'd wanted a fight; a chance to kill where the killing would be meaningful. And now here was an opponent who met all the qualifications—and Damon couldn't kill it because he couldn't find it. He sent a message, lambent with ferocity, in all directions.

I have already warned you once. Now I CHALLENGE *you. Show yourself*—OR ELSE STAY AWAY FROM ME*!*

He gathered Power, gathered it, gathered it again, thinking of all the different mortals who had contributed it. He held it, nurturing it, crafting it for its purpose, and raising its strength with all that his mind knew of fighting and of the skill and expertise of war. He held the Power until it felt as if he were holding a nuclear bomb in his arms. And then he let it go all at once, an explosion speeding in the opposite direction, away from him, nearing the speed of light.

Now, surely, he would feel the death throes of something enormously powerful and cunning—something that had managed to survive his previous strafings designed only for eldritch creatures.

Damon expanded his senses to their widest reach, waiting to hear or feel something shattering, combusting—something falling blind, with its own blood tumbling nearby, from a branch, from the air, from *somewhere*. From *somewhere* a creature should have plummeted to the ground or raked at it with huge dinosaur-like claws—a creature half-paralyzed and completely doomed, cooked from the inside out. But although he could feel the wind rising to a howl and huge black clouds pooling above him in response to his own mood, he still could sense no dark creature close enough to have entered his thoughts.

How strong was this thing? Where was it coming from?

Just for a moment, a thought flashed through his mind. A circle. A circle with a dot at its center. And the circle was the blast he'd shot away in all directions, and the dot was the only place his blast didn't reach. *Inside* him alre—

Snap! Suddenly his thoughts went blank. And then he began, sluggishly, slightly bewildered, to try to put the fractured pieces together. He had been thinking about the blast of Power he'd sent out, yes? And how he'd expected to feel something fall and die.

Hell, he couldn't even sense any ordinary animals bigger than a fox in the woods. Although his sweep of Power had been carefully made to affect only creatures of his kind of darkness, the ordinary animals had been so spooked that they'd gone running wildly from the area. He peered down. Hm. Except the trees around the car; and they weren't after him. Besides, whatever they were, they were only the pawns of an invisible killer. Not really sentient—not within the boundaries he had crafted so carefully.

Could he have been wrong? Half his fury had been for himself, for being so careless, so well-fed and confident that he'd let down his guard.

Well-fed . . . hey, maybe I'm drunk, he thought, and flashed the smile again at nothing, without even thinking about it. Drunk and paranoid and edgy. Pissed and pissed off.

Damon relaxed against the tree. The wind was scream-ing now, swirling and freezing, the sky full of roiling black clouds that cut out any light from the moon or stars. Just his kind of weather.

He was still edgy, but he couldn't find any reason to be. The only disturbance in the aura of the woods was the tiny crying of a mind inside the car, like a trapped bird with only one note. That would be the little one, the redheaded witch with the delicate neck. The one who'd been whining about life changing too much.

Damon gave a little more of his weight to the tree. He'd followed the car with his mind out of absent interest. It wasn't his fault that he'd caught them talking about him, but it did degrade their chances of rescue a bit.

He blinked slowly.

Odd that they'd had an accident trying not to run over a creature in approximately the same area he'd almost crashed the Ferrari trying to run one over. Pity he hadn't had a glimpse of their creature, but the trees were too thick.

The redheaded bird was crying again.

Well, do you want a change *now* or don't you, little witch? Make up your mind. You have to ask nicely.

And then, of course, *I* have to decide what kind of change you get.

Bonnie couldn't remember any more sophisticated prayer and so, like a tired child, she was
saying an old one: ". . . I pray the Lord my soul
to take. . . ." She had used up all her energy calling for
help and had gotten no response at all, just some feedback
noise. She was so sleepy now. The pain had gone away
and she was simply numb. The only thing bothering her
was the cold. But then, that could be taken care of, too.
She could just pull a blanket over herself, a thick, downy
blanket, and she would warm up. She knew it without
knowing how she knew.

The only thing that held her back from the blanket
was the thought of her mother. Her mother would be sad
if she stopped fighting. That was another thing she knew
without knowing how she knew. If she could just get a

message to her mother, explaining that she had fought as hard as she could, but that with the numbness and the cold, she couldn't keep it up. And that she had known she was dying, but that it hadn't hurt in the end, so there was no reason for Mom to cry. And next time she would learn from her mistakes, she promised . . . next time . . .

Damon's entry was meant to be dramatic, coordinated with a flash of lightning just as his boots hit the car. Simultaneously, he sent out another vicious lash of Power, this time directed at the trees, the puppets who were being controlled by an unseen master. It was so strong that he felt a shocked response from Stefan all the way back at the boardinghouse. And the trees . . . melted backward into the darkness. They'd ripped the top off as if the car had been a giant sardine can, he mused, standing on the hood. Handy for him.

Then he turned his attention to the human Bonnie, the one with the curls, who ought by rights to have been embracing his feet by now, and gasping out "Thank you!"

She wasn't. She was lying just as she had been in the embrace of the trees. Annoyed, Damon reached down to grab her hand, when he got a shock of his own. He sensed it before he touched it, smelled it before he felt it smear on his fingers. A hundred little pinpricks, each leaking blood. The evergreen's needles must have done that, taking blood from her or—no, pumping some resinous substance in. Some anesthetic to keep her still as it took whatever was the next step in its consumption of prey—something quite unpleasant, to judge by the manners of the creature so far. An injection of digestive juices seemed most likely.

Or perhaps simply something to keep her alive, like antifreeze for a car, he thought, realizing with another nasty shock just how cold she was. Her wrist was like ice. He glanced at the two other humans, the dark-haired girl with the disturbing, logical eyes, and the fair-haired boy who was always trying to pick a fight. He might just have cut this one too fine. It certainly looked bad for the other two. But he was going to save this one. Because it was his whim. Because she had called for his help so piteously. Because those creatures, those *malach*, had tried to make him watch her death, eyes half-focused on it as they took his mind off the present with a glorious daydream. *Malach*—it was a general word indicating a creature of darkness: a sister or brother of the night. But Damon thought it now as if the word itself were something evil, a sound to be spat or hissed.

He had no intention of letting *them* win. He picked Bonnie up as if she were a bit of dandelion fluff and slung her over one shoulder. Then he took off from the car. Flying without changing shape first was a challenge. Damon liked challenges.

He decided to take her to the nearest source of warm water, and that was the boardinghouse. He needn't disturb Stefan. There were half a dozen rooms in that warren that was making its genteel decline into the good Virginia mud. Unless Stefan was snoopy, he wouldn't go walking in on other folks' bathrooms.

As it turned out, Stefan was not only snoopy but *fast*. There was almost a collision: Damon and his burden came around a corner to find Stefan driving down the dark road with Elena, floating like Damon, bobbing behind the car as if she were a child's balloon.

Their first exchange of words was neither brilliant nor witty.

"What the hell are you doing?" exclaimed Stefan.

"What the hell are *you* doing?" Damon said, or began to say, when he noticed the tremendous difference in Stefan—and the tremendous Power that was Elena. While most of his mind simply reeled in shock, a small part of it immediately began to analyze the situation, to figure out how Stefan had gone from a nothing to a—a—

Good grief. Oh, well, might as well put a brave face on it.

"I felt a fight," Stefan said. "When did you become Peter Pan?"

"You should be glad you weren't in the fight. And I can fly because I have the Power, boy."

This was sheer bravado. In any case, it was perfectly correct, back when they were born, to address a younger relative as *ragazzo*, or "boy."

It wasn't now. And meanwhile the part of his brain that hadn't simply shut down was still analyzing. He could see, feel, do everything but *touch* Stefan's aura. And it was . . . unimaginable. If Damon hadn't been this close, hadn't been experiencing it firsthand, he wouldn't have believed it was possible for one person to have so much Power.

But he was looking at the situation with the same ability of cold and logical assessment that told him that his own Power—even after making himself drunk with the variety of women's blood he had taken in the last few days—his Power was nothing to Stefan's right now. And his cold and logical ability was also telling him that Stefan had been pulled out of bed for this, and that he hadn't had time—or hadn't been rational enough—to hide his aura.

"Well, now, look at you," Damon said with all the sarcasm that he could call up—and that turned out to be quite a lot. "Is it a halo? Did you get canonized while I wasn't looking? Am I addressing St. Stefan now?"

Stefan's telepathic response was unprintable. "Where are Meredith and Matt?" he added fiercely.

"Or," continued Damon, exactly as if Stefan hadn't spoken, "could it be that you merit congratulation for having learned the art of deception at last?"

"And what are you doing with Bonnie?" Stefan demanded, ignoring Damon's comments in turn.

"But you still don't seem to have a grasp of polysyllabic English, so I'll put this as simply as I can. You threw the fight."

"I threw the fight," Stefan said flatly, apparently seeing that Damon wasn't going to answer any of his questions until he'd told the truth. "I just thanked God that *you* seemed to be too mad or drunk to be very observant. I wanted to keep you and the rest of the world from figuring out just exactly what Elena's blood does. So you drove away without even trying to get a good look at her. And without suspecting that I could have shaken you off like a flea from the very beginning."

"I never thought you had it in you." Damon was reliving their little combat in all-too-vivid detail. It was true: he had never suspected that Stefan's performance had been entirely that—a performance—and that he could have thrown Damon down at any time and done whatever he'd wanted.

"And there's your benefactress." Damon nodded up to where Elena was floating, secured by—yes, it was true—secured by clothesline to the clutch. "Just a little lower than the angels, and crowned with glory and honor," he remarked, unable to help himself as he gazed up at her.

Elena was, in fact, so bright that to look at her with Power channeled to the eyes was like trying to stare straight into the sun.

"She seems to have forgotten how to hide as well; she's shining like a G0 star."

"She doesn't know how to lie, Damon." It was clear that Stefan's anger was steadily mounting. "Now tell me what's going on and what you've done to Bonnie."

The impulse to answer, *Nothing. Why, do you think I should?* was almost irresistible—*almost*. But Damon was facing a different Stefan than he'd ever seen before. This is not the little brother you know and love to trample into the ground, the voice of logic told him, and he heeded it.

"The other two huuu-mans," Damon said, drawing the word out to its full obscene length, "are in their auto-*mo*bile. And"—suddenly virtuous—"I was taking Bonnie to *your* place."

Stefan was standing by the car, at a perfect distance for examining Bonnie's outflung arm. The pinpricks turned into a smear of blood when he touched them, and Stefan examined his own fingers with horror. He kept repeating the experiment. Soon Damon would be drooling, a highly undignified behavior that he wished to avoid.

Instead, he concentrated on a nearby astronomical phenomenon.

The full moon, medium high, and white and pure as

snow. And Elena floating in front of it, wearing an old-fashioned high-necked nightgown—and little if anything else. As long as he looked at her without the Power needed to discern her aura, he could examine her as a girl rather than as an angel in the midst of blinding incandescence.

Damon cocked his head to get a better view of the silhouette. Yes, that was definitely the right apparel for her, and she should always stand in front of brilliant lights. If he—

Slam.

He was flying backward and to the left. He hit a tree, trying to make sure that Bonnie didn't hit it, too—she might break. Momentarily stunned, he floated—wafted really—down to the ground.

Stefan was on top of him.

"You," said Damon somewhat indistinctly through the blood in his mouth, "have been a naughty boy, boy."

"She made me. Literally. I thought she might die if I didn't take some of her blood—her aura was that swollen. Now you tell me what's wrong with Bonnie—"

"So you bled her despite your heroic unflagging resistance—"

Slam.

This new tree smelled of resin. I never particularly wanted to get acquainted with the insides of trees, Damon thought as he spat out a mouthful of blood. Even as a crow

I only use them when necessary.

Stefan had somehow snatched Bonnie out of the air while Damon was flying toward the tree. He was that fast now. He was very, very fast. Elena was a *phenomenon*.

"So now you have a secondhand idea what Elena's blood is like." *And* Stefan could hear Damon's private thoughts. Normally, Damon was always up for a fight, but right now he could almost hear Elena's weeping over her human friends, and something inside him felt tired. Very old—centuries old—and very tired.

But as for the question, well, *yes*. Elena was still bobbing aimlessly, sometimes spread-eagled and sometimes balled up like a kitten. Her blood was rocket fuel compared to the unleaded gasoline in most girls.

And Stefan wanted to fight. Wasn't even trying to hide it. I was right, Damon thought. For vampires, the urge to squabble is stronger than any other urge, even the need to feed or, in Stefan's case, the concern for his—what was the word? Oh, yes. *Friends*.

Now Damon was trying to elude a thrashing, trying to enumerate his assets, which weren't many, because Stefan was still holding him down. Thought. Speech. A penchant for fighting dirty that Stefan just couldn't seem to understand. Logic. An instinctive ability to find the chinks in his foe's armor . . .

Hmmm . . .

"Meredith and"—damn! What was that boy's *name*?— "her escort are dead by now, I think," he said innocently. "We can stay here and brawl, if that's what you want to call it, considering that I never laid a finger on you—or we can try to resuscitate them. Which will it be, I wonder?" He really did wonder about how much control Stefan had over himself right now.

As if Damon had zoomed out abruptly with a camera, Stefan seemed to become smaller. He had been floating a few feet above the ground; now he landed and looked about himself in astonishment, obviously unaware that he had been airborne.

Damon spoke in the pause while Stefan was most vulnerable. "I wasn't the one who hurt them," he added. "If you'll look at Bonnie"—thank badness, he knew *her* name—"you'll see that no vampire could do it. I think"—he added ingenuously, for shock value—"that the attackers were trees, controlled by malach."

"*Trees?*" Stefan barely took time to glance at Bonnie's pin-pricked arm. Then he said, "We need to get them indoors and into warm water. You take Elena—"

Oh, gladly. In fact I'd give anything, *anything*—

"—and this car with Bonnie right back to the boarding-house. Wake Mrs. Flowers. Do all you can for Bonnie. I'll go on ahead and get Meredith and Matt—"

That was it! Matt. Now if only he had a mnemonic—

"They're just up the road, right? That was where your first strafe of Power seemed to come from."

A strafe, was it? Why not be honest and just call it a feeble wash?

And while it was fresh in his mind . . . M for Mortal, A for Annoying, T for Thing. And there you had it. The pity was that it applied to all of them and yet not all of them were called MAT. Oh, damn—was there supposed to be another T at the end? Mortal, Annoying, Troublesome Thing? Annoying Terrible Thing?

"I said, is that all right?"

Damon returned to the present. "No, it's not all right. The other car's wrecked. It won't drive."

"I'll float it behind me." Stefan wasn't bragging, just making a statement of fact.

"It's not even in one piece."

"I'll bind the pieces. Come on, Damon. I'm sorry I strafed you; I had a completely wrong idea about what was going on. But Matt and Meredith may really be dying, and even with all my new Power, and all of Elena's, we may not be able to save them. I've raised Bonnie's core temperature a few degrees but I don't dare to stay and bring it up slowly enough. *Please*, Damon." He was putting Bonnie in the passenger seat.

Well, that *sounded* like the old Stefan, but coming from this powerhouse, the new Stefan, it had rather different undertones. Still, as long as Stefan *thought* he was a mouse, he was a mouse. End of discussion.

Earlier Damon had felt like Mount Vesuvius exploding. Now he suddenly felt as if he were *standing near* Vesuvius, and the mountain was rumbling. Ye gods! He actually felt seared just being this close to Stefan.

He called on all his considerable resources, mentally packing himself in ice, and hoped that at least a breath of coolness underlay his answer. "I'll go. See you later—hope the humans aren't dead yet."

As they parted, Stefan sent him a powerful message of disapproval—not strafing him with sheer elemental pain, as he had before when throwing Damon against the tree, but making sure that his opinion of his brother was stamped across every word.

Damon sent Stefan a last message as he went. *I don't understand*, he thought innocently toward the disappearing Stefan. *What's wrong with saying that I hope the humans are still alive? I've been in greeting card shops, you know*—he didn't mention that it wasn't for the cards but for the young cashiers—*and they had sections like "Hope you get well" and "Sympathy," which I suppose means that the previous card's spell wasn't strong enough. So what's wrong with saying "I hope they're not dead"?*

Stefan didn't even bother to answer. But Damon flashed a quick and brilliant smile anyway, as he turned the Porsche around and set off for the boardinghouse.

He tugged on the clothesline that kept Elena bobbing above him. She floated—nightgown billowing—above Bonnie's head—or rather where Bonnie's head should have been. Bonnie had always been small, and this freezing illness had her crumpled into the fetal position. Elena could practically sit on her.

"Hello, princess. Looking gorgeous, as always. And you're not too bad yourself."

It was one of the worst opening lines of his life, he thought dejectedly. But he wasn't feeling quite himself. Stefan's transformation had startled him—that must be what's wrong, he decided.

"Da . . . mon."

Damon started. Elena's voice was slow and hesitant . . . and absolutely beautiful: molasses dripping sweetness, honey falling straight from the comb. It was lower in pitch, he was sure, than it had been before her transformation, and it had become a true Southern drawl. To a vampire it resembled the sweet drip-drip of a newly opened human vein.

"Yes, angel. Have I called you 'angel' before? If not, it was purely an oversight."

And as he said this, he realized that that was another component to her voice, one he'd missed before: purity. The lancing purity of a seraph of seraphim. That should have put him off, but instead it just reminded him that Elena was someone to take seriously, never lightly.

I'd take you seriously or lightly or any way you prefer, Damon thought, if you weren't so stuck on my idiot younger brother.

Twin violet suns turned on him: Elena's eyes. She'd heard him.

For the first time in his life, Damon was surrounded by people more powerful than he was. And to a vampire, Power was everything: material goods, community position, trophy mate, comfort, sex, cash, candy.

It was an odd feeling. Not entirely unpleasant in regards to Elena. He liked strong women. He'd been looking for one strong enough for centuries.

But Elena's glance very effectively brought his thoughts back to their situation. He parked askew outside the boardinghouse, snatched up the stiffening Bonnie, and floated up the twisting, narrowing staircase towards Stefan's room. It was the only place he *knew* there was a bathtub.

There was barely room for three inside the tiny bathroom, and Damon was the one carrying Bonnie. He ran water into the ancient, four-footed tub based on what his exquisitely tuned senses said was five degrees above her current icy temperature. He tried to explain to Elena what he was doing, but she seemed to have lost interest and was floating round and round Stefan's bedroom, like a close-up of Tinkerbell caged. She kept bumping the closed window and then zooming over to the open door, looking out.

What a dilemma. Ask Elena to undress and bathe Bonnie, and risk her putting Bonnie in the tub wrong side up? Or ask Elena to do the job and watch over them both, but not touch—unless disaster struck? Plus, someone had to find Mrs. Flowers and get hot drinks going. Write a note and send Elena with it? There might be more casualties in here any moment now.

Then Damon caught Elena's eye, and all petty and conventional concerns seemed to drop away. Words appeared in his brain without bothering to come through his ears.

Help her. Please!

He turned back to the bathroom, lay Bonnie on the thick rug there and shelled her like a shrimp. Off with the sweatshirt, off with the summer top that went under it. Off with the small bra—A cup, he noticed sadly, discarding it, trying not to look at Bonnie directly. But he couldn't help but see that the prickling marks the tree had left were everywhere.

Off with the jeans, and then a small hitch because he had to sit and take each foot in his lap to get the tightly tied high-top sneakers off before the jeans would come past her ankles. Off with socks.

And that was all. Bonnie was left naked except for her

own blood and her pink silky underwear. He picked her up and put her in the tub, soaking himself in the process. Vampires associated baths with virgin's blood, but only the really crazy ones tried it.

The water in Bonnie's bathtub turned pink when he put her in. He kept the tap running because the tub was so large, and then sat back to consider the situation. The tree had been pumping something into her with its needles. Whatever it was, it wasn't good. So it ought to come out. Most sensible solution was to suck it as if it were a snakebite, but he was hesitant to try that until he was sure Elena wouldn't crush his skull if she found him methodically sucking Bonnie's upper body.

He would have to settle for next best. The bloody water didn't quite conceal Bonnie's diminutive form, but it helped to blur the details. Damon supported Bonnie's head against the edge of the tub with one hand, and with the other he began to squeeze and massage the poison out of one arm.

He knew he was doing the right thing when he smelled the resinous scent of pine. It was so thick and viscid itself that it hadn't yet disappeared into Bonnie's body. He was getting a small amount of it out this way, but was it enough?

Cautiously, watching the door and cranking his senses up to cover their broadest spectrum, Damon lifted Bonnie's hand to his lips as if he were going to kiss it. Instead, he took her wrist in his mouth and, suppressing every urge he had to bite, instead simply sucked.

He spat almost immediately. His mouth was full of resin. The massage wasn't enough by far. Even suction, if he could get a couple of dozen vampires and attach them all over Bonnie's little body like leeches, wouldn't be enough.

He sat back on his heels and looked at her, this fatally poisoned woman-child he'd as good as given his word to save. For the first time, he became aware that he was soaked to the waist. He gave an irritated glance toward the heavens and then shrugged out of his black bomber jacket.

What could he do? Bonnie needed medicine, but he had no idea what specific medicine she needed, and there was no witch he knew of to appeal to. Was Mrs. Flowers acquainted with arcane knowledge? Would she give it to him if she were? Or was she just a batty old lady? What was a generic medicine—for a human? He could give her over to her own people and let them try their bungling sciences—take her to a hospital—but they would be working with a girl who'd been poisoned by the Other Side, by the dark places they would never be allowed to see or understand.

Absently, he had been rubbing a towel over his arms and hands and black shirt. Now, he looked at the towel and decided that Bonnie deserved at least a sop to modesty, especially since he could think of no more work to be done on her. He soaked the towel and then spread it out and pushed it underwater to cover Bonnie from throat to feet. It floated in some places, sank in others, but generally did the job.

He turned the water temperature up again, but it made no difference. Bonnie was stiffening into the true death, young as she was. His peers in old Italy had had it right, he thought, a female like this was a *maiden*, no longer girl, not yet woman. It was especially apposite since any vampire could tell that she was a maiden in both senses.

And it had all been done under his nose. The lure, the pack-attack, the marvelous technique and synchronization—they had killed this maiden while he sat and watched. He'd applauded it.

Slowly, inside, Damon could feel something growing. It had sparked when he thought of the audacity of the malach, hunting his humans right under his nose. It didn't ask the question of when the group in the car had become *his* humans—he supposed it was because they had been so close lately that it seemed they were his to dispose of, to say whether they lived or died, or whether they became what he was. The growing thing surged when he'd thought of the way the malach had manipulated his thoughts, drawing him into a blissful contemplation of death in general terms, while death in very specific terms was going on right at his feet. And now it was reaching incendiary levels because he had been shown up too many times today. It really was unbearable. . . .

. . . and it was Bonnie. . . .

Bonnie, who had never hurt a—a harmless thing for malice. Bonnie, who was like a kitten, making airy pounces at no prey at all. Bonnie, with her hair that was called something strawberry, but that looked simply as if it was on fire. Bonnie of the translucent skin, with the delicate violet fjords and estuaries of veins all over her throat and inner arms. Bonnie, who had lately taken to looking at him sideways with her large childlike eyes, big and brown, under lashes like stars. . . .

His jaws and canines were aching, and his mouth felt as if it were on fire from the poisonous resin. But all that could be ignored, because he was consumed with one other thought.

Bonnie had called for his help for nearly half an hour before succumbing to the darkness.

That was what needed to be said. Needed to be examined. Bonnie had called for Stefan—who had been too far away and too busy with his angel—but she had called for Damon, too, and she had pleaded for his help.

And he had ignored it. With three of Elena's friends at his feet, he had ignored their agonies, had ignored

Bonnie's frenzied pleas not to let them die.

Usually, this sort of thing would only make him take off for some other town. But somehow he was still here and still tasting the bitter consequences of his act.

Damon leaned back with his eyes closed, trying to shut out the overwhelming smell of blood and the musty scent of . . . something.

He frowned and looked around. The little room was clean even to its corners. Nothing musty here. But the odor wouldn't go away.

And then he remembered.

12

It came back to him, all of it: the cramped aisles and the tiny windows and the musty smell of old books. He had been in Belgium some fifty years ago, and had been surprised to find an English-language book on such a subject still in existence. But there it was, its cover worn to a solid burnished rust, with nothing of the writing remaining, if there ever had been any. Pages were missing inside, so no one would ever know the author or the title, if either had ever been printed there. Every "receipt"—recipe, or charm, or spell—inside involved forbidden knowledge.

Damon could easily remember the simplest spell of all: "Ye Bloode of ye Samphire or Vampyre i*f* fair goode a*f* a general physic for all Maladie*f* or mischief Done by those who Dance in the Woode*f* at Moonspire."

These malach had certainly been doing mischief in the woods, and it was the month of Moonspire, the month of the "summer solstice" in the Old Tongue. Damon didn't want to leave Bonnie, and he certainly didn't want Elena to see what he was going to do next. Still supporting Bonnie's head above the warm pinkish water, he opened his shirt. There was a knife of ironwood in a sheath at his hip. He removed it and, in one quick motion, cut himself at the base of his throat.

Plenty of blood now. The problem was how to get her to drink. Sheathing the dagger, he lifted her out of the water and tried to put her lips to the cut.

No, that was *stupid*, he thought, with unaccustomed self-deprecation. She's going to get cold again, and you don't have any way to make her swallow. He let Bonnie lapse back into the water and thought. Then he pulled out the knife again and made another cut: this one on his arm, at the wrist. He followed the vein there until blood was not just dripping but streaming steadily out. Then he put that wrist to Bonnie's upturned mouth, adjusting the angle of her head with his other hand. Her lips were partly open and the dark red blood flowed beautifully. Periodically she swallowed. There was life in her yet.

It was just like feeding a baby bird, he thought, tremendously pleased with his memory, his ingenuity, and— well, just himself.

He smiled brilliantly at nothing in particular.

Now if it would only work.

Damon changed position slightly to be more comfortable and turned the hot water up again, all while holding Bonnie, feeding her, all—he knew—gracefully and without a wasted movement. This was fun. It appealed to his sense of the ridiculous. Here, right now, a vampire was not supping from a human, but was trying to save it from certain death by feeding it vampire blood.

More than that. He had followed all sorts of human traditions and customs by trying to strip Bonnie without compromising her maidenly modesty. That was exciting. Of course, he'd seen her body anyway; there had been no way to avoid that. But it was really more thrilling when he was *trying* to follow the rules. He'd never done that before.

Maybe that was how Stefan got his kicks. No, Stefan had Elena, who had been human, vampire, and invisible spirit, and now appeared to be living angel, if such a thing existed. Elena was kicky enough on her own. Yet he hadn't thought of her in *minutes*. It might even be a record of Elena-overlooking.

He'd better call her, maybe get her in here and explain how this was working so there was no reason to crush his skull. It would probably look better.

Damon suddenly realized he couldn't feel Elena's aura in Stefan's bedroom. But before he could investigate there was a crash, then pounding footsteps, and then another crash, much closer. And then the bathroom door was kicked open by Mortal Annoying Troublesome. . . .

Matt advanced menacingly, got his feet tangled, and looked down to untangle them. His tanned cheeks were swept with a sudden sunset. He was holding up Bonnie's small pink brassiere. He dropped it as if it had bitten him, picked it up again, and whirled around, only to cannon into Stefan, who was entering. Damon watched, entertained.

"How do you *kill* them, Stefan? Do you just need a stake? Can you hold him while—*blood*! He's feeding her blood!" Matt interrupted himself, looking as if he might attack Damon on his own. Bad idea, thought Damon.

Matt locked eyes with him. Confronting the monster, Damon thought, even more entertained. "Let . . . her . . . go." Matt spoke slowly, probably meaning to convey menace, but sounding, Damon thought, as if he thought that Damon was mentally impaired.

Mortally Unable To Talk, Damon mused. But that made . . . "Mutt," he said aloud, shaking his head slightly. Maybe, though, it would remind him in the future.

"*Mutt?* You're calling—? God, Stefan, please help me kill him! *He's killed Bonnie.*" The words spilled out of Matt in a single gushing flow, a single breath. Woefully, Damon saw his latest acronym go down in flames.

Stefan was surprisingly calm. He put Matt behind him and said, "Go and sit down with Elena and Meredith," in a way that was not a suggestion, and turned back to his brother. "You didn't feed from her," he said, and *this* was not a question.

"Swill poison? Not my kind of fun, little brother."

One corner of Stefan's mouth quirked up. He made no response to this, but simply looked at Damon with eyes that were . . . *knowing*. Damon bridled.

"I told the truth!"

"Going to take it up as a hobby?"

Damon started to release Bonnie, figuring that dropping her into bloodstained water would be the proper precursor to walking out of this dump, but . . .

But. She was his baby bird. She'd swallowed enough of his blood now that any more would begin to Change her seriously. And if the amount of blood he had already given her wasn't enough, it simply wasn't a remedy in the first place. Besides, the miracle worker was here.

He closed the cut on his arm enough to stop the bleeding and started to speak. . . .

And the door crashed open again.

This time it was Meredith, and she had Bonnie's bra. Both Stefan and Damon quailed. Meredith was, Damon thought, a very scary person. At least she took the time, which Mutt had not, to look over the trampled clothes on the bathroom floor. She said to Stefan, "How is she?" which Mutt had not, either.

"She's going to be fine," Stefan said and Damon was surprised at his feeling of . . . not relief, of course, but of a job well done. Plus, now he might avoid being thrashed to within an inch of his life by Stefan.

Meredith took a deep breath and closed her frightening eyes briefly. When she did that, her whole face glowed. Maybe she was praying. It had been centuries since Damon had prayed; and he had never had any prayer answered.

Then Meredith opened her eyes, shook herself, and started looking scary again. She nudged the pile of clothes on the floor and said, slowly and forcefully, "If the item that matches *this* is not still on Bonnie's body, there is going to be trouble."

She waved the now infamous bra like a flag.

Stefan looked confused. How could he not understand the mighty missing lingerie question? Damon wondered. How could anyone be such a . . . such an unobservant fool? Didn't Elena wear any—ever? Damon sat frozen, too arrested by the images in his own inner world to move for a moment. Then he spoke up. He had the answer to Meredith's riddle.

"Do you want to come and check?" he asked, turning his head virtuously away.

"Yes, I do."

He remained with his back to her as she approached the tub, plunged her hand into the warm pink water, and swished the towel a little. He heard her let out her breath in relief.

When he turned around she said, "There's blood on your mouth." Her dark eyes looked darker than ever.

Damon was surprised. He hadn't gone and pierced the redhead out of habit and then *forgotten* it, had he? But then he realized the reason.

"You tried to suck the poison out, didn't you?" Stefan said, throwing him a white face towel. Damon wiped the side Meredith had been looking at and came up with a bloody smear. No wonder his mouth had been stinging like fire. That poison was pretty nasty stuff, although it clearly didn't affect vampires the way it did humans.

"And there's blood on your throat," Meredith went on.

"Unsuccessful experiment," Damon said, and shrugged.

"So you cut your wrist. Pretty seriously."

"For a human, maybe. Is the press conference over?"

Meredith settled back. He could read her expression and he smiled inwardly. Extra! Extra! SCARY MEREDITH THWARTED. He knew the look of those who had to give up on cracking the Damon nut.

Meredith stood up. "Is there anything I can get him to stop his mouth bleeding? Something to drink, maybe?"

Stefan just looked stricken. Stefan's problem—well, a part of one of Stefan's many problems—was that he thought feeding was sinful. Even to talk about.

Maybe it was actually kickier that way. People relished anything they thought was sinful. Even vampires did. Damon was put out. How did you go back in time to when *anything* was sinful? Because he was sadly out of kicks.

With her back turned, Meredith was less scary. Damon risked an answer to the question of what he could drink.

"*You*, darling . . . you darling."

"One too many darlings," Meredith said mysteriously, and before Damon could figure out that she was simply making a point about linguistics, and not commenting on his personal life, she was gone. With the traveling bra.

Now Stefan and Damon were alone. Stefan came a step closer, keeping his eyes off the tub. You miss so much, you chump, Damon thought. That was the word he'd been searching for earlier. Chump.

"You did a lot for her," Stefan said, seeming to find it as hard to look at Damon as at the tub. This left him very little to stare at. He chose a wall.

"You told me you'd beat me up if I didn't. I've never cared for beatings." He flashed his dazzling smile at Stefan and kept it up until Stefan started to turn to look at him, and then turned it off immediately.

"You went beyond the call of duty."

"With you, little brother, one never knows where duty ends. Tell me, what does infinity look like?"

Stefan heaved a sigh. "At least you're not the kind of

bully who only terrorizes when he has the upper hand."

"Are you inviting me to 'step outside,' as they say?"

"No, I'm complimenting you on saving Bonnie's life."

"I didn't realize I had a choice. How, by the way, did you manage to cure Meredith and—and . . . how did you manage?"

"Elena kissed them. Didn't you even realize she was gone? I brought them back here, and she came downstairs and breathed into their mouths and it cured them. From what I've seen, she seems to be slowly turning from spirit to full human. I'm guessing it will take another few days, just from looking at her progress since she woke up until now."

"At least she's talking. Not much, but you can't ask for everything." Damon was remembering the view from the Porsche, with the top down and Elena bobbing like a balloon. "This little redhead hasn't said a word," Damon added querulously, and then shrugged. "Same difference."

"*Why*, Damon? Why not just admit that you care about her, at least enough to keep her living—and without even molesting her? You knew she couldn't afford to lose blood. . . ."

"It was an experiment," Damon explained painstakingly. And it was over now. Bonnie would wake or sleep, live or die, in Stefan's hands—not his. He was wet, he was uncomfortable, he was far enough from this night's meal to be hungry and cross. His mouth hurt. "You take her head now," he said brusquely. "I'm leaving. You and Elena and . . . Mutt can finish—"

"His name is Matt, Damon. It's not hard to remember."

"It is if you have absolutely no interest in him. There are too many lovely ladies in this vicinity to make him anything but last choice for a snack."

Stefan hit the wall hard. His fist broke through the ancient plastering. "Damn it, Damon, that's not all there is to humans."

"It's all I ask of them."

"You *don't* ask. That's the problem."

"It was a euphemism. It's all I plan to *take* from them, then. It's certainly all I'm interested in. Don't try to make-believe that it's anything more. There's no point in trying to find evidence for a pretty lie."

Stefan's fist flew out. It was his left fist, and Damon was supporting Bonnie's head on that side, so he couldn't lean away gracefully as he normally would. She was unconscious; she might take in a lungful of water and die immediately. Who knew about these humans, especially when they were poisoned?

Instead, he concentrated on sending all his shielding to the right side of his chin. He figured he could take a punch, even from the New Improved Stefan without losing his hold on the girl—even if Stefan broke his jaw.

Stefan's fist stopped a few millimeters away from Damon's face.

There was a pause; the brothers looked at each other across a distance of two feet.

Stefan took a deep breath and sat back. "Now will you admit it?"

Damon was genuinely puzzled. "Admit what?"

"That you care something for them. Enough to take a punch rather than letting Bonnie go underwater."

Damon stared, then began to laugh and found he couldn't stop.

Stefan stared back. Then he shut his eyes and half-turned away in pain.

Damon still had a case of the giggles. "And you th-thought that I cuh-cared about one little hu-hu-hu . . ."

"Why did you do it, then?" Stefan said tiredly.

"Whu-whu-whim. I t-told y-yuh-you. Just wuh-huh-huhuha . . ." Damon collapsed, punch-drunk from lack of food and from too many varying emotions.

Bonnie's head went underwater.

Both vampires dived for her, head butting each other as they collided over the center of the tub. Both fell back briefly, dazed.

Damon wasn't laughing anymore. If anything, he was fighting like a tiger to get the girl out of the water. Stefan was, too, and with his newly sharpened reflexes, he looked close to winning. But it was as Damon had thought just an hour or so earlier—neither one of them even considered cooperating to get the girl. Each was trying to do it alone, and each was impeding the other.

"Get out of my way, brat," Damon snarled, almost hissing in menace.

"You don't give a damn about her. *You* get out of the way—"

There was something like a geyser and Bonnie exploded upward from the water on her own. She spat out a mouthful and cried, "What's going on?" in tones to melt a heart of stone.

Which they did. Contemplating his bedraggled little bird, who was clutching the towel to her instinctively, with her fiery hair plastered to her head and her big brown eyes blinking between strands, something swelled in Damon. Stefan had run to the door to tell the others the good news. For a moment it was just the two of them: Damon and Bonnie.

"It tastes awful," Bonnie said woefully, spitting out more water.

"I know," Damon said, staring at her. The new thing he was feeling had swollen inside his soul until the pressure was almost too much to stand. When Bonnie said, "But I'm alive!" with an abrupt 180-degree turn in mood, her heart-shaped face flushing suddenly with joy, the fierce pride Damon felt in response was intoxicating. He and he alone had brought her back from the edge of icy death. Her poison-filled body had been cured by him; it was his blood that had dissolved and dispersed the toxin, *his* blood—

And then the swelling thing burst.

There was, to Damon, a palpable if not audible crack as the stone encasing his soul burst open and a great piece fell away.

With something inside him singing, he clutched Bonnie to him, feeling the wet towel through his raw silk shirt, and feeling Bonnie's slight body under the towel. Definitely a maiden, and not a child, he thought dizzily, whatever the writing on that infamous scrap of pink nylon had claimed. He clutched at her as if he needed her for blood—as if they were in hurricane-tossed seas and to let go of her would be to lose her.

His neck hurt fiercely, but more cracks were spreading all over the stone; it was going to explode completely, letting the *Damon* it held inside out—and he was too drunk on pride and joy, yes, joy, to care. Cracks were spreading in every direction, pieces of stone flying off . . .

Bonnie pushed him away.

She had surprising strength for someone with such a slight build. She pushed herself out of his arms completely. Her expression had changed radically again: now her face showed only fear and desperation—and, yes, revulsion.

"Help! Somebody, please, *help!*" Her brown eyes were

huge and now her face was white again.

Stefan had whirled around. All he saw was what Meredith saw, darting under his arm from the other room, or what Matt saw, trying to peer into the tiny, over-full bathroom: Bonnie fiercely clutching her towel, trying to make it cover her, and Damon kneeling by the bath, his face without expression.

"*Please* help. He heard me calling—I could *feel* him on the other end—but he just watched. He stood and *watched* us all dying. He wants all humans dead, with our blood running down white steps somewhere. Please, get him *away* from me!"

So. The little witch was more proficient than he had imagined. It wasn't unusual to recognize that someone was getting your transmissions—you got feedback—but to identify the individual took talent. Plus, she'd obviously heard the echoes of some of his thoughts. She was gifted, his bird . . . no, not his bird, not with her looking at him with a look as close to hatred as Bonnie could manage.

There was a silence. Damon had a chance to deny the charge, but why bother? Stefan would be able to gauge the truth of it. Maybe Bonnie, too.

Revulsion was flying from face to face, as if it were a swiftly-catching disease.

Now Meredith was hurrying forward, grabbing another towel. She had some kind of hot drink in her other hand—cocoa, by the smell. It was hot enough to be an effective weapon—no way to dodge all of that, not for a tired vampire.

"Here," she said to Bonnie. "You're safe. Stefan's here. I'm here. Matt's here. Take this towel; let's just put it around your shoulders."

Stefan had stood silently, watching all this—no, watching his brother. Now, his face hardening in finality, he said one word.

"Out."

Dismissed like a dog. Damon groped for his jacket behind him, found it, and wished that his groping for his sense of humor could be as successful. The faces around him were all the same. They could have been carved in stone.

But not stone as hard as that that was coming together again around his soul. That rock was remarkably quick to mend—and an extra layer was added, like the layering of a pearl, but not covering anything nearly so pretty.

Their faces were still all the same as Damon tried to get out of the small room that had too many people in it. Some of them were speaking; Meredith to Bonnie, Mutt—no, Matt—pouring out a stream of pure acidic hatred . . . but Damon didn't really hear the words. He could smell too much blood here. Everyone had little wounds. Their individual scents—different beasts in *the herd*—closed in on him. His head was spinning. He had to get out of here or he'd be snatching the nearest warm vessel and draining it dry. Now he was more than dizzy; he was too hot, too . . . *thirsty*.

Very, very thirsty. He had worked a long time without feeding and now he was surrounded by prey. *They* were circling *him*. How could he stop himself from grabbing just one of them? Would one really be missed?

Then there was the one he hadn't seen yet, and didn't want to see. To witness Elena's lovely features twisted into the same mask of revulsion he saw on every other face here would be . . . distasteful, he thought, his old sense of dispassion finally returning to him.

But it couldn't be avoided. As Damon came out of the bathroom, Elena was right in front of him, floating like an oversized butterfly. His eyes were drawn to exactly what he didn't want to see: her expression.

Elena's features didn't mirror the others. She looked worried, upset. But there wasn't a trace of the disgust or hatred that showed on all the other faces.

She even spoke, in that strange mind-speech that wasn't, somehow, like telepathy, but which allowed her to get in two levels of communication at once.

"Da—mon."

Tell about the malach. Please.

Damon just raised an eyebrow at her. Tell a bunch of humans about *himself*? Was she being deliberately ridiculous?

Besides, the malach hadn't really done anything. They

had distracted him for a few minutes, that was all. No point in blaming malach when all they had done was enhance his own views briefly. He wondered if Elena had any notion of the content of his little nighttime daydream.

"Da—mon."

I can see it. Everything. But, still, please . . .

Oh, well, maybe spirits got used to seeing *everybody's* dirty laundry. Elena made no response to that thought, so he was left in the dark.

In the dark. Which was what he was used to, where he had come from. They would all go their separate ways, the humans to their warm dry houses and he to a tree in the woods. Elena would stay with Stefan, of course.

Of course.

"Under the circumstances, I won't say *au revoir*," Damon said, flashing his dazzling smile at Elena, who looked gravely back at him. "We'll just say 'good-bye' and leave it at that."

There was no answer from the humans.

"Da—mon." Elena was crying now.

Please. Please.

Damon started out into the dark.

Please . . .

Rubbing at his neck, he kept going.

13

Much later that night, Elena couldn't sleep. She didn't want to be hemmed in inside the Tall Room, she said. Secretly, Stefan worried that she wanted to go outside and track the malach that had attacked the car. But he didn't think she was able to lie, now, and she kept bumping against the shut window, chiming to him that she just wanted air. Outside air.

"We should put some clothes on you."

But Elena was bewildered—and stubborn. *It's Night.... This is my Night Gown*, she said. *You didn't like my Day Gown.* Then she bumped the window again. Her "Day Gown" had been his blue shirt, which, belted, made a sort of very short chemise on her, coming to the middle of her thighs.

Right now what she wanted fit in with his own desires so completely that he felt . . . a bit guilty over the prospect. But he allowed himself to be persuaded.

They drifted, hand in hand, Elena like a ghost or angel in her white nightgown, Stefan all in black, feeling himself almost disappear where the trees obscured the moonlight. Somehow they ended up in the Old Wood, where skeletons of trees mixed with the living branches. Stefan stretched his newly improved senses to the widest but could only find the normal inhabitants of the forest, slowly and hesitantly returning after being frightened off by Damon's lash of Power. Hedgehogs. Deer. Dog-foxes, and one poor vixen with twin kits, who hadn't been able to run because of her children. Birds. All the animals that helped to make the forest the wondrous place it was.

Nothing that felt like malach or seemed as if it could do any harm.

He began to wonder if Damon had simply invented the creature that influenced him. Damon was a tremendously convincing liar.

He was telling the truth, Elena chimed. *But either it's invisible or it's gone now. Because of you. Your Power.*

He looked at her and found her looking at him with a mixture of pride and another emotion that was easily identified—but startling to see out of doors.

She tilted her face up, its classic lines pure and pale in the moonlight.

Her cheeks were rose pink with blushing, and her lips were slightly pursed.

Oh . . . hell, Stefan thought wildly.

"After all you've been through," he began, and made his first mistake. He took hold of her arms. There, some sort of synergy between his Power and hers started to bring them, in a very slow spiral, upward.

And he could feel the warmth of her. The sweet softness of her body. She still was waiting, eyes closed, for her kiss.

We can start all over again, she suggested hopefully.

And that was true enough. He wanted to give back to her the feelings she had given to him in his room. He wanted to hold her hard; he wanted to kiss her until she trembled. He wanted to make her melt and swoon with it.

He could do it, too. Not just because you learned a thing or two about women when you were a vampire, but because he knew Elena. They were really one at heart, one soul.

Please? Elena chimed.

But she was so young now, so vulnerable in her pure white nightgown, with her creamy skin flushing pink in anticipation. It couldn't be right to take advantage of someone like that.

Elena opened her violet-blue eyes, silvered by the moonlight, and looked right at him.

Do you want . . . She said it with sobriety in the mouth but mischief in her eyes. *. . . to see how many times you can make me say please?*

God, no. But that sounded so grown-up that Stefan helplessly took her into his arms. He kissed the top of her silky head. He kissed downward from there, only avoiding the little rosebud mouth that was still puckered in lonely supplication. *I love you. I love you.* He found that he was almost crushing her ribs and tried to let go, but Elena held on as tightly as she could, holding his arms to her.

Do you want—the chime was the same, innocent and ingenuous—*to see how many times I can make* you *say please?*

Stefan stared at her for a moment. Then, with a sort of wildness in his heart, he fell on the little rosebud mouth and kissed it breathless, kissed it until he himself was so dizzy that he had to let her go, just an inch or two.

Then he looked into her eyes again. A person could lose themselves in eyes like that, could fall forever into their starry violet depths. He wanted to. But more than that, he wanted something else.

"I want to kiss you," he whispered, right at the portal of her right ear, nipping it.

Yes. She was definite about that.

"Until you faint in my arms."

He felt the shiver go through her body. He saw the violet eyes go misty, half closing. But to his surprise he got back an immediate, if slightly breathless, "Yes," from Elena out loud.

And so he did.

Just short of swooning, with little shivers going through her, and little cries that he tried to stop with his own mouth, he kissed her. And then, because it was Time, and because the shivers were starting to have a painful edge to them, and Elena's breath was coming so quick and hard when he let her breathe that he really was afraid that she might pass out, he solemnly used his own fingernail to open a vein in his neck for her.

And Elena, who once had been only human, and would have been horrified by the idea of drinking another person's blood, clasped herself to him with a small choked sound of joy. And then he could feel her mouth warm, warm against the flesh of his neck, and he felt her shudder hard, and he felt the heady sensation of having his blood drawn out by the one he loved. He wanted to pour his entire being out in front of Elena, to give her everything that he was, or ever would be. And he knew that this was the way she had felt, letting him drink her blood. That was the sacred bond they shared.

It made him feel that they had been lovers since the beginning of the universe, since the very first dawning of the very first star out of the darkness. It was something very primitive, and very deeply ingrained in him. When he first felt the flow of blood into her mouth, he had to stifle a cry against her hair. And then he was whispering to her, fierce, involuntary things about how he loved her and how they could never be parted, and endearments and absurdities wrenched from him in a dozen different languages. And then there were no more words, only feelings.

And so they slowly spiraled up in the moonlight, the white nightgown sometimes wrapping itself around his black-clad legs, until they reached the top of the trees, living and standing but dead.

It was a very solemn, very private ceremony of their own, and they were far too lost in joy to look out for any danger. But Stefan had already checked for that, and he knew that Elena had, too. There was no danger; there was only the two of them, drifting and bobbing with the moon shining down like a benediction.

One of the most useful things Damon had learned lately—more useful than flying, although that had been something of a kick—was to shield his presence absolutely.

He had to drop all his barriers, of course. They would show up even in a casual scan. But that didn't matter, because if no one could see him, no one could find him. And therefore he was safe. Q.E.D.

But tonight, after walking out of the boardinghouse, he had gone out to the Old Wood to find himself a tree to sulk in.

It wasn't that he minded what human trash thought of him, he thought venomously. It would be like worrying what a chicken thought of him just before he wrung its neck. And, of all things he cared *least* about, his brother's opinion was number one.

But Elena had been there. And even if she had understood—had made efforts to get the others to understand—it was just too humiliating, being thrown out in front of her.

And so he had retired, he thought bitterly, into the only retreat he could call home. Although that was a little ridiculous, since he could have spent the night in Fell's Church's best hotel (its only hotel) or with any number of sweet young girls who might invite a weary traveler in for a drink . . . of water. A wave of Power to put the parents to sleep, and he could have had shelter, as well as a warm and willing snack, until morning.

But he was in a vicious mood, and he just wanted to be alone. He was a little afraid to hunt. He wouldn't be able to control himself with a panicked animal in his present state of mind. All he could think of was ripping and tearing and making somebody very, very unhappy.

The animals were coming back, though, he noticed, careful to use only ordinary senses and nothing that would betray his presence. The night of horror was over for them, and they tended to have very short memories.

Then, just as he had been reclining on a branch, wishing that Mutt, at least, had sustained some sort of painful and lasting injury, *they* had appeared. Out of nowhere, seemingly. Stefan and Elena, hand in hand, floating like a pair of happy wingèd Shakespearean lovers, as if the forest was *their* home.

He hadn't been able to believe it at first.

And then, just as he was about to call down thunder and sarcasm on them, they had started their love scene.

Right in front of his eyes.

Even floating up to his level, as if to rub it in. They'd begun kissing and caressing and . . . more.

They'd made an unwilling voyeur out of him, although he'd become more angry and less unwilling as time passed and their caresses had become more passionate. He'd had to grind his teeth, when Stefan had offered Elena his blood. Had wanted to scream that there had been a time when this girl had been his for the taking, when he could have drained her dry and she would have died happily in his arms, when she had obeyed the sound of his voice instinctively and the taste of his blood would make her reach heaven in his arms.

As she obviously was in Stefan's.

That had been the worst. He'd had to dig his nails into his palms when Elena had wrapped herself around Stefan like a long, graceful snake and had fastened her mouth against his neck, as Stefan's face had tipped toward the sky, with his eyes shut.

For the love of all the demons in hell, why couldn't they just get done with it?

That was when he noticed that he wasn't alone in his well-chosen, commodious tree.

There was someone else there, sitting calmly right beside him on the big branch. They must have appeared while he was engrossed in the love scene and his own fury, but still, that made them very, very good. No one had snuck up on him like that in over two centuries. Three, perhaps.

The shock of it had sent him tumbling off the branch—without turning on his vampire ability to float.

A long lean arm reached out to catch him, to haul him to safety, and Damon found himself gazing into a pair of laughing golden eyes.

Who the hell *are you?* he sent. He didn't worry about it being picked up by the lovers in the moonlight. Nothing short of a dragon or an atomic bomb would catch their attention now.

I'm the hell Shinichi, the other boy replied. His hair was the strangest Damon had seen in a while. It was smooth and shiny and black everywhere except for a fringe of uneven dark red at the tips. The bangs he tossed carelessly out of his eyes ended in crimson and so did the little wisps all round his collar—for he wore it slightly long. It looked as if tongues of dancing, flaring flame were licking at the ends of it, and gave singular emphasis to his answer: *I'm the hell Shinichi.* If anyone could pass as a devil come up straight from Hell, this boy could.

On the other hand, his eyes were the pure golden eyes of an angel. *Most people just call me Shinichi alone,* he added soberly to Damon, letting those eyes crinkle a little to show that it was a joke. *Now you know my name. Who are you?*

Damon simply looked at him in silence.

14

Elena woke up the next morning in Stefan's narrow bed. She recognized this before she was fully awake and hoped to heaven that she had given Aunt Judith some reasonable excuse last night. Last night—the very concept was extremely fuzzy. What had she been dreaming to make this wakening seem so extraordinary? She couldn't remember—jeez, she couldn't remember anything!

And then she remembered everything.

Sitting up with a jolt that would have sent her flying off the bed had she attempted it yesterday, she searched her recollections.

Daylight. She remembered daylight, full light on her—and she didn't have her ring. She took a frantic look at both hands. No ring. And she was sitting up in a shaft of sunlight and it wasn't hurting her. It wasn't possible. She knew, she remembered with a raw memory that pervaded every cell of her body, that daylight would *kill* her. She had learned that lesson with a single touch of a sunbeam to her hand. She would never forget the searing, scalding pain: the touch had imprinted a behavior on her forever. Go nowhere without the lapis lazuli ring that was beautiful in itself, but more beautiful in the knowledge that it was her savior. Without it, she might, she *would* . . .

Oh. *Oh.*

But she already *had*, hadn't she?

She'd died.

Not simply Changed as she had when she'd become a vampire, but died the true death that no one came back from. In her own personal philosophy, she ought to have disintegrated into nameless atoms, or gone straight to hell.

Instead she hadn't really *gone* anywhere. She'd had some dreams about fatherly or motherly people giving her advice—and of wanting very much to help people, who were suddenly much easier to understand. School bully? She had watched sadly as his drunken father took his own outrages out on him night after night. That girl who never got her homework done? She was expected to raise three younger sisters and brothers while her mother lay in bed all day. Just getting the baby fed and cleaned took all the time she had. There was always a reason behind any behavior, and now she could see it.

She had even communicated with people through their dreams. And then one of the Old Ones had arrived in Fell's Church, and it was all she could do to stand his interference in the dreams and not run away. He caused the humans to call for Stefan's help—and Damon had accidentally been summoned, too. And Elena had helped them all she could even when it had been almost unbearable, because Old Ones knew about love and which buttons to push and how to make your enemies run in all the right directions. But they had fought him—and they had won. And Elena, in trying to heal Stefan's mortal wounds, had somehow ended up mortal again herself: naked, lying on the ground of the Old Wood, with Damon's jacket over her, while Damon himself had disappeared without waiting for thanks.

And that awakening had been of basic things: things of the senses: touch, taste, hearing, sight—and of the heart, but not of the head. Stefan had been so good to her.

"And now, what am I?" Elena said aloud, staring as she turned her hands over and over, marveling at the solid, mortal flesh that obeyed the laws of gravity. She *had* said that she'd give up flying for him. Someone had taken her at her word.

"You're beautiful," Stefan answered absently, not moving. Then suddenly he rocketed up. *"You're talking!"*

"I know I am."

"And making sense!"

"Thank you kindly."

"And in sentences!"

"I've noticed."

"Go on, then, and say something long—please," Stefan said as if he didn't believe it.

"You've been hanging out too much with my friends," Elena said. "That sentence has Bonnie's impudence, Matt's courtesy, and Meredith's insistence on the facts."

"Elena, it's you!"

Instead of keeping up the silly dialogue with "Stefan, it *is* me!" Elena stopped to think. Then, carefully she got out of bed and took a step. Stefan hastily looked away, handing her a robe. *Stefan? Stefan?*

Silence.

When Stefan turned around after a decent interval, he saw Elena kneeling in the sunlight holding the robe.

"Elena?" She knew that to him, she looked like a very young angel in meditation.

"Stefan."

"But you're crying."

"I'm human again, Stefan." She lifted a hand, let it fall into the clutches of gravity. "I'm human again. No more, no less. I guess it just took me a few days to get fully back on track."

She looked into his eyes. They were always such *green* green eyes. Like green crystal with some offside light behind them. Like a summer leaf held up before the sun.

I can read your mind.

"But I can't read yours, Stefan. I can only get a general sense, and even that may be going . . . we can't count on anything."

Elena, I have all I want in this room. He patted the bed. *Sit by me and I can say "all I want is on this bed."*

Instead she got up and threw herself at him, arms around his neck, legs tangled with his. "I'm still very young," she whispered, holding him tightly. "And if you count it in days, we haven't had many days together like this, but—"

"I'm still far too old for you. But to be able to look at you and see *you* looking back at me—"

"Tell me you'll love me forever."

"I'll love you forever."

"No matter what happens."

"Elena, Elena—I've loved you as mortal, as vampire, as pure spirit, as spiritual child—and now as human again."

"Promise we'll be together."

"We'll be together."

"No. Stefan, this is *me*." She pointed to her head as if to emphasize that behind her gold-flecked blue eyes there was a bright active mind spinning in overdrive. "I *know* you. Even if I can't read your mind I can read your face. All the old fears—they're back, aren't they?"

He looked away. "I will never leave you."

"Not for a day? Not for an hour?"

He hesitated and then looked up at her. *If that's what you really want. I won't leave you, even for an hour.* Now he was projecting, she knew, for she could hear him.

"I release you from all your promises."

"But, Elena, I mean them."

"I know. But when you do go, I don't want you to have the guilt of breaking them looming over you as well."

Even without telepathy, she could tell what he was thinking to the tiniest shade of a nuance: *Humor her. After all, she'd just woken up. She was probably a little confused.* And she wasn't interested in becoming less confused, or in making him less confused. That must be why she was nipping his chin gently. And kissing him. Certainly, Elena thought, one of the two of them was confused. . . .

Time seemed to stretch and then stop around them. And then nothing was confusing at all. Elena knew that Stefan knew what she wanted, and he wanted whatever she wanted him to do.

Bonnie stared at the numbers on her phone, concerned. Stefan was calling. Then she ran a hasty hand through her hair, fluffing the curls out, and took the video call.

But instead of Stefan it was Elena. Bonnie started to giggle, started to tell her not to play with Stefan's grown-up toys—and then she stared.

"*Elena?*"

"Am I going to get this every time? Or only from my sister-witch?"

"*Elena?*"

"Awake and good as new," Stefan said, getting in the picture. "We called as soon as we woke up—"

"*Ele*—but it's noon!" Bonnie blurted out.

"We've been occupied with this and that," Elena cut in smoothly, and oh, wasn't it good to hear Elena talk that way! Half innocent and wholly smug about it, making you want to shake her and beg her for every wicked detail.

"*Elena,*" Bonnie gasped, using the nearest wall for support, and then sliding down it, and allowing an armload of socks, shirts, pajamas, and underwear to shower down onto the carpet, while tears began to leak out of her eyes. "Elena, they said you'd have to leave Fell's Church—will you?"

Elena bridled. "They said *what?*"

"That you and Stefan would have to leave for your own good."

"*Never in this world!*"

"Little lovely lo—" began Stefan, and then abruptly he stopped, opening and shutting his mouth.

Bonnie stared. It had happened at the bottom of the screen, out of sight, but she could almost swear that

Stefan's little lovely love had just elbowed him in the stomach. "Ground zero, two o'clock?" Elena was asking.

Bonnie snapped back to reality. Elena never gave you time for reflection. "I'll *be* there!" she cried.

"Elena," Meredith breathed. And then "Elena!" like a half-chocked sob. "Elena!"

"Meredith. Oh, don't make me cry, this blouse is pure silk!"

"It's pure silk because it's my pure silk sari blouse, that's why!"

Elena suddenly looked as innocent as an angel. "You know, Meredith, I seem to have grown much taller lately—"

"If the end of that sentence is 'so it really fits *me* better'"—Meredith's voice was threatening—"then I'm warning you, Elena Gilbert . . ." She broke off, and both girls began to laugh and then to cry. "You can have it! Oh, you can have it!"

"Stefan?" Matt waved his phone—first cautiously, then banging it into the wall of the garage. "I can't see—" He stopped, swallowed. "E-le-na?" The word came out slowly, with a pause between each syllable.

"Yes, Matt. I'm back. Even up here." She pointed to her forehead. "Will you meet with us?"

Matt, leaning on his newly purchased, almost-running car, was muttering, "Thank God, thank God," over and over.

"Matt? I can't see you. Are you okay?" Shuffling sounds. "I think he fainted."

Stefan's voice: "Matt? She *really* wants to see you."

"Yeah, yeah." Matt lifted his head up, blinking at the phone. "Elena, Elena . . ."

"I'm so sorry, Matt. You don't have to come—"

Matt laughed shortly. "Are you *sure* you're Elena?"

Elena smiled the smile that had broken a thousand hearts. "In that case—Matt Honeycutt, I insist that you come and meet with us at Ground Zero at two o'clock. Is that more like it?"

"I think you've almost got it down. The old Elena Imperial Manner." He coughed theatrically, sniffed, and said, "Sorry—I've got a little cold; or allergies, maybe."

"Don't be silly, Matt. You're bawling like a baby and so am I," Elena said. "And so were Bonnie and Meredith, when I called them. So *I've* been crying nearly all day—and at this rate I'll have to scramble to get a picnic ready and be on time. Meredith's planning to pick you up. Bring something to drink or eat. Love ya!"

Elena put down the phone, breathing hard.

"Now *that* was tough."

"He still loves you."

"He'd rather that I stayed a baby all my life?"

"Maybe he liked the way you used to say 'hello' and 'good-bye.'"

"Now you're teasing me." Elena quivered her chin.

"Never in this world," Stefan said softly. Then, suddenly, he grabbed her hand. "Come on—we're going shopping for a picnic and a car, too," he said, pulling her up.

Elena startled both of them by flying up so quickly that Stefan had to grab her by the waist to keep her from shooting toward the ceiling.

"I thought you had gravity!"

"So did I! What do I do?"

"Think heavy thoughts!"

"What if it doesn't work?"

"We'll buy you an anchor!"

At two o'clock Stefan and Elena arrived at the Fell's Church graveyard in a brand-new red Jaguar; Elena was wearing dark glasses under a scarf with all her hair pinned up under it, a muffler around her lower face, and black lace mitts borrowed from Mrs. Flowers' younger days, which she admitted she didn't know why she was wearing. She made quite a picture, Meredith said, with the violet sari top and jeans. Bonnie and Meredith had already spread a cloth for a picnic, and the ants were sampling sandwiches and grapes and low-fat pasta salad.

Elena told the story of how she had woken up this morning, and then there was more hugging and kissing and crying than the males could stand.

"You want to see the woods around here? Check if those malach things are around?" Matt said to Stefan.

"They'd better not be," Stefan said. "If the trees this far from where you had your accident are infested—"

"Not good?"

"Serious trouble."

They were about to go when Elena called them back.

"You can stop looking all male and superior," she added. "Suppressing your emotions is *bad* for you. *Expressing* them keeps you well balanced."

"Listen, you're tougher than I thought," Stefan said. "Having picnics at a cemetery?"

"We used to find Elena here all the time," Bonnie said, pointing to a nearby headstone with a celery stick.

"It's my parents' gravesite," Elena explained simply. "After the accident—I always felt closer to them here than anywhere. I would come here when things got bad, or when I needed to have a question answered."

"Did you ever get any answers?" Matt asked, taking a home-preserved cucumber pickle from a glass jar and passing the jar on.

"I'm not sure, even now," Elena said. She had taken

off the dark glasses, muffler, headscarf, and mitts. "But it always made me feel better. Why? Do you have a question?"

"Well—yeah," Matt said unexpectedly. Then he flushed as he suddenly found himself the center of attention. Bonnie rolled over to stare at him, the stalk of celery at her lips, Meredith scooted in, Elena sat up. Stefan, who had been leaning against an elaborate headstone with unconscious vampire grace, sat down.

"What is it, Matt?"

"I was going to say, you don't look right today," Bonnie said anxiously.

"Thank *you*," Matt snapped.

Tears pooled in Bonnie's brown eyes. "I didn't mean—"

But she didn't get to finish. Meredith and Elena drew in protectively around her in the solid phalanx of what they called "velociraptor sisterhood." It meant that anybody messing with one of them was messing with them all.

"Sarcasm instead of chivalry? That's hardly the Matt I know." Meredith spoke with one eyebrow raised.

"She was only trying to be sympathetic," Elena pointed out quietly. "And that was a cheap comeback."

"Okay, okay! I'm sorry—*really* sorry, Bonnie"—he turned toward her, looking ashamed—"It was a nasty thing to say and I know you were only trying to be nice. I just—I don't really know what I'm doing or saying. Anyway, do you want to hear the thing," he finished, looking defensive, "or not?"

Everyone did.

"Okay, here it is. I went to visit Jim Bryce this morning—you remember him?"

"Sure. I went out with him. Captain of the basketball team. Nice guy. A little bit young, but . . ." Meredith shrugged.

"Jim's okay." Matt swallowed. "Well, it's just—I don't want to gossip or anything, but—"

"Gossip!" the three girls commanded him in unison, like a Greek chorus.

Matt quailed. "Okay, okay! Well—I was supposed to be over there at ten o'clock, but I got there a little early, and—well, Caroline was there. She was leaving."

There were three little shocked gasps and a sharp look from Stefan.

"You mean you think she spent the night with him?"

"Stefan!" Bonnie began. "This isn't how proper gossip goes. You never just outright say what you think—"

"No," Elena said evenly. "Let Matt answer. I can remember enough from before I could talk to be worried about Caroline."

"More than worried," Stefan said.

Meredith nodded. "It's not gossip; it's necessary information," she said.

"Okay, then." Matt gulped. "Well, yeah, that was what I thought. He said she'd come early to see his little sister, but Tamra is only about fifteen. And he turned bright red when he said it."

There were sober glances between the others.

"Caroline's always been . . . well, sleazy . . ." began Bonnie.

"But I've never heard that she even gave Jim a second glance," finished Meredith.

They looked to Elena for an answer. Elena slowly shook her head. "I certainly can't see any earthly reason for her visiting Tamra. And besides"—she looked up quickly at Matt—"you're holding out on us somehow. What else happened?"

"Something *more* happened? Did Caroline flash her lingerie?" Bonnie was laughing until she saw Matt's red face. "Hey—c'mon, Matt. This is *us*. You can tell us anything."

Matt drew in a deep breath and shut his eyes.

"Okay, well—as she was going out, I think—I think Caroline . . . propositioned me."

"She did *what*?"

"She would *never*—"

"How, Matt?" Elena asked.

"Well—Jim thought she'd left, and he went to the

garage to get his basketball, and I turned around and suddenly Caroline was back again, and she said—well, it doesn't matter what she said. But it was about her liking football better than basketball and did I want to be a sport."

"And what did you say?" Bonnie breathed, fascinated.

"I didn't say anything. I just stared at her."

"And then Jim came back?" Meredith suggested.

"No! And then Caroline left—she gave me this look, you know, that made things pretty clear as to what she meant—and then *Tami* came in." Matt's honest face was flaming by now. "And then—I don't know how to say it. Maybe Caroline said something about me to make her do it to me, because she—she . . ."

"Matt." Stefan had scarcely spoken until this point; now he leaned forward and spoke quietly. "We're not asking just because we want to gossip. We're trying to find out if there's something seriously wrong happening in Fell's Church. So—please—just tell us what happened."

att nodded, but he was blushing to the fair roots of his hair. "Tami . . . pressed herself against me."

There was a long pause.

Meredith said levelly, "Matt, do you mean she hugged you? Like a biiiiiig hug? Or that she . . ." She stopped, because Matt was already shaking his head vehemently.

"It was no innocent biiiiiig hug. We were alone, in the doorway there, and she just . . . well, I couldn't believe it. She's only fifteen, but she acted like an adult woman. I mean . . . not that I've ever had an adult woman do *that* to me."

Looking embarrassed but relieved at having got this off his chest, Matt's gaze went from face to face. "So what do you think? Was it just a coincidence that Caroline was there? Or did she . . . say something to Tamra?"

"No coincidence," Elena said simply. "It'd be too *much* of a coincidence: Caroline coming on to you and then Tamra acting like that. I know—I used to know Tami Bryce. She's a nice little girl—or she used to be."

"She still is," Meredith said. "I told you, I went out with Jim a few times. She's a very nice girl, and not at all mature for her age. I don't think she would normally do anything inappropriate, unless . . ." She stopped, looking into the middle distance, and then shrugged without finishing her sentence.

Bonnie looked serious now. "But we have to stop this," she said. "What if she does that to some guy who's not nice and shy like Matt? She's going to get herself assaulted!"

"That's the whole problem," Matt said, turning red again. "I mean, it's pretty difficult. . . . If she had been some other girl, that I was going on a date with—not that I go out with other girls on dates . . ." he added hastily, glancing at Elena.

"But you *should* be going out on dates," Elena said firmly. "Matt, I don't want eternal fidelity from you—there's nothing I'd like better than to see you dating a nice girl." As if by accident, her gaze wandered over to Bonnie, who was now trying to crunch celery very quietly and neatly.

"Stefan, you're the only one who can tell us what to

do," Elena said, turning to him.

Stefan was frowning. "I don't know. With only two girls, it's pretty hard to draw any conclusions."

"So we're going to wait and see what Caroline—or Tami—does next?" Meredith asked.

"Not just wait," Stefan said. "We've got to find out more about it. You guys can keep an eye on Caroline and Tamra Bryce, and I can do some research on it."

"Damn!" Elena said, hitting the ground with one fist. "I can almost—" She stopped suddenly and looked at her friends. Bonnie had dropped her celery, gasping, and Matt had choked on his Coke, going into a coughing fit. Even Meredith and Stefan were staring at her. "What?" she said blankly.

Meredith recovered first. "It's just that yesterday you were—well, very young angels don't swear."

"Just because I died a couple of times, it means I have to say 'darn' for the rest of my life?" Elena shook her head. "*Not*. I'm me and I'm going to stay me—whoever I am."

"Good," said Stefan, leaning over to kiss the top of her head. Matt looked away and Elena gave Stefan an almost dismissive pat, but thinking, *I love you forever*, and knowing that he would pick it up even if she couldn't hear his thought in return. In fact she found she *could* pick up his general response to it, a warm rose color seemed to hang around him.

Was this what Bonnie saw and called an aura? She realized that most of the day she'd seen him with a light, cool, emerald sort of shadowing around him—if shadows could be light. And the green was returning now as the pink faded away.

Immediately she glanced over the rest of the picnickers. Bonnie was surrounded by a roselike color, shading to the palest of pinks. Meredith was a deep and profound violet. Matt was a strong clear blue.

It reminded her that up until yesterday—*only yesterday?*—she'd seen so many things that no one else could see. Including something that had scared her silly.

What had it *been*? She was getting flashes of images—little details that were scary enough by themselves. It could be as small as a fingernail or as large as an arm. Bark-like texture, at least on the body. Insect-like antennae, but far too many of them, and moving like whips, faster than any insect ever moved them. She had the general crawly feeling she got whenever she thought about insects. It was a bug, then. But a bug built on a different body plan than any insect she knew of. It was more like a leech in that respect, or a squid. It had a completely circular mouth, with sharp teeth all around, and far too many tentacles that looked like thick vines whipping around in back.

It could attach itself to a person, she thought. But she had a terrible feeling that it could do more.

It could turn transparent and pull itself inside you and

you would feel no more than a pinprick.

And *then* what would happen?

Elena turned to Bonnie. "Do you think that if I show you what something looks like, you could recognize it again? Not with your eyes, but with your psychic senses?"

"I guess it depends on what the 'something' is," Bonnie answered cautiously.

Elena glanced over at Stefan, who gave her briefest of nods.

"Then shut your eyes," she said.

Bonnie did so, and Elena put her fingertips on Bonnie's temples, with her thumbs gently brushing Bonnie's eyelashes. Trying to activate her White Powers—something that had been so easy before today—was like striking two rocks together to make a fire and hoping one was flint. Finally she felt a small spark, and Bonnie jerked backward.

Bonnie's eyes snapped open. "*What was that?*" she gasped. She was breathing hard.

"That's what I saw—yesterday."

"*Where?*"

Elena said slowly, "Inside Damon."

"But what does it mean? Was he controlling it? Or . . . or . . ." Bonnie stopped and her eyes widened.

Elena finished the sentence for her. "Was it controlling him? I don't know. But here's one thing I do know, almost for certain. When he ignored your Calling, Bonnie, he was being influenced by the malach."

"The question is, *if not Damon*, who was controlling it?" Stefan said, standing up again restlessly. "I picked that up, and the kind of creature Elena showed you—it's not something with a mind of its own. It needs an outside brain to control it."

"Like another vampire?" Meredith asked quietly.

Stefan shrugged. "Vampires usually just ignore them, because vampires can get what they want without them. It would have to be a very strong mind to get a malach like that to possess a vampire. Strong—and evil."

"Those," Damon said with biting grammatical precision, from where he was sitting on a high limb of an oak, "are they. My younger brother and his . . . associates."

"Marvelous," murmured Shinichi. He had draped himself even more gracefully and languidly against the oak than Damon had. It had become an unspoken contest. Shinichi's golden eyes had flared once or twice—Damon had seen it—upon seeing Elena and at the mention of Tami.

"Don't even try to tell me you're not involved with those rowdy girls," Damon added dryly. "From Caroline to Tamra and onward, that's the idea, isn't it?"

Shinichi shook his head. His eyes were on Elena and he began to sing a folksong softly.

"With cheeks like blooming roses
And hair like golden wheat . . ."

"I wouldn't try it on *those* girls." Damon smiled without humor. His eyes were narrow. "Granted, they look about as strong as wet tissue paper—but they're tougher than you'd think, and they're toughest of all when one of them is in danger."

"I told you, it's not me doing it," Shinichi said. He looked uneasy for the first time since Damon had seen him. Then he said, "Although I might know the originator."

"Do tell," Damon suggested, still narrow-eyed.

"Well—did I mention my younger twin? Her name is Misao." He smiled winningly. "It means maiden."

Damon felt an automatic stirring of appetite. He ignored it. He was too relaxed to think of hunting, and he wasn't at all sure that *kitsune*—fox-spirits, which Shinichi claimed to be—could be hunted. "No, you *didn't* mention her," Damon said, absently scratching at the back of his neck. That mosquito bite was gone, but it had left behind a furious itching. "It must have somehow slipped your mind."

"Well, she's here somewhere. She came when I did, when we saw the flare of Power that brought back . . . Elena."

Damon felt sure that the hesitation before the mention of Elena's name was a fake. He tilted his head at the *don't think you're fooling me* angle and waited.

"Misao likes to play games," Shinichi said simply.

"Oh, yes? Like backgammon, chess, Go Fish, that sort of thing?"

Shinichi coughed theatrically, but Damon caught the glint of red in his eye. My, he really *was* overprotective of her, wasn't he? Damon gave Shinichi one of his most incandescent smiles.

"I love her," the young man with the black hair licked by fire said, and this time there was an open warning in his voice.

"Of course you do," Damon said in soothing tones. "I can see that."

"But, well, her games usually have the effect of destroying a town. Eventually. Not all at once."

Damon shrugged. "This flyspeck of a village isn't going to be missed. Of course, I get my girls out alive first." Now it was his voice that held an open warning.

"Just as you like." Shinichi was back to his normal, submissive self. "We're allies, and we'll keep to our deal. Anyway, it would be a shame to waste . . . all that." His gaze drifted to Elena again.

"By the way, we won't even discuss the little fiasco with your malach and me—or hers, if you insist. I'm pretty sure I've vaporized at least three of them, but if I see another one, our business relationship is over. I make a bad enemy,

Shinichi. You don't want to find out how bad."

Shinichi looked suitably impressed as he nodded. But the next moment he was gazing at Elena again, and singing.

> "*. . . hair like golden wheat*
> *all a-down her milk-white shoulders;*
> *My pretty pink, my sweet . . .*"

"And I'll want to meet this Misao of yours. For her protection."

"And I know she wants to meet you. She's caught up in her game at the moment, but I'll try to tear her away from it." Shinichi stretched luxuriously.

Damon looked at him for a moment. Then, absentmindedly, he too stretched.

Shinichi was watching him. He smiled.

Damon wondered about that smile. He had noticed that when Shinichi smiled, two little flames of crimson could be seen in his eyes.

But he was really too tired to think about it right now. Simply too relaxed. In fact he suddenly felt very sleepy. . . .

"So we're going to be looking for these malach things in girls like Tami?" Bonnie asked.

"Exactly like Tami," said Elena.

"And you think," Meredith said, watching Elena closely, "that Tami got it somehow from Caroline."

"Yes. I know, I know—the question is: where did Caroline get it from? And that I *don't* know. But, again, we don't know what happened to her when she was kidnapped by Klaus and Tyler Smallwood. We don't know anything about what she's been doing for the last week—except that it's clear she never really stopped hating us."

Matt held his head in his hands. "And then what are we going to *do?* I feel as if I'm responsible somehow."

"No—Jimmy's responsible, if anyone is. If he—you know, let Caroline spend the night—and then let her talk about it with his fifteen-year-old sister. . . . Well, it doesn't make him *guilty*, but he sure could have been a little more subtle," Stefan said.

"And that's where *you're* wrong," Meredith told him. "Matt and Bonnie and Elena and I have known Caroline for *ages* and *we know what she's capable of*. If anyone qualifies as their sister's keeper—it's us. And I think we're in serious delinquency of duty. I vote we stop by her house."

"So do I," Bonnie said sadly, "but I'm not looking forward to it. Besides, what if she *doesn't* have one of those malach things in her?"

"That's where the research comes in," Elena said. "We need to find out who's behind it all. Someone strong enough to influence Damon."

"Wonderful," Meredith said, looking grim. "And given the power of the ley lines, we only have every single person in Fell's Church to choose from."

Fifty yards west and thirty feet straight up, Damon was struggling to keep awake.

Shinichi reached up to brush fine hair the color of night and flames licking upward off his forehead. Under his lowered lids he was watching Damon intently.

Damon meant to be watching him as intently, but he was simply too drowsy. Slowly, he imitated Shinichi's motion, brushing a very few strands of silky black hair off his own forehead. His lids drooped inadvertently, just a little more than before. Shinichi was still smiling at him.

"So we have our deal," he murmured. "We get the town, Misao and I, and you don't stand in our way. We get the rights to the power of the ley lines. You get your girls safely out . . . and you get your revenge."

"Against my sanctimonious brother and that . . . that Mutt!"

"Matt." Shinichi had sharp ears.

"Whatever. I just won't have Elena hurt, is all. Or the little red-headed witch."

"Ah, yes, sweet Bonnie. I wouldn't mind one or two like her. One for Samhain and one for the Solstice."

Damon snorted drowsily. "There aren't two like her; I don't care where you look. I won't have her hurt either."

"And what about the tall, dark-haired beauty . . . Meredith?"

Damon woke up. "*Where?*"

"Don't worry; she's not coming to get you," Shinichi said soothingly. "What do you want *done* with her?"

"Oh." Damon lounged back again in relief, easing his shoulders. "Let her go her own way—as long as it's far away from mine."

Shinichi seemed to deliberately relax back against his branch. "Your brother will be no problem. So it's really just that other boy down there," he murmured. He had a very insinuating murmur.

"Yes. But my brother—" Damon was almost asleep now, in the exact position that Shinichi had taken.

"I told you, he'll be taken care of."

"Mm. I mean, good."

"So we have a deal?"

"Mm-hmm."

"Yes?"

"Yes."

"We have a deal."

This time, Damon didn't respond. He was dreaming. He dreamed that Shinichi's angelic golden eyes snapped open suddenly to look at him.

"Damon." He heard his name, but in his dream it was too much trouble to open his eyes. He could see without opening them, anyway.

In his dream, Shinichi leaned over him, hovering directly over his face, so that their auras mixed and they would have shared breath if Damon had been breathing. Shinichi stayed that way a long time, as if he were testing Damon's aura, but Damon knew that to an outsider he would appear to be out on all channels and frequencies. Still, in his dream Shinichi hung over him, as if he were trying to memorize the crescent of dark lashes on Damon's pale cheek or the subtle curve of Damon's mouth.

Finally, the dream-Shinichi put his hand under Damon's head and stroked the spot where the mosquito bite had itched.

"Oh, growing up to be a fine big lad, aren't you?" he said to something Damon couldn't see—to something *inside* him. "You could almost take full control against his own strong will, couldn't you?"

Shinichi sat for a moment, as if watching a cherry blossom fall, then shut his eyes.

"I think," he whispered, "that that's what we'll try, not too long from now. Soon. Very soon. But first, we have to gain his trust; get rid of his rival. Keep him blurred, angry, vain, off balance. Keep him thinking of Stefan, of his hatred for Stefan, who took his angel, while *I* take care of what needs to be done here."

Then he spoke directly to Damon. "Allies, indeed!" He laughed. "Not while I can put my finger on your very soul. Here. Do you feel it? What I could make you do . . ."

And then again he seemed to address whatever creature was already inside Damon: "But right now . . . a little feast to help you grow up much faster and get much stronger."

In the dream, Shinichi made a gesture, and lay back, encouraging previously invisible malach to come up the trees. They slunk up and slid up the back of Damon's neck. And then, hideously, they slipped inside him, one by one, through some cut he hadn't known he had. The feeling of their soft, flabby, jellyfish-like bodies was almost unbearable . . . slipping inside of him. . . .

Shinichi sang softly.

"Oh, come a' tae me, ye fair pretty maidens
Haste ye lassies tae my bosom
Come tae me by sunlight or moonlight
While the roses still are in blossom . . ."

In his dream, Damon was angry. Not because of the nonsense about malach inside him. That was ludicrous. He was angry because he knew that the dream-Shinichi was watching Elena as she began to pack up the remains of the picnic. He was watching every motion she made with an obsessive closeness.

"They blossom ever where you tread
. . . Wild roses bloody red."

"Extraordinary girl, your Elena," the dream-Shinichi added. "If she lives, I think she'll be mine for a night or so." He stroked the remaining strands of hair off Damon's forehead gently. "Extraordinary aura, don't you think? I'll make sure her death is beautiful."

But Damon was in one of those dreams where you can neither move nor speak. He didn't answer.

Meanwhile, dream-Shinichi's dream-pets continued to climb the trees and pour themselves, like Jell-O, inside him. One, two, three, a dozen, two dozen of them. *More.*

And Damon could not wake, even though he sensed more malach coming from the Old Wood. They were neither dead, nor living, neither man nor maiden, mere capsules of Power that would allow Shinichi to control Damon's mind from far away. Endlessly, they came.

Shinichi kept watching the flow, the bright sparkle of internal organs sparkling into Damon. After a while he sang again,

"Days are precious, dinna lose them
Flo'ers will fade and so will ye . . .

Come to me, ye fair young maidens
While young and fair ye still may be."

Damon dreamed that he heard the word "forget" as if whispered by a hundred voices. And even as he tried to remember what to forget, it dissolved and disappeared.

He woke up alone in the tree, with an ache that filled his entire body.

tefan was surprised to find Mrs. Flowers waiting for them when they returned from their picnic. And, also unusually, she had something to say that didn't involve her gardens.

"There is a message for you upstairs," she said, jerking her head toward the narrow staircase. "It came from a dark young fellow—he looked somewhat like you. He wouldn't leave a word with me. Just asked where to leave a message."

"Dark fellow? Damon?" Elena asked.

Stefan shook his head. "What would he want to be leaving me messages for?"

He left Elena with Mrs. Flowers and hastened up the crazy, zigzagging stairs. At the top he found a piece of paper stuffed under the door.

It was a Thinking of You card, sans envelope. Stefan, who knew his brother, doubted that it had been paid for— with money, at least. Inside, in heavy black felt-tipped pen, were the words:

DON'T NEED THIS.
THOUGHT ST. STEFAN MIGHT.
MEET ME TONIGHT AT THE TREE
WHERE THE HUMANS CRASHED.
NO LATER THAN 4:30 A.M.
I'LL GIVE YOU THE SCOOP.
D.

That was all . . . except for a Web address.

Stefan was about to throw the note in the wastebasket when curiosity assailed him. He turned on the computer, directed it to the proper website, and watched. For a while, nothing happened. Then very dark gray letters on a black screen appeared. To a human, it would have appeared to be a completely blank screen. To vampires, with their higher visual acuity, the gray on black was faint but clear.

Tired of that lapis lazuli?
Want to take a vacation in Hawaii?
Sick of that same old liquid cuisine?
Come and visit Shi no Shi.

Stefan started to close the page, but something stopped him. He sat and stared at the inconspicuous little ad beneath the poem until he heard Elena at the door. He quickly closed the computer and went to take the picnic basket from her. He said nothing about the note or what he'd seen on the computer screen. But as the night went on, he thought more and more.

"Oh! Stefan, you'll break my ribs! You squeezed all my breath out!"

"I'm sorry. I just need to hold you."

"Well, I need to hold you, too."

"Thank you, angel."

Everything was quiet in the room with the high ceiling. One window was open, letting the moonlight through. In the sky, even the moon seemed to creep stealthily along, and the shaft of moonlight followed it on the hardwood floor.

Damon smiled. He had had a long, restful day and now he meant to have an interesting night.

Getting through the window wasn't quite as easy as he'd expected. When he arrived as a huge, glossy black crow, he was expecting to balance on the windowsill and change to human form to open the window. But the window had a trap on it—it was linked by Power to one of the sleepers inside. Damon puzzled over it, preening himself viciously, afraid to put any tension on that thin link, when something arrived beside him in a flutter of wings.

It looked like no respectable crow ever registered in the sighting book of any ornithologist. It was sleek enough, but its wings were tipped with scarlet, and it had golden, shining eyes.

Shinichi? Damon asked.

Who else? came the reply as a golden eye fixed on him. *I see you have a problem. But it can be fixed. I'll deepen their sleep so that you can cut the link.*

Don't! Damon said reflexively. *If you so much as touch either of them, Stefan will—*

The answer came in soothing tones. *Stefan's just a boy, remember? Trust me. You do trust me, don't you?*

And it worked out exactly as the demonically colored bird said it would. The sleepers inside slept more deeply, and then more deeply still.

A moment later the window opened, and Damon changed form and was inside. His brother and . . . and *she* . . . the one he always *had* to watch . . . *she* was lying asleep, her golden hair lying across the pillow and lying across his brother's body.

Damon tore his eyes away. There was a medium-sized, slightly outdated computer on the desk in the corner. He went over to it and without the slightest hesitation turned it on. The two on the bed never stirred.

Files . . . aha. *Diary*. How original a name. Damon opened it and examined the contents.

Dear Diary,

I woke up this morning and—marvel of marvels—I'm me *again. I walk, talk, drink, wet the bed (well, I haven't yet, but I'm sure I could if I tried).*

I'm back.

It's been one hell of a journey.

I died, dearest Diary, I really died. And then I died as a vampire. And don't expect me to describe what happened either time—believe me; you had to be there.

The important thing is that I was gone, but now I'm back again—and, oh, dear patient friend who has been keeping my secrets since kindergarten . . . I am so glad to be back.

On the debit side, I can never live with Aunt Judith or Margaret again. They think I'm "resting in peace" with the angels. On the credit side, I can live with Stefan.

This is the compensation for all I've been through—I don't know how to compensate those who went to the very gates of Hell for me. Oh, I'm tired and—might as well say it—eager for a night with my darling.

I'm very happy. We had a fine day, laughing and loving, and watching each of my friends' faces as they saw me alive*! (And not* insane, *which I gather is how I have been acting the past few days. Honestly, you'd think Great Spirits Inna Sky could have dropped me off with my marbles all in order. Oh, well.)*

Love ya,

Elena

Damon's eyes skimmed over these lines impatiently. He was looking for something quite different. Ah. Yes. This was more like it:

> *My dearest Elena,*
> *I knew you would look here sooner or later. I hope you never have to see it at all. If you're reading this, then Damon is a traitor, or something else has gone terribly wrong.*

A traitor? That seemed a little strong, Damon thought, hurt, but also burning with an intense desire to get on with his task.

> *I'm going out to the woods to talk to him tonight—if I don't come back, you'll know*

where to start asking questions.

The truth is that I don't exactly under-stand the situation. Earlier today, Damon sent me a card with a Web address on it. I've put the card under your pillow, love.

Oh damn, thought Damon. It was going to be hard to get that card without waking her. But he had to do it.

Elena, follow this Web link. You'll have to dither with the brightness controls because it's been created for vampire eyes only. What the link seems to be saying is that there is a place called Shi no Shi—*literally translated, it says, as* the Death of Death, *where they can remove this curse which has haunted me for almost half a millennium. They use magic and science in combination to restore former vampires to simple men and women, boys and girls.*

If they truly can do this, Elena, we can be together for as long as ordinary people live. That's all I ask of life.

I want it. I want to have the chance to stand before you as an ordinary breathing, eating human.

But don't worry. I'm just going to talk with

Damon about this. *You don't need to command me to stay. I would never leave you with all the goings-on in Fell's Church right now. It's too dangerous for you, especially with your new blood and your new aura.*

I realize that I'm trusting Damon more than I probably should. But of one thing I am certain: he would never harm you. *He loves you. How can he help it?*

Still, I have to meet with him at least, on his terms, alone at a particular location in the wood. Then we'll see what we see.

As I said before, if you're reading this letter, it means that something has gone drastically wrong. Defend yourself, love. Don't be afraid. Trust yourself. And trust your friends. They can all help you.

I trust Matt's instinctive protectiveness for you, Meredith's judgment, and Bonnie's intuition. Tell them to remember that.

I'm hoping that you never have to read this,

with all my love, my heart, my soul,
Stefan

P.S. Just in case, there is $20,000 in hundred-dollar bills under the second floorboard from the wall, across from the bed. Right now the rocking

chair is over it. You'll see the crack easily if you
move the chair.

Carefully, Damon deleted the words in this file. Then, with one corner of his mouth quirked up, he carefully, silently typed in new words with a rather different meaning. He read them over. He smiled brilliantly. He'd always fancied himself a writer; no formal training of course, but he felt he had an instinctive flair for it.

And that was Step One accomplished, Damon thought, saving the file with his words instead of Stefan's.

Then, noiselessly, he walked to where Elena was sleeping, spooned behind Stefan on the narrow bed.

Now for Step Two.

Slowly, very slowly, Damon slipped his fingers under the pillow on which Elena's head rested. He could feel Elena's hair where it spilled on her pillow in the moonlight, and the ache that it awoke was more in his chest than in his canines. Inching his fingers under the pillow, he searched for something smooth.

Elena murmured in her sleep and suddenly turned over. Damon almost jumped back into the shadows, but Elena's eyes were shut, her lashes a thick inky crescent on her cheeks.

She was facing him now, but strangely Damon didn't find himself tracing the blue veins in her fair, smooth skin. He found himself staring hungrily at her slightly parted lips. They were . . . almost impossible to resist. Even in sleep they were the color of rose petals, slightly moist, and parted that way. . . .

I could do it very lightly. She would never know. I could, I know I could. I feel invincible tonight.

As he bent toward her his fingers touched cardboard.

It seemed to jerk him out of a dream world. What had he been thinking? Risking everything, all his plans, for a *kiss*? There would be plenty of time for kisses—and other, much more important things—later.

He slipped the little card out from under the pillow and put it in his pocket.

Then he became a crow and vanished from the window-sill.

Stefan had long ago perfected the art of sleeping only until a certain moment, then awakening. He did this now, glancing at the clock on the mantelpiece to confirm that it was four A.M. exactly.

He didn't want to awaken Elena.

He dressed soundlessly and exited the window by the same route his brother had—only as a hawk. Somewhere, he was sure Damon was being made a fool by someone using malachs to make him their puppet. And Stefan, still pumped up with Elena's blood, felt that he had a duty to stop them.

The note Damon had delivered had directed him to

the tree where the humans had crashed. Damon would also want to continually revisit that tree until he'd traced the malach puppets to their puppeteer.

He swooped, drifted, and once almost gave a mouse a heart attack by stooping down on it suddenly before rocketing skyward again.

And then, in midair, as he saw evidence of a car hitting a tree, he changed from a glorious hawk to a young man with dark hair, a pale face, and intensely green eyes.

He drifted, light as a snowflake, down to the ground and gazed in each direction, using all his vampire senses to test the area. He could feel nothing of a trap; no animosity, just the unmistakable signs of the trees' violent fight. He stayed human to climb the tree that bore the psychic imprint of his brother.

He wasn't chilly as he climbed the oak his brother had been lounging in when the accident had taken place at his feet. He had too much of Elena's blood running through him to feel the cold. But he was aware that this area of the forest was particularly cold; that something was keeping it that way. Why? He'd already claimed the rivers and forests that ran through Fell's Church, so why take up lodging here without telling him? Whatever it was, it would have to present itself before him eventually, if it wanted to stay in Fell's Church. Why wait? he wondered, as he squatted on the branch.

He felt Damon's presence coming at him long before

his senses would have noticed it in the days before Elena's transformation, and he kept himself from flinching. Instead he turned with his back to the trunk of the tree and looked outward. He could feel Damon speeding toward him, faster and faster, stronger and stronger—and then Damon should have been there, standing before him, but he wasn't.

Stefan frowned.

"It always pays to look up, little brother," advised a charming voice above him, and then Damon, who had been clinging to the tree like a lizard, did a forward flip and landed on Stefan's branch.

Stefan said nothing, merely examining his older brother. At last he said, "You're in good spirits."

"I've had a sumptuous day," Damon said. "Shall I name them off to you? There was the greeting-card shop girl . . . Elizabeth, and my dear friend Damaris, whose husband works in Bronston, and little young Teresa who volunteers at the library, and . . ."

Stefan sighed. "Sometimes I think you could remember the name of every girl you've bled in your life, but you forget my name on a regular basis," he said.

"Nonsense . . . little brother. Now, since Elena has undoubtedly explained to you just what happened when I tried to rescue your miniature witch—Bonnie—I feel I'm due an apology."

"And since *you* sent me a note that I can only construe

as provocative, I really feel *I'm* due an explanation."

"Apology first," Damon rapped out. And then, in long-suffering tones, "I'm sure you think it's bad enough, having promised Elena when she was dying that you would look after me—forever. But you never seem to realize that I had to promise the same thing, and I'm not exactly the caretaking type. Now that she's not dead anymore, maybe we should just forget it."

Stefan sighed again. "All right, all right. I apologize. I was wrong. I shouldn't have thrown you out. Is that enough?"

"I'm not sure you really mean it. Try it once more, with feel—"

"Damon, what in God's name was the website about?"

"Oh. I thought it was rather clever: they got the colors so close that only vampires or witches or such could read it, whereas humans would just see a blank screen."

"But how did you find out about it?"

"I'll tell you in a moment. But just think of it, little brother. You and Elena, on the perfect little honeymoon, just two more humans in a world of humans. The sooner you go, the sooner you can sing 'Ding Dong, the Corpse Is Dead'!"

"I still want to know how you *just happened* to come across this website."

"All right. I admit it: I've been suckered into the age of technology at last. I have my own website. And a very helpful young man contacted me just to see whether I really meant the things I said on it or if I was just a frustrated idealist. I figured that description fit you."

"You—a website? I don't believe—"

Damon ignored him. "I passed the message along because I'd already heard of the place, the *Shi no Shi*."

"The *Death of Death*, it said."

"That's how it was translated to me." Damon turned a thousand-kilowatt smile on Stefan, boring into him, until finally Stefan turned away, feeling as if he'd been exposed to the sun without his lapis ring.

"As a matter of fact," Damon went on chattily, "I've invited the fellow himself to come and to explain it to you."

"You did *which*?"

"He should be here at 4:44 exactly. Don't blame me for the timing; it's something special to him."

And then with very little fuss, and certainly no Power at all that Stefan could discern, something landed in the tree above them and dropped down to their branch, changing as it did.

It was, indeed, a young man, with fire-tipped black hair and serene golden eyes. As Stefan swung toward him, he held up both hands in a gesture of helplessness and surrender.

"Who the hell are you?"

"I'm the hell Shinichi," the young man said easily. "But, as I told your brother, most people call me just

Shinichi. Of course, it's up to you."

"And you know all about the Shi no Shi."

"Nobody knows all about it. It's a place—and an organization. I'm a little partial to it because"—Shinichi looked shy—"well, I guess I just like to help people."

"And now you want to help me."

"If you truly want to become human . . . I know a way."

"I'll just leave the two of you to talk about it, shall I?" said Damon. "Three's a crowd, especially on this branch."

Stefan looked at him sharply. "If you have any slightest thought of stopping by the boardinghouse . . ."

"With Damaris already waiting for me? Honestly, little brother." And Damon changed to crow form before Stefan could ask him to give his sworn word.

Elena turned over in bed, reaching automatically for a warm body next to her. What her fingers found, however, was a cool, Stefan-shaped hollow. Her eyes opened. "Stefan?"

The darling. They were so in tune that it was like being one person—he always knew when she was about to wake up. He'd probably gone down to get her breakfast—Mrs. Flowers always had it steaming hot for him when he went down (further proof that she was a witch of the white variety)—and Stefan brought up the tray.

"Elena," she said, testing her old-new voice just to hear herself talk. "Elena Gilbert, girl, you have had too many breakfasts in bed." She patted her stomach. Yes, definitely in need of exercise.

"All right, then," she said, still aloud. "Start with limbering up and breathing. Then some mild stretching." All of which, she thought, could be put aside when Stefan showed up.

But Stefan didn't show up, even when she lay exhausted from a full hour's routine.

And he wasn't coming up the stairs, bringing up a cup of tea, either.

Where was he?

Elena looked out their one-view window and caught a glimpse of Mrs. Flowers below.

Elena's heart had begun beating hard during her aerobic exercise and had never really slowed down properly. Though it was likely impossible to start a conversation with Mrs. Flowers this way she shouted down, "Mrs. Flowers?"

And, wonder of wonders, the lady stopped pinning a sheet on the clothesline and looked up. "Yes, Elena dear?"

"Where's Stefan?"

The sheet billowed around Mrs. Flowers and made her disappear. When the billow straightened out, she was gone.

But Elena had her eyes on the laundry basket. It was still there. She shouted, "Don't go away!" and hastened to put on jeans and her new blue top. Then, hopping down the stairs as she buttoned, she burst out into the back garden.

"Mrs. Flowers!"

"Yes, Elena dear?"

Elena could just see her between billowing yards of white fabric. "Have you seen Stefan?"

"Not this morning, dear."

"Not at *all*?"

"I get up with the dawn, regular. His car was gone then, and it hasn't come back."

Now Elena's heart was pounding in good earnest. She'd always been afraid of something like this. She took one deep breath and ran back up the staircase without pausing.

Note, note . . .

He'd never leave her without a note. And there was no note on his pillow. Then she thought of *her* pillow.

Her hands scrabbled frantically under it, and then under his pillow. At first she didn't turn the pillows over, because she wanted so badly for the note to be there—and because she was so afraid of what it might say.

At last, when it was clear that there was nothing under those pillows but the bed sheet, she flipped them and stared at the empty white blankness for a long time. Then she pulled the bed away from the wall, in case the note had fallen down behind it.

Somehow she felt that if she just kept looking, she must find it. In the end she'd shaken out all the bedding and ended up staring at the white sheets again, accusingly, ever so often running her hands over them.

And that ought to be good, because it meant Stefan hadn't *gone* somewhere—except that she'd left the closet door open and she could see, without even meaning to, a bunch of empty hangers.

He'd taken all his clothes.

And emptiness on the bottom of the closet.

He'd taken every pair of shoes.

Not that he had ever owned much. But everything that he needed to make a trip away was gone—and he was gone.

Why? Where? How *could* he?

Even if it turned out that he'd left in order to scout them out a new place to live, how *could* he? He'd get the fight of his life when he came back—

—if he came back.

Chilled to the bone, aware that tears were running unmeant and almost unnoticed down her cheeks, she was about to call up Meredith and Bonnie when she thought of something.

Her diary.

17

In the first days after she'd come back from the afterlife, Stefan had always put her to bed early, made sure she was warm, and then allowed her to work on his computer with her, writing a diary of sorts, with her thoughts on what had happened that day, always adding his impressions.

Now she called up the file desperately, and desperately scrolled to the end.

And there it was.

My dearest Elena,
I knew you would look here sooner or later. I hope it was sooner.
Darling, I believe that you're able to take care of yourself now, and I've never seen

a stronger or more independent girl.

And that means it's time. Time for me to go. I can't stay any longer without turning you into a vampire again—something we both know can't happen.

Please forgive me. Please forget me. Oh, love, I don't want to go, but I have to.

If you need help, I've gotten Damon to give his word to protect you. He would never hurt you, and whatever mischief is going on in Fell's Church won't dare touch you with him around.

My darling, my angel, I'll always love you. . . .

Stefan

P.S. To help you go on with your real life, I've left money to pay Mrs. Flowers for the room for the next year. Also, I've left you $20,000 in hundred-dollar bills under the second floorboard from the wall, across from the bed. Use it to build a new future, with whomever you choose.

Again, if you need anything, Damon will help you. Trust his judgement if you're in need of advice. Oh, lovely little love, how can I go? Even for your own sake?

Elena finished the letter.

And then she just sat there.

After all her hunting, she'd found the answer.

And she didn't know what to do now but scream.

If you need help go to Damon. . . . Trust Damon's judgment. . . . It couldn't be a more blatant ad for Damon if Damon had written it himself.

And Stefan was gone. And his clothes were gone. And his boots were gone.

He'd left her.

Make a new life. . . .

And that was how Bonnie and Meredith found her, alarmed by an hour-long bounce-back of their telephone calls. It was the first time they hadn't been able to get through to Stefan since he'd arrived, at their request, to slay a monster. But that monster was now dead, and Elena . . .

Elena was sitting in front of Stefan's closet.

"He even took his shoes," she said emotionlessly, softly. "He took everything. But he paid for the room for a year. And yesterday morning he bought me a Jaguar."

"Elena—"

"Don't you see?" Elena cried. "*This* is my Awakening. Bonnie predicted that it would be sharp and sudden and that I would need both of you. And Matt?"

"He wasn't mentioned by name," Bonnie said gloomily.

"But I think we'll need his help," Meredith said grimly.

"When Stefan and I were first together—before *I* became a vampire—I always knew," Elena whispered, "that there would come a time when he would try to leave me for my own good." Suddenly she hit the floor with her fist, hard enough to hurt herself. "I knew, but I thought I would be there to talk him out of it! He's so noble—so self-sacrificing! And now—he's *gone*."

"You really don't care," Meredith said quietly, watching her, "whether you stay human or become a vampire."

"You're right—I *don't* care! I don't care about anything, as long as I can be with him. When I was still half a spirit, I knew that nothing could Change me. Now I'm human and as susceptible as any other human to the Change—but it doesn't matter."

"Maybe that's the Awakening," Meredith said, still quietly.

"Oh, maybe him not bringing her breakfast is an awakening!" Bonnie, said, exasperated. She'd been staring into a flame for more than thirty minutes, trying to get psychically in touch with Stefan. "Either he won't—or he can't," she said, not seeing Meredith's violently shaking head until after the words were out.

"What do you mean 'can't'?" Elena demanded, popping back off the floor from where she was slumped.

"I don't know! Elena, you're hurting me!"

"Is he in danger? Think, Bonnie! Is he going to be hurt because of me?"

Bonnie looked at Meredith, who was telegraphing "no" with every inch of her elegant body. Then she looked at Elena, who was demanding the truth. She shut her eyes. "I'm not sure," she said.

She opened her eyes slowly, waiting for Elena to explode. But Elena did nothing of the kind. She merely shut her own eyes slowly, her lips hardening.

"A long time ago, I swore I'd have him, even if it killed us both," she said quietly. "If he thinks he can just walk away from me, for my own good or for any other reason . . . he's wrong. I'll go to Damon first, since Stefan seems to want it so much. And then I'm going after him. Someone will give me a direction to start in. He left me twenty thousand dollars. I'll use that to follow him. And if the car breaks down, I'll walk; and when I can't walk anymore, I'll crawl. But I *will* find him."

"Not alone, you won't," Meredith said, in her soft, reassuring way. "We're with you, Elena."

"And then, if he's done this of his own free will, he's going to get the bitch-slapping of his *life*."

"Whatever you want, Elena," Meredith said, still soothingly. "Let's just find him first."

"All for one and one for all!" Bonnie exclaimed. "We'll get him back and we'll make him sorry—or we won't," she added hastily as Meredith again began shaking her head. "Elena, don't! Don't cry," she added, the instant before Elena burst into tears.

* * *

"So Damon was the one to say he'd take care of Elena, and Damon should have been the one last to see Stefan this morning," Matt said, when he had been fetched from his house and the situation was explained to him.

"Yes," Elena said with quiet certainty. "But Matt, you're wrong if you think Damon would do anything to keep Stefan away from me. Damon's not what you all think. He really was trying to save Bonnie that night. And he truly felt hurt when you all hated him."

"This is what is called 'evidence of motive,' I think," Meredith remarked.

"No. It's character evidence—evidence that Damon *does* have feelings, that he can care for human beings," Elena countered. "And he would never hurt Stefan, because—well, because of me. He knows how I would feel."

"Well, why won't he answer me, then?" Bonnie said querulously.

"Maybe because the last time he saw us all together, we were glaring at him as if we hated him," said Meredith, who was always fair.

"Tell him I beg his pardon," Elena said. "Tell him that I want to talk with him."

"I feel like a communications satellite," Bonnie complained, but she clearly put all her heart and strength into each call. At last, she looked completely wrung out and exhausted.

And, at last, even Elena had to admit it was no good.

"Maybe he'll come to his senses and start calling *you*," Bonnie said. "Maybe tomorrow."

"We're going to stay with you tonight," Meredith said. "Bonnie, I called your sister and told her you'd be with me. Now I'm going to call my dad and tell him I'll be with you. Matt, you're not invited—"

"Thanks," Matt said dryly. "Do I get to walk home, too?"

"No, you can take my car home," Elena said. "But please bring it back here early tomorrow. I don't want people to start asking about it."

That night, the three girls prepared to make themselves comfortable, schoolgirl fashion, in Mrs. Flowers' spare sheets and blankets (no wonder she washed so many sheets today—she must have known somehow, Elena thought), with the furniture pushed to the walls and the three makeshift sleeping bags on the floor. Their heads were together and their bodies radiated out like the spokes of a wheel.

Elena thought, So this is the Awakening.

It's the realization that, after all, I can be left alone again. And, oh, I'm grateful to have Meredith and Bonnie sticking with me. It means more than I can tell them.

She had gone automatically to the computer, to write a little in her diary. But after the first few words she'd found herself crying again, and had been secretly glad when Meredith took her by the shoulders and more or less forced her to drink hot milk with vanilla, cinnamon, and nutmeg, and when Bonnie had helped her into her pile of sleeping blankets and then held her hand until she went to sleep.

Matt had stayed late, and the sun was setting as he drove home. It was a race against darkness, he thought suddenly, refusing to be distracted by the Jaguar's expensive new-car smell. Somewhere in the back of his mind, he was pondering. He hadn't wanted to say anything to the girls, but there was something about Stefan's farewell note that bothered him. The only thing was, he had to make sure it wasn't just his injured pride speaking.

Why hadn't Stefan ever mentioned *them*? Elena's friends from the past, her friends in the here and now. You'd think he'd at least give the girls a mention, even if he'd forgotten Matt in the pain of leaving Elena permanently.

What else? There definitely was something else, but Matt couldn't bring it to mind. All he got was a vague, wavering image about high school last year and—yeah, Ms. Hilden, the English teacher.

Even as Matt was daydreaming about this, he was

taking care with his driving. There was no way to avoid the Old Wood entirely on the long, single-lane road that led from the boardinghouse to Fell's Church proper. But he was looking ahead, keeping alert.

He saw the fallen tree even as he came around the corner and hit the brakes in time to come to a screeching stop, with the car at an almost ninety-degree angle to the road.

And then he had to think.

His first instinctive reaction was: call Stefan. He can just lift the tree right off the ground. But he remembered fast enough that that thought was knocked away by a question. Call the girls?

He couldn't make himself do it. It wasn't just a question of masculine dignity—it was the solid reality of the mature tree in front of him. Even if they all worked together, they couldn't move that thing. It was too big, too heavy.

And it had fallen from the Old Wood so that it lay directly across the road, as if it wanted to separate the boardinghouse from the rest of the town.

Cautiously, Matt rolled down the driver's side window. He peered into the Old Wood to try to see the tree's roots, or, he admitted to himself, any kind of movement. There was none.

He couldn't see the roots, but this tree looked far too

healthy to have just fallen over on a sunny summer afternoon. No wind, no rain, no lightning, no beavers. No lumberjacks, he thought grimly.

Well, the ditch on the right side was shallow, at least, and the tree's crown didn't quite reach it. It might be possible—

Movement.

Not in the forest, but on the tree right in front of him. Something was stirring the tree's upper branches, something more than wind.

When he saw it, he still couldn't believe it. That was part of the problem. The other part was that he was driving Elena's car, not his old jalopy. So while he was frantically groping for a way to shut the window, with his eyes glued to the *thing* detaching itself from the tree, he was groping in all the wrong places.

And the final thing was simply that the beast was fast. Much too fast to be real.

The next thing Matt knew, he was fighting it off at the window.

Matt didn't know what Elena had shown Bonnie at the picnic. But if this wasn't a malach, then what the hell was it? Matt had lived around woods his entire life, and he'd never seen any insect remotely like this one before.

Because it was an insect. Its skin looked bark-like, but that was just camouflage. As it banged against the half-raised car window—as he beat it off with both hands—he could hear and feel its chitinous exterior. It was as long as his arm, and it seemed to fly by whipping its tentacles in a circle—which should be impossible, but here it was stuck halfway inside the window.

It was built more like a leech or a squid than like any insect. Its long, snakelike tentacles looked almost like vines, but they were thicker than a finger and had large suckers on them—and inside the suckers was something sharp. Teeth. One of the vines got around his neck, and he could feel the suction and the pain all at once.

The vine had whipped around his throat three or four times, and it was tightening. He had to use one hand to reach up and rip it away. That meant only one hand available to flail at the headless thing—which suddenly showed it had a mouth, if no eyes. Like everything else about the beast, the mouth was radially symmetrical: it was round, with its teeth arranged in a circle. But deep inside that circle, Matt saw to his horror as the bug drew his arm in, was a pair of pincers big enough to cut off a finger.

God—no. He clenched his hand into a fist, desperately trying to batter it from the inside.

The burst of adrenaline he had after seeing *that* allowed him to pull the whipping vine from around his throat, the suckers coming free last. But now his arm had been swallowed up past the elbow. Matt made himself strike at the insect's body, hitting it as if it were a shark, which was the other thing it reminded him of.

He had to get his arm out. He found himself blindly prying the bottom of the round mouth open and merely snapping off a chunk of exoskeleton that landed in his lap. Meanwhile the tentacles were still whirling around, thumping against the car, looking for a way in. At some point it was going to realize that all it had to do was fold those thrashing vine-like things and it could squeeze its body through.

Something sharp grazed his knuckles. The pincers! His arm was almost completely engulfed. Even as Matt was focused entirely on how to get out, some part of him wondered: where's its stomach? This beast isn't *possible*.

He had to get his arm free *now*. He was going to lose his hand, as sure as if he'd put it in the garbage disposal and turned it on.

He'd already undone his seat belt. Now with one violent heave, he threw his body to the right, toward the passenger seat. He could feel the teeth raking his arm as he dragged it past them. He could see the long, bloody furrows it left in his arm. But that didn't matter. All that mattered was getting his arm *out*.

At that moment his other hand found the button that controlled the window. He mashed it upward, dragging his wrist and hand out of the bug's mouth just as the window closed on it.

What he expected was a crackling of chiton and black blood gushing out, maybe eating through the floor of Elena's new car, like that scuttling thing in *Alien*.

Instead the bug vaporized. It simply . . . turned transparent and then turned into tiny particles of light that disappeared even as he stared at them.

He was left with one arm with long bloody scratches on it, swelling sores on his throat, and scraped knuckles on the other hand. But he didn't waste time counting his injuries. He had to make it out of there; the branches were stirring again and he didn't want to wait to see whether it was wind.

There was only one way. The ditch.

He put the car in drive and floored it. He headed for the ditch, hoping that it wasn't too deep, hoping that the tree wouldn't somehow foul the tires.

There was a sharp plunge that made his teeth clash together, catching his lip between them. And then there was the crunch of leaves and branches under the car, and for a moment all movement stopped, but Matt kept his foot pressed as hard as he could on the accelerator, and suddenly he was free, and being thrown around as the car careened in the ditch. He managed to get control of it and swerved back onto the road just in time to make a sharp left turn where it curved abruptly and the ditch ran out.

He was hyperventilating. He took curves at nearly fifty miles an hour, with half his attention on the Old Wood— until suddenly, blessedly, a solitary red light stared at him like a beacon in the dusk.

The intersection with Mallory. He had to force himself to screech to another rubber-burning stop. A hard right turn and he was sailing away from the woods. He'd have to loop around a dozen neighborhoods to get home, but at least he'd stay clear of any large groves of trees.

It was a big loop, and now that the danger was over, Matt was starting to feel the pain of his furrowed arm. By the time he was pulling the Jaguar up to his house, he was also feeling dizzy. He sat under a streetlight and then let the car coast into the darkness beyond. He didn't want anyone to see him so rattled.

Should he call the girls *now*? Warn them not to go out tonight, that the woods were dangerous? But they already knew that. Meredith would never let Elena go to the Old Wood, not now that Elena was human. And Bonnie would kick up a huge noisy fuss if anyone even mentioned going out in the dark—after all, Elena had shown her those *things* that were out there, hadn't she?

Malach. An ugly word for a genuinely hideous creature.

What they really needed was for some official people to go out and clear the tree away. But not at night. Nobody else was likely to be using that lonely road tonight, and sending people out there—well, it was like handing them over to the malach on a platter. He would call the police about it first thing tomorrow. They'd get the right people out there to move that thing.

It was dark, and later than he'd imagined. He probably should call the girls, after all. He just wished his head would clear. His scratches itched and burned. He was finding it hard to think. Maybe if he just took a moment to breathe . . .

He leaned his forehead against the steering wheel. And then the dark closed in.

18

Matt woke, fuzzily, to find himself still behind the steering wheel of Elena's car. He stumbled into his house, almost forgetting to lock the car, and then fumbling with keys to unlock the back door. The house was dark; his parents were asleep. He made it up to his bedroom and collapsed on the bed without even taking off his shoes.

When he woke again, he was startled to find it was nine A.M. and his mobile phone was ringing in his jeans pocket.

"Mer'dith?"

"We thought you were coming over early this morning."

"I am, but I've got to figure out *how* first," Matt said—or rather, croaked. His head felt twice its usual size and his arm at least four times too big. Even so, something in the back of his mind was calculating how to get to the boardinghouse without taking the Old Wood Road at all. Finally a few neurons lit up and showed him.

"Matt? Are you still there?"

"I'm not sure. Last night . . . God, I don't even *remember* most of last night. But on the way home—look, I'll tell you when I get there. First I have to call the police."

"The *police*?"

"Yeah . . . look . . . just give me an hour, okay? I'll be there in an hour."

When he finally arrived at the boardinghouse, it was closer to eleven than to ten. But a shower had cleared his head, even if it hadn't done much for his throbbing arm. When he did appear, he was engulfed in worried femininity.

"Matt, *what happened*?"

He told them everything he could remember. When Elena, with set lips, undid the Ace bandage he had wrapped around his arm, they all winced. The long scratches were clearly badly infected.

"They're poisonous, then, these malach."

"Yes," Elena said tersely. "Poisonous to body and mind."

"And you think one of these can get *inside* people?" Meredith asked. She was doodling on a notebook page, trying to draw something that looked like what Matt had described.

"Yes."

For just a moment Elena's and Meredith's eyes met—then both looked down. At last Meredith said, "And how do we know whether one is inside . . . someone . . . or not?"

"Bonnie should be able to tell, in trance," Elena said evenly. "Even I might be able to tell, but I'm not going to use White Power for that. We're going down to see Mrs. Flowers."

She said it in that special way that Matt had learned to recognize long ago, and it meant that no argument would do any good. She was putting her foot down, and that was that.

And the truth was that Matt didn't feel very much like arguing. He hated to complain—he'd played through football games with a broken collarbone, a sprained knee, a turned ankle—but this was different. His arm felt in danger of exploding.

Mrs. Flowers was downstairs in the kitchen, but on the family room table were four glasses of iced tea.

"I'll be right with you," she called through the swinging half-door that divided the kitchen from where they were standing. "Drink the tea, especially the young man who's injured. It'll help him relax."

"Herbal tea," Bonnie whispered to the others, as if this were some trade secret.

The tea wasn't all that bad, although Matt would've

preferred a Coke. But when he thought of it as medicine, and with the girls all watching him like hawks, he managed to get over half of it down before the landlady came out.

She was wearing her gardening hat—or at least a hat with artificial flowers on it that looked as if it had been used for gardening. But on a cookie tray, she had a number of instruments, all gleaming as if they'd just been boiled.

"Yes, dear, I am," she said to Bonnie, who had stood up in front of Matt protectively. "I used to be a nurse, just like your sister. Women weren't encouraged to be doctors then. But all my life I've been a witch. Gets kind of lonely, doesn't it?"

"It wouldn't be so lonely," Meredith said, looking puzzled, "if you lived closer to town."

"Ah, but then I'd have people staring at my house all the time, and children daring each other to run and touch it, or to throw a stone through my window, or adults peering at me every time I went shopping. And how could I ever keep my garden in peace?"

It was the longest speech any of them had ever heard her make. It took them so by surprise that it was a moment before Elena said, "I don't see how you can keep your garden in peace out *here*. What with all the deer and rabbits and other animals."

"Well, most of it is *for* the animals, you see." Mrs.

Flowers smiled beatifically and her face seemed to light up from within. "They surely enjoy it. But they don't enjoy the herbs I grow for putting on scrapes and cuts and sprains and such. And perhaps they know I'm a witch, too, since they always leave me a bit of the garden for myself and maybe a guest or two."

"Why are you telling me all of this now?" Elena demanded. "Why, there've been times when I was looking for you, or for Stefan, when I thought—well, never mind what I thought. But I wasn't always sure you were our friend."

"The truth is that I've gotten solitary and unsociable in my old age. But now you've lost your young man, haven't you? I wish I had gotten up a little earlier this morning. Then I might have been able to speak to him. He left the money for a year's rental of the room on the kitchen table. I've always had a soft spot for him, and that's the truth."

Elena's lips were trembling. Matt hastily and heroically lifted his wounded arm. "Can you help at all with this?" he asked, peeling the Ace bandage away again.

"Oh, my, my. And what sort of critter gave you these?" Mrs. Flowers said, examining the scratches while the three girls winced.

"We think it was a malach," Elena said quietly. "Do you know anything about those?"

"I've heard the word, yes, but I don't know anything specific. How long ago did you get them?" she asked Matt. "They look more like tooth marks than claw marks."

"They are," Matt said grimly, and he described the malach to her as best he could. It was partly to keep himself distracted, because Mrs. Flowers had picked up one of the gleaming instruments from the cookie tray and was starting to do things to his red and swollen arm.

"Hold as still as you can on this towel," she said. "These have already scabbed over, but they need to be opened and drained and cleaned out properly. It's going to hurt. Why don't one of you young women hold his hand to help keep his arm steady?"

Elena started to stand but Bonnie beat her to it, almost leaping over Meredith to take Matt's hand in both of her own.

The draining and cleaning were painful, but Matt managed to bear it without making a sound, even giving Bonnie a sort of sickly grin as blood and pus trickled out of his arm. The lancing hurt at first, but the release of pressure felt good, and when the wounds were drained and clean and then packed with a cold herbal compress, they felt blessedly cool and ready to heal properly.

It was while he was trying to thank the old woman that he noticed Bonnie staring at him. In particular, at his neck. Suddenly she giggled.

"What? What's funny?"

"The bug," she said. "It gave you a hickey. Unless you did something else last night that you didn't tell us about."

Matt could feel himself flush as he pulled his collar up higher. "I did tell you about it, and it was the malach. It had a sort of tentacle with suckers around my neck. It was trying to strangle me!"

"I remember now," Bonnie said meekly. "I'm sorry."

Mrs. Flowers even had an herbal ointment for the mark the sucker tentacle had left—and one for Matt's scraped knuckles. After she'd applied them, Matt felt so good that he was able to look sheepishly at Bonnie, who was watching him with big brown eyes.

"I know, it does look like a hickey," he said. "I saw it this morning in the mirror. And I've got another one lower down, but at least my collar covers that one." He snorted and reached into his shirt to apply more ointment. The girls laughed—a release of the tension that they'd all been feeling.

Meredith had started back up the narrow stairway to what everyone still thought of as Stefan's room, and Matt automatically followed her. He didn't realize that Elena and Bonnie were hanging back until he was halfway up the stairs, and then Meredith motioned him onward.

"They're just conferring," Meredith said, in her quiet, no-nonsense voice.

"About *me*?" Matt swallowed. "It's about that thing Elena saw inside Damon, right? The invisible malach. And whether or not I've got one—inside me—right now."

Meredith, never one to soft-pedal anything, simply nodded. But she put a hand briefly on his shoulder as they entered the dim, high-ceilinged bedroom.

Shortly after, Elena and Bonnie came up, and Matt could tell at once by their faces that the worst-case scenario wasn't true. Elena saw his expression and immediately went to him and hugged him. Bonnie followed, more shyly.

"Feel okay?" Elena said, and Matt nodded.

"I feel fine," he said. Like wrestling alligators, he thought. Nothing was nicer than hugging soft, soft girls.

"Well, the consensus is that you don't have anything inside you that doesn't belong there. Your aura seems clear and strong now that you're not in pain."

"Thank God," Matt said, and he meant it.

It was at that moment that his mobile phone rang. He frowned, puzzled at the number displayed, but he answered it.

"Matthew Honeycutt?"

"Yes."

"Hold, please."

A new voice came on: "Mr. Honeycutt?"

"Uh, yeah, but—"

"This is Rich Mossberg of the Fell's Church Sheriff's Department. You called this morning to report a fallen tree midway down Old Wood Road?"

"Yes, I—"

"Mr. Honeycutt, we don't like prank calls of this sort. We frown upon them, in fact. It takes up the valuable time of our officers, and besides, it happens to be a crime to make a false report to the police. If I wanted to, Mr. Honeycutt, I could charge you with this crime and make you answer to a judge. I don't see just what you find so amusing about it."

"I wasn't—I don't find *anything* amusing about it! Look, last night—" Matt's voice trailed off. What was he going to say? *Last night I was waylaid by a tree and a monster bug?* A small voice inside him added that the Fell's Church Sheriff's officers seemed to spend most of their valuable time hanging around the Dunkin' Donuts in the city square, but the next words he heard shut it up.

"*In fact*, Mr. Honeycutt, under the authority of Virginia State Code, Section 18.2-461, making a false police report is punishable as a Class 1 misdemeanor. You could be looking at a year in jail or a twenty-five-thousand-dollar fine. Do you find *that* amusing, Mr. Honeycutt?"

"Look, I—"

"Do you, in fact, *have* twenty-five thousand dollars, Mr. Honeycutt?"

"No, I—I—" Matt waited to be cut off and then he realized that he wasn't going to be. He was sailing off the edge of the map into some unknown region. What to say? *The malach took the tree away*—or *maybe it moved by itself?* Ludicrous. Finally, in a creaky voice he managed, "I'm sorry they didn't find the tree. Maybe . . . somehow it got moved."

"Maybe somehow it got moved," the sheriff repeated expressionlessly. "In fact maybe somehow it moved itself the way that all those stop signs and yield signs keep moving themselves away from intersections. Does that ring a bell, Mr. Honeycutt?"

"No!" Matt felt himself flush deeply. "I would never move any kind of street sign." By now the girls were clustered around him, as if they could somehow help by appearing as a group. Bonnie was gesturing vigorously, and her indignant expression made it clear that she wanted to tell the sheriff off personally.

"In fact, Mr. Honeycutt," Sheriff Mossberg cut in, "we called your home number first, since that's the phone you used to place the report. And your mother said that she hadn't seen you at all last night."

Matt ignored the little voice that wanted to snap, *Is that a crime?* "That was because I got held up—"

"By a self-propelled tree, Mr. Honeycutt? In fact we had already had another call about your house last night. A member of Neighborhood Watch reported a suspicious car roughly in front of your house. According to your mother, you recently totaled your own car, isn't that right, Mr. Honeycutt?"

Matt could see where this was going and he didn't like it. "Yes," he heard himself say, while his mind worked desperately for a plausible explanation. "I was trying to avoid running over a fox. And—"

"Yet there was a report of a brand new Jaguar lingering in front of your house, just far enough away from the street-light to be—inconspicuous. A car so new that it had no license plates. Was that, in fact, *your* car, Mr. Honeycutt?"

"Mr. Honeycutt's my father!" Matt said desperately. "I'm Matt. And it was my friend's car—"

"And your friend's name is . . . ?"

Matt stared at Elena. She was making wait gestures, obviously trying to think. To say *Elena Gilbert* would be suicidal. The police, of all people, knew that Elena Gilbert was dead. Now Elena was pointing around the room and mouthing words at him.

Matt shut his eyes and said the words, "Stefan Salvatore. But he gave the car to his girlfriend?" He knew he was ending his sentence so that it sounded like a question, but he could hardly believe Elena's coaching.

Now the sheriff was beginning to sound tired and exasperated. "Are *you* asking *me*, Matt? So you were driving the brand-new car of your friend's girlfriend. And her name is . . . ?"

There was a brief moment when the girls seemed to disagree and Matt hung in limbo. But then Bonnie threw her arms up and Meredith moved forward, pointing to herself.

"Meredith Sulez," Matt said weakly. He heard the hesitation in his own voice and he repeated, huskily but with more conviction, "Meredith Sulez."

Now Elena was whispering rapidly in Meredith's ear.

"And the car was purchased where? Mr. Honeycutt?"

"Yes," Matt said. "Just a second—" He put the phone into Meredith's outstretched hand.

"This is Meredith Sulez," Meredith said smoothly, in the polished, relaxed tones of a classical music disk jockey.

"Miss Sulez, you've heard the conversation so far?"

"*Ms.* Sulez, please, Sergeant. I have."

"Did you, in fact, lend your car to Mr. Honeycutt?"

"I did."

"And where is Mr."—there was a shuffling of paper—"Stefan Salvatore, the original owner of the car?"

He's not asking her where they bought it, Matt

thought. He must know.

"My boyfriend is away from town right now," Meredith said, still in the same refined, unflappable voice. "I don't know when he'll be back. When he is, shall I have him call you?"

"That might be wise," Sheriff Mossberg said dryly. "These days very few cars are bought with cash on the line, especially brand-new Jaguars. I'd like your driver's license number, also. And, in fact, I'd very much like to speak to Mr. Salvatore when he returns."

"That may be very soon," Meredith said, a bit slowly, but following Elena's coaching. Then she recited her driver's license number from memory.

"Thank you," Sheriff Mossberg said briefly. "That will be all for—"

"May I just say one thing? Matt Honeycutt would never, ever remove stop signs or yield signs. He's a very conscientious driver and was a leader in his high school class. You can speak to any of Robert E. Lee High School's teachers or even the principal if she's not on vacation. Any one of them will tell you the same thing."

The sheriff didn't seem to be impressed. "You can tell him from me that I'll be keeping an eye on him in the future. In fact it might be a good idea if he stopped in the Sheriff's Department today or tomorrow," he said, and then the phone went dead.

Matt burst out, "Stefan's girlfriend? You, Meredith? What if the car dealer says the girl was a blond? How are we going to work that out?"

"We aren't," Elena said simply from behind Meredith. "Damon is. All we have to do is to find him. I'm sure he can take care of Sheriff Mossberg with a little mind control—if the price is right. And don't worry about me," she added gently. "You're frowning, but everything is going to be fine."

"You believe that?"

"I'm sure of it." Elena gave him another hug and a kiss on the cheek.

"I'm supposed to stop by the Sheriff's Department today or tomorrow, though."

"But not alone!" Bonnie said, and her eyes were sparkling with indignation. "And when Damon goes with you, Sheriff Mooseburger will end up being your best friend."

"All right," Meredith said. "So what are we doing today?"

"The problem," Elena returned, tapping an index finger against her upper lip, "is that we've got too many problems at once and I don't want anybody—and I mean anybody—going out alone. It's clear that there are malach in the Old Wood, and that they're trying to do unfriendly-type things to us. Kill us, for one."

Matt basked in the warm relief of being believed. The

conversation with Sheriff Mossberg had shaken him more than he wanted to show.

"So we make up task forces," Meredith said, "and we split the jobs between them. What problems do we need to plan for?"

Elena ticked off the problems with her fingers. "One problem is Caroline. I really think someone should try to see her, at the very least to try and find out if she has one of those *things* inside her. Another problem is Tami—and who knows who else? If Caroline is . . . contagious somehow, she might have spread it to some other girl—or guy."

"Okay," Meredith said, "and what else?"

"Someone needs to contact Damon. Try to find out from him anything he knows about Stefan leaving, and also try to get him to go in to headquarters with us to influence Sheriff Mossberg."

"Well, you'd better be on that last team, since you're the only one Damon's likely to talk to," said Meredith. "And Bonnie should be on it, so she can keep—"

"No. No Calling today," Bonnie pleaded. "I'm so sorry, Elena, but I just can't, not without a day of rest between. And besides, if Damon wants to talk to you, all you need to do is to walk—not *into* the forest, but *near* it—and call to him yourself. He knows everything that's going on. He'll know you're there."

"Then I should go with Elena," Matt reasoned. "Since that sheriff is my problem. I'd like to go by the place where I saw the tree—"

At once there was a protest from all three girls.

"I said I'd *like* to," Matt said. "Not that we should plan for it. That's one spot we know is too dangerous."

"All right," Elena said. "So Bonnie and Meredith will visit Caroline, and you and I will go Damon hunting, all right? I'd rather go Stefan hunting, but we just don't have enough information yet."

"Right, but before you go, maybe stop by Jim Bryce's house. Matt has an excuse to stop by anytime—he knows Jim. And you can check on Tami's progress as well," Meredith suggested.

"Sounds like plans A, B, and C," Elena said, and then, spontaneously, they all laughed.

It was a clear day, with a hot sun shining overhead.

In the sunlight, despite the minor annoyance of Sheriff Mossberg's call, they all felt strong and capable.

None of them had any idea that they were about to walk into the worst nightmare of their lives.

Bonnie stood back as Meredith knocked at the front door of the Forbes home.

After a while of no answer and silence inside, Meredith knocked again.

This time Bonnie could hear whisperings and Mrs. Forbes hissing something, and Caroline's distant laughter.

Finally, just as Meredith was about to ring the bell—the height of discourtesy between neighbor and neighbor in Fell's Church—the door opened. Bonnie neatly slipped a foot in, keeping it from being shut again.

"Hi, Mrs. Forbes. We just . . ." Meredith faltered. "We just wanted to see if Caroline was any better," she finished in a tinny-sounding voice. Mrs. Forbes looked as if she'd seen a ghost—and she'd spent all night running from it.

"No, she's not. Not better. She's still—sick." The woman's voice was hollow and distant and her eyes scanned the ground just over Bonnie's right shoulder. Bonnie felt fine hairs on her arms and the back of her neck stand up.

"Okay, Mrs. Forbes." Even Meredith sounded false and hollow.

Then someone said suddenly, "Are *you* all right?" and Bonnie realized it was her own voice.

"Caroline . . . isn't well. She's . . . not seeing anyone," whispered the woman.

An iceberg seemed to glide down Bonnie's spine. She wanted to turn and run from this house and its aura of malevolence. But at that moment Mrs. Forbes suddenly slumped. Meredith was barely able to break her fall.

"She's fainted," Meredith said tersely.

Bonnie wanted to say, *Well, put her on the rug inside and*

run! But they could hardly do that.

"We've got to take her inside," Meredith said flatly. "Bonnie, are you okay to go?"

"No," Bonnie said just as flatly, "but what choice do we have?"

Mrs. Forbes, small as she was, was heavy. Bonnie held her feet and followed Meredith, step by reluctant step, into the house.

"We'll just put her on her bed," Meredith said. Her voice was shaky. There was something about the house that was terribly unsettling—as if waves of pressure kept bearing down on them.

And then Bonnie saw it. Just a glimpse as they stepped into the living room. It was down the hallway, and it could have been the play of light and shadow there, but it looked for all the world like a person. A person scuttling like a lizard—but not on the floor. On the ceiling.

att was knocking at the Bryces' door, with Elena at his side. Elena had disguised herself by stuffing all her hair into a Virginia Cavaliers baseball cap and wearing wraparound sunglasses from one of Stefan's drawers. She was also wearing an overlarge maroon and navy Pendleton shirt donated by Matt, and a pair of Meredith's outgrown jeans. She felt sure that no one who had known the old Elena Gilbert would ever recognize her, dressed like this.

The door opened very slowly to reveal not Mr. or Mrs. Bryce, nor Jim, but Tamra. She was wearing—well, close to nothing. She had on a thong bikini bottom, but it looked handmade, as if she'd cut a regular bikini bottom with scissors—and it was beginning to come apart. On top she had two round decorations made of cardboard with sequins pasted on and a few strands of colored tinsel. On her head she wore a paper crown, which was clearly where she'd gotten the tinsel. She'd made an attempt to glue strands onto the bikini bottoms as well. The result looked like what it was: a child's attempt to make an outfit for a Las Vegas showgirl or stripper.

Matt immediately turned around and stood facing away, but Tami threw herself at him and plastered herself to his back.

"Matt Honey-butt," she cooed. "You came back. I knew you would. But why'd you bring this ugly old whore with you? How can we—"

Elena stepped forward, then, because Matt had whirled with his hand up. She was sure that Matt had never struck a female in his life, especially a child, but he was also over-sensitive about one or two subjects. Like her.

Elena managed to get between Matt and the surprisingly strong Tamra. She had to hide a smile when contemplating Tami's costume. After all, only a few days ago, she hadn't understood the human nakedness taboo at all. Now she got it, but it didn't seem nearly as important as it once had. People were born with their own perfectly good skins on. There was no real reason, in her mind, to wear false skins over those, unless it was cold or somehow uncomfortable without them. But society said that to be naked was to be wicked. Tami was trying to be wicked, in her own childish way.

"Get your hands off me, you old whore," Tamra snarled as Elena held her away from Matt, and then she added several rather lengthy expletives.

"Tami, where are your parents? Where's your brother?" Elena said. She ignored the obscene words—they were just sounds—but saw that Matt had gone white around the lips.

"You apologize to Elena right now! Apologize for talking that way!" he demanded.

"Elena's a stinking corpse with worms in her eye sockets," Tamra sang glibly. "But my friend says she was a whore when she was alive. A real"—a string of four-letter words that made Matt gasp—"cheap whore. *You* know. Nothing's cheaper than something that comes free."

"Matt, just don't pay any attention," Elena said under her breath, and she repeated, "Where are your parents and Jim?"

The answer was littered with more expletives, but it amounted to the story—truthful or not—that Mr. and Mrs. Bryce had gone away on vacation for a few days, and that Jim was with his girlfriend, Isobel.

"Okay, then, I guess I'll just have to help you get into some more decent clothes," Elena said. "First, I think you need a shower to get these Christmas doodads off—"

"Just try-hy-hy! Just try-hy-hy!" The answer was

somewhere between the whinny of a horse and human speech. "I glued them on with PermaStick!" Tami added and then began giggling on a high and hysterical note.

"Oh, my God—Tamra, do you realize that if there isn't some solvent for this, you may need surgery?"

Tami's answer was foul. There was also a sudden foul smell. No, not a smell, Elena thought: a choking, gut-curdling stench.

"Oops!" Tami gave that high, glassy giggle again. "Pardon *moi*. At least it's *natural* gas."

Matt cleared his throat. "Elena—I don't think we should be here. With her folks gone and all . . ."

"They're afraid of me," Tamra giggled. "Aren't *you*?"—very suddenly in a voice that had dropped several octaves.

Elena looked Tamra in the eye. "No, I'm not. I just feel sorry for a little girl who was in the wrong place at the wrong time. But Matt's right, I guess. We have to go."

Tami's whole manner seemed to change. "I'm so sorry. . . . I didn't realize I had guests of that ca*l*iber. Don't go, please, Matt." Then she added in a confidential whisper to Elena, "Is he any good?"

"What?"

Tami nodded at Matt, who immediately turned his back to her. He looked as if he felt a terrible, repulsive fascination for Tami's ridiculous appearance.

"Him. Is he any good in the sack?"

"Matt, look at this." Elena held up a small tube of glue. "I think she actually did PermaStick that stuff to her skin. We have to call Child Protective Services or whatever, because nobody took her to the hospital right away. Whether her parents knew about this behavior or not, they shouldn't have just left her."

"I just hope *they're* all right. Her family," Matt said grimly as they walked out the door, with Tami coolly following them to the car, and shouting lurid details about "what a good time" they had had, "the three of them."

Elena glanced at him uneasily from her place in the passenger seat—with no ID or driver's license, of course, she knew she shouldn't drive. "Maybe we'd better take her to the police first. My God, that poor family!"

Matt said nothing for a long time. His chin was set, his mouth grim. "I feel somehow as if I'm responsible. I mean, I knew there was something wrong with her—I should have told her parents then."

"Now you're sounding like Stefan. You're not responsible for everyone you meet."

Matt gave her a grateful glance, and Elena continued, "In fact I'm going to ask Bonnie and Meredith to do one other thing, which proves you're not. I'm going to ask them to check on Isobel Saitou, Jim's girlfriend. *You've* never had any contact with her, but Tami might have."

"You mean you think she's got it, too?"

"That's what I hope Bonnie and Meredith will find out."

Bonnie stopped dead, almost losing her hold on Mrs. Forbes's feet. "I am not going into that bedroom."

"You have to. I can't manage her alone," Meredith said. Then she added cajolingly, "Look, Bonnie, if you go in with me, I'll tell you a secret."

Bonnie bit her lip. Then she shut her eyes and let Meredith guide her, step by step, farther into this house of horror. She knew where the master bedroom was—after all, she had played here since childhood. All the way down the hall, then turn left.

She was surprised when Meredith came to a sudden stop after only a few steps. "Bonnie."

"Well? What?"

"I don't want to frighten you, but—"

This had the immediate effect of terrifying Bonnie. Her eyes snapped open. "What? *What?*" Before Meredith could answer she glanced over her shoulder in fear and saw what.

Caroline was behind her. But not standing. She was crawling—no, she was scuttling, the way she had on Stefan's floor. Like a lizard. Her bronze hair, unkempt, hung down over her face. Her elbows and knees stuck out at impossible angles.

Bonnie screamed, but the pressure of the house seemed to choke the scream back down her throat. The only effect it had was to make Caroline look up at her with a quick reptilian movement of her head.

"Oh, my God—Caroline, what happened to your face?"

Caroline had a black eye. Or rather, a purplish-red eye that was so swollen that Bonnie knew it would have to turn black in time. On her jaw was another purple swelling bruise.

Caroline didn't answer, unless you counted the sibilant hiss she gave while scuttling forward.

"Meredith, run! She's right behind me!"

Meredith quickened her pace, looking frightened—all the more frightening to Bonnie because almost nothing could shake her friend. But as they lurched forward, with Mrs. Forbes bouncing between them, Caroline scuttled right under her mother and into the door of her parents' room, the master bedroom.

"Meredith, I won't go in th—" But they were already stumbling through the door. Bonnie shot quick darting glances into every corner. Caroline was nowhere to be seen.

"Maybe she's in the closet," Meredith said. "Now, let me go first and put her head on the far side of the bed. We can adjust her later." She backed around the bed, almost dragging Bonnie with her, and dumped Mrs. Forbes's upper torso so that her head rested on pillows. "Now just pull her and put her legs down on the other side."

"I can't do it. I can't! Caroline's *under* the bed, you know."

"She can't be under the bed. There's only about a five-inch clearance," Meredith said firmly.

"She's there! I *know* it. And"—rather fiercely—"you promised you'd tell me a secret."

"All right!" Meredith gave a complicit glance through her disheveled dark hair. "I telegraphed Alaric yesterday. He's so far out in the boonies that telegraph is the only way to reach him, and it may be days before my message gets to him. I had an idea that we were going to need his advice. I feel bad, asking him to do projects that aren't for his doctorate, but—"

"Who cares about his doctorate? God *bless* you!" cried Bonnie thankfully. "You did just right!"

"Then come on and swing Mrs. Forbes' feet around the bottom of the bed. You can do it if you lean in."

The bed was a California king-size. Mrs. Forbes was lying at an angle across it, like a doll thrown on the floor. But Bonnie halted near the foot of the bed. "Caroline's going to grab me."

"No, she won't. Come on, Bonnie. Just get Mrs. Forbes'

legs and give one big heave. . . ."

"If I get that close to the bed, she'll *grab* me!"

"Why should she?"

"Because she knows what scares me! And now that I've said it, she *definitely* will."

"If she grabs you, I'll come and kick her in the face."

"Your leg's not that long. It would bang on the metal bed-frame thingummy—"

"Oh, for God's sake, Bonnie! Just help me *heeeeeeere!*" The last word was a full-fledged scream.

"Meredith—" began Bonnie, and then she screamed, too.

"*What is it?*"

"*She's grabbing me!*"

"*She can't be!* She's grabbing *me*! Nobody has arms that long!"

"Or that strong! Bonnie! *I can't make her let go!*"

"*Neither can I!*"

And then any words were drowned in screaming.

After dropping Tami off with the police, driving Elena around the woods known as the Fell's State Park was . . . well, a walk in the park. Every so often they would stop. Elena would go a few steps into the trees and stand, Calling—however you did that. Then she came back to the Jaguar, looking discouraged.

"I'm not sure that Bonnie wouldn't be better at this," she said to Matt. "If we can brace ourselves to go out at night."

Matt shuddered involuntarily. "Two nights were enough."

"Do you know, you never told me your story from that first night. Or at least, not when I could understand words, spoken words."

"Well, I was driving around like this, except almost on the other side of the Old Wood—near the Lightning-Split Oak area . . . ?"

"Right."

"When right in the middle of the road something appears."

"A fox?"

"Well, it was red in the headlights, but it wasn't like any fox I've ever seen. And I've been driving this road since I could drive."

"A wolf?"

"Like a werewolf, you mean? But, no—I've seen wolves by moonlight and they're bigger. This was right in between."

"In other words," Elena said, narrowing her lapis lazuli eyes, "a custom-made creature."

"Maybe. It sure was different from the malach that chewed my arm up."

Elena nodded. Malach could take all sorts of different

forms, from what she understood. But they were siblings in one way: they all used Power and they all needed a diet of Power to live. And they could be manipulated by a stronger Power than they had.

And they were venomous enemies of humans.

"So all we really know is that we don't know anything."

"Right. That was the place back there, where we saw it. It just suddenly appeared in the middle of the—*hey*!"

"Go right! Right *here*!"

"Just like that! It was just like that!"

The Jaguar screeched almost to a stop, turning right, not into a ditch but into a small lane that no one would notice unless they were looking directly at it.

When the car stopped, they both stared up the lane, breathing hard. Neither had to ask whether the other had seen a reddish creature zip across the road, bigger than a fox but smaller than a wolf.

They looked up at the narrow lane.

"The million-dollar question: should we go in?" Matt asked.

"No KEEP OUT signs—and hardly any houses on this side of the wood. Across the street and down a way there's the Dunstans'."

"So we go in?"

"We go in. Just go slowly. It's later than I thought."

* * *

Meredith, of course, was the one to calm down first. "All *right*, Bonnie," she said. "Stop it! Now! It's not going to do any good here!"

Bonnie didn't think she *could* stop it. But Meredith had that special look in her dark eyes; the one that meant she was serious. The look she'd had before laying Caroline out on Stefan's floor.

Bonnie made a supreme effort and found that somehow she was able to hold in the next shriek. She looked dumbly at Meredith, feeling her own body shake.

"Good. Good, Bonnie. Now." Meredith swallowed. "Pulling doesn't do any good, either. So I'm going to try . . . peeling her fingers off. If anything happens to me; if I get—pulled under the bed or anything, then you *run*, Bonnie. And if you can't run, then you call Elena and Matt. You call until you get an answer."

Bonnie managed something almost heroic then. She refused to picture Meredith being pulled under the bed. She wouldn't let herself imagine how that would look as Meredith, struggling, disappeared, or how she would feel, all alone, after that. They'd both left their purses with their mobile phones in the entryway to carry Mrs. Forbes, so Meredith wasn't saying to call them in any normal sense. She meant Call them.

A sudden radical burst of indignation swept through

Bonnie. Why did girls carry purses anyway? Even the efficient, reliable Meredith often did it. Of course Meredith's purses were usually designer handbags that enhanced her outfits and were full of useful things like small notebooks and keychain flashlights, but still . . . a boy would have his mobile phone in his pocket.

From now on, I'm wearing a waist pouch, Bonnie thought, feeling as if she were raising a rebel flag for girls everywhere, and for just a moment also feeling her panic recede.

Then she saw Meredith stooping, a hunched figure in the dim light, and at the same moment she felt the grip on her own ankle tighten. Despite herself she glanced down, and saw the outline of Caroline's tanned fingers and long bronze nails against the creamy white of the rug.

Panic burst out in her again, full force. She made a choked sound that was a strangled scream, and to her own astonishment she spontaneously hit trance and began to Call.

It wasn't the fact that she was Calling that surprised her. It was what she was saying.

Damon! Damon! We're trapped at Caroline's house and she's gone crazy! Help!

It flowed out of her like an underwater well that had been suddenly tapped, releasing a geyser.

Damon, she's got me by the ankle—and she won't let go! If she pulls Meredith under, I don't know what I'll do! Help me!

Vaguely, because the trance was good and deep, she heard Meredith say, "Ah-hah! It feels like fingers, but actually it's a vine. It must be one of those tentacles that Matt told us about. I'm—trying—to break one of the loops—off . . ."

All at once there was a rustling from under the bed. And not just from one place, either, but a massive whipping and shaking that actually bounced the mattress up and down, even with poor little Mrs. Forbes on it.

There must be dozens of those insects under there.

Damon, it's those things*! Lots of them. Oh, God, I think I'm going to faint. And if I faint—and if Caroline pulls me under . . . Oh, please come and help!*

"Damn!" Meredith was saying. "I don't know how Matt managed to do this. It's too tight, and—and I think there's more than one tentacle here."

It's all over, Bonnie sent in quiet conclusion, feeling herself start to go at the knees. *We're going to die.*

"Undoubtedly—that's the problem with humans. But not just *yet*," a voice said from behind her, and a strong arm went around her, taking up her weight easily. "Caroline, the fun's over. I mean it. Let *go!*"

"Damon?" Bonnie gasped. "Damon? You came!"

"All that wailing gets on my nerves. It doesn't mean—"

But Bonnie wasn't listening. She wasn't even thinking.

She was still half in trance and not responsible (she decided later) for her own actions. She wasn't *herself*. It was someone else who went into rapture when the grip on her ankle loosened, and someone else who whirled around in Damon's grip and threw her arms around his neck and kissed him on the mouth.

It was someone else, too, who felt Damon startle, with his arms still around her, and who noticed that he made no attempt to pull away from the kiss. That person also noticed, when at last she leaned back, that Damon's skin, pale in the dim light, looked almost as if he had flushed.

And that was when Meredith straightened up slowly, painfully, from the other side of the bed, which was still jouncing up and down. She hadn't seen anything of the kiss, and looked at Damon as if she couldn't believe he was really here.

She was at a great disadvantage, and Bonnie knew she knew it. This was one of those situations where anyone else would have been too flustered to speak, or even stammer.

But Meredith just took a deep breath and then said quietly, "Damon. Thank you. Do you think—would it be too much trouble to make the malach let go of me, as well?"

Now Damon looked like his old self. He gave a brilliant smile aimed at something no one else could see and said sharply, "And as for the rest of you down there—heel!" He snapped his fingers.

The bed stopped moving instantly.

Meredith stepped away, and closed her eyes for a moment in relief.

"Thank you again," she said, with the dignity of a princess, but fervently. "And now, do you think you could do anything about Caro—"

"Right now," Damon cut in even more roughly than usual, "I have to run." He glanced at the Rolex on his wrist. "It's past 4:44, and I had an appointment I'm already late for. Come around here and prop up this dizzy bundle. She's not quite ready to stand by herself."

Meredith hastened to switch places with him. At that point, Bonnie discovered that her legs were no longer wobbling.

"Wait a minute, though," Meredith said rapidly. "Elena *needs* to talk to you—*desperately*—"

But Damon was gone, as if he'd mastered the art of simply disappearing, not even waiting for Bonnie's thanks. Meredith looked astonished, as if she'd been certain that the mention of Elena's name would stop him, but Bonnie had something else on her mind.

"Meredith," Bonnie whispered, putting two fingers to her lips in amazement. "I kissed him!"

"What? *When?*"

"Before you stood up. I—don't even know how it happened but I did it!"

She expected some kind of explosion from Meredith.

Instead, Meredith looked at her thoughtfully and murmured, "Well, maybe it wasn't such a bad thing to do, after all. What I don't understand is why he turned up in the first place."

"Uh. That was me, too. I Called him. I don't know how that happened either—"

"Well, there's no point in trying to figure it out in here." Meredith turned toward the bed. "Caroline, are you coming out of there? Are you going to stand up and have a normal conversation?"

There was a menacing and reptilian hiss from under the bed, along with the whipping of tentacles and another noise that Bonnie had never heard before but which terrified her instinctively, like the snapping of giant pincers.

"That's answer enough for me," she said, and grabbed Meredith to drag her out of the room.

Meredith didn't need dragging. But for the first time today they heard Caroline's taunting voice, lifted childishly high.

"Bonnie and Damon sitting in a tree
K-I-S-S-I-N-G.
First comes love, then comes marriage;
Then there comes a vampire in a baby carriage."

Meredith paused in the hallway. "Caroline, you know that that isn't going to help matters. Come out—"

The bed went into a frenzy, bucking and heaving. Bonnie turned and ran, and she knew Meredith was right behind her. They still didn't manage to outpace the sing-song words:

"You're not *my* friends; you're the *whore's* friends. Just you wait! Just you *wait*!"

Bonnie and Meredith grabbed their purses and left the house.

"What time is it?" Bonnie asked, when they were safely in Meredith's car.

"Almost five."

"It seemed like so much longer!"

"I know, but we've got hours of daylight left. And, come to that, I have a text message from Elena."

"About Tami?"

"I'll tell you about it. But first—" It was one of the few times Bonnie had seen Meredith look awkward. Finally she blurted, "How was it?"

"How was what?"

"Kissing Damon, you nitwit!"

"hhhh." Bonnie melted back into the bucket seat. "It was like . . . *kapow! Zap! Zowie!* Like . . . fireworks."

"You're smirking."

"I am not smirking," Bonnie said with dignity. "I am smiling in fond remembrance. Besides—"

"Besides, if you hadn't Called him, we'd still be stuck in that horror of a room. Thank you, Bonnie. You saved us." Abruptly Meredith was at her most serious and sincere.

"I guess Elena was maybe right when she said he didn't hate all humans," Bonnie said slowly. "But, you know, I just realized. I couldn't see his aura at all. All I could see was black: smooth hard black, like a shell around him."

"Maybe that's how he protects himself. He makes a

shell so no one can see inside."

"Maybe," Bonnie said, but there was worried note in her voice. "And what about that message from Elena?"

"It says that Tami Bryce is definitely acting strangely and that she and Matt are going out to check out the Old Wood."

"Maybe that's who they're going to meet—Damon, I mean. At 4:44, like he said. Too bad we can't call her."

"I know," Meredith said grimly. Everyone in Fell's Church knew that there was no reception in the Old Wood or the cemetery area. "But go ahead and try anyway."

Bonnie did, and as usual got a no-service message. She shook her head. "No good. They must already be in the woods."

"Well, what she wants is for us to go ahead and get a look at Isobel Saitou—you know, because she's Jim Bryce's girlfriend." Meredith made a turn. "That reminds me, Bonnie: did you get a look at *Caroline's* aura? Do you think she has one of those things—inside her?"

"I guess so. I saw her aura, and yuck, I never want to see it again. She used to be a kind of deep bronzy-green, but now she's muddy brown with black lightning zigzagging all through. I don't know if that means one of those things was inside her, but she sure didn't mind cuddling up to them!" Bonnie shuddered.

"Okay," Meredith said soothingly. "I know what I

would say if I had to make a guess—and if you're going to be sick, I'll stop."

Bonnie gulped. "I'm all right. But we're seriously going to Isobel Saitou's house?"

"We're very seriously going there. As a matter of fact, we're almost there. Let's just brush our hair, take a few deep breaths, and get it over with. How well do you know her?"

"Well, she's smart. We didn't have any classes together. But we both got out of athletics at the same time—she had a jumpy heart or something, and I used to get that terrible asthma. . . ."

"From any exertion except dancing, which you could keep up all night," Meredith said dryly. "I don't know her very well at all. What's she like?"

"Well, nice. Looks a bit like you, except Asian. Shorter than you—Elena's height, but skinnier. Sort of pretty. A little shy—the quiet type, you know. Sort of hard to get to know. And . . . nice."

"Shy and quiet and nice sounds good to me."

"Me, too," Bonnie said, pressing her sweaty hands together between her knees. What sounded even better, she thought, was for Isobel to be not at home.

However, there were several cars parked in front of the Saitou house. Bonnie and Meredith knocked on the door hesitantly, mindful of what had happened the last time they had done this.

It was Jim Bryce who answered, a tall, lanky boy who hadn't filled out yet and stooped a bit. What Bonnie found amazing was the change in his face as he recognized Meredith.

When he'd answered he'd looked awful; his face white under a medium tan, his body somehow crumpled. When he saw Meredith, some of the color came to his cheeks and he seemed to . . . well, to smooth out like a piece of paper. He stood taller.

Meredith didn't say a word. She just stepped forward and put her arms around him. He clutched at her as if he was afraid she'd run away, and buried his face in her dark hair.

"Meredith."

"Just breathe, Jim. Breathe."

"You don't know what it's been like. My parents left because my great-grandpa's really sick—I think he's dying. And then Tami—Tami—"

"Tell me slowly. And keep breathing."

"She threw knives, Meredith. Butcher knives. She got me in the leg here." Jim plucked at his jeans to show a small slit of a hole in the fabric over the lower part of one thigh.

"Have you had a tetanus shot recently?" Meredith was at her most efficient.

"No, but it's not really a big cut. It's a puncture wound, mainly."

"Those are exactly the kind that are most dangerous.

You need to call Dr. Alpert right away." Old Dr. Alpert was an institution in Fell's Church: a doctor who even made house calls, in a country where carrying around a little black bag and stethoscope was pretty much unheard-of behavior.

"I *can't*. I can't leave. . . ." Jim jerked his head backward toward the interior of the house as if he couldn't bring himself to say a name.

Bonnie tugged at Meredith's sleeve. "I have a very bad feeling about this," she hissed.

Meredith turned back to Jim. "You mean Isobel? Where are *her* parents?"

"Isa-chan, I mean Isobel, I just call her Isa-chan, you know . . ."

"It's all right," said Meredith. "Just say what comes naturally. Go on."

"Well, Isa-chan only has her grandma, and Grandma Saitou doesn't even come downstairs much. I made her lunch a while ago and she thought I was—Isobel's father. She gets . . . confused."

Meredith glanced at Bonnie, and said, "And Isobel? Is she confused, too?"

Jim shut his eyes, looking utterly miserable. "I wish you'd go in and, well, just talk to her."

Bonnie's bad feeling was only getting worse. She really couldn't stand another scare like the one at Caroline's house—and she certainly didn't have the strength to Call again, even if Damon weren't in a hurry to get some-where.

But Meredith knew all this, and Meredith was giving her the sort of look that couldn't be denied. It also promised that Meredith would protect Bonnie, no matter what.

"Is she hurting anybody? Isobel?" Bonnie heard her-self ask as they crossed through the kitchen and toward a bedroom at the end of the hallway.

She could hardly hear Jim's whispered, "Yeah."

And then, as Bonnie groaned internally, he added, "Herself."

Isobel's room was just what you'd expect from a quiet and studious girl. At least one side was. The other side looked as if a tidal wave had picked everything up and thrown it down again randomly. Isobel was sitting in the middle of this mess like a spider on a web.

But that wasn't what made Bonnie's gut churn. It was what Isobel was doing. She had laid out beside her what looked a lot like Mrs. Flowers' kit for cleaning out wounds, but she wasn't healing anything.

She was piercing herself.

She had already done her lip, her nose, one eyebrow, and her ears, many times. Blood was dripping from all these places, dripping and falling onto the unmade sheets of her bed. Bonnie saw all that as Isobel looked up at them with a frown, except that the frown was only half there. On the pierced side, the eyebrow didn't move at all.

Her aura was shattered orange with black lashings through it.

Bonnie knew, all at once, that she was going to be sick. She knew it with the deep knowledge that overcame all embarrassment and which sent her flying to a wastebasket she didn't even remember seeing. Thank God, it had a white plastic bag lining it, she thought, and then she was completely occupied for a few minutes.

Her ears recorded a voice, even as she was thinking she was glad she hadn't had lunch.

"My God, *are you crazy?* Isobel, what have you done to yourself? Don't you know the kind of infections you can get . . . the veins you can hit . . . the muscles you can paralyze . . . ? I think you've already pierced the muscle in your eyebrow—*and you shouldn't still be bleeding unless you've hit veins or arteries.*"

Bonnie retched dryly into the wastebasket, and spat.

And just then she heard a meaty thud.

She looked up, half knowing what she would see. But it still was a shock. Meredith was doubled over from what must have been a punch in the stomach.

The next thing Bonnie knew, she was beside Meredith. "Oh, my God, did she *stab* you?" A stab wound . . . deep enough into the abdomen . . .

Meredith clearly couldn't get her breath. From somewhere a bit of advice from her sister Mary, the nurse, floated into Bonnie's mind.

Bonnie pounded with both fists on Meredith's back, and suddenly Meredith took a huge gulp of air.

"Thanks," she was saying weakly, but Bonnie was already dragging her away, away from the laughing Isobel and a collection of the world's longest nails and the rubbing alcohol and other things that she had on a breakfast tray beside her.

Bonnie got to the door and almost collided with Jim, who had a wet washcloth in his hand. For her, she supposed. Or maybe for Isobel. All Bonnie was interested in was making Meredith pull up her top to make absolutely, positively sure that there were no holes in her.

"I got it—out of her hand—before she punched me," Meredith said, still breathing painfully as Bonnie anxiously scanned the area above her low-rise jeans. "I'll have a bruise, that's all."

"She hit you, too?" Jim said in dismay. Except that he didn't say it. He whispered it.

You poor guy, Bonnie thought, finally satisfied that Meredith wasn't perforated. What with Caroline and your sister Tami and your girlfriend, you don't have the first idea of what's going on. How could you?

And if we told you, you'd just think we were two more crazy girls.

"Jimmy, you *have* to call Dr. Alpert right away, and

then I think they're going to have to go to the hospital in Ridgemont. Isobel's already done permanent damage to herself—God knows how much. *All* those piercings are almost certainly going to be infected. When did she start this?"

"Um, well . . . she first started acting weird after Caroline came to see her."

"Caroline!" Bonnie blurted, confused. "Was she crawling?"

Jim gave her a look. "Huh?"

"Never mind Bonnie; she was joking," Meredith said easily. "Jimmy, you don't have to tell us about Caroline if you don't want to. We—well, we know she was over at your house."

"Does *everybody* know?" Jim asked miserably.

"No. Just Matt, and he only told us so that somebody could go check on your little sister."

Jim looked guilty and stricken at once. The words poured out of him as if they'd been bottled up and now the cork was out of the bottle.

"I don't know what's going on anymore. All I can tell you is what happened. It was a couple days ago—late evening," Jim said. "Caroline came over, and—I mean, I never even had a crush on her. It's like, sure, she's good-looking, and my parents were away and all, but I never thought I was the kind of guy . . ."

"Never mind that now. Just tell us about Caroline and Isobel."

"Well, Caroline came over wearing this outfit that was—well, the top was practically transparent. And she just—she said, did I want to dance and it was, like, slow dancing and she—she, like, *seduced* me. That's the truth. And the next morning she left—just about the time Matt came. That was the day before yesterday. And then I noticed Tami acting—crazy. Nothing I could do would stop her. And then I got a phone call from Isa-chan and—I've never heard her so hysterical. Caroline must have gone straight from my house to her house. Isa-chan said she was going to kill herself. And so I ran over here. I had to get away from Tami anyway because me being there at home just seemed to make it worse."

Bonnie looked at Meredith and knew that they were both thinking the same thing: *and somewhere in there, both Caroline and Tami propositioned Matt, too.*

"Caroline must have told her everything." Jim gulped. "Isa-chan and I haven't—we were waiting, you know? But all Isa-chan would say to me was that I was going to be sorry. 'You'll be sorry; just wait and see,' over and over and over. And, God, I *am* sorry."

"Well, now you can stop being sorry and start calling the doctor. Right *now*, Jimmy." Meredith gave him a swat on the behind. "And then you need to call your parents.

Don't give me those big brown puppy-dog eyes. You're over eighteen; I don't know what they can do to you for leaving Tami alone all this time."

"But—"

"But me no buts. I *mean* it, Jimmy."

Then she did what Bonnie knew she would, but was dreading. She approached Isobel again. Isobel's head was down; she was pinching her navel with one hand. In the other, she held a long, shining nail.

Before Meredith could even speak, Isobel said, "So you're in on it, too. I heard the way you called him 'Jimmy.' You're all trying to take him away from me. All you bitches are trying to hurt me. *Yurusenai! Zettai yurusenai!*"

"Isobel! Don't! Can't you see that you're hurting *yourself?*"

"I'm only hurting myself to take away the pain. You're the one who's really doing it, you know. You're pricking me with needles inside."

Bonnie jumped inside her own skin, but not just because Isobel suddenly gave a vicious thrust of the nail. She felt heat sweep up into her cheeks. Her heart began to pound even faster than it was already going.

Trying to keep one eye on Meredith, she pulled her mobile phone out of her back pocket where she'd stashed it after the visit to Caroline's house.

Still with half her attention on Meredith, she went on

the Internet and rapidly entered just two search words. Then, as she made a couple of selections from her hits, she realized that she could never absorb all the information in a week, much less a few minutes. But at least she had a start.

Just now, Meredith was backing away from Isobel. She put her mouth close to Bonnie's ear and whispered, "I think we're just antagonizing her. Did you get a good look at her aura?"

Bonnie nodded.

"Then we probably should leave the room, at least."

Bonnie nodded again.

"Were you trying to call Matt and Elena?" Meredith was eyeing the mobile phone.

Bonnie shook her head and turned the phone so Meredith could see her two search words. Meredith stared, then lifted dark eyes to Bonnie's in a kind of horrified recognition.

Salem witches.

21

"It actually makes a horrible kind of sense," Meredith said. They were in Isobel's family room, waiting for Dr. Alpert. Meredith was at a beautiful desk made of some black wood ornamented with designs in gilt, working at a computer that had been left on. "The Salem girls accused people of hurting them—witches, of course. They said they were pinching them and 'pricking them with pins.'"

"Like Isobel blaming us," Bonnie said, nodding.

"And they had seizures and contorted their bodies into 'impossible positions.'"

"Caroline looked as if she were having seizures in Stefan's room," said Bonnie. "And if crawling like a lizard isn't contorting your body into an impossible position . . . here, I'll try it." She got down on the Saitous' floor and tried to stick her elbows and knees out the way

Caroline had. She couldn't do it.

"See?"

"Oh, my God!" It was Jim at the doorway of the kitchen, holding—almost dropping—a tray of food. The smell of miso soup was sharp in the air, and Bonnie wasn't sure if it made her feel hungry or if she was too sick to ever be hungry again.

"It's okay," she told him hastily, standing up. "I was just . . . trying something out."

Meredith stood up too. "Is that for Isobel?"

"No, it's for Obaasan—I mean Isa-chan's grandma—Grandma Saitou—"

"I told you to call everybody whatever comes out naturally. Obaasan is fine, just like Isa-chan," Meredith said softly and firmly to him.

Jim relaxed a hair. "I tried to get Isa-chan to eat, but she just throws the trays at the wall. She says that she can't eat; that somebody's choking her."

Meredith glanced significantly at Bonnie. Then she turned back to Jim. "Why don't you let me take it? You've been through a lot. Where is she?"

"Upstairs, second door on the left. If—if she says anything weird, just ignore it."

"All right. Stay near Bonnie."

"*Oh*, no," Bonnie said hastily. "Bonnie is going with." She didn't know if it was for her own protection or Meredith's, but she was going to stick like glue.

Upstairs, Meredith turned the hall light on carefully with her elbow. Then they found the second door on the left, which turned out to have a doll-like old lady in it. She was in the exact center of the room, lying on the exact center of a futon. She sat up and smiled when they came in. The smile turned a wrinkled face almost into the face of a happy child.

"Megumi-chan, Beniko-chan, you came to see me!" she exclaimed, bowing where she sat.

"Yes," Meredith said carefully. She put the tray down beside the old lady. "We came to see you—Ms. Saitou."

"Don't play games with me! It's Inari-chan! Or are you mad at me?"

"All these *chans*. I thought 'Chan' was a Chinese name. Isn't Isobel Japanese?" whispered Bonnie from behind Meredith.

One thing, the doll-like old woman was not, was deaf. She burst into laughter, bringing up both hands to cover her mouth girlishly. "Oh, don't tease me before I eat. *Itadakimasu!*" She picked up the bowl of miso soup and began to drink it.

"I think *chan* is something you put at the end of someone's name when you're friends, the way Jimmy was saying *Isa-chan*," Meredith said aloud. "And *Eeta-daki-mass-u* is something you say when you start eating. And that's *all* I know."

Part of Bonnie's mind noted that the "friends" Grandma

Saitou had just happened to have names starting with *M* and *B*. Another part was calculating where this room was with relation to the rooms below it, Isobel's room in particular.

It was directly above it.

The tiny old woman had stopped eating and was watching her intently. "No, no, you're not Beniko-chan and Megumi-chan. I know it. But they do visit me sometimes, and so does my dear Nobuhiro. Other things do, too, unpleasant things, but I was raised a shrine maiden—I know how to take care of *them*." A brief look of knowing satisfaction passed over the innocent old face. "This house is possessed, you know." She added, *"Kore ni wa kitsune ga karande isou da ne."*

"I'm sorry, Ms. Saitou—what was that?" Meredith asked.

"I said, there's a kitsune involved in this somehow."

"A kit-su-nay?" Meredith repeated, quizzically.

"A fox, silly girl," the old woman said cheerfully. "They can turn into anything they like, don't you know? Even humans. Why, one could turn into *you* and your best friend wouldn't know the difference."

"So—a sort of were-fox, then?" Meredith asked, but Grandma Saitou was rocking back and forth now, her gaze on the wall behind Bonnie. "We used to play a circle game," she said. "All of us in a circle and one in the middle, blindfolded. And we would sing a song. *Ushiro no shounen daare?* Who is standing behind you? I taught it to my children, but I made up a little song in English to go with it."

And she sang, in the voice of the very old or the very young, with her eyes fixed innocently on Bonnie all the while.

"Fox and turtle
Had a race.

Who's that far behind you?

Whoever came in
Second place

Who's that near behind you?

Would make a nice meal
For the winner.

Who's that close behind you?

Lovely turtle soup
For dinner!

Who's that right behind you?"

Bonnie felt hot breath on her neck. Gasping, she whirled around—and screamed. And *screamed*.

Isobel was there, dripping blood onto the mats that covered the floor. She had somehow managed to get past Jim and to sneak into the dim upstairs room without anyone seeing or hearing her. Now she stood there like some distorted goddess of piercing, or the hideous embodiment of every piercer's nightmare. She was wearing only a pair of very brief bikini bottoms. Otherwise she was naked except for the blood and the different kinds of hoops and studs and needles she had put through the holes. She had pierced every area Bonnie had ever heard that you *could* pierce, and a few that Bonnie hadn't dreamed of. And every hole was crooked and bleeding.

Her breath was warm and fetid and nauseating—like rotten eggs.

Isobel flicked her pink tongue. It wasn't pierced. It was worse. With some kind of instrument she had cut the long muscle in two so that it was forked like a snake's.

The forked, pink thing licked Bonnie's forehead.

Bonnie fainted.

Matt drove slowly down the almost invisible lane. There was no street sign to identify it, he noticed. They went up a little hill and then down sharply into a small clearing.

"'Keep away from faerie circles,'" Elena said softly, as

if she were quoting. "'And old oaks . . .'"

"What are you talking about?"

"Stop the car." When he did, Elena stood in the center of the clearing. "Don't you think it has a faerie sort of feeling?"

"I don't know. Where'd the red thing go?"

"In here somewhere. I saw it!"

"Me, too—and did you see how it was bigger than a fox?"

"Yes, but not as big as a wolf."

Matt let out a sigh of relief. "Bonnie just won't believe me. And you saw how quickly it moved—"

"Too quickly to be something natural."

"You're saying we didn't really see anything?" Matt said almost fiercely.

"I'm saying we saw something *super*natural. Like the bug that attacked you. Like the trees, for that matter. Something that doesn't follow the laws of this world."

But search as they would, they couldn't find the animal. The bushes and shrubs between the trees reached from the ground up in a dense circle. But there was no evidence of a hole or a hide or a break in the dense thicket.

And the sun was sliding down in the sky. The clearing was beautiful, but there was nothing of interest to them.

Matt had just turned to say so to Elena when he saw her stand up quickly, in alarm.

"What's—?" He followed her gaze and stopped.

A yellow Ferrari blocked the way back to the road.

They hadn't passed a yellow Ferrari on their way in. There was only room for one car on the one-lane road.

Yet there the Ferrari stood.

Branches broke behind Matt. He whirled.

"Damon!"

"Whom were you expecting?" The wraparound Ray-Bans concealed Damon's eyes completely.

"We weren't expecting *anyone*," Matt said aggressively. "We just turned in here." The last time he'd seen Damon, when Damon had been banished like a whipped dog from Stefan's room, he'd wanted to punch Damon in the mouth very much, Elena knew. She could feel that he wanted it again now.

But Damon wasn't the same as he'd been when he'd left that room. Elena could see danger rising off him like heat waves.

"Oh, I *see*. This is—your *private* area for—*private* explorations," Damon translated, and there was a note of complicity in his voice that Elena disliked.

"No!" Matt snarled. Elena realized she was going to have to keep him under control. It was dangerous to antagonize Damon in this mood. "How can you even say that?" Matt went on. "Elena belongs to Stefan."

"Well—we belong to each other," Elena temporized.

"Of course you do," said Damon. "One body, one heart, one soul." For a moment there was something there—an expression inside the Ray-Bans, she thought, that was murderous.

Instantly, though, Damon's tone changed to an expressionless murmur. "But then, why are *you two* here?" His head, turning to follow Matt's movement, moved like a predator tracking prey. There was something more disquieting than usual about his attitude.

"We saw something red," Matt said before Elena could stop him. "Something like what I saw when I had that accident."

Prickles were now running up and down Elena's arms. Somehow she wished Matt hadn't said that. In this dim, quiet clearing in the evergreen grove, she was suddenly very much afraid.

Stretching her new senses to their utmost—until she could feel them distending like a gossamer garment pushed thin all around her, she felt the wrongness there, too, and felt it pass out of the reach of her mind. At the same time she felt birds go quiet all that long distance away.

What was most disturbing was to turn just then, just as the birdsong stopped, and find Damon turning at the same instant to look at her. The sunglasses kept her from knowing what he was thinking. The rest of his face was a mask.

Stefan, she thought helplessly, longingly.

How could he have left her—*with this*? With no warning, no idea of his destination, no way of ever contacting him again . . . It might have made sense to him, with his desperate desire not to make her into something he loathed in himself. But to leave her with Damon in this mood, and all of her previous powers gone—

Your own fault, she thought, cutting short the flood of self-pity. You were the one who harped on brotherhood. You were the one who convinced him Damon was to be trusted. Now you deal with the consequences.

"Damon," she said, "I've been looking for *you*. I wanted to ask you—about Stefan. You do know that he's left me."

"Of course. I believe the saying goes, for your own good. He left me to be your bodyguard."

"Then you saw him two nights ago?"

"Of course."

And—of course—you didn't try to stop him. Things couldn't have turned out better for you, Elena thought. She had never wished more for the abilities she'd had as a spirit, not even when she'd realized Stefan was really gone and beyond her all-too-human reach.

"Well, I'm not just letting him leave me," she said flatly, "for my own good or for any other reason. I'm going to follow him—but first I need to know where he might have gone."

"You're asking *me*?"

"Yes. Please. Damon, I have to find him. I need him. I—" She was starting to choke up, and she had to be stern with herself.

But just then she realized that Matt was whispering very softly to her. "Elena, stop. I think we're just making him mad. Look at the sky."

Elena felt it herself. The circle of trees seemed to be leaning in all around them, darker than before, menacing. Elena tilted her chin slowly, looking up. Directly above them, gray clouds were pooling, piling in on themselves, cirrus overwhelmed by cumulus, turning to thunderheads— centered exactly over the spot where they stood.

On the ground, small whirlwinds began to form, lifting handfuls of pine needles and fresh green summer leaves off saplings. She had never seen anything like it before, and it filled the clearing with a sweet but sensuous smell, redolent of exotic oils and long, dark winter nights.

Looking at Damon, then, as the whirlwinds lifted higher and the sweet scent encircled her, resinous and aromatic, closing in until she knew it was soaking into her clothes and being impressed into her very flesh, she knew she had overstepped herself.

She couldn't protect Matt.

Stefan told me to trust Damon in his note in my diary. Stefan knows more about him than I do, she thought desperately. But we both know what Damon wants, ultimately. What he's always wanted. Me. My blood . . .

"Damon," she began softly—and broke off. Without looking at her, he held out a hand with the palm toward her.

Wait.

"There's something I have to do," he murmured. He bent down, every movement as unconsciously and economically graceful as a panther's, and picked up a small broken branch of what looked like ordinary Virginia pine. He waved it slightly, appraisingly, hefting it in his hand as if to feel weight and balance. It looked more like a fan than a branch.

Elena was now looking at Matt, trying with her eyes to tell him all the things she was feeling, foremost of which was that she was sorry: sorry that she had gotten him into this; sorry that she'd ever cared for him; sorry that she'd kept him bound into a group of friends who were so intimately intertwined with the supernatural.

Now I know a little bit of what Bonnie must have felt this last year, she thought, being able to see and predict things without having the slightest power to stop them.

Matt, jerking his head, was already moving stealthily toward the trees.

No, Matt. *No. No!*

He didn't understand. Neither did she, except to feel that the trees were only keeping their distance because of Damon's presence here. If she and Matt were to venture into the forest; if they left the clearing or even stayed in it too long . . . Matt could see the fear on her face, and his own face reflected grim understanding. They were trapped.

Unless—

"Too late," Damon said sharply. "I told you, there's something I have to do."

He had apparently found the stick he was looking for. Now he raised it, shook it slightly, and brought it down in a single motion; slashing sideways as he did.

And Matt convulsed in agony.

It was a kind of pain he had never dreamed of before: pain that seemed to come from *inside* himself, but from everywhere, every organ in his body, every muscle, every nerve, every bone, releasing a different type of pain. His muscles ached and cramped as if they were strained to their ultimate flexion, but were being forced to flex farther still. Inside, his organs were on fire. Knives were at work in his belly. His bones felt the way his arm had when he had shattered it once, when he was nine years old and a car had broadsided his dad's. And his nerves—if there was a switch on nerves that could be set from "pleasure" to "pain"—his had been set to "anguish." The touch of clothes on his skin was unbearable. The currents of air passing were agony. He endured fifteen seconds of it and passed out.

"Matt!" For her part, Elena had been frozen, her muscles locked, unable to move for what seemed like forever. Suddenly released, she ran to Matt, pulled him up into her lap, stared into his face.

Then she looked up.

"Damon, *why*? Why?" Suddenly she realized that although Matt wasn't conscious, he was still writhing in pain. She had to keep herself from screaming the words, to only speak forcefully. "Why are you *doing* this? Damon! *Stop it.*"

She stared up at the young man dressed all in black: black jeans with a black belt, black boots, black leather jacket, black hair, and those damned Ray-Bans.

"I told you," Damon said casually. "It's something I need to do. To watch. Painful death."

"*Death!*" Elena stared at Damon in disbelief. And then she began gathering all her Power, in a way that had been so easy and instinctual just days ago while she had been mute and not subject to gravity, and that was so difficult and so foreign right now. With determination, she said, "If you don't let him go—*now*—I'll hit you with everything I've got."

He laughed. She'd never seen Damon really laugh before, not like this. "And you expect that I'll even notice your tiny Power?"

"Not *that* tiny." Elena weighed it grimly. It was no more than the intrinsic Power of any human being—the Power that vampires took from humans along with the blood they drank—but since becoming a spirit, she knew how to use it. How to attack with it. "I think you'll feel it, Damon. Let him go—NOW!"

"Why do people always assume that volume will succeed when logic won't?" Damon murmured.

Elena let him have it.

Or at least she prepared to. She took the deep breath necessary, held her inner self still, and imagined herself holding a ball of white fire, and then—

Matt was on his feet. He looked as if he'd been *dragged* to his feet and was being held there like a puppet, and his eyes were involuntarily watering, but it was better than Matt writhing on the ground.

"You owe me," Damon said to Elena casually. "I'll collect later."

To Matt he said, in the tones of a fond uncle, with one of those instantaneous smiles that you could never be quite sure you saw, "Lucky for me that you're a hardy specimen, isn't it?"

"Damon." Elena had seen Damon in his *let's-play-with-weaker-creatures* mood, and it was the one she liked least. But there was something off today; something she couldn't understand. "Let's get down to it," she said, while the hairs on her arms and the back of her neck rose again. "What do you *really* want?"

But he didn't give the answer she expected.

"I was officially appointed as your caretaker. I'm officially taking care of you. And for one thing, I don't think you should be without my protection and companionship while my little brother is gone."

"I can handle myself," Elena said flatly, waving a hand so they could get down to the real issue.

"You're a very pretty girl. Dangerous and"—flash smile—"unsavory elements could be after you. I insist you have a bodyguard."

"Damon, right now the thing I need most is to be protected from *you*. You know that. What is this really about?"

The clearing was . . . pulsing. Almost as if it were something organic, breathing. Elena had the feeling that beneath her feet—beneath Meredith's old, rugged hiking boots—the ground was moving slightly, like a great sleeping animal, and the trees were like a beating heart.

For what? The forest? There was more dead wood than live here. And she could swear that she knew Damon well enough to know that he didn't like trees or woods.

It was at times like this that Elena wished she still had wings. Wings and the knowledge—the hand motions, the Words of White Power, the white fire inside her that would allow her to know the truth without trying to figure it out, or to simply blast annoyances back to Stonehenge.

It seemed that all she'd been left with was being a greater temptation to vampires than ever, and her wits.

Wits had worked up until now. Maybe if she didn't let Damon know how afraid she was, she could win a stay of execution for them.

"Damon, I thank you for being concerned about me.

Now would you mind leaving Matt and me for a moment so that I can tell if he's still breathing?"

From inside the Ray-Bans, she thought she could discern a single flash of red.

"Somehow I thought you might say that," Damon said. "And, of course, it's your right to have consolation after being so treacherously abandoned. Mouth-to-mouth resuscitation, for example."

Elena wanted to swear. Carefully, she answered, "Damon, if Stefan appointed you as my bodyguard, then he hardly 'treacherously abandoned' me, did he? You can't have it both—"

"Just indulge me in one thing, all right?" Damon said in the voice of one whose next words are going to be *Be careful* or *Don't do anything I wouldn't do.*

There was silence. The dust devils had stopped whirling. The smell of sun-warmed pine needles and pine resin in this dim place was making her languid, dizzy. The ground was warm, too, and the pine needles were all aligned, as if the slumbering animal had pine needles for fur. Elena watched dust motes turn and sparkle like opals in the golden sunlight. She knew she wasn't at her best right now; not her sharpest. Finally, when she was sure her voice would be steady, she asked, "What do you want?"

"A kiss."

onnie was disturbed and confused. It was dark.

"All right," a voice that was brusque and calming at once was saying. "That's two possible concussions, one puncture wound in need of a tetanus shot—and—well, I'm afraid I've got to sedate your girl, Jim. And I'm going to need help, but you're not allowed to move at all. You just lie back and keep your eyes shut."

Bonnie opened her own eyes. She had a vague memory of falling forward onto her bed. But she wasn't at home; she was still at the Saitou house, lying on a couch.

As always, when in confusion or fear, she looked for Meredith. Meredith was just returning from the kitchen with a makeshift ice pack. She put it on Bonnie's already wet forehead.

"I just fainted," Bonnie explained, as she herself figured it out. "That's all."

"I know you fainted. You cracked your head pretty hard on the floor," Meredith replied, and for once her face was perfectly readable: worry and sympathy and relief were all visible. She actually had tears pooling in her eyes. "Oh, Bonnie, I couldn't get to you in time. Isobel was in the way, and those tatami mats don't cushion the floor much—and you've been out for almost half an hour! You *scared* me."

"I'm sorry." Bonnie fumbled a hand out a blanket she seemed to be wrapped in and gave Meredith's hand a squeeze. It meant *velociraptor sisterhood is still in action*. It also meant *thank you for caring*.

Jim was sprawled on another couch holding an ice pack to the back of his head. His face was greenish-white. He tried to stand up but Dr. Alpert—it was her voice that was both crusty and kind—pushed him back onto the couch.

"You don't need any more exertion," she said. "But I do need an assistant. Meredith, can you help me with Isobel? It sounds as if she's going to be quite a handful."

"She hit me in the back of the head with a lamp," Jim warned them. "Don't ever turn your back on her."

"We'll be careful," Dr. Alpert said.

"You two stay *here*," Meredith added firmly.

Bonnie was watching Meredith's eyes. She wanted to get up to help them with Isobel. But Meredith had that special look of determination that meant it was better not to argue.

As soon as they left, Bonnie tried to stand up. But immediately she began to see the pulsating gray nothingness that meant she was going to pass out again.

She lay back down, teeth gritted.

For a long time there were crashes and shouts from Isobel's room. Bonnie would hear Dr. Alpert's voice raised, and then Isobel's, and then a third voice—not Meredith, who never shouted if she could help it, but what sounded like Isobel's voice, only slowed down and distorted.

Then, finally, there was silence, and Meredith and Dr. Alpert came back carrying a limp Isobel between them. Meredith had a bloody nose and Dr. Alpert's short pepper-and-salt hair was standing on end, but they had somehow gotten a T-shirt onto Isobel's abused body and Dr. Alpert had managed to hang on to her black bag as well.

"Walking wounded, stay where you are. We'll be back to lend you a hand," the doctor said in her terse way.

Next Dr. Albert and Meredith made another trip to take Isobel's grandmother with them.

"I don't like her color," Dr. Albert said briefly. "Or the tick of her tocker. We might as well all go get checked up."

A minute later they returned to help Jim and Bonnie to Dr. Albert's SUV. The sky had clouded over, and the sun was a red ball not far from the horizon.

"Do you want me to give you something for the pain?" the doctor asked, seeing Bonnie eyeing the black bag.

Isobel was in the very back of the SUV, where the seats had been folded down.

Meredith and Jim were in the two seats in front of her, with Grandma Saitou between them, and Bonnie—at Meredith's insistence—was in the front with the doctor.

"Um, no, it's okay," Bonnie said. Actually, she had been wondering whether the hospital actually could cure Isobel of infection any better than Mrs. Flowers' herbal compresses could.

But although her head throbbed and ached and she was developing a lump the size of a hard-boiled egg on her forehead, she didn't want to cloud her thinking. There was something nagging at her, some dream or something she'd had while Meredith said she'd been unconscious.

What *was* it?

"All right then. Seat belts on? Here we go." The SUV pulled away from the Saitou house. "Jim, you said Isobel has a three-year-old sister asleep upstairs, so I called my granddaughter Jayneela to come over here. At least it will be somebody in the house."

Bonnie twisted around to look at Meredith. They both spoke at once.

"Oh, no! She can't go in! *Especially* not into Isobel's room! Look, please, you have to—" Bonnie babbled.

"I'm really not sure if that's a good idea, Dr. Alpert," Meredith said, no less urgently but much more coherently.

"Unless she does stay away from that room and maybe has someone with her—a boy would be good."

"A boy?" Dr. Alpert seemed bewildered, but the combination of Bonnie's distress and Meredith's sincerity seemed to convince her. "Well, Tyrone, my grandson, was watching TV when I left. I'll try to get him."

"Wow!" Bonnie said involuntarily. "That's the Tyrone who's offensive tackle on the football team next year, huh? I heard that they call him the Tyre-minator."

"Well, let's say I think he'll be able to protect Jayneela," Dr. Alpert said after making the call. "But we're the ones with the, ah, *overexcited* girl in the vehicle with us. From the way she fought the sedative, I'd say she's quite a 'terminator' herself."

Meredith's mobile phone beeped out the tune it used for numbers not in its memory, and then announced, "Mrs. T. Flowers is calling you. Will you take the—" In a moment Meredith had hit the *talk* button.

"Mrs. Flowers?" she said. The hum of the SUV kept anything Mrs. Flowers might be saying from Bonnie and the others, so Bonnie went back to concentrating on two things: what she knew about the "victims" of the Salem "witches," and what that elusive thought while she was unconscious had been.

All of which promptly flew away when Meredith put down her mobile phone.

"What was it? What? *What?*" Bonnie couldn't get a clear view of Meredith's face in the dusk, but it looked pale, and when she spoke she *sounded* pale, too.

"Mrs. Flowers was doing some gardening and she was about to go inside when she noticed that there was something in her begonia bushes. She said it looked as if someone had tried to stuff something down between the bush and a wall, but a bit of fabric stuck up."

Bonnie felt as if the wind had been knocked out of her. "*What was it?*"

"It was a duffel bag, full of shoes and clothes. Boots. Shirts. Pants. All Stefan's."

Bonnie gave a shriek that caused Dr. Alpert to swerve and then recover, the SUV fishtailing.

"Oh, my God; oh, my God—*he didn't go!*"

"Oh, I think he went all right. Just not of his own free will," Meredith said grimly.

"*Damon*," Bonnie gasped, and slumped back into her own seat, tears welling up in her eyes and overflowing. "I couldn't help wanting to believe . . ."

"Head getting worse?" Dr. Alpert asked, tactfully ignoring the conversation that had not included her.

"No—well, yes, it is," Bonnie admitted.

"Here, open the bag and give me a look inside. I've got samples of this and that . . . all right, here you go. Anybody see a water bottle back there?"

Jim listlessly handed one over. "Thanks," Bonnie said, taking the small pill and a deep gulp. She had to get her head right. If Damon had kidnapped Stefan, then she should be Calling for him, shouldn't she? God only knew where he would end up this time. Why hadn't any of them even thought of it as a possibility?

Well, first, because the new Stefan was supposed to be so strong, and second, because of the note in Elena's diary.

"That's it!" she said, startling even herself. It had all come flooding back, everything that she and Matt had shared. . . .

"Meredith!" she said, oblivious to the side look which Dr. Alpert gave her, "while I was unconscious I talked with *Matt*. He was unconscious, too—"

"Was he hurt?"

"God, yes. Damon must have been doing something awful. But he said to ignore it, that something had been bothering him about the note Stefan left for Elena ever since he saw it. Something about Stefan talking to the English teacher about how to spell *judgment* last year. And he just kept saying, *Look for the backup file. Look for the backup . . . before Damon does.*"

She stared at Meredith's dim face, aware as they cruised slowly to stop at an intersection that Dr. Alpert and Jim were both staring at her. Tact had its limits.

Meredith's voice broke the silence. "Doctor," she said, "I'm going to have to ask you something. If you take a left here and another one at Laurel Street and then just drive for about five minutes to Old Wood, it won't be too far out of your way. But it'll let me get to the boardinghouse where the computer Bonnie's talking about is. You may think I'm crazy, but I *need* to get to that computer."

"I know you're not crazy; I'd have noticed it by now." The doctor laughed mirthlessly. "And I have heard some things about young Bonnie here . . . nothing bad, I promise, but a little difficult to believe. After seeing what I saw today, I think I'm beginning to change my opinion about them." The doctor abruptly took a left turn, muttering, "Somebody's taken the stop sign from this road, too." Then she continued, to Meredith, "I can do what you ask. I'd drive you all the way to the old boardinghouse—"

"No! That would be much too dangerous!"

"—but I've got to get Isobel to a hospital as soon as possible. Not to mention Jim. I think he really does have a concussion. And Bonnie—"

"Bonnie," Bonnie said, enunciating distinctly, "is going to the boardinghouse, too."

"No, Bonnie! I'm going to *run*, Bonnie, do you understand that? I'm going to *run* as fast as I can—and I can't let you hold me up." Meredith's voice was grim.

"I won't hold you up, I swear it. You go ahead and run.

I'll run, too. My head feels fine, now. If you have to leave me behind, you *keep on running*. I'll be coming after you."

Meredith opened her mouth and then closed it again. There must have been something in Bonnie's face that told her any kind of argument would be useless, Bonnie thought. Because that was the truth of the matter.

"Here we are," Dr. Alpert said a few minutes later. "Corner of Laurel and Old Wood." She pulled a small flashlight out of her black bag and shone it in each of Bonnie's eyes, one after another. "Well, it still doesn't look as if you have concussion. But you know, Bonnie, that my medical opinion is that you shouldn't be running any-where. I just can't force you to accept to take treatment if you don't want it. But I can make you take this." She handed Bonnie the small flashlight. "Good luck."

"Thank you for everything," Bonnie said, for an instant laying her pale hand on Dr. Alpert's long-fingered, dark brown one. "You be careful, too—of fallen trees and of Isobel, and of something red in the road."

"Bonnie, I'm leaving." Meredith was already outside the SUV.

"And lock your doors! And don't get out until you're away from the woods!" Bonnie said, as she tumbled down from the vehicle beside Meredith.

And then they ran. Of course, all that Bonnie had said about Meredith running in front of her, leaving her behind, was nonsense, and they both knew it. Meredith seized Bonnie's hand as soon as Bonnie's feet had touched the road and began running like a greyhound, dragging Bonnie along with her, at times seeming to whirl her over dips in the road.

Bonnie didn't need to be told how important speed was. She wished desperately that they had a car. She wished a lot of things, primarily that Mrs. Flowers lived in the middle of town and not way out here on the wild side.

At last, as Meredith had foreseen, she was winded, and her hand so slick with sweat that it slipped out of Meredith's hand. She bent almost double, hands on her knees, trying to get her breath.

"Bonnie! Wipe your hand! We have to run!"

"Just—give me—a minute—"

"We don't have a minute! Can't you *hear* it? *Come on!*"

"I just *need*—to get—my breath."

"Bonnie, look behind you. And don't scream!"

Bonnie looked behind her, screamed, and then discovered that she wasn't winded after all. She took off, grabbing Meredith's hand.

She could hear it, now, even above her own wheezing breath and the pounding in her ears. It was an insect sound, not a buzzing but still a sound that her brain filed under *bug*. It sounded like the *whipwhipwhip* of a helicopter, only much higher in pitch, as if a helicopter could have insect-like tentacles instead of blades. With that one glance, she had made out an entire gray mass of those tentacles, with heads in front—and all the heads were open to show mouths full of white sharp teeth.

She struggled to turn on the flashlight. Night was falling, and she had no idea how long it would be until moonrise. All she knew was that the trees seemed to make everything darker, and that *they* were after her and Meredith.

The malach.

The whipping sound of tentacles beating the air was much louder now. Much closer. Bonnie didn't want to turn around and see the source of it. The sound was pushing her body beyond all sane limits. She couldn't help hearing over and over Matt's words: *like putting my hand in a garbage disposal and turning it on. Like putting my hand in a garbage disposal . . .*

Her hand and Meredith's were covered with sweat again. And the gray mass was definitely overtaking them. It was only half as far away as it had been at first, and the whipping noise was getting higher-pitched.

At the same time her legs felt like rubber. Literally. She couldn't feel her knees. And now they felt like rubber dissolving into gelatin.

Vipvipvipvipveeee . . .

It was the sound of one of them, closer than the

rest. Closer, closer, and then it was in front of them, its mouth open in an oval shape with teeth all around the perimeter.

Just like Matt had said.

Bonnie had no breath to scream with. But she needed to scream. The headless thing with no eyes or features—just that horrible mouth—had turned ahead of them and was coming right for her. And her automatic response—to beat at it with her hands—could cost her an arm. Oh God, it was coming for her *face*. . . .

"There's the boardinghouse," gasped Meredith, giving her a jerk that lifted her off her feet. *"Run!"*

Bonnie ducked, just as the malach tried to collide with her. Instantly, she felt tentacles *whipwhipwhip* into her curly hair. She was abruptly yanked backward to a painful stumble and Meredith's hand was torn out of hers. Her legs wanted to collapse. Her guts wanted her to scream.

"Oh, God, Meredith, it's got me! Run! *Don't let one get you!"*

In front of her, the boardinghouse was lit up like a hotel. Usually it was dark except for maybe Stefan's window and one other. But now it shone like a jewel, just beyond her reach.

"Bonnie, shut your eyes!"

Meredith hadn't left her. She was still here. Bonnie could feel vine-like tentacles gently brushing her ear, lightly tasting her sweaty forehead, working toward her face, her throat . . . She sobbed.

And then there was a sharp, loud crack mixed with a sound like a ripe melon bursting, and something damp scattered all over her back. She opened her eyes. Meredith was dropping a thick branch she had been holding like a baseball bat. The tentacles were already sliding out of Bonnie's hair.

Bonnie didn't want to look at the mess behind her.

"Meredith, you—"

"*Come on—run!*"

And she was running again. All the way up the gravel boardinghouse driveway, all the way up the path to the door. And there, in the doorway, Mrs. Flowers was standing with an old-fashioned kerosene lamp.

"Get in, get in," she said, and as Meredith and Bonnie skittered to a stop, sobbing for air, she slammed the door shut behind them. They all heard the sound that came next. It was like the sound the branch had made—a sharp crack plus a bursting, only much louder, and repeated many times over, like popcorn popping.

Bonnie was shaking as she took her hands away from her ears and slid down to sit on the entry-hall rug.

"What in heaven's name have you girls been doing to yourselves?" Mrs. Flowers said, eyeing Bonnie's forehead, Meredith's swollen nose, and their general state of sweaty exhaustion.

"It takes too—long to explain," Meredith got out.

"Bonnie! You can sit down—upstairs."

Somehow or other Bonnie made it upstairs. Meredith went at once to the computer and turned it on, collapsing on the desk chair in front of it. Bonnie used the last of her energy to pull off her top. The back was stained with nameless insect juices. She crumpled it into a ball and threw it into a corner.

Then she fell down on Stefan's bed.

"What exactly did Matt say?" Meredith was getting her breath back.

"He said *Look in the backup*—or *Look for the backup file* or something. Meredith, my head . . . it isn't good."

"Okay. Just relax. You did great out there."

"I made it because you saved me. Thanks . . . again. . . ."

"Don't worry about it. But I don't understand," Meredith added in her talking-to-herself murmur. "There's a backup file of this note in the same directory, but it's no different. I don't see what Matt meant."

"Maybe he was confused," Bonnie said reluctantly. "Maybe he was just in a lot of pain and sort of off his head."

"Backup file, backup file . . . wait a minute! Doesn't Word automatically save a backup in some weird place, like under the administrator directory or somewhere?" Meredith was clicking rapidly through directories. Then she said, in a disappointed voice, "No, nothing there."

She sat back, letting her breath out sharply. Bonnie knew what she must be thinking. Their long and desperate run through danger couldn't all be for nothing. It *couldn't*.

Then, slowly, Meredith said, "There are a lot of temp files in here for one little note."

"What's a temp file?"

"It's just a temporary storage of your file while you're working on it. Usually it just looks like gibberish, though." The clicking started again. "But I must as well be thorough—*oh!*" She interrupted herself. The clicking stopped.

And then there was dead silence.

"What is it?" Bonnie said anxiously.

More silence.

"Meredith! Talk to me! *Did you find a backup file?*"

Meredith said nothing. She seemed not even to hear. She was reading with what looked like horrified fascination.

cold *frisson* went down Elena's back, the most delicate of shivers. Damon didn't *ask* for kisses. This wasn't *right*.

"No," she whispered.

"Just one."

"I'm not going to kiss you, Damon."

"Not me. Him." Damon denoted "him" with a tilt of his head toward Matt. "A kiss between you and your former knight."

"You want *what?*" Matt's eyes snapped open and he got the words out explosively before Elena could open her mouth.

"You'd like it," Damon's voice had dropped to its softest, most insinuating tones. "You'd like to kiss her. And there's no one to stop you."

"Damon." Matt struggled up out of Elena's arms. He

seemed, if not entirely recovered, perhaps eighty percent of the way there, but Elena could hear his heart laboring. Elena wondered how long he'd lain feigning unconsciousness to get his strength back. "The last thing I knew you were trying to kill me. That doesn't exactly get you on my good side. Second, people just don't go around kissing girls because they're pretty or their boyfriend takes a day off."

"Don't they?" Damon hiked an eyebrow in surprise. "I do."

Matt just shook his head, dazed. He seemed to be trying to keep one idea fixed in his mind. "Will you move your car so we can leave?" he said.

Elena felt as if she were watching Matt from very far away; and as if he was caged somewhere with a tiger and didn't know it. The clearing had become a very beautiful, wild, and dangerous place, and Matt didn't know that either. Besides, she thought with concern, he's *making* himself stand up. We *need* to leave—and quickly, before Damon does anything else to him.

But what was the real way out?

What was Damon's real agenda?

"You can go," Damon said. "As soon as she kisses you. Or you kiss her," he added, as if making a concession.

Slowly, as if he realized what it was going to mean, Matt looked at Elena and then back at Damon. Elena tried to communicate silently with him, but Matt wasn't in the mood. He looked Damon in the face and said, "No way."

Shrugging, as if to say, *I did everything I could*, Damon lifted the shaggy pine rod—

"No," cried Elena. "Damon, I'll do it."

Damon smiled *the* smile and held it for a moment, until Elena looked away and went to Matt. His face was still pale, cool. Elena leaned her cheek against his and said almost soundlessly into his ear, "Matt, I've dealt with Damon before. And you can't just defy him. Let's play along—for now. Then maybe we can get away." And then she made herself say, "For me? Please?"

The truth was that she knew too much about stubborn males. Too much about how to manipulate them. It was a trait she'd come to hate, but right now she was too busy trying to think of ways to save Matt's life to debate the ethics of pressuring him.

She wished it were Meredith or Bonnie instead of Matt. Not that she would wish such pain on anyone, but Meredith would be coming up with Plans C and D even as Elena came up with A and B. And Bonnie would already have lifted tear-filled, heart-melting brown eyes to Damon. . . .

Suddenly Elena thought of the single red flash she'd seen under the Ray-Bans, and she changed her mind. She wasn't sure she wanted Bonnie around Damon now.

Of all of the guys she'd known, Damon had been the only one Elena couldn't break.

Oh, Matt was stubborn, and Stefan could be impossible sometimes. But they both had brightly colored buttons somewhere inside them, labeled PUSH ME, and you just had to fiddle with the mechanism a little—okay, sometimes more than a little—and eventually even the most challenging male could be mastered.

Except one . . .

"All right, kiddies, enough time out."

Elena felt Matt pulled from her arms and held up—she didn't know by what, but he was standing. Something held him in place, upright, and she knew it wasn't his muscles.

"So where were we?" Damon was walking back and forth, with the Virginia pine branch in his right hand, tapping it on his left palm. "Oh, that's *right*"—as if making a great discovery—"the girl and the stalwart knight are going to kiss."

In Stefan's room, Bonnie said, "For the last time, Meredith, did you find a backup file for Stefan's note or not?"

"No," Meredith said in a flat voice. But just as Bonnie was about to collapse again, Meredith said, "I found a different note completely. A letter, really."

"A *different* note? What does it say?"

"Can you stand up at all? Because I think you'd better have a look at this."

Bonnie, who had only just gotten back her breath, managed to hobble over to the computer.

She read the document on the screen—complete except for what seemed to be its final words, and gasped.

"Damon did something to Stefan!" she said, and felt her heart plummet and all her internal organs follow it. So Elena had been wrong. Damon *was* evil, through and through. By now, Stefan might even be . . .

"Dead," Meredith said, her mind obviously following the same track that Bonnie's had taken. She lifted dark eyes to Bonnie's. Bonnie knew that her own eyes were wet. "How long," Meredith asked, "has it been since you called Elena or Matt?"

"I don't know; I don't know what time it is. But I called twice after we left Caroline's house and once at Isobel's; and when I've tried after that, I either get a message that their mailboxes are full or it won't connect at all."

"That's about exactly what I've gotten. If they went near the Old Wood—well, you know what it does to phone reception."

"And now, even if they come out of the woods, we can't leave them a message because we've filled up their voicemail—"

"E-mail," Meredith said. "Good old e-mail; we can use that to send Elena a message."

"Yes!" Bonnie punched the air. Then she deflated. She hesitated for an instant and then almost whispered, "No." Words from Stefan's real note kept echoing in her mind: *I trust Matt's instinctive protectiveness for you,*

Meredith's judgment, and Bonnie's intuition. Tell them to remember that.

"You can't tell her what Damon's done," she said, even as Meredith began busily typing. "She probably already knows—and if she doesn't, it'll just make more trouble. She's with Damon."

"Matt told you that?"

"No. But Matt was out of his mind with pain."

"Couldn't it have been from those—bugs?" Meredith looked down at her ankle where several red welts still showed on the smooth olive flesh.

"It could be, but it wasn't. It didn't feel like the trees, either. It was just... pure pain. And I don't know, not for certain, how I know that it's Damon doing it. I just—know."

She saw Meredith's eyes unfocus and knew that she was thinking about Stefan's words, too. "Well, my judgment tells me to trust you," she said. "By the way, Stefan spells 'judgment' the preferred American way," she added. "Damon spells it with an *e*. That may have been what was bothering Matt."

"As if Stefan would really leave Elena alone with everything that's been going on," Bonnie said indignantly.

"Well, Damon fooled all of us and made us think so," Meredith pointed out. Meredith tended to point out things like that.

Bonnie started suddenly. "I wonder if he stole the money?"

"I doubt it, but let's see." Meredith pulled the rocking chair away, saying, "Grab me a hanger."

Bonnie grabbed one from the closet and grabbed herself one of Elena's tops to put on at the same time. It was too big, since it was Meredith's top given to Elena, but at least it was warm.

Meredith was using the hooked end of the wire hanger on all sides of the floorboard that looked most promising. Just as she managed to pry it up, there was a knock at the open door. They both jumped.

"It's only me," said the voice of Mrs. Flowers from behind a large duffel bag and a tray of bandages, mugs, sandwiches, and strong-smelling cheesecloth bags like the ones she'd used on Matt's arm.

Bonnie and Meredith exchanged a glance and then Meredith said, "Come in and let us help you." Bonnie was already taking the tray, and Mrs. Flowers was dumping the duffel bag on the floor. Meredith continued prying the board up.

"Food!" Bonnie said gratefully.

"Yes, turkey-and-tomato sandwiches. Help yourselves. I'm sorry I was away so long, but you can't hurry the poultice for swellings," Mrs. Flowers said. "I remember, long ago, my younger brother always said—oh, my goodness gracious!" She was staring at the place where the floorboard had been. A good-sized hollow was filled with hundred-dollar bills, neatly wrapped in packets with bank-bands still around them.

"Wow," Bonnie said. "I never saw so much money!"

"Yes." Mrs. Flowers turned and began distributing cups of cocoa and sandwiches. Bonnie bit into a sandwich hungrily. "People used to simply put things behind the loose brick in the fireplace. But I can see that the young man needed more space."

"Thank you for the cocoa and sandwiches," Meredith said after a few minutes spent wolfing them down while working on the computer at the same time. "But if you want to treat us for bruises and things—well, I'm afraid we just can't wait."

"Oh, come." Mrs. Flowers took a small compress that smelled to Bonnie like tea and pressed it to Meredith's nose. "This will take the swelling down in minutes. And you, Bonnie—sniff out the one that's for that bump on your forehead."

Once again Meredith's and Bonnie's eyes met. Bonnie said, "Well, if it's only a few minutes—I don't know what we're doing next anyway." She looked the poultices over and picked a round one that smelled of flowers and musk to put on her forehead.

"Exactly right," Mrs. Flowers said without turning around to look. "And of course, the long thin one is for Meredith's ankle."

Meredith drank the last of her cocoa, then reached down to gingerly touch one of the red marks. "That's okay—" she began, when Mrs. Flowers interrupted.

"You're going to need that ankle at full capacity when we go out."

"'When we go out'?" Meredith stared at her.

"Into the Old Wood," Mrs. Flowers clarified. "To find your friends."

Meredith looked horrified. "If Elena and Matt are in the Old Wood, then I agree: *we* have to go look for them. But *you* can't go, Mrs. Flowers! And we don't know where they are, anyway."

Mrs. Flowers drank from the cup of cocoa in her hand, looking thoughtfully at the one window that wasn't shuttered. For a moment Meredith thought she hadn't heard or didn't mean to answer. Then she said, slowly, "I daresay you all think I'm just a batty old woman who's never around when there's trouble at hand."

"We would never think that," Bonnie said staunchly, but thinking that they'd found out more about Mrs. Flowers in the last two days than in the entire nine months since Stefan had moved in here. Before that, all she'd ever heard were ghost stories or rumors about the crazy old lady in the boardinghouse. She'd been hearing them since she could remember.

Mrs. Flowers smiled. "It's not easy having the Power

and never being believed when you use it. And then, I've lived for so long—and people don't like that. It worries them. They start to make up ghost stories or rumors—"

Bonnie felt her eyes go round. Mrs. Flowers just smiled again and nodded gently. "It's been a real pleasure having a polite young man in the house," she said, taking the long poultice from the tray and wrapping it around Meredith's ankle. "Of course, I had to get over my prejudices. Dear Ma*ma* always said that if I kept the place, I might have to take in boarders, and to be sure not to take in foreigners. And then of course, the young man is a vampire as well—"

Bonnie almost sprayed cocoa across the room. She choked, then went into a spasm of coughing. Meredith had her no-expression expression on.

"—but after a while I got to understand him better and to sympathize with his problems," Mrs. Flowers continued, ignoring Bonnie's attack of coughing. "And now, the blond girl is involved as well . . . poor young thing. I often speak to Ma*ma*"—still with the accent on the second syllable—"about it."

"How old is your mother?" Meredith asked. Her tone was one of polite inquiry, but to Bonnie's experienced eyes her expression was one of slightly morbid fascination.

"Oh, she died back at the turn of the century."

There was a pause, and then Meredith rallied.

"I'm so sorry," she said. "She must have lived a long—"

"I should have said, the turn of the *previous* century. Back in 1901, it was."

This time it was Meredith who had the choking fit. But she was more quiet about it.

Mrs. Flowers' gentle gaze had drifted back to them. "I was a medium in my day. On vaudeville, you know. So hard to achieve a trance in front of a roomful of people. But, yes, I really am a White Witch. I have the Power. And now, if you've finished your cocoa, I think it's time we went into the Old Wood to find your friends. Even though it's summertime, my dears, you'd both better dress warmly," she added. "I have."

24

No peck on the lips was going to satisfy Damon, Elena thought. On the other hand, Matt was going to need outright seduction before he would give in. Fortunately Elena had broken the Matt Honeycutt code long ago. And she planned to be remorseless in using what she had learned on his weakened, susceptible body.

But Matt could be far too stubborn for his own good. He allowed Elena to put her soft lips against his, he allowed her to put her arms around him. But when Elena tried to do some of the things he liked most—like running her nails down his spine, or touching her tongue tip lightly to his closed lips—he clamped his teeth shut. He wouldn't put an arm around her.

Elena let go of him and sighed. Then she felt a crawling

sensation between her shoulder blades, as if she were being watched but a hundred times stronger. She glanced back to see Damon standing at a distance with his Virginia pine rod, but she couldn't find anything unusual. She glanced back once more—and had to cram a fist into her mouth.

Damon was *there*; right behind her; so close that you couldn't have gotten two fingers between the front of her body and the front of his. She didn't know why her arm hadn't hit him. Her whirl actually trapped her in between two male bodies.

But how had he done it? There had been no time to travel the distance of the clearing from where Damon had been standing to one inch behind her in the second that she had glanced away. Nor had there been any sound as he'd walked across the pine needles toward them; like the Ferrari, he was just—there.

Elena swallowed the scream that was desperately trying to get out of her lungs, and tried to breathe. Her own body was rigid with fear. Matt was trembling slightly behind her. Damon was leaning in, and all she could smell was the sweetness of pine resin.

Something's wrong with him. Something's wrong.

"You know what," Damon said, leaning forward even farther so that she had to lean backward against Matt, so that, even spooned against Matt's shaking body, she was looking straight into the Ray-Bans from a distance of three inches. "That gets you a grade of a D minus."

Now Elena was shaking as well as Matt. But she had to get a grip on herself, had to meet this aggression head-on. The more passive she and Matt were, the more time Damon had to think.

Elena's mind was in feverish scheming mode. He may not be reading our minds, she thought, but he can certainly tell if we're telling the truth or lying. That's normal for a vampire who drinks human blood. What can we make of that? What can we do with it?

"That was a greeting kiss," she said boldly. "It's to identify the person that you're meeting, so you'll always know them afterwards. Even—even prairie hamsters do it. Now—please—could we move just a little, Damon? I'm getting crushed."

And this is just much too provocative a position, she thought. For everybody involved.

"One more chance," Damon said, and this time he didn't smile. "I want to see a kiss—a real kiss—between you. Or else."

Elena twisted in the tight space. Her eyes searched Matt's. They had, after all, been boyfriend and girlfriend for quite a while last year. Elena saw the look in Matt's blue eyes: he *wanted* to kiss her, as much as he could want anything after that pain. And he realized that she'd had to go through all that fancy footwork to save him from Damon.

Somehow, we'll get out, Elena thought to him. Now, will you cooperate? Some boys didn't have buttons in the selfish sensations area of their brain. Some, like Matt, had buttons labeled HONOR or GUILT.

Now Matt held still as she took his face between her hands, tilting it down and going up on her toes to kiss him, because he'd grown so much. She thought of their first real kiss, in his car on the way home from a minor school dance. He'd been terrified, his hands damp, his whole interior quaking. She'd been cool, experienced, gentle.

And so she was now, drawing a warm tongue tip to melt his frozen lips apart. And just in case Damon was eavesdropping on her thoughts, she kept them strictly on Matt, on his sunshiny looks and his warm friendship and on the gallantry and courtesy that he had always shown to her, even when she broke up with him. She wasn't aware when his arms went around her shoulders or when he took control of the kiss, like a person dying of thirst who's finally found water. She could see it clearly in his mind: he'd never thought he'd kiss Elena Gilbert like this again.

Elena didn't know how long it lasted. Finally she unwound her arms from around Matt's neck and stepped back.

And then she realized something. It was no accident

that Damon had sounded like a film director. He was holding up a palm-sized video camera, staring into the viewfinder. He'd captured the whole thing.

With Elena clearly visible. She had no idea what had happened to the disguising baseball cap and dark glasses. Her hair was disordered and her breathing came quickly, involuntarily. The blood had risen to the surface of her skin. Matt didn't look much more together than she felt.

Damon looked up from the viewfinder.

"What do you want that for?" Matt growled in tones completely unlike his normal voice. The kiss had affected him, too, Elena thought. More so than her.

Damon picked up his branch again and again waved the end of it like a Japanese fan. Pine aroma wafted by Elena. He looked considering, as though he might ask for a retake, then changed his mind, smiled brilliantly at them, and tucked the video camera into a pocket.

"All you need to know is that it was a perfect take."

"Then we're leaving." The kiss seemed to have given Matt new strength, even if it was for saying the wrong type of things. "Right now."

"Oh, no, but keep that dominant, aggressive attitude. As you remove her shirt."

"*What?*"

Damon repeated the words in the tones of a director giving an actor complicated instructions.

"Undo the buttons of her shirt, please, and take it off."

"You're *crazy*." Matt turned and looked at Elena, stopped aghast to see the expression on her face, the single tear running down the eye not hidden.

"Elena . . ."

He moved around, but she moved too. He couldn't get her to look him in the face. At last, she stopped, stood with her eyes down and leaking tears. He could *feel* the heat radiating from her cheeks.

"Elena, let's fight him. Don't you remember how you fought the bad things in Stefan's room?"

"But this is worse, Matt. I've never felt anything this bad before. This strong. It's—pressing on me."

"You don't mean we should give in to him . . . ?" That was what Matt *said* and he sounded as if he were on the verge of being ill. What his clear blue eyes said was simpler. They said: *No. Not if he kills me for refusing.*

"I mean . . ." Elena turned suddenly back to Damon. "Let him go," she said. "This is between you and me. Let's settle it ourselves." She was damned well going to save Matt, even if he didn't want to be saved.

I'll do what you want, she thought as hard as she could to Damon, hoping he would pick some of it up. After all, he'd bled her against her will—at least initially—before. She could live through him doing it again.

"Yes, you'll do *everything* I want," Damon said, proving that he could read her thoughts even more clearly than she'd imagined. "But the question is, after how much?" He didn't say how much what. He didn't have to. "Now, I know I just gave you an order," he added, half turning toward Matt but with his eyes still on Elena, "because I can still see you picturing it in your mind. But—"

Elena saw the look in Matt's eyes then, and the flaming of his cheeks, and she knew—and immediately tried to hide the knowledge from Damon—what he was going to do.

He was going to commit suicide.

"If we can't talk you out of it, we can't talk you out of it," Meredith said to Mrs. Flowers. "But—there are things out there—"

"Yes, dear, I know. And the sun is going down. It's a bad time to be outside. But as my mother always said, two witches are better than one." She gave Bonnie an absent smile. "And as you very kindly did not say before, I am very old. Why, I can remember the days before the first motorcars and airplanes. I might have knowledge that would help you in your quest for your friends—and on the other hand, I am dispensable."

"You certainly are not," Bonnie said fervently. They were using up Elena's wardrobe now, piling on the clothes.

Meredith had picked up the duffel bag with Stefan's clothes in it and dumped it on his bed, but the first time she picked up a shirt, she dropped it again.

"Bonnie, you might take something of Stefan's with you as we go," she said. "See if you get any impressions from it. Um, maybe you too, Mrs. Flowers?" she added. Bonnie understood. It was one thing to let somebody call themselves a witch; it was another thing to call someone very much your senior one.

The last layer of Bonnie's wardrobe was one of Stefan's shirts, and Mrs. Flowers tucked one of his socks in her pocket.

"But I won't go out the front door," Bonnie said adamantly. She couldn't even bear to imagine the mess.

"All right, so we go out the back," Meredith said, flipping Stefan's lamp off. "Come on."

They were actually walking out the back door when the front doorbell rang.

They all three exchanged glances. Then Meredith wheeled, "It could be them!" And she hastened back to the dim front of the house. Bonnie and Mrs. Flowers followed more slowly.

Bonnie shut her eyes as she heard the door open. When there were no immediate exclamations about the mess, she opened them a slit.

There was no sign that anything unusual had happened

outside the door. No smashed insect bodies—no dead or dying bugs on the front porch.

Hairs on the back of Bonnie's neck rose. Not that she wanted to see the malach. But she did want to know what had happened to them. Automatically, one hand went to her hair, to feel if a tendril had been left behind. Nothing.

"I'm looking for Matthew Honeycutt." The voice cut into Bonnie's reverie like a hot knife through butter, and Bonnie's eyes snapped all the way open.

Yes, it was Sheriff Rich Mooseburger and he was all there, from shiny boots to crisp collar. Bonnie opened her mouth, but Meredith spoke first.

"This is not Matt's house," she said, her tone quiet, her voice even.

"In fact I have already been to the Honeycutt house. And to the Sulez house and the McCulloughs'. Every one of them, in fact, suggested that if Matt weren't at one of those places, he might be out here with you."

Bonnie wanted to kick him in the shins. "Matt hasn't been stealing stop signs! He would never, ever, *ever* do something like that. And I wish to God I knew where he was, but I don't. None of us do!" She stopped, with the feeling that she might have said too much.

"And your names are?"

Mrs. Flowers took over. "This is Bonnie McCullough,

and Meredith Sulez. I am Mrs. Flowers, the owner of this boardinghouse, and I believe I can second Bonnie's remarks about the stop signs—"

"In fact this is more serious than missing road signs, ma'am. Matthew Honeycutt is under suspicion of assaulting a young woman. There is considerable physical evidence to support her story. And she claims that they have known each other since childhood, so there can be no mistake as to identity."

There was a moment of stunned silence, and then Bonnie almost shouted, "She? She *who?*"

"Miss Caroline Forbes is the complainant. And I would in fact suggest, if any of the three of you should *happen* to see Mr. Honeycutt, that you advise him to turn himself in. Before he is taken by force into custody." He took a step toward them as if threatening to come through the door, but Mrs. Flowers silently barred the way.

"*In fact*," Meredith said, regaining her composure, "I'm sure you realize that you need a warrant to enter these premises. Do you have one?"

Sheriff Mossberg didn't answer. He made a sharp little right turn, walked down the pathway to his sheriff's car, and disappeared.

att lunged at Damon in a rush that clearly demonstrated the skills that had gotten him a college football scholarship. He accelerated from utter stillness to a blur of motion, trying to tackle Damon, to bring him down.

"Run," he shouted, at the same instant. *"Run!"*

Elena stood still, trying to come up with Plan A after this disaster. She had been forced to watch Stefan's humiliation at Damon's hands at the boardinghouse, but she didn't think she could stand to see this.

But when she looked again, Matt was standing about a dozen yards from Damon, white-faced and grim, but alive and on his feet. He was preparing to rush Damon again.

And Elena . . . couldn't run. She knew that it would probably be the best thing—Damon might punish Matt briefly but most of his attention would be turned to hunting her down.

But she couldn't be sure. And she couldn't be sure that the punishment wouldn't kill Matt, or that he would be able to get away before Damon found her and had leisure time to think of him again.

No, not *this* Damon, pitiless and remorseless as he was.

There must be some way—she could almost feel wheels spinning in her own head.

And then she saw it.

No, not that . . .

But what else was there to do?

Matt was, indeed, rushing Damon again, and this time as he went for him, lithe and unstoppable and fast as a darting snake, she saw what Damon did. He simply sidestepped at the last moment, just when Matt was about to ram him with a shoulder. Matt's momentum kept him going, but Damon simply turned in place and faced him again. Then he picked up his damned pine branch. It was broken at the end where Matt had trampled it.

Damon frowned at the stick, then shrugged, lifting it—and then both he and Matt stopped frozen. Something came sailing in from the sidelines to settle on the ground between them. It lay there, stirring in the breeze.

It was a maroon and navy Pendleton shirt.

Both of the boys turned slowly toward Elena, who was wearing a white lacy camisole. She shivered slightly and wrapped her arms around herself. It seemed unusually cold for this time of evening.

Very slowly, Damon lowered the pine branch.

"Saved by your *inamorata*," he said to Matt.

"I know what that means and it's not true," Matt said. "She's my friend, not my girlfriend."

Damon just smiled distantly. Elena could feel his eyes on her bare arms. "So . . . on to the next step," he said.

Elena wasn't surprised. Heartsick but not surprised. Neither was she surprised to see, when Damon turned to look from her to Matt and back, a flash of red. It seemed to be reflected on the inside of his sunglasses.

"Now," he said to Elena. "I think we'll put you over there on that rock, sort of half reclining. But first—another kiss." He looked back at Matt. "Get with the program, Matt; you're wasting time. First, maybe you kiss her hair, then she throws her head back and you kiss her neck, while she puts her arms around your shoulders. . . ."

Matt, thought Elena. Damon had said *Matt*. It had slipped out so easily, so innocently. Suddenly her entire brain, and her body, too, seemed to be vibrating as if to a single note of music, seemed to be flooded by an icy shower-bath. And what the note was saying was not shocking, because it was something that somehow, at a subliminal level, she already knew. . . .

That's not Damon.

This wasn't the person she had known for—was it

really only nine or ten months? She had seen him when she was a human girl, and she had defied him and desired him in equal measure—and he had seemed to love her best when she was defying him.

She had seen him when she was a vampire and had been drawn to him with all her being, and he had cared for her as if she were a child.

She had seen him when she was a spirit, and from the afterlife she had learned a great deal.

He was a womanizer, he could be callous, he drifted through his victims' lives like a chimera, like a catalyst, changing other people while he himself remained unchanging and unchanged. He mystified humans, confused them, used them—leaving them bewildered, because he had the charm of the devil.

And never once had she seen him break his word. She had a rock-bottom feeling that this wasn't something that was a decision, it was so much a part of Damon, lodged so deep in his subconscious, that even he couldn't do anything to change it. He couldn't break his word. He'd starve first.

Damon was still talking to Matt, giving him orders. ". . . and then take off her . . ."

So what about his word to be her bodyguard, to keep her from harm?

He was talking to her now. "So you know when to throw your head back? After he—"

"*Who are you?*"

"What?"

"You heard me. *Who are you?* If you had really seen Stefan off and promised him to take care of me, none of this would have happened. Oh, you might be messing with Matt, but not in front of me. You're not—Damon's not stupid. He knows what a bodyguard is. He knows that watching Matt in pain hurts me as well. You're not Damon. Who . . . are . . . you?"

Matt's strength and fast-as-a-rattlesnake speed hadn't done any good. Maybe a different approach would work. As Elena spoke, she had been very slowly reaching up to Damon's face. Now, with one motion, she pulled his sunglasses off.

Eyes red as fresh new blood shone out at her.

"*What have you done?*" she whispered. "What have you done to Damon?"

Matt was out of the range of her voice but had been inching around, trying to get her attention. She wished fervently that Matt would just make a run for it himself. Here, he was just another way for this creature to blackmail her.

Without seeming to move quickly, the Damon-thing reached down and snatched the sunglasses from her hand. It was too fast for her to resist.

Then he seized her wrist in a painful grip.

"This would be a lot easier on both of you if you'd

cooperate," he said casually. "You don't seem to realize what might happen if you make me angry."

His grip was forcing her down, forcing her to kneel. Elena decided not to let it. But unfortunately her body didn't want to cooperate; it sent urgent messages of pain to her mind, of agony, of burning, searing agony. She had thought that she could ignore it, could stand to let him break her wrist. She was wrong. At some point something in her brain blacked out completely, and the next thing she knew she was on her knees with a wrist that felt three times the right size and burned fiercely.

"Human weakness," Damon said scornfully. "It will get you every time. . . . You should know better than to disobey me, by now."

Not Damon, Elena thought, so vehemently that she was surprised the imposter didn't hear her.

"All right," Damon's voice continued above her as cheerfully as if he'd simply given her a suggestion. "You go sit on that rock, leaning backward, and Matt, if you'll just come over here, facing her." The tone was of polite command, but Matt ignored it and was beside her already, looking at the finger marks on Elena's wrist as if he didn't believe them.

"Matt stands up, Elena sits, or the opposite one gets the full treatment. Have fun, kiddies." Damon had the palm-camera out again.

Matt consulted Elena with his eyes. She looked at the

imposter and said, enunciating carefully, "Go to hell, who-ever you are."

"Been there, done that, bought the brimstone," the not-Damon creature rattled off. He gave Matt a smile that was both luminescent and terrifying. Then he waggled the pine branch.

Matt ignored it. He waited, his face stoic, for the pain to hit.

Elena struggled up to stand by him. Side by side, they could defy Damon.

Who seemed for a moment to be out of his mind. "You're trying to pretend you're not afraid of me. But you will be. If you had any sense, you would be now."

Belligerently, he took a step toward Elena. *"Why aren't you afraid of me?"*

"Whoever you are, you're just an oversized bully. You've hurt Matt. You've hurt me. I'm sure you can kill us. But we're not afraid of bullies."

"You will be afraid." Now Damon's voice had dropped to a menacing whisper. "Just wait."

Even as something was ringing in Elena's ears, telling her to listen to those last words, to make a connection—who did that sound like?—the pain hit.

Her knees were knocked out by it. But she wasn't just kneeling now. She was trying to roll into a ball, trying to curl around the agony. All rational thought was swept from her head. She sensed Matt beside her, trying to hold her, but she could no more communicate with him than she could fly. She shuddered and fell to her side, as if having a seizure. Her entire universe was pain, and she only heard voices as if they came from far away.

"Stop it!" Matt sounded frantic. *"Stop it! Are you crazy? That's* Elena, *for God's sake! Do you want to* kill her?"

And then the not-Damon-thing advising him mildly, "I wouldn't try that again," but the only sound Matt made was a scream of primal rage.

"Caroline!" Bonnie was raging, pacing back and forth in Stefan's room while Meredith did something else with the computer. "How *dare* she?"

"She doesn't dare try to attack Stefan or Elena out-right—there's the oath," Meredith said. "So she's thought this up to get at all of us."

"But Matt—"

"Oh, Matt's handy," Meredith said grimly. "And unfortunately there's the matter of the physical evidence on both of them."

"What do you mean? Matt doesn't—"

"The scratches, my dear," put in Mrs. Flowers, looking sad, "from your razor-toothed bug. The poultice I put on will have healed them so that they'll look like a girl's fingernail scratches—about now. And the mark it left on your neck . . ." Mrs. Flowers coughed delicately. "It looks like what in my day was called a 'love bite.' Perhaps a sign of a tryst that ended in force? Not that your friend would ever do anything like that."

"And remember how Caroline looked when we saw her, Bonnie?" Meredith said dryly. "Not the crawling around—I'll bet anything she's walking just fine now. But her face. She had a black eye coming in and a swollen cheek. Perfect for the time frame."

Bonnie felt as if everyone was two steps ahead of her. "*What* time frame?"

"The night the bug attacked Matt. It was the morning after that that the sheriff called and talked to him. Matt admitted that his mother hadn't seen him all night, and that Neighborhood Watch guy saw Matt drive up to his house and, basically, pass out."

"That was from the bug poison. He'd just been fighting the malach!"

"We know that. But they'll say he'd just come back from attacking Caroline. Caroline's mother will hardly be fit to testify—you saw how she was. So who's to say that Matt wasn't over at Caroline's? Especially if he was planning assault."

"We are! We can vouch for him—" Bonnie suddenly stumbled to a halt. "No, I guess it was after he left that this was supposed to have happened. But, no, this is all wrong!" She took up pacing again. "I saw one of those bugs up close and it was exactly the way Matt described. . . ."

"And what's left of it now? Nothing. Besides, they'll

say that you would say *anything* for him."

Bonnie couldn't stand just walking aimlessly around anymore. She had to get to Matt, had to warn him—if they could even find him or Elena. "I thought *you* were the one who couldn't wait a minute to find them," she said accusingly to Meredith.

"I know; I was. But I had to look something up—and besides I wanted one more try at that page only vampires are supposed to read. The *Shi no Shi* one. But I've tweaked the screen in all the ways I can think of, and if there's something written here, I certainly can't find it."

"Best not to waste more time on it, then," Mrs. Flowers said. "Come get into your jacket, my dear. Shall we take the Yellow Wheeler or not?"

For just a moment Bonnie had a wild vision of a horse-drawn vehicle, a sort of Cinderella carriage but not pumpkin-shaped. Then she remembered seeing Mrs. Flowers' ancient Model T—painted yellow—parked inside what must be the old stables that belonged to the boardinghouse.

"We did better when we were on foot than we *or* Matt did in a car," said Meredith, giving the computer monitor controls a final vicious click. "We're more mobile than—oh, my God! *I did it!*"

"Did what?"

"The website. Come look at this."

Both Bonnie and Mrs. Flowers came over to the

computer. The screen was bright green with thin, faint, dark green writing.

"*How* did you do it?" Bonnie demanded as Meredith bent to get a notebook and pen to copy down what they saw.

"I don't know. I just tweaked the color settings one last time—I'd already tried it for Power Saver, Low Battery, High Resolution, High Contrast, and every combination I could think of."

They stared at the words.

Tired of that lapis lazuli?
Want to take a vacation in Hawaii?
Sick of that same old liquid cuisine?
Come and visit Shi no Shi.

After that came an ad for the "Death of Death," a place where vampires could be cured of their cursed state and become human again. And then there was an address. Just a city road, no mention of what state, or, for that matter, what city. But it was a Clue.

"Stefan didn't mention a road address," Bonnie said.

"Maybe he didn't want to scare Elena," Meredith said grimly. "Or maybe, when he looked at the page, the address wasn't there."

Bonnie shivered. "*Shi no Shi*—I don't like the sound of it. And don't laugh at me," she added to Meredith defensively. "Remember what Stefan said about trusting my intuition?"

"Nobody's laughing, Bonnie. We need to get to Elena and Matt. What does your intuition tell you about that?"

"It says that we're going to get into trouble, and that Matt and Elena are in trouble already."

"Funny, because that's just what my judgment tells me."

"Are we ready, now?" Mrs. Flowers handed out flash-lights.

Meredith tried hers and found it had a strong, steady beam.

"Let's do it," she said, automatically flipping off Stefan's lamp again.

Bonnie and Mrs. Flowers followed her down the stairs, out of the house, and onto the street they had run from not so long ago. Bonnie's pulse was racing, her ears ready for the slightest *whipwhip* sound. But except for the beams of their flashlights, the Old Wood was completely dark and eerily silent. Not even the sound of birdsong broke the moonless night.

They plunged in, and in minutes they were lost.

Matt woke up on his side and for a moment didn't know where he was. Outdoors. Ground. Picnic? Hiking? Fell asleep?

And then he tried to move and agony flared like a

geyser of flame, and he remembered everything. That *bastard*, torturing Elena, he thought.

Torturing Elena.

It didn't go together, not with *Damon*. What was it Elena had been saying to him at the end that had made him so angry?

The thought nagged at him, but it was just another unanswered question, like Stefan's note in Elena's diary.

Matt realized that he could move, if very slowly. He looked around, moving his head by careful increments until he saw Elena, lying near him like a broken doll. He hurt and he was desperately thirsty. She would feel the same way. The first thing was to get her to a hospital; the kind of muscular contractions brought on by that degree of pain could break an arm or even a leg. They were certainly strong enough to cause a sprain or dislocation. Not to mention Damon spraining her wrist.

That was what the practical, sensible part of him was thinking. But the question that kept going around in his mind still made him reel in complete astonishment.

He *hurt* Elena? The way he hurt me? I don't believe it. I knew he was sick, twisted, but I never heard of him hurting the girls. And never, never Elena. *Never*. But me—if he treats me the way he treats Stefan, he'll kill me. I don't have a vampire's resilience.

I have to get Elena out of this before he kills me. I can't leave her alone with him.

Instinctively, somehow, he knew that Damon was still around. This was confirmed when he heard some little noise, turned his head too fast, and found himself staring at a blurred and wobbling black boot. The blur and wobble were the result of turning too quickly, but as quickly as he'd turned, he'd suddenly felt his face pressed into the dirt and pine needles on the ground of the clearing.

By The Boot. It was on his neck, grinding his face into the dirt now. Matt made a wordless sound of pure fury and grabbed at the leg above the boot with both hands, trying to get a purchase and throw Damon off. But while he could grasp the smooth leather of the boot, moving it in any direction was impossible. It was as if the vampire in the boot could turn himself to iron. Matt could feel the tendons in his throat stand out, his face turn red, and his muscles bunch under his shirt as he made a violent effort to heave Damon off. At last, exhausted, chest heaving, he lay still.

In that very same instant, The Boot was lifted. Exactly, he realized, at the moment when he was too tired to lift his head himself. He made a supreme effort and lifted it a few inches.

And The Boot caught him under the chin and lifted his face a little higher.

"What a pity," Damon said with infuriating contempt. "You humans are so weak. It's no fun to play with you at all."

"Stefan . . . will come back," Matt got out, looking up at Damon from where he was unintentionally groveling on the ground. "Stefan will kill you."

"Guess what?" Damon said conversationally. "Your face is all messed up on one side—scratches, you know. You've got sort of a Phantom of the Opera thing going on."

"If he doesn't, I will. I don't know how, but I will. I swear it."

"Careful what you promise."

Just as Matt got his arm working enough to prop him up—exactly then, to the millisecond—Damon reached out and grabbed him painfully by a handful of hair, yanking his head up.

"Stefan," Damon said, looking straight down into Matt's face and forcing Matt to look up at him, no matter how Matt tried to turn his face away, "was only powerful for a few days because he was drinking the blood of a very powerful spirit who hadn't yet adapted to Earth yet. But look at her now." He twisted his grip on Matt's hair again, more painfully. "Some spirit. Lying there in the dirt. Now the Power is back where it should be. Do you understand? *Do* you—boy?"

Matt just stared at Elena. "How could you do that?" he whispered finally.

"An object lesson in what it means to defy me. And surely you wouldn't want me to be sexist and leave her out?" Damon *tched*. "You have to keep up with the times."

Matt said nothing. He had to get Elena out of this.

"Worrying about the girl? She's just playing possum now. Hoping I'll ignore her and concentrate on you."

"You're a liar."

"So I'll concentrate on you. Speaking of keeping up with the times, you know—except for the scratches and things, you're a fine-looking young man."

At first the words meant nothing to Matt. When he understood them, Matt could feel his blood freeze in his body.

"As a vampire, I can give you an informed and honest opinion. And as a vampire, I'm getting very thirsty. There's you. And then there's the girl who's still pretending to be asleep. I'm sure you can see what I'm getting at."

I believe in you, Elena, Matt thought. He's a liar, and he'll always be a liar. "Take my blood," he said wearily.

"Are you sure?" Now Damon sounded solicitous. "If you resist, the pain is horrible."

"Just get it over with."

"Whatever you like." Damon knelt fluidly on one knee, at the same time twisting his grip on Matt's hair, making Matt wince. The new grip dragged Matt's upper body across Damon's knee, so that his head was thrown back, his neck arched and exposed. In fact Matt had never felt so exposed, so helpless, so vulnerable in his life.

"You can always change your mind," Damon taunted him.

Matt shut his eyes, stubbornly saying nothing.

At the last moment, though, as Damon bent with fangs exposed, Matt's fingers almost involuntarily, almost as if it were something his body was doing *apart* from his mind, clenched themselves into a fist and he suddenly, unpredictably, brought the fist swinging up to deal a violent blow to Damon's temple. But—serpent-quick—Damon reached up and caught the blow almost nonchalantly in an open hand, and held Matt's fingers in a crushing grip— just as razor-sharp fangs opened a vein in Matt's throat and an open mouth fastened on his exposed throat, sucking and drinking the blood that sprayed upward.

Elena—awake but unable to move from where she had fallen, unable to make a sound or turn her head—was forced to listen to the entire exchange, forced to hear Matt's groan as his blood was taken against his will, as he resisted to the last.

And then she thought of something that, as dizzy and frightened as she was, almost made her pass out in fear.

26

Ley lines. Stefan had spoken of them, and with the influence of the spirit world still on her, she had seen them without trying. Now, still lying on her side, channeling what remained of that Power to her eyes, she looked at the earth.

And that was what made her mind go gray in terror.

As far as she could see there were lines converging here from all directions. Thick lines that glowed with a cold phosphorescence, medium-sized lines that had the dull shine of bad mushrooms in a cellar, and tiny lines that looked like perfectly straight cracks of the outer surface layer of the world. They were like veins and arteries and nerves just under the skin of the clearing-beast.

No wonder it seemed alive. She was lying on a massive convergence of ley lines. And if the cemetery was worse than this—she couldn't imagine what it might look like.

If Damon had somehow found a way to tap into that Power . . . no wonder he seemed different, arrogant, undefeatable. Ever since he had released her to drink Matt's blood, she had kept shaking her head, trying to shake off the humiliation with it. But now finally she stopped as she tried to calculate a way to make use of this Power. There had to be a way to do it.

The grayness wouldn't clear from her vision. Finally Elena realized that it was not because she was faint, but because it was getting dark—twilight outside the clearing, true darkness coming into it.

She tried again to lift herself up, and this time she succeeded. Almost immediately a hand was extended to her and, automatically, she took it, letting it draw her to her feet.

She faced—whoever it was, Damon or whatever was using his features or his body. Despite the almost-darkness, he still wore those wraparound sunglasses. She could make nothing out of the rest of his face.

"Now," the thing in the sunglasses said. "You're going to come with me."

It was nearing full dark, and they were in the clearing that was a beast.

This place—it was unwholesome. She was afraid of the clearing as she had never been afraid of a person or creature. It resounded with malevolence, and she couldn't shut her ears to it.

She had to keep thinking, and keep thinking straight, she thought.

She was terribly frightened for Matt; frightened that Damon had taken too much blood or had played too hard with his toy; breaking it.

And she was afraid of this Damon thing. She was also worried about the influence this place might have had on the real Damon. The woods around them shouldn't have any effect on vampires, except to hurt them. Was the possible-Damon inside the possessor hurt? If he could understand anything of what was happening, could he distinguish that hurt from his hurt and anger at Stefan?

She didn't know. She did know that there had been a terrible look in his eyes when Stefan had told him to get out of the boardinghouse. And she did know that there were creatures in the forest, malach, that could influence a person's mind. She was afraid, deeply afraid, that the malach were using Damon now, blackening his darkest desires and twisting him into something horrible, something he had never been even at his worst.

But how could she be sure? How could she know whether or not there was something else behind the malach, something that controlled *them*? Her soul was telling her that this might be the case, that Damon might be completely unconscious of what his body was doing, but that might just be wishful thinking.

Certainly all she could sense around her were small, evil creatures. She could feel them encircling the clearing, strange insect-like beings like the one that had attacked Matt. They were in a furor of excitement, whipping their tentacles around to make a noise almost like a buzzing helicopter.

Were they influencing Damon now? Certainly, he had never before hurt any of the other humans she knew the way he had today. She had to get all three of them out of this place. It was diseased, contaminated. Once again she felt a wave of longing for Stefan, who might know what to do in this situation.

She turned, slowly, to look at Damon.

"May I call someone to come and help Matt? I'm afraid to leave him here; I'm afraid *they'll* get him." Just as well to let him know that she knew *they* were hiding in the liverwort and the rhododendron and mountain holly bushes all around.

Damon hesitated; he seemed to consider it. Then he shook his head.

"We wouldn't want to give them too many clues to where you are," he said cheerily. "It'll be an interesting experiment to see if the malach do get him—and how they do it."

"It wouldn't be an interesting experiment for *me*." Elena's voice was flat. "Matt is my friend."

"Nevertheless, we'll leave him here for now. I don't trust you—even to give *me* a message to Meredith or Bonnie—to send on my phone."

Elena didn't say anything. As a matter of fact, he was right not to trust her, as she and Meredith and Bonnie had worked out an elaborate code of harmless-sounding phrases as soon as they knew that Damon was after Elena. A lifetime ago for her—literally—but she could still remember them.

Silently, she simply followed Damon to the Ferrari.

She was responsible for Matt.

"You're not putting up much of an argument this time, and I wonder what you're plotting."

"I'm plotting that we might as well get on with it. If you'll tell me what 'it' is," she said, more bravely than she felt.

"Well, now what 'it' is, is up to you." Damon gave Matt a kick in the ribs in passing. He was now pacing in a circle around the clearing, which seemed smaller than ever, a circle which didn't include her. She took a few paces toward him—and slipped. She didn't know how it happened. Maybe the giant animal breathed. Maybe it was just the slick pine needles under her boots.

But one moment she was heading for Matt and the next her feet had gone out from under her and she was heading for the ground with nothing to grab onto.

And then, smoothly and unhurriedly, she was in Damon's

arms. With centuries of Virginian etiquette behind her she automatically said, "Thank you."

"My pleasure."

Yes, she thought. That's all it means. It is *his* pleasure, and that's all that matters.

That was when she noticed that they were headed for her Jaguar.

"*Oh*, no, we don't," she said.

"Oh, yes, we will—if I please," he said. "Unless you want to see your friend Matt suffer like that again. At some point his heart *will* give out."

"Damon." She pushed her way out of his arms, standing on her own feet. "I don't understand. This isn't like you. Take what you want and go."

He just kept looking at her. "I was doing just that."

"You don't have to"—for the life of her, she couldn't keep a tremor out of her voice—"take me anywhere special to take my blood. And Matt won't know. He's out."

For a long moment there was silence in the clearing. Utter silence. The night birds and the crickets stopped making their music. Suddenly Elena felt as if she were on some kind of thrill ride that plummeted down, leaving her stomach and organs still at the top. Then Damon put it in words.

"I want *you*. Exclusively."

Elena braced herself, trying to keep a clear head despite the fog that seemed to be invading it.

"You know that that's not possible."

"I know that it was possible for Stefan. When you were with him, you didn't think about anything but him. You couldn't see, couldn't hear, couldn't feel anything but him."

Elena's gooseflesh now covered her whole body. Speaking carefully around the obstruction in her throat, she said, "Damon, did you do something to Stefan?"

"Now, why would I want to do something like that?"

Very low, Elena said, "You and I both know why."

"Do you mean," Damon started out speaking casually, but his voice grew more intense as he gripped her shoulders, "so that you would see nothing but *me*, hear nothing but *me*, think of nothing but *me*?"

Still quietly, still controlling her terror, Elena said, "Take off the sunglasses, Damon."

Damon glanced upwards and around as if to reassure himself that no last ray of sunset could pierce the green-gray world that surrounded them. Then with one hand, he stripped off the sunglasses.

Elena found herself looking into eyes that were so black there seemed to be no difference between iris and pupil. She . . . turned a switch in her brain, did something so that all her senses were tuned onto Damon's face, his expression, the Power circulating through him.

His eyes were still as black as the depths of an

unexplored cave. No red. But then, he'd had time, this time to get ready for her.

I believe what I saw before, Elena thought. With my *own* eyes.

"Damon, I'll do anything, anything you want. But you have to tell me. *Did you do something to Stefan?*"

"Stefan was still high on *your* blood when he left you," he reminded her, and before she could speak to deny this—"and, to answer your question precisely, I don't know where he is. On that, you have my word. But in any case, it's true, what you were thinking earlier," he added, as Elena tried to step away, to get out of the grip he had on her upper arms. "*I'm* the only one, Elena. The only one you haven't conquered. The only one you can't manipulate. Intriguing, isn't it?"

Suddenly, in spite of her fear, she was furious. "Then why hurt Matt? He's just a friend. What's he got to do with it?"

"Just a friend." And Damon began to laugh the way he had before, eerily.

"Well, I know *he* didn't have anything to do with Stefan leaving," Elena snapped.

Damon turned on her, but by then the clearing was so dim that she couldn't read his expression at all. "And who said *I* did? But that doesn't mean I'm not going to make use of the opportunity." He picked Matt up easily and held up something that shone silver from his other hand.

Her keys. From her jeans pocket. Taken, no doubt, when she was lying unconscious on the ground.

She could tell nothing from his voice, either, except that it was bitter and grim—all usual if he were talking about Stefan. "With your blood in him, I couldn't have killed my brother if I had tried, the last time I saw him," he added.

"*Did* you try?"

"As a matter of fact, no. You have my word on that as well."

"And you don't know where he is?"

"No." He hefted Matt.

"What do you think you're doing?

"Taking him with us. He's hostage for your good behavior."

"*Oh*, no," Elena said flatly, pacing. "This is between you and me. You've hurt Matt enough." She blinked and once again almost screamed to find Damon much too close, much too fast. "I'll do whatever you want. *Whatever* you want. But not here out in the open and not with Matt around."

Come on, Elena, she was thinking. Where's that vampy behavior when you want it? You used to be able to vamp any guy; now, just because he's a vampire, you can't do it?

"Take me somewhere," she said softly, intertwining

her arm with his free one, "but in the Ferrari. I don't want to go in my car. Take me in the Ferrari."

Damon paced back to the trunk of the Ferrari, unlocked it, and looked inside. Then he looked at Matt. It was clear that the tall, well-built boy wasn't going to fit in to the trunk . . . at least, not with all his limbs attached.

"Don't you even *think* about it," Elena said. "Just put him in the Jaguar with the keys and he'll be safe enough—lock him in." Elena fervently prayed that what she was saying was true.

For a moment Damon said nothing, then he looked up with a smile so brilliant she could see it in the dusk. "All right," he said. He dumped Matt on the ground again. "But if you try to run while I move the cars, I run *him* over."

Damon, Damon, will you never understand? Humans don't *do* that to their friends, Elena thought as he brought the Ferrari out so he could bring the Jaguar in, so he could dump Matt in it.

"All right," she said in a small voice. She was afraid to look at Damon. "Now—what do you want?"

Damon inclined from the waist in a very graceful bow, indicating the Ferrari. She wondered what would happen once she got in. If he were any normal attacker—if there wasn't Matt to think about—if she didn't fear the forest even more than she feared him . . .

She hesitated and then got into Damon's car.

Inside, she pulled her camisole out of her jeans to conceal the fact that she wasn't wearing a seat belt. She doubted Damon ever wore a seat belt or locked his doors or anything like that. Precautions weren't his thing. And now she prayed that he had other matters on his mind.

"Seriously, Damon, where are we going?" she said as he got into the Ferrari.

"First, how about one for the road?" Damon suggested, his voice fake-jocular.

Elena had expected something like this. She sat passively as Damon took her chin in fingers that trembled slightly, and tilted it up. She shut her eyes as she felt the double-snakebite pinch of razor-sharp fangs piercing her skin. She kept her eyes shut as her attacker fastened his mouth on the bleeding flesh and began to drink deeply. Damon's idea of "one for the road" was just what she would have expected: enough to put both of them in danger. But it wasn't until she actually began to feel as if she would pass out any minute that she shoved at his shoulder.

He held on for a few more very painful seconds just to show who was Boss here. Then he let go of her, licking his lips avidly, his eyes actually gleaming at her *through* the Ray-Bans.

"Exquisite," he said. "Unbelievable. Why you're—"

Yeah, tell me I'm a bottle of single malt scotch, she thought. That's the way to my heart.

"Can we go now?" she asked pointedly. And then, as she suddenly remembered Damon's driving habits, she added deliberately, "Be careful; this road twists and turns a lot."

It had the effect she had hoped for. Damon hit the accelerator and they shot out of the clearing at high speed. Then they were taking the sharp turns of the Old Wood faster than Elena had ever driven through here; faster than anyone had dared go with her as a passenger before.

But still, they were *her* roads. From childhood on she had played here. There was only one family who lived right on the perimeter of the Old Wood, but their driveway was on the right side of the road—her side—and she got herself ready for it. He would take the sudden curve to the left just before the second curve that was the Dunstans' driveway—and on the second curve she would jump.

There was no sidewalk edging Old Wood Road, of course, but at that point there was a heavy growth of rhododendron and other bushes. All she could do was pray. Pray that she didn't snap her neck on impact. Pray that she didn't break an arm or leg before she limped through the few yards of woods to the driveway. Pray that the Dunstans were home when she pounded on their door and pray that they listened when she told them not to let the vampire in behind her.

She saw the curve. She didn't know why the Damon-thing couldn't read her mind, but apparently he couldn't. He wasn't speaking and his only precaution against her trying to get out seemed to be speed.

She was going to get hurt, she knew that. But the worst part of any hurt was fear, and she wasn't afraid.

As he rounded the curve, she pulled the handle and pushed open the door as hard as she could with her hands while she kicked it as hard as she could with her feet. The door swung open, quickly being caught by centrifugal force, as were Elena's legs. As was Elena.

Her kick alone took her halfway out of the car. Damon grabbed for her and got only a handful of hair. For a moment she thought he would keep her in, even without keeping hold of her. She tumbled over and over in the air, floating, remaining about two feet off the ground, reaching out to grab fronds, branches of bushes, anything she could use to slow her velocity. And in this place where magic and physics met; she was able to do it, to slow while still floating on Damon's power, although it took her much farther from the Dunstans' house than she wanted.

Then she did hit the ground, bounced, and did her best to twist in the air, to take the impact on her buttock or the back of a shoulder, but something went wrong and her left heel hit first—*God!*—and tangled, swinging her around completely, slamming her knee into concrete—*God, God!*—flipping her in the air and bringing her down on her right arm so hard it seemed to be trying to drive it into her shoulder.

She had the wind knocked out of her by the first blow and was forced to hiss air in by the second and third.

Despite the flipping, flying universe, there was one sign she couldn't miss—an unusual spruce growing into the road that she had noticed ten feet behind her when she'd exploded out of the car. Tears were pouring uncontrollably down her cheeks as she pulled at tendrils of bush that had entangled her ankle—and a good thing, too. A few tears might have blurred her vision, made her afraid—as she had been with the last two explosions of pain—that she might pass out. But she was out on the road, her eyes were washed clear, she could see the spruce and the sunset both directly ahead, and she was thoroughly conscious. And that meant that if she headed for the sunset but at a forty-five-degree angle to her right, she couldn't miss the Dunstans'; driveway, house, barn, cornfield were all there to guide her after perhaps twenty-five steps in the woods.

She had barely stopped rolling when she was pulling at the bush that had thwarted her and getting to her feet just as she pulled the last entangling stems from her hair.

The calculation about the Dunstans' house happened instantaneously in her head, even as she turned and saw the crushed swath she'd cut through the greenery and the blood on the road.

At first she looked at her skinned hands in bewilderment; they couldn't have left such a gory trail. And they hadn't. One knee had been skinned—flayed, really—right through her jeans—and one seriously messed up leg, less bloody but causing her sheets of pain like white lighting even while she was not trying to move it. Two arms with quite a lot of skin removed.

No time to find out how much or to figure out what she'd done to her shoulder. A *screeeeeeech* of brakes ahead. Lord, he's slow. No, I'm fast, hyped up by pain and terror. Use it!

She ordered her legs to sprint into the forest. Her right leg obeyed, but when she swiveled her left and it hit the ground fireworks went off behind her eyes. She was in a state of hyper-alertness; she saw the stick even as she was falling. She rolled over once or twice, which caused dull red flares of pain to go off in her head, and then she was able to grab it. It might have been specially designed for a crutch, around underarm height and blunt on one end but sharp on the other. She tucked it under her left arm and somehow willed herself up from her place in the mud: boosting off with her right leg and catching herself on the crutch so that she scarcely had to touch her left foot to the ground.

She'd got turned around in the fall and had to twist to right herself again—but there she saw it, the last remains of sunset and the road behind her. Head forty-five-degrees right from that glow, she thought. Thank God, it was her right arm that was messed up; this way she could support herself with her left shoulder on the crutch. Still without a moment's hesitation, without giving Damon an extra millisecond to follow her, she plunged in her chosen direction into the forest.

Into the Old Wood.

hen Damon woke up, he was wrestling with the wheel of the Ferrari. He was on a narrow road, heading almost straight into a glorious sunset—and the passenger door was waving open.

Once again, only the combination of almost instantaneous reflex and perfectly designed automobile allowed him to keep out of the wide, muddy ditches on either side of the one-lane road. But he managed it and ended up with the sunset at his back, gazing at the long shadows down the road and wondering what the hell had just happened to him.

Was he sleep-driving now? The passenger door—why was it open?

And then something happened. A long, thin thread,

slightly waving, almost like a single strand of gossamer, lit up as the reddish sunlight hit it. It was dangling from the top of the passenger window, which was shut, with the roof down.

He didn't bother to pull the car to one side, but stopped in the middle of the road and went around to look at that hair.

In his fingers, held toward the light, it turned white. But turned toward the dark of the forest, it showed its true color: gold.

A long, slightly waving, golden hair.

Elena.

As soon as he had identified it, he got back into the car and began to backtrack. Something had ripped Elena right out of his car without putting so much as a scratch on the paint. What could have done that?

How had he managed to get Elena to go for a spin anyway? And why couldn't he remember? Had they both been attacked . . . ?

When he backtracked, however, the marks by the passenger's side of the road told the entire grisly story. For some reason, Elena had been frightened into jumping out of the car—or some power had pulled her. And Damon, who now felt as if there were steam rising from his skin, knew that in all the woods there were only two creatures that could have been responsible.

He sent out a scouting probe, a simple circle that was meant to be undetectable, and almost lost control of the car again.

Merda! That blast had come out as a sphere-shaped killing strafe—birds were dropping out of the sky. It tore through the Old Wood, through Fell's Church, which surrounded it, and into the areas beyond, before finally dying out hundreds of miles away.

Power? He wasn't a vampire, he was Death Incarnate. Damon had a vague thought of pulling over and waiting until the turmoil inside himself had stopped. Where had such Power come from?

Stefan would have stopped, would have dithered around, wondering. Damon just grinned savagely, gunned the engine, and sent thousands of probes raining from the sky, all attuned to catch a fox-shaped creature running or hiding in the Old Wood.

He got a hit in a tenth of a second.

There. Under a black cohosh bush, if he wasn't mistaken—under some unspeakable bush, anyway. And Shinichi knew he was coming.

Good. Damon sent a wave of Power directly at the fox, catching it in a *kekkai*, a sort of invisible rope-barrier that he tightened deliberately, slowly, around the struggling animal. Shinichi fought back, with killing force. Damon used the kekkai to pick him up bodily and slam the little fox body into the ground. After a few of these slams Shinichi decided to stop fighting and played dead instead. That was fine with Damon. It was the way he thought Shinichi looked best, except for the bit about playing.

At last he had to stash the Ferrari between two trees and ran swiftly to the bush where Shinichi was now fighting the barrier around him to get into human form.

Standing back, eyes narrowed, arms crossed on his chest, Damon watched the struggle for a while. Then he let up enough on the kekkai's field to allow the change.

And the instant Shinichi became human, Damon's hands were around his throat.

"Where is Elena, *kono bakayarou*?" In a lifetime as a vampire you learned a lot of curse words. Damon preferred to use those of a victim's native language. He called Shinichi everything he could think of, because Shinichi was fighting, and was Calling telepathically for his sister. Damon had some choice things to say about *that* in Italian, where hiding behind your younger twin sister was . . . well, good for a *lot* of creative cursing.

He felt another fox-shape racing at him—and he realized that Misao intended to kill. She was in her true shape as a kitsune: just like the russet thing he'd tried to run over while driving with Damaris. A fox, yes, but a fox with two, three . . . six tails altogether. The extra ones usually were invisible, he gathered, as he neatly caught her in a kekkai as well. But she was ready to show them, ready to use all her powers to rescue her brother.

Damon contented himself with holding her as she struggled vainly within the barrier, and saying to Shinichi, "Your baby sister fights better than you do, *bakayarou*. Now, *give me Elena*."

Shinichi changed forms abruptly and leaped for Damon's throat, sharp white teeth in evidence, top and bottom. They were both too keyed up, too high on testosterone—and Damon, on his new Power—to let it go.

Damon actually felt the teeth scrape his throat before he got his hands again around the fox's neck. But this time Shinichi was showing his tails, a fan that Damon didn't bother to count.

Instead he stomped one neat boot on the fan and *pulled* with his other two hands. Misao, watching, shrieked in anger and anguish. Shinichi thrashed and arched, golden eyes fixed on Damon's. In another minute his spine would crack.

"I'll enjoy that," Damon told him sweetly. "Because I'll bet that Misao knows whatever you know. Too bad you won't be here to see *her* die."

Shinichi, rabid with fury, seemed willing to die and condemn Misao to Damon's mercies just to avoid losing the fight. But then his eyes darkened abruptly, his body went limp, and words appeared faintly in Damon's mind.

. . . hurts . . . can't . . . think . . .

Damon regarded him gravely. Now, Stefan, at this point, would release a good deal of the pressure on the kitsune so the poor little fox could think, Damon, on the other hand, increased the pressure briefly, then released it back to the previous level.

"Is that better?" he asked solicitously. "Can the cute little foxie think now?"

You . . . bastard . . .

Angry as he was, Damon suddenly remembered the point of all this.

"*What happened to Elena?* Her trail runs out up against a tree. Is she *inside* it? You have seconds left to live, now. Talk."

"Talk," seconded another voice, and Damon barely glanced up at Misao. He'd left her relatively unguarded and she'd found power and room to change into her human shape. He took it in instantaneously, dispassionately.

She was small-boned and petite, looking like any Japanese schoolgirl, except that her hair was just like her brother's—black tipped with red. The only difference was that the red in her hair was lighter and brighter—a truly brilliant scarlet. The bangs that fell into her eyes had blazing fiery tips, and so did the silky dark hair falling over her shoulders. It was striking but the only neurons that lit in Damon's mind in response were connected to fire and danger and deception.

She might have fallen into a trap, Shinichi managed.

A trap? Damon frowned. *What kind of trap?*

I'll take you to where you can look into them, Shinichi said evasively.

"And the fox can suddenly think again. But you know what? I don't think you're cute at all," Damon whispered, then dropped the kitsune on the ground. Shinichi-as-a-human fountained up, and Damon dropped the barrier just long enough to let the fox in human form try to take his head off with one punch. He leaned away from it easily, and returned it with a blow that knocked Shinichi back into the tree hard enough to bounce. Then, while the kitsune was still dazed and glassy-eyed, he picked him up, slung him over one shoulder, and started back to the car.

What about me? Misao was trying to curb furious and sound pathetic, but she really wasn't very good at it.

"You're not cute, either," Damon said, recklessly. He could get to like this super-Power thing. "But if you mean, when do you get out, it's when I get Elena back. Safe and healthy, with all her bits attached."

He left her cursing. He wanted to get Shinichi to wherever they had to go while the fox was still dazed and in pain.

* * *

Elena was counting. Go straight one, go straight two—untangle crutch from creeper, three, four, go straight five—it was definitely getting darker now, go straight six, caught by something in hair, *yank*, seven, eight, go straight—damn! A fallen tree. Too high to scramble over. She'd have to go around it. All right, to the right, one, two, three—a long tree—seven steps. Seven steps back—now, *sharp* right turn and keep walking. Much as you'd like to, you can't count any of those steps. So you're at nine. Straighten yourself because the tree was perpendicular—dear heaven, it's pitch dark now. Call that eleven and—

—she was flying. What had caused her crutch to slip, she didn't know, couldn't tell. It was too dark to go frisking around, maybe finding herself a case of poison oak. What she had to do was to think about things, to think so that this all-pervading hellish pain in her left leg would quiet down. It hadn't helped her right arm either—that instinctive windmilling, trying to catch something and save herself. God, that fall had hurt. The whole side of her body hurt so much—

But she had to get to civilization because she believed only civilization could help Matt.

You have to get up again, Elena.

I'm *doing* it!

Now—she couldn't see anything, but she had a pretty good idea which way she'd been pointed when she'd fallen. And if she was wrong, she would hit the road and be able to backtrack.

Twelve, thirteen—she kept counting, kept talking to herself. When she reached twenty she felt relief and joy. Any minute now, she'd hit the driveway.

Any minute now, she'd hit it.

It was pitch black out, but she was careful to scuff the ground so she would know, the minute she hit it.

Any . . . minute . . . now . . .

When Elena reached forty she knew she was in trouble.

But where could she have gone so far wrong? Every time some small obstacle had made her turn right, she'd turned carefully left the next time. And there was that whole line of landmarks in her way, the house, the barn, the small cornfield. How could she have gotten lost? *How?* It had only been half a minute in the forest . . . only a few steps in the Old Wood.

Even the trees were changing. Where she had been, near the road, most of the trees had been hickory or tulip. Now she was in a thicket of white oaks and red oaks . . . and conifers.

Old oaks . . . and on the ground, needles and leaves that muffled her foot-hops into soundlessness.

Soundlessness . . . but she needed help!

"Mrs. Dunstan! Mr. Dunstan! Kristin! Jake!" She threw the names out into a world that was doing its best to muffle her voice. In fact, in the darkness she could discern a certain swirling wispy grayness that seemed to be—yes—it was fog.

"Mrs. Dunstaa—a-aan! Mr. Dunstaa-aa-an! Kriiiissstiiiinnn! Jaaa-aaake!"

She needed shelter; she needed help. Everything hurt, most of all her left leg and right shoulder. She could just imagine what a sight she would make: covered in mud and leaves from falling every few feet, her hair in a wild mop from being caught on trees, blood everywhere. . . .

One good thing: she certainly didn't look like Elena Gilbert. Elena Gilbert had long silky hair that was always perfectly coifed or charmingly *dishabille*. Elena Gilbert set the fashions in Fell's Church and would never be seen wearing a torn camisole and jeans covered with mud. Whoever they thought this forlorn stranger was, they wouldn't think she was Elena.

But the forlorn stranger was feeling a sudden qualm. She'd walked through woods all her life and never had her hair caught once. Oh, of course she had been able to see then, but she didn't remember having to step out of her way often to avoid it.

Now, it was as if the trees were deliberately reaching down to catch and snag her hair. She had to hold her body clumsily still and try to whip her head away in the worst cases—she couldn't manage to stay upright and get the tendril torn out as well.

But painful as the tearing at her hair was, nothing scared her like the grabbing at her legs.

Elena had grown up playing in this forest, and there had always been plenty of room to walk without hurting herself. But now . . . things were reaching out, fibrous tendrils were grabbing at her ankle just where it hurt most. And then it was agony to try to rip with her fingers at these thick, sap-coated, stinging roots.

I'm frightened, she thought, putting into words at last what all her feelings had been since she stepped into the darkness of the Old Wood. She was damp with dew and sweat, her hair was as wet as if she'd been standing in the rain. It was so dark! And now her imagination began to work, and unlike most people's imaginations it had genuine, solid information to work *with*. A vampire's hand seemed to tangle in her hair. After an endless time of agony in her ankle and her shoulder, she had twisted the "hand" out of her hair—to find another curling stalk.

All right. She would ignore the pain and get her bearings here, here where there was a remarkable tree, a massive white pine that had a huge hole in its center, big enough for Bonnie to get into. She would put that flat at her back and then walk straight west—she couldn't see stars because of the cloud cover, but she *felt* that west was to her left. If she were correct, it would bring her to the road. If she were wrong and it was north, it would take her to the Dunstans'. If it were south, it would eventually take her to another curve of the road. If it were east . . . well, it would be a long walk, but it would eventually take her to the creek.

But first she would gather all her Power, all the Power she'd been unconsciously using to dull the pain and give her strength—she would gather it and light up this place so she could see if the road was visible—or, better, a house—from where she stood. It was only a human's power but, again, the knowledge of how to use it made all the difference, she thought. She gathered the Power in one tight white ball and then loosed it, twisting to look around before it dissipated.

Trees. Trees. Trees.

Oaks and hickories, white pine and beech. No high ground to get to. In every direction, nothing but trees, as if she were lost in some grimly enchanted forest and could never get out.

But she *would* get out. Any of those directions would take her to people eventually—even east. Even east, she could just follow the stream until it led to people.

She wished she had a compass.

She wished she could see the stars.

She was trembling all over, and it wasn't just from the cold. She was injured; she was terrified. But she had to forget about that. Meredith wouldn't cry. Meredith wouldn't be terrified. Meredith would find a sensible way to get out.

She had to get help for Matt.

Gritting her teeth to ignore the pain, Elena started off. If any of her wounds had happened to her in isolation, she would have made a big fuss about it, sobbing and writhing over the injury. But with so many different pains, it had all melted into one terrible agony.

Be careful now. Make sure you're going straight and not tilting off at an angle. Pick your next target in your straight line of sight.

The problem was that by now it was too dark to see much of anything. She could just make out deeply grooved bark straight ahead. A red oak probably. All right, go to it. Hop—*oh, it hurts*—hop—*the tears washing down her cheeks*—hop—*just a little farther*—hop—*you can make it*—hop. She put her hand out on shaggy bark. All right. Now, look straight in front of you. Ah. Something gray and rough and massive ahead—maybe a white oak. Hop to it—*agony*—hop—*somebody help me*—hop—*how long will it take?*—hop—*not that far now*—hop. *There.* She put her hand on the wide rough bark.

And then she did it again.

And again.

And again. And again. And again.

* * *

"What is it?" Damon demanded. He'd been forced to let Shinichi lead once they were out of the car again, but he still kept the kekkai loosely around him and he still watched every move the fox made. He didn't trust him as far as—well, the fact was, he didn't trust him at all. "What's behind the barrier?" he said again, more roughly, tightening the noose around the kitsune's neck.

"Our little cabin—Misao's and mine."

"And it wouldn't possibly be a trap, would it?"

"If you think so, fine! I'll go in alone. . . ." Shinichi had finally changed into a half-fox, half-human form: black hair to his waist, with ruby-colored flames licking up from the ends, one silky tail with the same coloration behind him waving behind him, and two silky, crimson-tipped twitching ears on top of his head.

Damon approved aesthetically, but more important, he now had a ready-made handle. He caught Shinichi by the tail and twisted.

"*Stop that!*"

"I'll stop it when I get Elena—unless you waylaid her deliberately. If she's hurt, I'm going to take whoever harmed her and cut him into slivers. His life is forfeit."

"No matter who it was?"

"No matter who."

Shinichi was quivering slightly.

"Are you cold?"

" . . . just . . . admiring your resolve." More inadvertent quivering. Almost shaking his entire body. *Laughter?*

"At Elena's discretion, I would keep them alive. But in agony." Damon twisted the tail harder. "Move!"

Shinichi took another step and a charming country cabin came into view, with a gravel path leading up between wild creepers that loaded the porch and hung down like pendants.

It was exquisite.

Even as the pain grew, Elena began to have hope. No matter how turned around she was, she *had* to come out of the forest at some point. She had to make it. The ground was solid—no sign of mushiness or slanting downward. She wasn't headed for the creek. She was headed for the road. She could tell.

She fixed her sights on a distant, smooth-barked tree. Then she hopped to it, the pain almost forgotten in her new feeling of certainty.

She fell against the massive, peeling, ash-gray tree. She was resting against it when something bothered her. Her dangling leg. Why wasn't it bumping painfully against the trunk? It had knocked continually against all the other trees when she turned to rest. She pulled back from the tree, and, as if she knew it were important, gathered all her Power and let it go in a burst of white light.

The tree with the huge hole in it, the tree she had started from, was in front of her.

For a moment Elena stood completely still, wasting Power, holding the light. Maybe it was some different . . .

No. She was on the other side of the tree, but it was the same one. That was *her* hair caught in the peeling gray bark. That dried blood was *her* handprint. Below it was where her bloody leg had left a mark—fresh.

She'd walked straight out and come straight back to this tree.

"*Noooooooooooooo!*"

It was the first vocalized sound she'd made since she'd fallen out of the Ferrari. She'd endured all that pain in silence, with little gasps or sharp breaths, but she'd never cursed and screamed. Now she wanted to do both.

Maybe it wasn't the same tree—

Nooooooo, nooooooo, noooooooooooo!

Maybe her Power would come back and she'd see that she'd only hallucinated—

No, no, no, no, no, no!

It just wasn't possible—

Nooooooo!

Her crutch slipped from under her arm. It had dug into her armpit so deeply that the pain there rivaled the other pains. Everything hurt. But worst was her mind. She had a picture in her mind of a sphere like the Christmas snow globes you shook to make snow or glitter fall through liquid. But this sphere had trees all over the inside. From top to bottom, side to side, all trees, all pointing toward the middle. And herself, wandering inside this lonely sphere . . . no matter where she went, she'd find more trees, because that was all there were in this world she'd stumbled into.

It was a nightmare, but something like it was real.

The trees were intelligent, too, she realized. The little creeping vines, the vegetation; even now it was pulling her crutch away from her. The crutch was moving as if being passed from hand to hand by very small people. She reached out and just barely grabbed the end of it.

She didn't remember having fallen to the ground, but here she was. And there was a smell, a sweet, earthy, resinous aroma. And here were creepers, testing her, tasting her. With delicate little touches, they wound into her hair so that she couldn't pick her head up. Then she could feel them tasting her body, her shoulder, her bloody knee. Nothing about it mattered.

She squeezed her eyes shut, her body heaving with sobs. The creepers were pulling at her wounded leg now, and instinctively she jerked away. For a moment the pain woke her up and she thought, *I've got to get to Matt*, but the next moment that thought was dulled, too. The sweet, resinous smell remained. The creepers felt their way across her moving chest, across her breasts. They encircled her stomach.

And then they began to tighten.

By the time Elena realized the danger, they were restricting her breathing. She couldn't expand her chest. As she let out her breath, they only tightened again, working together: all the little creepers like one giant anaconda.

She couldn't tear them away. They were tough and springy and her nails couldn't cut through them. Working her fingers under a handful, she pulled as hard as she could, scraping with her nails and twisting. Finally one fiber sprang loose with the sound of a harp's string breaking and a wild whipping in the air.

The rest of the creepers pulled tighter.

She was having to fight to get air now, fight not to contract her chest. Creepers were delicately touching her lips, swaying over her face like so many thin cobras, then suddenly striking and going taut around her cheek and head.

I'm going to die.

She felt a deep regret. She had been given the chance of a second lifetime—a third, if you counted her life as a vampire—and she hadn't done anything with it. Nothing but pursue her own pleasure. And now Fell's Church was in peril and Matt was in immediate danger, and not only was she not going to help them, she was going to give up and die right here.

What would be the right thing to do? The spiritual thing? Cooperate with evil now, and hope she'd have the chance to destroy it later? Maybe. Maybe all she needed to do was to ask for help.

The feeling of breathlessness was leaving her light-headed. She would never have believed it of Damon, that he would put her through all this, that he would allow her to be killed. Just days ago she had been defending him to Stefan.

Damon and the malach. Maybe she was his offering to them. They certainly demanded a lot.

Or maybe it was just that he wanted her to beg for help. He might be waiting in the darkness quite close, his mind centered on hers, waiting for a whispered *please*.

She tried to spark the last of her Power. It was almost depleted, but like a match, with repeated striking she managed to get a tiny white flame.

Now she visualized the flame going into her forehead. Into her head. Inside. There.

Now.

Through the fiery agony of not being able to draw a breath, she thought: *Bonnie. Bonnie. Hear me.*

No answer—but she wouldn't hear one.

Bonnie, Matt is in a clearing in a lane off the Old Wood. He may need blood or some other help. Look for him. In my car.

Don't worry about me. It's too late for me. Find Matt.

And that's all I can say, Elena thought wearily. She had a vague, sad intuition that she hadn't gotten Bonnie to hear her. Her lungs were exploding. This was a terrible way to die. She was going to be able to exhale one more time, and then there would be no more air. . . .

Damn you, Damon, she thought, and then she concentrated all her thoughts, all her mind's reach on memories of Stefan. On the feeling of being held by Stefan, on Stefan's sudden leaping smile, on Stefan's touch.

Green eyes, leaf green, a color like a leaf held up to sunlight . . .

The decency he had somehow managed to retain, untainted . . .

Stefan . . . I love you. . . .

I'll always love you. . . .

I've loved you. . . .

I love . . .

28

att had no idea what time it was, but it was deep dusk under the trees. He was lying sideways in Elena's new car, as if he'd been tossed in and forgotten. His entire body was in pain.

This time he awoke and immediately thought, Elena. But he couldn't see the white of her camisole anywhere, and when he called, first softly, then shouting, he got no answer.

So now he was feeling his way around the clearing, on hands and knees. Damon seemed to have gone and that gave him a spark of hope and courage that lit up his mind like a beacon. He found the discarded Pendleton shirt—considerably trampled. But when he couldn't find another soft warm body in the clearing, his heart crashed down somewhere around his boots.

And then he remembered the Jaguar. He fumbled frantically in one pocket for the keys, came up empty, and finally discovered, inexplicably, that they were in the ignition.

He lived through the agonizing moment when the car wouldn't start, and then was shocked to see the brightness of its headlights. He puzzled briefly about how to turn the car while making sure he wasn't running a limp Elena over, then dug through the glove compartment box, flinging out manuals and pairs of sunglasses. Ah, and one lapis lazuli ring. Someone was keeping a spare here, just in case. He put it on; it fit well enough.

At last his fingers closed over a flashlight, and he was free to search the clearing as thoroughly as he wanted to.

No Elena.

No Ferrari either.

Damon had taken her somewhere.

All right, then, he would track them. To do that he had to leave Elena's car behind, but he had already seen what these monsters could do to cars, so that wasn't saying much.

He would have to be careful with the flashlight, too. Who knew how much charge the batteries had left?

For the hell of it, he tried calling Bonnie's mobile phone, and then her home phone, and then the boardinghouse. No signal, even though according to the phone itself, there should have been. No need to question why, either—this was the Old Wood, messing with things as usual. He didn't even ask himself why it was Bonnie's number he called first, when Meredith would probably be more sensible.

He found the tracks of the Ferrari easily. Damon had sped out of here like a bat . . . Matt smiled grimly as he finished the sentence in his mind.

And then he'd driven as if to get out of the Old Wood. This was easy, it was clear that either Damon had been going too fast for proper control or that Elena had been fighting, because in a number of places, mainly around corners, the tire tracks showed up clearly against the soft ground beside the road.

Matt was especially careful not to step on anything that might be a clue. He might have to backtrack at some point. He was careful, too, to ignore the quiet noises of the night around him. He knew the malach were out there, but he refused to let himself think about them.

And he never even asked himself why he was doing this, deliberately going into danger instead of retreating from it, instead of trying to drive the Jaguar out of the Old Wood. After all, Stefan hadn't left *him* as bodyguard.

But then you couldn't trust anything that Damon might say, he thought.

And besides—well, he'd always kept one eye out for

Elena, even before their first date. He might be clumsy, slow, and weak in comparison to their enemies now, but he would always try.

It was pitch-dark now. The last remnants of twilight had left the sky, and if Matt looked up he could see clouds and stars—with trees leaning in ominously from either side.

He was getting toward the end of the road. The Dunstans' house should be coming up on the right pretty soon. He'd ask them if they'd seen—

Blood.

At first his mind flew to ridiculous alternatives, like dark red paint. But his flashlight had caught reddish brown stains on the roadside just as the road made a sharp curve. That was *blood* on the road there. And not just a little blood.

Being careful to walk well around the red-brown marks, running his flashlight over and over the far side of the road, Matt began to put together what must have happened.

Elena had jumped.

Either that or Damon had pushed her out of a speeding car—and after all the trouble he'd taken to get her, that didn't make much sense. Of course, he might have already bled her until he was satisfied—Matt's fingers went up to his sore neck instinctively—but then, why take her in the car at all?

To kill her by pushing her out?

A stupid way to do it, but maybe Damon had been counting on his little pets to take care of the body.

Possible, but not very likely.

What *was* likely?

Well, the Dunstans' house was coming up on this side of the road, but you couldn't see it from here. And it would be just like Elena to jump out of a speeding car as it rounded a sharp corner. It would take brains, and guts, and a breathtaking trust in sheer luck that it wouldn't kill her.

Matt's flashlight slowly traced the devastation of a long hedge of rhododendron bushes just off the road.

My God, that's what she did. Yeah. She jumped out and tried to roll. Jeez, she was lucky not to break her neck. But she kept rolling, grabbing at roots and creepers to stop herself. That's why they're all torn up.

A bubble of elation was rising in Matt. He was doing it. He was tracking Elena. He could see her fall as clearly as if he'd been there.

But then she got flipped by that tree root, he thought as he continued to follow her trail. That would have hurt. And she'd slammed down and rolled on the concrete for a bit—that must have been agony; she'd left a lot of blood here, and then back into the bushes.

And then what? The rhododendron showed no more

signs of her fall. What had happened here? Had Damon reversed the Ferrari fast enough and gotten her back?

No, Matt decided, examining the earth carefully. There was only one set of footprints here, and it was Elena's. Elena had gotten up here—only to fall down again, probably from injury. And then she'd managed to get up again, but the marks were weird, a normal footprint on one side and a deep but small indentation on the other.

A crutch. She found herself a crutch. Yeah, and that dragging mark was the mark of her bad foot. She walked up to this tree, and then around it—or hopped, actually, that's what it looked like. And then she'd headed for the Dunstans'.

Smart girl. She was probably unrecognizable by now, and anyway, who cared if they noticed the resemblance between her and the late, great Elena Gilbert? She could be Elena's cousin from Philadelphia.

So she'd gone, one, two, three . . . eight steps—and there was the Dunstan house. Matt could see lights. Matt could smell horses. Excitedly, he ran the rest of the way—taking a few falls that didn't do his aching body any good, but still heading straight for the back porch light. The Dunstans weren't front porch people.

When he got to the door, he pounded on it almost frenziedly. He'd found her. He'd found Elena!

It seemed a long time before the door opened a crack.

Matt automatically wedged his foot in the crack while thinking, Yes, good, you're cautious people. Not the type to let a vampire in after you'd just seen a girl covered in blood.

"Yes? What do you want?"

"It's me, Matt Honeycutt," he said to the eye that he could see peering out of the slit of open door. "I've come for El—for the girl."

"What girl are you talking about?" the voice said gruffly.

"Look, you don't have to worry. It's me—Jake knows me from school. And Kristin knows me, too. I've come to help."

Something in the sincerity of his voice seemed to strike a chord in the person behind the door. It was opened to reveal a large, dark-haired man who was wearing an undershirt and needed a shave. Behind him, in the living room was a tall, thin, almost gaunt woman. She looked as if she had been crying. Behind both of them was Jake, who'd been a year senior to Matt at Robert E. Lee High.

"Jake," Matt said. But he got no answer back except a dull look of anguish.

"*What's wrong?*" Matt demanded, terrified. "A girl came by here a while ago—she was hurt—but—but—you let her in, right?"

"No girl's come by here," said Mr. Dunstan flatly.

"She had to have. I followed her trail—she left a trail

in *blood*, do you understand, almost up to your *door*." Matt wasn't letting himself think. Somehow, if he kept telling the facts loudly enough, they would produce Elena.

"More trouble," Jake said, but in a dull voice that went with his expression.

Mrs. Dunstan seemed the most sympathetic. "We heard a voice out in the night, but when we looked, there was no one there. And we have troubles of our own."

It was then, right on cue, that Kristin burst into the room. Matt stared at her with a feeling of déjà vu. She was dressed up something like Tami Bryce. She had cut off the bottoms of her jeans shorts until they were practically nonexistent. On top she was wearing a bikini top, but with—Matt hastily turned his eyes away—two big round holes cut just where Tami had had round pieces of cardboard. And she'd decorated herself with glitter glue.

God! She's only, what, twelve? Thirteen? How could she possibly be acting this way?

But the next moment, his whole body was vibrating in shock. Kristin had pasted herself against him and was cooing, "Matt Honey-butt! You came to see me!"

Matt breathed carefully to get over his shock. *Matt Honey-butt*. She couldn't know that. She didn't even go to the same school as Tami did. Why would Tami have called her and—told her something like that?

He shook his head, as if to clear it. Then he looked at

Mrs. Dunstan, who had seemed kindest. "Can I use your phone?" he asked. "I need—I *really need* to make a couple of calls."

"The phone's been down since yesterday," Mr. Dunstan said harshly. He didn't try to move Kristin away from Matt, which was odd because he was clearly angry. "Probably a fallen tree. And you know mobile phones don't work out here."

"But—" Matt's mind spun into overdrive. "You really mean that no teenage girl came up to your house asking for help? A girl with blond hair and blue eyes? I swear, I'm not the one who hurt her. I swear I want to help her."

"Matt Honey-butt? I'm making a tattoo, just for you." Still pressed up behind him, Kristin extended her left arm. Matt stared at it, horrified. She had obviously used needles or a pin to prick holes in her left forearm, and then opened a fountain pen's cartridge of ink to supply the dark blue color. It was your basic prison-type tattoo, done by a child. The straggling letters M A T were already visible, along with a smudge of ink that was probably going to be another T.

No wonder they weren't thrilled about letting me in, Matt thought, dazed. Now Kristin had both arms around his waist, making it hard to breathe. She was on tiptoe, talking to him, whispering rapidly some of the obscene things Tami had said.

He stared at Mrs. Dunstan. "Honest, I haven't even seen Kristin for—it must be nearly a year. We had an end of the year carnival, and Kristin helped with the pony rides, but . . ."

Mrs. Dunstan was nodding slowly. "It's not your fault. She's been acting the same way with Jake. Her own brother. And with—with her father. But I'm telling *you* the truth; we haven't seen any other girl. No one but you has come to the door today."

"Okay." Matt's eyes were watering. His brain, attuned first of all to his own survival, was telling him to save his breath, not to argue. Telling him to say, "Kristin—I really can't breathe—"

"But I *love* you, Matt Honey-butt. I don't want you to *ever* leave me. Especially for that old whore. That old whore with worms in her eye-sockets . . ."

Again Matt felt the sense of the world rocking. But he couldn't gasp. He didn't have the air. Pop-eyed, he turned helplessly toward Mr. Dunstan, who was closest.

"Can't—breathe—"

How could a thirteen-year-old be so strong? It was taking both Mr. Dunstan and Jake to pry her off him. No, even that wasn't working. He was beginning to see a gray network pulsating before his eyes. He needed air.

There was a sharp crack that ended with a meaty sound.

And then another. Suddenly he could breathe again.

"No, Jacob! No more!" Mrs. Dunstan cried. "She let him go—don't hit her anymore!"

When Matt's vision cleared, Mr. Dunstan was doing up his belt. Kristin was wailing, "Just you *waaa*-hate! Just you *waa-haate!* You'll be *sor*-ry!" Then she rushed from the room.

"I don't know if this helps or makes it worse," Matt said when he'd gotten his breath back, "but Kristin isn't the only girl acting this way. There's at least one other one in the town—"

"All I care about is my Kristin," Mrs. Dunstan said. "And that . . . *thing* isn't her."

Matt nodded. But there was something he needed to do now. He had to find Elena.

"If a blond girl does come to the door and asks for help, will you please let her in?" he asked Mrs. Dunstan. "Please? But don't let any guys in—not even me if you don't want," he blurted.

For a moment his eyes and Mrs. Dunstan's eyes met, and he felt a connection. Then she nodded and hastened to get him out of the house.

All right, Matt thought. Elena was headed for here, but she didn't quite get here. So look at the signs.

He looked. And what the signs showed him was that, within a few feet of the Dunstan property, she had inexplicably turned sharply right, deeply into the forest.

Why? Had something scared her? Or had she—Matt felt sick to his stomach—somehow been tricked into hobbling on and on, until at last she left all human help behind?

All he could do was to follow her into the woods.

29

"Elena!"

Something was bothering her.

"Elena!"

Please, no more pain. She couldn't feel it right now, but she could remember . . . oh, no more fighting for air . . .

"*Elena!*"

No . . . just let it be. Mentally, Elena pushed away the thing that bothered her ears and her head.

"*Elena, please . . .*"

All she wanted was sleep. Forever.

"*Damn you*, Shinichi!"

Damon had picked up the snow globe with the miniature forest when Shinichi found Elena's smudged glow radiating from it. Inside it, dozens of spruce, hickory, pine, and other trees grew—all from a perfectly transparent inner membrane. A miniature person—given that someone could be miniaturized and placed into such a globe, would see trees ahead, trees behind, trees in every direction—and could walk a straight line and come back to their starting point no matter which way they went.

"It's an amusement," Shinichi had said sullenly, watching him intently from under his lashes. "A toy, for children, usually. A play-trap."

"And you find *this* amusing?" Damon had smashed the globe against the driftwood coffee table in the exquisite cabin which was Shinichi's secret hideout. That was when he had discovered why these were games for children— the globe was unbreakable.

After that Damon had taken a moment—just one moment—to get hold of himself. Elena had perhaps seconds to live. He needed to be precise with his words.

After that single moment, a long flow of words had spilled out from his lips, mostly in English, and mostly without unnecessary curses or even insults. He didn't care about insulting Shinichi. He had simply threatened—no, he had *sworn*—to carry out on Shinichi the kind of violence that he had seen sometimes in a long life filled with humans and vampires with skewed imaginations. Eventually, it had gotten through to Shinichi that he was serious, and Damon had found himself inside the globe with a drenched Elena in front of him. She was lying at his feet, and she was worse off than his worst fears had allowed him to picture. She had a dislocated right arm with multiple fractures and a hideously shattered left tibia.

Horrified as he had been to imagine her staggering through the forest of the globe, blood streaming from her right arm from shoulder to elbow, left leg dragging behind her like a wounded animal's, this was worse. Her hair had been soaking with sweat and mud, straggling over her face. And she'd been out of her mind, literally, delirious, talking to people who weren't there.

And she was turning blue.

She had been able to snap exactly one creeper with all her effort. Damon clawed up huge armfuls of them, ripping them from the earth viciously if they tried to fight or wrap around his wrists. Elena gasped in one deep breath just as suffocation would have killed her, but she didn't regain consciousness.

And she wasn't the Elena he remembered. When he'd picked her up, he'd felt no resistance, no acceptance, nothing. She didn't know him. She was delirious with fever, exhaustion, and pain, but in one moment of half-consciousness had kissed his hand through her damp, disheveled hair, whispering "Matt . . . Find . . . Matt." She didn't know who he was—she scarcely knew who *she* was, but her concern was for her friend. The kiss had gone through his hand and up his arm like the touch of a branding iron, and since then he'd been monitoring her mind, trying to divert the agony she was feeling away— away anywhere—into the night—into himself.

He turned back to Shinichi and, in a voice like an icy wind, said, "You'd better have a way to cure all her wounds—now."

The charming cabin was surrounded by the same evergreens, hickory, and pines as grew in the snow globe. The fire burned violet and green as Shinichi poked it.

"This water is just about ready to boil. Make her drink tea made with this." He handed Damon a blackened flagon—once beautiful chased silver; now a battered remnant of what it had been—and a teapot with some broken leaves and other unsavory-looking things at the bottom. "Make sure she drinks a good three quarters of a cup, and she'll fall asleep and wake up almost as good as new."

He dug an elbow into Damon's ribs. "Or you can just let her have a few sips—heal her partway, and then let her know it's in your power to give her more . . . or not. You know . . . depending on how cooperative she is . . ."

Damon remained silent and turned away. If I have to look at him, he thought, I'll kill him. And I might need him again.

"And if you really want to accelerate the healing, add some of your blood. Some people like to do it that way," Shinichi added, his voice picking up speed with excitement again. "See how much pain a human can take, you know, and then when they're dying, you can just feed them tea and blood and start over . . . if they remember you from last time—which they hardly ever do; they'll usually go through more pain just to get a chance to fight you . . . ," he giggled, and Damon thought he sounded not quite sane.

But when he had suddenly turned to Shinichi, he had to hold himself very still inside. Shinichi had become a blazing, glowing, outline of himself, with tongues of light lapping from his projection, rather like close-up solar flares. Damon was nearly blinded, and knew he was meant to be. He clutched the silver flagon as if he were holding on to his own sanity.

Maybe he was. He had a blank space in his mind— and then there were suddenly memories of trying to find Elena . . . or Shinichi. Because Elena had abruptly been absent from his company, and it could only be the fault of the kitsune.

"There's a modern bathroom here?" Damon asked Shinichi.

"There's whatever you want; just decide before you open a door and unlock it with this key. And now . . ."

Shinichi stretched, his golden eyes half shut. He ran a languid hand through his shiny black hair tipped with flame. "Now, I think I'll go sleep under a bush."

"Is that all you ever do?" Damon made no attempt to keep the biting sarcasm out of his voice.

"And have fun with Misao. And fight. And go to the tournaments. They—well, you'll have to come and see one for yourself."

"I don't care to go anywhere." Damon didn't want to know what this fox and his sister considered fun.

Shinichi reached out and took the miniature cauldron full of boiling water off the fire. He poured the boiling water over the collection of tree bark, leaves, and other detritus in the battered metal teapot.

"Why don't you go find a bush *now*?" Damon said— and it wasn't a suggestion. He'd had enough of the fox, who had served his purpose now anyway, and he didn't care a bit about whatever mischief Shinichi might make for other people. All he wanted was to be alone—with Elena.

"Remember; get her to drink it all if you want to keep her for a while. She's pretty much unsalvageable without it." Shinichi poured through a fine sieve the infusion of dark green tea. "Better try before she wakes up."

"Will you just *get out of here*?"

* * *

When Shinichi stepped through the dimensional crack, taking care to turn just the right way so as to reach the real world, and not some other globe, he was steaming. He wanted to go back and thrash Damon within an inch of his life. He wanted to activate the malach inside Damon and cause him to . . . well, of course, not *quite* kill sweet Elena. She was a blossom with nectar untasted, and Shinichi was in no hurry to see her buried underground.

But as for the rest of the idea . . . yes, he decided. Now he knew what he would do. It would be simply delicious to watch Damon and Elena make up, and then, during the Moonspire Festival tonight, to bring back the monster. He could let Damon go on believing they were "allies," and then, in the middle of their little spree—let the possessed Damon loose. Show that he, Shinichi, had been in control all along.

He would punish Elena in ways she had never dreamed about and she would die in delicious agony . . . at Damon's hand. Shinichi's tails quivered a little ecstatically at the thought. But for now, let them laugh and joke together. Revenge only ripened with time, and Damon was really quite difficult to control when he was raging.

It hurt to admit that, just as his tail—the physical one in the center—hurt from Damon's abominable cruelty to animals. When Damon was in a passion it took every ounce of Shinichi's concentration to control him.

But at Moonspire Damon would be calm, would be placid. He'd be pleased with himself, as he and Elena would undoubtedly have laid some absurd plot to try to stop Shinichi.

That would be when the fun would begin.

Elena would make a beautiful slave while she lasted.

With the kitsune gone, Damon felt that he could behave more naturally. Keeping a firm grasp on Elena's mind, he picked up the cup. He tried a sip of the mixture himself before trying it on her and found it tasted just slightly less nauseating than it smelled. However, Elena really had no choice, she could not do anything of her own volition, and little by little, the mixture went down.

And then a dose of his blood went down. Again, Elena was unconscious and had no choice in the matter.

And then she'd gone to sleep by herself.

Damon paced restlessly. He had a memory that was more like a dream floating around in his head. It was of Elena trying to throw herself out of a Ferrari going about 100 kilometers an hour, to get away from—what?

Him?

Why?

Not, in any case, the best of beginnings.

But that was *all* he could remember! Damn it! Whatever came right before it was a total blank. Had he hurt Stefan?

No, Stefan was gone. It had been the other boy with her, Mutt. *What had happened?*

Damn it to *hell*! He had to figure out what had happened so he could explain it all to Elena when she woke up. He wanted her to believe him, to trust him. He didn't want Elena as a one-night bleeder. He wanted her to *choose* him. He wanted her to see how much better suited she was to him than to his mousy, milksop brother.

His princess of darkness. That was what she was *meant* to be. With him as king, consort, whatever she wished. When she saw things more clearly, she would understand that it didn't matter. That nothing mattered except them being together.

He viewed her body, veiled under the sheet, with dispassion—no, with positive *guilt. Dio mio*—what if he hadn't found her? He couldn't get the picture out of his mind of how she'd looked, stumbling forward like that . . . lying there breathless . . . kissing his hand . . .

Damon sat down and pinched the bridge of his nose. Why had she been in the Ferrari with him? She'd been angry—no, not angry. Furious was closer but so frightened . . . of *him*. He could picture that clearly now, the moment of her throwing herself out of the speeding car, but he couldn't remember anything before it.

Was he going out of his mind?

What had been done to her? No . . . Damon forced his

thoughts away from the easy question and made himself ask the *real* question. What had *he* done to her? Elena's eyes, blue with golden flecks, like lapis lazuli, were easy to read even without telepathy. What had . . . *he* . . . done to her that was so frightening that she would jump out of a speeding car to get away from him?

He'd been taunting the fair-haired boy. Mutt . . . Gnat . . . whatever. The three of them had been together, and he and Elena had been . . . damn! From there to his awakening at the steering wheel of the Ferrari, all was a shimmering blank. He could remember saving Bonnie at Caroline's house; he could remember being late for his 4:44 A.M. meeting with Stefan; but after that, things began to fragment. *Shinichi, maledicalo!* That fox! He knew more about this than he was telling Damon.

I have always . . . been stronger . . . than my enemies, he thought. I have always . . . remained . . . in . . . control.

He heard a slight sound and was by Elena in an instant. Her blue eyes were shut, but the lashes were fluttering. Was she waking up?

He made himself turn down the sheet by her shoulder. Shinichi had been right. There was a lot of dried blood, but he could sense that the blood flow itself was more normal. But there was something horribly wrong . . . no, he wouldn't believe it.

Damon barely kept himself from screaming in

frustration. The damn fox had left her with a dislocated shoulder.

Things were definitely not going well for him today.

Now what? Call for Shinichi?

Never. He felt he couldn't look at the fox again tonight without wanting to murder him.

He was going to have to put her shoulder back in the socket alone. It was a procedure usually only attempted by two people, but what could he do?

Still keeping Elena in an iron mind-grip, making sure she *couldn't* awaken, he grasped her by the arm and began the painful business of dislocating the humerus even farther, pulling the bone away so that he could finally release pressure and hear the sweet *pop* that meant that the long arm bone had slipped back into the socket. Then he let go. Elena's head was tossing from side to side, her lips parched. He poured some more of Shinichi's magical bone-knitting tea into the battered cup, then lifted her head gently from the left side to put the cup to her lips. He let her mind have some freedom, then, and she started to lift her right hand and then dropped it.

He sighed and tilted her head, tipping the silver flagon so that the tea trickled into her mouth. She swallowed obediently. It all reminded him of Bonnie . . . but Bonnie hadn't been so terribly hurt. Damon knew he couldn't return Elena to her friends in this condition; not with her camisole and jeans shredded, and dried blood everywhere.

Maybe he could do something about that. He went to the second door off the bedroom, thought, *bathroom— modern bathroom*, and unlocked and opened the door. It was exactly what he'd imagined: a pristine, white, sanitary place with a large heap of towels piled, ready for guests, on the bathtub.

Damon ran warm water over one of the washcloths. He knew better by now than to strip Elena and dump her in warm water. It was what she needed, but if anyone ever found out, her friends would have his beating heart torn out of his chest and staked on a pike. He didn't even have to think about that—he simply knew it.

He went back to Elena and began to gently stroke dried blood off her shoulder. She murmured, shaking her head, but he kept it up until the shoulder at least looked normal, exposed as it was by torn cloth.

Then he got another washcloth and went to work on her ankle. This was still swollen—she wasn't going to be running away anytime soon. Her tibia, the first of the two bones in the lower leg, had grown properly together again. It was more evidence that Shinichi and the *Shi no Shi* had no need for money, or they could simply put this tea on the market and make a fortune.

"We look at things . . . differently," Shinichi had said,

fixing Damon with those strange golden eyes. "Money doesn't mean much to us. What does? The deathbed agonies of an old rogue who fears he's going to hell. Watching him sweat, trying to remember encounters he's long forgotten. A baby's first conscious tear of loneliness. The emotions of an unfaithful wife when her husband catches her with her lover. A maiden's . . . well, her first kiss and her first night of discovery. A brother willing to die for his brother. Things like that."

And many other things that couldn't be mentioned in polite company, Damon thought. A lot were about pain. They were emotional leeches, sucking up the feelings of mortals to make up for the emptiness of their own souls.

He could feel the sickness inside him again as he tried to imagine—to calculate—the pain Elena must have felt, leaping out of his car. She must have expected an agonizing death—but it was still better than staying with him.

This time, before entering the door that had been a white-tiled bathroom, he thought, *Kitchen, modern, with plenty of ice packs in the freezer.*

Nor was he disappointed. He found himself in a strongly masculine kitchen, with chrome appliances and black-and-white tiling. In the freezer: six ice packs. He took three back to Elena and put one around her shoulder, one at her elbow, and one around her ankle. Then he went back into the kitchen's spotless beauty for a glass of ice-cold water.

Tired. So tired.

Elena felt as if her body were weighted with lead.

Every limb . . . every thought . . . lapped in lead.

For instance, there was something she was supposed to be doing—or not doing—right now. But she couldn't make the thought come to the surface of her mind. It was too heavy. Everything was too heavy. She couldn't even open her eyes.

A scraping sound. Someone was near, on a chair. Then there was liquid coolness on her lips, just a few drops, but it stimulated her to try to hold the cup herself and drink. Oh, delicious water. It tasted better than anything she'd ever had before. Her shoulder hurt terribly, but it was worth the pain to drink and drink—no! The glass was being pulled away. She tried, feebly, to hang onto it, but it was pulled out of her grasp.

Then she tried to touch her shoulder, but those gentle, invisible hands wouldn't let her, not until they had washed her own hands with warm water. After that they packed the ice packs around her and wrapped her like a mummy in a sheet. The cold numbed her immediate feelings of pain, although there were other pains, deep inside. . . .

It was all too difficult to think about. As the hands

removed the ice packs again—she was shivering with cold now—she let herself lapse back into sleep.

Damon treated Elena and dozed, treated and dozed. In the perfectly appointed bathroom, he found a tortoiseshell hairbrush and a comb. They looked serviceable. And one thing he knew for certain: Elena's hair had never looked like this in her life—or unlife. He tried to stroke the brush gently through her hair and found that the tangles were much harder to get out than he'd imagined. When he pulled harder on the brush, she moved and murmured in that strange sleep-language of hers.

And, finally, it was the hair brushing that did it. Elena, without opening her eyes, reached up and took the brush from his hand and then, when it hit a major tangle, frowned, reached up to grasp a fistful and try to get the brush through it. Damon sympathized. He'd had long hair at times during his centuries of existence—when it couldn't be helped, and though his hair was as naturally fine as Elena's, he knew the frustrated feeling that you were ripping your hair out by the roots. Damon was about to take the brush from her again, when she opened her eyes.

"What—?" she said, and then she blinked.

Damon had tensed, ready to push her into mental blackout if it were necessary. But she didn't even try to hit him with the brush.

"What . . . happened?" What Elena was feeling was clear: she didn't like this. She was unhappy about another awakening with only a vague idea of what had been going on when she slept.

As Damon, poised for fight or flight, watched her face, she slowly began to put together what had happened to her.

"Damon?" She gave him that no-holds-barred lapis gaze.

It said, *Am I being tortured, or treated, or are you just an interested bystander, enjoying somebody's pain while drinking a glass of cognac?*

"They *cook* with cognac, princess. They *drink* Armagnac. And I don't drink . . . either," Damon said. He spoiled the entire effect by adding hastily, "That's not a threat. I swear to you, Stefan left me as your bodyguard."

This was technically true if you considered the facts: Stefan had yelled, "You'd better make sure nothing happens to Elena, you double-dealing bastard, or I'm going to find a way to come back and rip off your—" The rest had been muffled in the fight, but Damon had gotten the gist. And now he took the assignment seriously.

"Nothing else will hurt you, if you'll allow me to watch over you," he added, now getting into the area of the fictitious, since whoever had frightened or pulled her out of the car had obviously been around when he had. But nothing would get her in the future, he swore to himself. However he had blundered this last time, from now on there would be no further attacks on Elena Gilbert—or someone would die.

He wasn't trying to spy on her thoughts, but as she stared into his eyes for a long moment, they projected with total clarity—and utter mystery—the words: I knew I was right. It was someone else all along. And he knew that under her pain, Elena felt a huge sense of satisfaction.

"I hurt my shoulder." She reached up with her right hand to grip it, but Damon stopped her.

"You dislocated it," Damon said. "It's going to hurt for a while."

"And my ankle . . . but someone . . . I remember being in the woods and looking up and it was *you*. I couldn't breathe but you tore the creepers off me and you picked me up in your arms. . . ." She looked at Damon in bewilderment. "*You* saved me?"

The statement had the sound of a question, but it wasn't. She was wondering over something that seemed impossible. Then she began to cry.

A baby's first conscious tear of loneliness. The emotions of an unfaithful wife when her husband catches her with her lover . . .

And maybe a young girl's weeping when she believes that her enemy has saved her from death.

Damon ground his teeth in frustration. The thought

that Shinichi might be watching this, feeling Elena's emotions, savoring them . . . it was impossible to bear. Shinichi would give Elena her memory back again, he was certain of that. But at a time and place most amusing to him.

"It was my job," he said tightly. "I'd sworn to do it."

"Thank you," Elena gasped between her sobs. "No, please—don't turn away. I really mean it. Ohhh—is there a box of tissues—or anything *dry*?" Her body was heaving with sobs again.

The perfect bathroom had a box of tissues. Damon brought it back to Elena.

He looked away as she used them, blowing her nose again and again as she sobbed. Here there was no enchanted and enchanting spirit, no grim and sophisticated fighter of evil, no dangerous coquette. There was only a girl broken by pain, gasping like a wounded doe, sobbing like a child.

And undoubtedly his brother would know what to say to her. He, Damon, had no idea of what to do—except that he knew he was going to kill for this. Shinichi would learn what it meant to tangle with Damon when Elena was involved.

"How do you feel?" he asked brusquely. No one would be able to say he'd taken advantage of this—no one would be able to say he'd hurt her only to . . . to make use of her.

"You gave me your blood," Elena said wonderingly,

and as he looked quickly down at his rolled-up sleeve, she added, "No—it's just a feeling I know. When I first—came back to Earth, after the spirit life. Stefan would give me his blood, and eventually I would feel . . . this way. Very warm. A little uncomfortable."

He swung around and looked at her. "Uncomfortable?"

"Too full—here." She touched her neck. "We think it's a symbiotic thing . . . for vampires and humans who live together."

"For a vampire Changing a human into a vampire, you mean," he said sharply.

"Except I didn't Change when I was part spirit still. But then—I turned back human." She hiccupped, tried a pathetic smile, and used the brush again. "I'd ask you to look at me and see that I haven't Changed, but . . ." She made a helpless little motion.

Damon sat and imagined what it would have been like, taking care of the spirit-child Elena. It was a tantalizing idea.

He said bluntly, "When you said you were a little uncomfortable before, did you mean that *I* should take some of your blood?"

She half glanced away, then looked back. "I told you I was grateful. I told you that I felt . . . too full. I don't know how *else* to thank you."

Damon had had centuries of training in discipline or he would have thrown something across the room. It was a situation to make you laugh . . . or weep. She was offering herself to him as thanks for rescue from suffering that he should have saved her from, and had failed.

But he was no hero. He wasn't like St. Stefan, to refuse this ultimate of prizes; whatever condition she was in.

He wanted her.

att had given up on clues. As far as he could tell, something had caused Elena to bypass the Dunstan house and barn completely, hopping on and on until she got to a squashed and torn bed of thin creeping vines. They hung limp from Matt's fingers, but they reminded him, disquietingly, of the feeling of the bug's tentacles around his neck.

And from there on there was no sign of human movement. It was as if a UFO had beamed her up.

Now, from making forays to all sides until he had lost the patch of creepers, he was lost in the deep Wood. If he wanted to, he could fantasize that all sorts of noises were all around him. If he wanted to, he could imagine that the light of the flashlight was no longer as bright as it had been, that it had a sickly yellowish tinge. . . .

All this time, while searching, he had kept as quiet as possible, realizing that he might be trying to sneak up on something that didn't want to be snuck up on. But now, somewhere inside him, something was swelling up and his ability to stop it was weakening by the second.

When it burst out of him, it startled him as much as it might have any possible listeners.

"Ellleeeeeeeeeeeeeeeenaaaa!"

From the time when he'd been a child, Matt had been taught to say his nighttime prayers. He didn't know much else about church, but he did have a deep and sincere feeling that there was Someone or Something out there that looked after people. That somewhere and somehow it all made sense, and that there were reasons for everything.

That belief had been severely tested during the past year.

But Elena's return from the dead had swept away all his doubts. It had seemed to prove everything that he'd always wanted to believe in.

You wouldn't give her back to us for just a few days, and then take her away again? he wondered, and the wondering was really a form of praying. You wouldn't— would You?

Because the thought of a world without Elena, without her *sparkle*; her strong will; her way of getting into crazy adventures—and then getting out of them, even more crazily—well, it was too much to lose. The world would be painted in drab grays and dark browns again without her. There would be no fire-engine reds, no flashes of parakeet green, no cerulean, no daffodil, no mercury silver—and no gold. No sprinkles of gold in endless blue lapis lazuli eyes.

"Elllleeeeeeenaaaa! Damn you, you answer me! It's Matt, Elena! Elleeeeee—"

He broke off quite suddenly and listened. For a moment his heart leaped and his whole body started. But then he made out the words he could hear.

"Eleeeeeenaaa? Maaaatt? Where are you?"

"Bonnie? *Bonnie! I'm here!*" He turned his flashlight straight up, slowly twisting it in a circle. "Can you see me?"

"Can you see us?"

Matt pivoted slowly. And—yes—there were the beams of one flashlight, two flashlights, three!

His heart leaped to see *three* beams. "I'm coming toward you," he shouted, and suited the action to the word. Secrecy had been long ago left behind. He was running into things, yanking at tendrils that tried to grab his ankles, but bellowing all the while, "Stay where you are! I'm coming to you!"

And then the flashlight beams were right in front of him, blinding him, and somehow he had Bonnie in his arms, and Bonnie was crying. That at least lent the situation some normality. Bonnie was crying against his chest and he was looking at Meredith, who was smiling anxiously, and at . . . Mrs. Flowers? It had to be, she was wearing that gardening hat with the artificial flowers on it, as well as what looked like about seven or eight woolly sweaters.

"Mrs. Flowers?" he said, his mouth finally catching up with his brain. "But—where's Elena?"

There was a sudden droop in the three people watching him, as if they had been on tiptoes for news, and now they had slumped in disappointment.

"We haven't seen her," Meredith said quietly. "*You* were with her."

"I *was* with her, yeah. But then Damon came. *He hurt her*, Meredith"—Matt felt Bonnie's arms clench on him. "He had her rolling on the ground having seizures. I think he's going to kill her. And—he hurt me. I guess I blacked out. When I woke up she was gone."

"He took her away?" Bonnie asked fiercely.

"Yeah, but . . . I don't understand what happened next." Painfully, he explained about Elena seemingly jumping out of the car and the tracks that led nowhere.

Bonnie shivered in his arms.

"And then some other weird stuff happened," Matt said. Slowly, faltering sometimes, he did his best to explain about Kristin, and the similarities to Tami.

"That is . . . just plain weird," Bonnie said. "I thought I had an answer, but if Kristin hasn't had any contact with any of the other girls . . ."

"You were probably thinking something about the Salem witches, dear," said Mrs. Flowers. Matt still couldn't get used to Mrs. Flowers *talking* to them. She went on, "But you don't really know with whom Kristin has been in the last few days. Or with whom Jim has been, for that matter. Children have quite a lot of freedom in this day and age, and he might be—what do they call it?—a *carrier*."

"Besides, even if this is possession, it may be an entirely different kind of possession," Meredith said. "Kristin lives out in the Old Wood. The Old Wood is full of these insects—these malach. Who knows whether it happened when she simply stepped outside her door? Who knows what was waiting for her?"

Now Bonnie was shaking in Matt's arms. They'd turned out all the flashlights but one, to conserve energy, but it sure made for spooky surroundings.

"But what about the telepathy?" Matt said to Mrs. Flowers. "I mean, I don't believe for a minute that *real* witches were attacking those Salem girls. I think they were repressed girls who had mass hysteria when they all got together, and somehow everything got out of hand. But how could Kristin know to call me—to call me—the same name that Tamra did?"

"Maybe we've all got it all wrong," Bonnie said, her voice buried somewhere in Matt's solar plexus. "Maybe it's not like Salem at all, where the—the hysteria spread out horizontally, if you see what I mean. Maybe there's somebody on top here, who's spreading it wherever they want to."

There was a brief silence, and then Mrs. Flowers murmured, "'Out of the mouths of babes and sucklings . . .'"

"You mean you think that's right? But then who is it that's on top? Who's doing all of this?" Meredith demanded. "It can't be Damon because Damon saved Bonnie twice— and me once." Before anyone could muster words to ask about *that*, she was going on. "Elena was pretty sure that something was possessing *Damon*. So who else is it?"

"Somebody we haven't met yet," Bonnie muttered ominously. "Somebody we aren't going to like."

With perfect timing there was the crackle of a branch behind them. As one person, as one body, they turned to look.

"What I really want," Damon said to Elena, "is to get you warm. And that either means cooking you something hot so you'll warm up from the inside or putting you in the tub so you'll warm up from the outside. And considering what happened last time—"

"I . . . don't feel I can eat anything. . . ."

"Come on, it's an American tradition. Apple soup? Mom's homemade chicken pie?"

She chuckled in spite of herself, then winced. "It's apple pie and Mom's homemade chicken soup. But you didn't do badly, for a start."

"Well? I promise not to mix the apples and the chicken together."

"I could try some soup," Elena said slowly. "And, oh, Damon I'm so thirsty just for plain water. Please."

"I know, but you'll drink too much, get pains. I'll make soup."

"It comes in little cans with red paper on them. You pull the tab on top to make it come off . . . ." Elena stopped as he turned to the door.

Damon knew she had serious doubts about the entire project, but he also knew that if he brought her anything passably drinkable she would drink it. Thirst did that to you.

He was unliving proof of the example.

As he went through the door there was a sudden horrendous noise, like a pair of kitchen choppers coming together. It nearly took off his—his rear from top to bottom, by the sound of it.

"*Damon!*" A voice crying weakly through the door. "Damon, are you all right? Damon! Answer me!"

Instead, he turned around, studied the door, which

looked perfectly normal, and opened it. Anyone watching him open it would have wondered because he put a key in the unlocked door, said "Elena's room" and then unlocked and opened the door.

When he got inside, he ran.

Elena was lying in a hopeless tangle of sheets and blankets on the floor. She was trying to get up, but her face was blue-white with pain.

"What pushed you off the bed?" he said. He was going to kill Shinichi *slowly*.

"Nothing. I heard a terrible sound just as the door shut. I tried to get to you, but—"

Damon stared at her. *"I tried to get to you, but—"* This broken, hurting, exhausted creature had tried to rescue *him*? Tried so hard that she'd fallen off her bed?

"I'm sorry," she said, with tears in her eyes. "I can't get used to gravity. Are you hurt?"

"Not as much as you are," he said, purposely keeping his voice rough, his eyes averted. "I did something stupid, leaving the room, and the house . . . reminded me."

"What are you talking about?" said the woebegone Elena, dressed only in sheets.

"This key," Damon held it up for her to see. It was golden and could be worn as a ring, but two wings folded out and made a beautiful key.

"What's wrong with it?"

"The way I used it. This key has the power of the kit-sune in it, and it will unlock anything and take you any-where, but the way it works is that you put it into the lock, say where you want to go, and then turn the key. I forgot to do that in leaving your room."

Elena looked puzzled. "But what if a key doesn't have a lock in it? Most bedroom doors don't have locks."

"This key goes into any door. You might say it makes its own lock. It's a kitsune treasure—which I shook out of Shinichi when I was so angry about you being hurt. He'll be wanting it back soon." Damon's eyes narrowed and he smiled faintly. "I wonder which of us will end up keep-ing it. I noticed another one in the kitchen—a spare, of course."

"Damon, all this about magical keys is interesting, but if you could let me get off the floor . . ."

He was contrite at once. Then came the question of whether to put her on the bed or not.

"I'll take the bath," Elena said in a small voice. She unsnapped the top of her jeans and tried to scoot out of them.

"Wait a minute! You might faint and drown. Lie down and I promise to get you clean, if you're willing to try and eat." He had new reservations about the house.

"Now undress on the bed and pull the sheet over you. I do wicked massages," he added, turning away.

"Look, you don't have to not look. It's something I haven't understood since I . . . came back," Elena said. "Modesty taboos. I don't see why anyone should be ashamed of their body." (This came to him in a rather muffled voice.) "I mean for anyone who says God made us, God made us without clothes, even after Adam and Eve. If it's so important, why didn't he make us with diapers on?"

"Yes, actually, what you're saying reminds me of what I once said to the Dowager Queen of France," Damon said, determined to keep her undressing while he gazed at a crack in one of the wooden panels of the wall. "I said that if God were both omnipotent and omniscient, then He surely knew our destinies beforehand, and why were the righteous doomed to be born as sinfully naked as the damned?"

"And what did she say?"

"Not a word. But she giggled and tapped me three times on the back of my hand with her fan, which I was later told was an invitation for an assignation. Alas, I had other obligations. Are you on the bed still?"

"Yes, and I'm under a sheet," Elena said wearily. "If she were *Dowager* Queen, I expect you were glad," she added in a half-bewildered voice. "Aren't they the old mothers?"

"No, Anne of Austria, Queen of France, kept her

remarkable beauty to the end. She was the only redhead that—"

Damon stopped, groping wildly for words as he faced the bed. Elena had done as he had asked. He just hadn't realized how much she would look like Aphrodite arising from the ocean. The ruffled white of the sheet came up to the warmer milk-white of her skin. She needed cleaning, certainly, but just knowing that under that thin sheet she was magnificently naked was enough to make him lose his breath.

She had rolled her clothes into a ball and thrown them into the farthest corner of the room. He didn't blame her.

He didn't think. He didn't give himself time. He simply held out his hands and said, "Lemon-thyme chicken consommé, hot, in a Mikasa cup—and plum flower oil, very warm, in a vial."

Once the broth was duly consumed and Elena was lying on her back again, he began to gently massage her with the oil. Plum flower always made for a good start. It numbed the skin and the senses to pain, and it provided a basis for the other, more exotic, oils he planned to use on her.

In a way, it was much better than dumping her in a modern bath or Jacuzzi. He knew where her injuries were; he could heat the oils to the appropriate temperature for any of them. And instead of a barely mobile Jacuzzi head spouting water against a bruise, he could avoid anything too sensitive—in the painful sense.

He started with her hair, adding a very, very light coating of oil that would make the worst tangles easy to brush out. After the oiling, her hair shone like gold against her skin—honey on cream. Then he began with the muscles in her face: tiny strokes with his thumbs over her forehead to smooth it and relax it, forcing her to relax along with his movements. Slow, circular swirls at her temples, with only the lightest of pressure. He could see the thin blue veins traced here, and he knew that deep pressure could put her to sleep.

He then proceeded to upper arms, her forearms, her hands, taking her apart with ancient strokes and the correct ancient essences to go with them, until she was nothing but a loose, boneless thing under the sheet: sleek and soft and yielding. He flashed his incandescent smile for a moment while pulling a toe until it popped—and then the smile turned ironic. He could have what he wanted of her, now. Yes, she was in no mood to refuse anything. But he hadn't counted on what the damned sheet would do to *him*. Everyone knew that a scrap of covering, no matter how simple, always drew attention to the taboo area as pure nakedness did not. And massaging Elena by inches this way only focused him on what lay beneath the snowy fabric.

After a while Elena said drowsily, "Aren't you going to

tell the end of the story? About Anne of Austria, who was the only redhead to . . ."

". . . to, ah, remain a natural redhead to the end of her life," Damon murmured. "Yes. It was said that Cardinal Richelieu was her lover."

"Isn't that the wicked Cardinal from the *The Three Musketeers*?"

"Yes, but perhaps not so wicked as he was portrayed there, and certainly an able politician. And, some say, the real father of Louis . . . now turn over."

"It's a strange name for a king."

"Hm?"

"Louis Now Turn Over," Elena said, turning over and showing a flash of creamy thigh while Damon tried to eye various other parts of the room.

"Depends on the naming traditions of the individual's native country," Damon said wildly. All he could see were replays of that glimpse of thigh.

"What?"

"What?"

"I was asking you—"

"Are you warm now? All done," Damon said and, unwisely, patted the highest curve of terrain under the towel.

"Hey!" Elena reared up, and Damon—faced by an entire body of pale rose-gold and perfumed and sleek—and with muscles like steel under the silken skin—precipitately fled.

He came back after an appropriate interval with a calming offering of more soup. Elena, dignified under her sheet, which she had made into a toga, accepted. She didn't even try to swat him on the bottom when his back was turned.

"What *is* this place?" she wondered instead. "It can't be the Dunstans'—they're an old family, with an old house. They used to be farmers."

"Oh, let's just call it a little pied-à-terre of my own in the woods."

"Ha," Elena said. "I knew you weren't sleeping in trees."

Damon found himself trying not to smile. He'd never been with Elena when the situation hadn't been life-or-death. Now, if he said he'd found he loved her mind after having massaged her naked under a sheet—no . . . No one would ever believe him.

"Feeling better?" he asked.

"As warm as chicken-apple soup."

"I'm never going to hear the end of that, am I?"

He made her stay on the bed while he thought up nightgowns, all sizes and styles, and robes, too—and slippers, all in the instant of walking to what had been a bathroom, and was pleased to find that it was now a walk-in closet with everything anyone could want in terms of night attire. From silky lingerie to good old-fashioned sleeping gowns to night-caps, this wardrobe had it all. Damon emerged with a double armful and gave Elena her choice.

She picked a high-necked white nightgown made out of some modest fabric. Damon found himself stroking a regal sky-blue gown trimmed with what looked like genuine Valenciennes lace.

"Not my style," Elena said, quickly tucking it under some other robes.

Not your style around *me*, Damon thought, amused. And a wise little lass you are, too. You don't want to tempt me into doing anything you might be sorry for tomorrow.

"All right—and then you can get a good night's sleep—" He broke off, for she was suddenly looking at him with astonishment and distress.

"Matt! Damon, we were looking for *Matt*! I just remembered. We were looking for him and I—I don't know. I got hurt. I remember falling and then I was here."

Because I carried you here, Damon thought. Because this house is just a thought in Shinichi's mind. Because the only permanent things inside it are we two.

Damon took in a deep breath of air.

Let us at least have the dignity of walking out of your trap on our own feet—or should I say, using your own key? Damon thought to Shinichi. To Elena, he said, "Yes, we're looking for what's-his-face. But you took a bad fall. I wish—I would like to ask you—that you stay here and recuperate while *I* go look for him."

"You think you know where Matt is?" That was the entire sentence distilled for her. That was all she heard.

"Yes."

"Can we go *now?*"

"Won't you let me go alone?"

"No," Elena said simply. "I have to find him. I wouldn't sleep at all if you went out alone. Please, can't we go now?"

Damon sighed. "All right. There were some"—(there

will be now)— "clothes that will fit you in the closet. Jeans and things. I'll get them," he said. "As long as I really, really can't convince you to lie down and rest while I look for him."

"I can make it," Elena promised. "And if you go without me, I'll just jump out a window and follow you."

She was serious. He went and got the promised pile of clothes and then turned his back while Elena put on an identical version of the jeans and Pendleton shirt she had been wearing, whole and un-bloodstained. Then they left the house, Elena brushing her hair vigorously, but glancing back every step or so.

"What are you doing?" Damon asked, just when he had decided to carry her.

"Waiting for the house to disappear." And when he gave her his best *what're you talking about?* look, she said, "Armani jeans, just my size? La Perla camisoles, same? Pendleton shirts, two sizes too big, just like the one I was wearing? That place is either a warehouse or it's magic. My bet's on magic."

Damon picked her up as a way to shut her up, and walked to the passenger's door of the Ferrari. He wondered if they were in the real world now or in another of Shinichi's globes.

"Did it disappear?" he asked.

"Yup."

What a pity, he thought. He'd have liked to keep it.

He could try to renegotiate the bargain with Shinichi, but there were other, more important things to think of. He gave Elena a slight squeeze, thinking, other, *much, much* more important things.

In the car he made sure of three small facts. First, that click which his brain automatically registered as passenger buckled up really did mean that Elena had her seat buckle properly fastened. Second, that the doors were locked—from *his* master control. And third, that he drove quite slowly. He didn't think that anyone in Elena's shape would be throwing themselves out of cars again in the near future, but he wasn't taking any chances.

He had no idea how long this spell was going to work. Elena must eventually come out of her amnesia. It was only logical, since he seemed to be, and he'd been awake much longer than she had. Pretty soon she would remember ... what? That he'd taken her in the Ferrari against her will (bad but forgivable—he couldn't know she'd launch herself out)? That he'd been teasing Mike or Mitch or whoever and her in the clearing? He himself had a vague picture of this—or was it another dream.

He wished he knew what the truth was. When would *he* remember everything? He'd be in a much stronger bargaining position once he did.

And it was hardly possible that Mac was getting

hypothermia in a midsummer snowstorm even if he were still in that clearing right now. It was a chilly night, but the worst the boy could expect was a twinge of rheumatism when he was around eighty.

The vital thing was that they *didn't* find him. He might have some unpleasant truths to tell.

Damon noticed Elena making the same gesture again. A touch to her throat, a grimace, a deep breath.

"Are you carsick?"

"No, I'm . . ." In the moonlight he could see her blush come and go; could sense her heat with detectors in his face. She flushed deeply. "I explained," she said, "about feeling . . . too full. That's what it is now."

What was a vampire to do?

Say, *I'm sorry—I've given it up for Moonspire*?

Say, *I'm sorry—you'll hate me in the morning*?

Say, *To hell with the morning; this seat reclines two inches*?

But what if they got to the clearing and found that something really had happened to Mutt—Gnat—the boy? Damon would regret it for the rest of the remaining twenty seconds of his life. Elena would call battalions of sky spirits down on his head. Even if no one else believed in her, Damon did.

He found himself saying, as smoothly as ever he'd spoken to a Page or a Damaris, "Will you trust me?"

"What?"

"Will you trust me for another fifteen or twenty minutes, to go to a certain place I think what's his name might be?" *If he is—my bet is that you remember everything and you never want to see me again in your life—then you'll be spared a long search. If he isn't—and the car isn't either; it's my lucky day and Mutt wins the prize of a lifetime—and then we go on looking.*

Elena was watching him intently. "Damon, do you *know* where Matt is?"

"No." Well, that was true enough. But she was a bright little trinket, a pretty little pink, and more than all that, she was clever. . . . Damon broke off his polyrhythmic contemplations on Elena's intelligence. Why was he thinking in poetry? Was he really going crazy? He'd wondered that before—hadn't he? Didn't it prove you weren't crazy if you wondered if you were? The truly insane never doubted their sanity, right? Right. Or did they? And surely all this talking to himself couldn't be good for *anyone*.

Merda.

"All right, then. I'll trust you."

Damon let out a breath he didn't need and headed the car toward the clearing.

It was one of the more exciting gambles of his life. On one hand, there *was* his life—Elena would find some way or other of killing him if he'd killed Mark, he was certain. And on the other hand . . . a taste of paradise. With a willing

Elena, an eager Elena, an open Elena . . . he swallowed. He found himself doing the thing closest to praying that he'd done in half a millennium.

As they rounded the corner on the road to the little lane, he kept himself in hyper-alertness, the engine a bare hum, the night air bringing all kinds of information to vampire senses. He was thoroughly aware that an ambush could have been set up for him. But the lane was deserted. And as he suddenly hit the accelerator to reveal the little clearing, he found it blessedly, bleakly, blankly empty of either cars or of college-aged young men whose names started with "M."

He relaxed against the seatback.

Elena had been watching him.

"You thought he might be here."

"Yes." And now was the time for the real question. Without asking her this, the whole thing was a sham, a fraud. "Do *you* remember this place?"

She glanced around. "No. Should I?"

Damon smiled.

But he took the precaution of driving on up another three hundred yards, into a different clearing, just in case she should have a sudden attack of memory.

"There were malach in the other clearing," he explained easily. "This one is guaranteed monster-free." Oh, what a liar, I am, I am, he rejoiced. Have I still got it or what?

He'd been . . . disturbed ever since Elena had come back from the Other Side. But if that first night it had discomfited him into literally giving her the shirt off his back—well, there were still no words for how he'd felt when she'd stood before him newly returned from the afterlife, her skin glowing in the dark clearing, naked without shame or the concept of shame. And during her massage, where veins traced out lines of blue comet fire against an inverse sky. Damon was feeling something he hadn't felt for five hundred years.

He was feeling desire.

Human desire. Vampires didn't feel that. It was all sublimated into the need for the blood, always the blood. . . .

But he was feeling it.

He knew why, too. Elena's aura. Elena's blood. She'd brought back with her something more substantial than wings. And while the wings had faded, this new talent seemed to be permanent.

He realized that it was a very long time since he'd felt this, and that therefore he might be quite wrong. But he didn't think so. He thought that Elena's aura would make the most fossilized of vampires stand up and blossom into virile young men once again.

He leaned away as far as the crowded confines of the Ferrari would allow. "Elena, there's something I should tell you."

"About Matt?" She gave him a straightforward, intelligent glance.

"Nat? No, no. It's about you. I know you were surprised that Stefan would leave you in the care of somebody like *me*."

There was no room for privacy in the Ferrari and he was sharing her body warmth already.

"Yes, I was," she said simply.

"Well, it may have something to do with—"

"It may have had something to do with how we decided that my aura would give even old vampires the jigsies. From now on, I'll need strong protection because of that, Stefan said."

Damon didn't know what the jigsies were, but he was prepared to bless them for getting a delicate point across to a lady. "I think," he said carefully, "that of all things, Stefan would want you to have protection from the evil folk drawn here from all over the globe, and above all other things that you not be forced to—to, um, jigsy—if it was not your wish."

"And now he's *left* me—like a selfish, stupid, idealistic idiot, considering all the people in the world who might want to jigsy me."

"I agree," Damon said, careful of keeping the lie of Stefan's willing departure intact. "And I've already promised what protection I can offer. I really will do my best,

Elena, to see that no one gets near you."

"Yes," said Elena, "but then something like this"—she made a little gesture probably to indicate Shinichi and all the problems brought about by his arrival—"comes up and nobody knows how to deal with it."

"True," said Damon. He had to keep shaking himself and reminding himself of his real purpose here. He was here to . . . well, he wasn't on St. Stefan's side. And the thing was, it was easy enough. . . .

There she was, brushing her hair out . . . a fair pretty maiden sat brushing her hair out . . . the sun in the sky was nonesuch so gold. . . . Damon shook himself *hard*. Since when had he gotten into ye Olde English folksongs? What was *wrong* with him?

To have something to say, he asked, "How are you feeling?"—just, as it happened, as she lifted her hand to her throat.

She grimaced. "Not bad."

And that made them look at each other. And then Elena smiled and he had to smile back, at first just a quirk of the lip, and then a full smile.

She was . . . damn it, she was *everything*. Witty, enchanting, brave, smart . . . and beautiful. And he knew that his eyes were saying all that and that she wasn't turning away.

"We might—take a little walk," he said, and bells rang

and trumpets played fanfares, and confetti came raining down and there was a release of doves. . . .

In other words, she said, "All right."

They picked a little path off the clearing that looked easy to Damon's night-acquainted vampire eyes. Damon didn't want her on her feet too much. He knew that she still hurt and that she didn't want him to know it or to pamper her. Something inside him said, "Well, then, wait until she says she's tired and help her to sit down."

And something else beyond his control, sprang out at the first little hesitation of her foot, and he picked her up, apologizing in a dozen different languages, and generally acting the fool until he had her seated on a comfortably carved wooden bench with a back to it and a very light traveling blanket over her knees. He kept adding, "You'll tell me if there's something—anything—else you want?" He accidentally sent to her a snippet of his thoughts of possible contenders, which were, a glass of water, him sitting beside her, and a baby elephant, which he had earlier seen in her mind that she admired very much.

"I'm very sorry, but I don't think I do elephants," he said, on his knees, making the footstool more comfortable for her, when he caught a random thought of hers: that he was not so different from Stefan as he seemed.

No other name could have caused him to do what he

did then. No other word, or concept, could have such effect on him. In an instant the blanket was off, the footstool had disappeared, and he was holding Elena bent backward with the slender column of her neck fully exposed to him.

The difference, he told her, *between me and my brother is that he is still hoping somehow to slip in through some side door into heaven. I'm not such a moaning ninny about my fate.* I know where I'm going. *And I don't*—he gave her a smile with all canines fully extended—*give a damn about it.*

Her eyes were wide—he'd startled her. And startled her into an unintentional, thoroughly honest response. Her thoughts were projected toward him, easy to read. *I know—and, I'm like that, too. I want what I want. I'm not as good as Stefan. And I don't know—*

He was enthralled. *What don't you know, sweetheart?*

She just shook her head, eyes shut.

To break the deadlock, he whispered into her ear, "What about this, then:

Say I'm bold
And say I'm bad
Say—you vanities
—I'm vainer.
But you Erinyes, just add
I kissed Elena."

Her eyes flew open. "Oh, no! Please, Damon." She was whispering. "Please! Please not now!" And she swallowed miserably. "Besides, you asked me if I'd like a drink, and then suddenly it's no drink. I wouldn't mind *being* a drink if you'd like, but first, I'm *so* thirsty—as thirsty as you are, maybe?"

She did the little tap-tap-tap under her chin again.

Damon's insides melted.

He held out his hand and it closed around the stem of a delicate crystal glass. He swirled the splash of liquid in it expertly, tested it for bouquet—ah, exquisite—then gently rolled it on his tongue. It was the real thing. *Black Magic* wine, grown from Clarion Loess Black Magic grapes. It was the only wine most vampires would drink—and there were apocryphal stories of how it had kept them on their feet when their other thirst could not be assuaged.

Elena was drinking hers, her blue eyes wide above the deep violet of the wine as he told her some of its story. He loved to watch her when she was like this—investigating with all her senses fully aroused. He shut his eyes and remembered some choice moments from the past. Then he opened them again to find Elena, looking very much the thirsty child, eagerly gulping down—

"Your *second* glass . . . ?" He'd discovered the first goblet at her feet. "Elena, where did you get another one?"

"I just did what you did. Held out my hand. It's not as

if it were hard liquor, is it? It tastes like grape juice, and I was dying for a drink."

Could she really be that naïve? True, Black Magic wine didn't have the sharp odor or taste of most alcohol. It was subtle, created for the fastidious vampire palate. Damon knew that the grapes were grown in the soil, loess, that a grinding glacier leaves behind. Of course, that process was only for the long-lived vampires, as it took ages to build up enough loess. And when the soil was ready, the grapes were grown and processed, from graft to foot-stomped pulp in ironwood vats, without ever seeing the sun. That was what gave it its black velvet, dark, delicate taste. And now . . .

Elena had a "grape juice" mustache. Damon wanted very much to kiss it away.

"Well, someday you can tell people you drank two glasses of Black Magic in under a minute, and impress them," he said.

But she was doing the tap-tap-tapping again under her chin.

"Elena, do you want to have some of your blood drawn?"

"Yes!" She said it in the ringing-bell tones of someone who has finally been asked the right question.

She was drunk.

She flung both arms backward, draping them against

the bench, which conformed to accept her body's every new motion. It had become a black suede couch with a high back: a divan, and just now, Elena's slender neck was resting on the highest point of that back, her throat exposed to the air. Damon turned away with a little moan. He wanted to get Elena to civilization. He was worried about her health, mildly concerned about . . . Mutt's; and now . . . he couldn't have *anything* he wanted. He could hardly bleed her when she was drunk.

Elena made a different sort of sound that might have been his name. "D'm'n?" she mumbled. Her eyes had filled with tears.

Just about anything that a nurse might have to do for a patient, Damon had done for Elena. But it seemed she didn't want to unswallow two glasses of Black Magic in front of him.

"'M'shick," Elena got out, with a dangerous hiccup at the end. She gripped Damon's wrist.

"Yes, this is not the kind of wine to guzzle. Wait, just sit up straight and let me try . . ." And maybe because he said the words without thinking, without thinking of being rude, without thinking of manipulating her one way or another, it was all right. Elena obeyed him and he put two fingers on either side of her temples and pressed slightly. For a split second there was a near disaster, and then Elena was breathing slowly and calmly. She was still affected by the wine, but she wasn't drunk any longer.

And the time was now. He had to tell her the truth at last.

But first, he needed to wake up.

"A triple espresso, please," he said, holding out his hand. It appeared instantly, aromatic and black as his soul. "Shinichi says espresso alone is an excuse for the human race."

"Whoever Shinichi is, I agree with him or her. A triple espresso, please," Elena said to the magic that was this forest, this snowflake globe, this universe. Nothing happened.

"Maybe it's only attuned to my voice right now," Damon said, flashing her a reassuring smile, and then he fetched her espresso with a wave.

To his surprise, Elena was frowning.

"You said 'Shinichi.' Who's that?

Damon wanted nothing less than for Elena to get involved with the kitsune, but if he was really going to tell all she was going to have to. "He's a *kitsune*, a fox spirit," he said. "And the person who gave me that Web address that sent Stefan running."

Elena's expression froze over.

"Actually," Damon said, "I find that I would rather get you home before taking the next step."

Elena lifted exasperated eyes to the sky, but let him pick her up and carry her back to the car.

He had just realized where the best place to tell her was.

It was just as well that they didn't urgently need to get to any place that was out of the Old Wood right now. They didn't find any road that did not lead to dead ends, little clearings, or trees. Elena seemed so unsurprised at finding the little lane that led to their small but perfectly appointed house that he said nothing as they entered and he took new inventory of what they had.

They had one bedroom with one large, luxurious bed. They had a kitchen. And a living area. But any of these rooms could become any kind of room you chose simply by thinking of it before opening the door. Moreover, there were the keys—left behind by what Damon was realizing was a seriously shaken Shinichi—that allowed the doors to do more. Insert a key in a door and announce what you wanted and there you were—even, it seemed, if it should be outside Shinichi's territory in spacetime. In other words, they *seemed* to link to the real outside world, but Damon wasn't entirely sure about that. *Was* it the real world or just another of Shinichi's play-traps?

What they had right now was a long spiraling stairway to an open-air observatory with a widow's walk around it, just like the roof of the boardinghouse. There was even a room just like Stefan's, Damon noted as he carried Elena up the stairs.

"We're going all the way up?" Elena sounded bewildered.

"All the way."

"And what are we *doing* up here?" Elena asked, when he had her settled in a chair with a footstool and a light blanket on the roof.

Damon sat down on a rocker, rocking a little, his arms wrapped around one knee, his face tilted to the clouded sky.

He rocked once more, stopped, and turned to face her. "I suppose we're here," he said, in the light self-mocking tone that meant he was very serious, "so that I can tell you the truth, the whole truth, and nothing but the truth."

32

"Who is it?" a voice was saying from the forest darkness. "Who's out there?"

Bonnie had seldom been as grateful to anyone as she was to Matt for holding on to her. She needed people contact. If she could only bury herself deep enough in other people, she would be safe somehow. She just barely managed not to scream as the dimming flashlight swung onto a surrealistic scene.

"Isobel!"

Yes, it really was Isobel, not at the Ridgemont hospital at all, but here in the Old Wood. She was standing at bay, almost naked except for blood and mud. Right here, against this background, she looked like both prey and a sort of forest goddess, a goddess of vengeance, and of hunted things, and of punishment for any being who stood in her way. She was winded, breathing hard, with bubbles of saliva coming out of her mouth, but she wasn't broken. You only had to see her eyes, shining red, to see that.

Behind her, stepping on branches and letting loose the occasional grunt or curse, were two other figures, one tall and thin but bulbous on top, and one shorter and stouter. They looked like gnomes trying to follow a wood nymph.

"*Dr. Alpert!*" Meredith seemed just barely able to sound like her ordinary controlled self.

At the same time, Bonnie saw that Isobel's piercings were much worse. She'd lost most of her studs and hoops and needles, but there was blood and, already, pus, coming out of the holes where they had been.

"Don't scare her," Jim's voice whispered out of the shadows. "We've been tracking her since we had to stop." Bonnie could feel Matt, who had drawn in air to shout, suddenly choke it off. She could also see why Jim looked so top-heavy. He was carrying Obaasan, Japanese-style, on his back, with her arms around his neck. Like a backpack, Bonnie thought.

"*What happened to you?*" Meredith whispered. "We thought you'd gone to the hospital."

"Somehow, a tree fell across the road while we were letting you off, and we couldn't get around it to get to the hospital, or anywhere else. Not only that, but it was a tree with a hornet's nest or something inside it. Isobel woke up like *that*"—the doctor snapped her fingers—"and when she heard the hornets she scrambled out and ran from them. We ran after her. I don't mind saying I would have done the same if I'd been alone."

"Did anybody see these hornets?" Matt asked, after a moment.

"No, it had just turned dark. But we heard them all right. Weirdest thing I ever heard. Sounded like hornet a foot long," Jim said.

Meredith was now squeezing Bonnie's arm from the other side. Whether to keep her silent or to encourage her to speak, Bonnie had no idea. And what could she say? "Fallen trees here only stay fallen until the police *make the decision* to look for them?" "Oh, and watch out for the hellish streams of bugs as long as your arm?" "And by the way, there's probably one inside Isobel right now?" *That* would really freak Jim out.

"If I knew the way back to the boardinghouse, I would drop these three off there," Mrs. Flowers was saying. "They're not part of this."

To Bonnie's surprise, Dr. Alpert did not take exception to the statement that she herself was "not part of it." Nor did she ask what Mrs. Flowers was doing with the two teenagers out in the Old Wood at this hour. What she said was even more astonishing: "We saw the lights as you started shouting. It's right back there."

Bonnie felt Matt's muscles tighten up against her. "Thank God," he said. And then, slowly, "But that's not possible. I left the Dunstans' about ten minutes before we met, and that's right on the other side of the Old Wood from the boardinghouse. It would take at least forty-five minutes to walk it."

"Well, possible or not, we saw the boardinghouse, Theophilia. All the lights were on, from top to bottom. It was impossible to mistake. Are you sure you're not underestimating time?" she added, to Matt.

Mrs. Flowers' name is Theophilia, Bonnie thought, and had to curb an urge not to giggle. The tension was getting to her.

But just as she was thinking it, Meredith gave her another nudge.

Sometimes she thought that she, and Elena, and Meredith had a sort of telepathy with each other. Maybe it wasn't true telepathy, but sometimes just a look, just a glance, could say more than pages and pages of argument. And sometimes—not always, but sometimes—Matt or Stefan would seem to be part of it. Not that it was like real telepathy, with voices as clear in your head as they would be in your ears, but sometimes the boys seemed to be . . . on the girls' channel.

Because Bonnie knew exactly what that nudge meant. It meant that Meredith had turned the lamp off in Stefan's room on the top of the house, and that Mrs. Flowers had turned the downstairs lights off as they left. So while Bonnie had a very vivid image of the boardinghouse with lights blazing, that image couldn't be reality, not now.

Someone is trying to mess with us was what Meredith's nudge meant. And Matt was on the same wavelength, even if it was for a different reason. He leaned very slightly back at Meredith, with Bonnie in between.

"But maybe we should head back toward the Dunstans'," Bonnie said in her most babyish, heart-rending voice. "They're just normal people. They could protect us."

"The boardinghouse is just over that rise," Dr. Alpert said firmly. "And I really would appreciate your advice on how to slow down Isobel's infections," she added to Mrs. Flowers.

Mrs. Flowers fluttered. There was no other word for it. "Oh, goodness, what a compliment. One thing would be to wash the dirt out of the wounds immediately."

This was so obvious and so unlike Mrs. Flowers that Matt squeezed Bonnie hard just as Meredith leaned in on her. *Yeehaw!* Bonnie thought. Do we have this telepathy thing going or not! So it's Dr. Alpert who's the dangerous one, the liar.

"That's it, then. We head for the boardinghouse," Meredith said calmly. "And Bonnie, don't worry. We'll take care of you."

"We sure will," Matt said, giving her one last hard squeeze. It meant *I get it. I know who's not on our side.* Aloud, he added, in a fake stern voice, "It's no good going to the Dunstans' anyway. I already told Mrs. Flowers and the girls about this, but they've got a daughter who's like Isobel."

"Piercing herself?" Dr. Alpert said, sounding startled and horrified at the thought.

"No. She's just acting pretty strangely. But it's not a good place." Squeeze.

I got it a long time ago, Bonnie thought in annoyance. I'm supposed to shut up now.

"Lead the way, please," murmured Mrs. Flowers, seeming more fluttery than ever. "Back to the boarding-house."

And they let the doctor and Jim lead the way. Bonnie kept up a mumbling complaint in case anyone was listening. And she, and Matt, and Meredith all kept an eye on the doctor and Jim.

"Okay," Elena said to Damon, "I'm dolled up like some-body on the deck of an ocean liner, I'm keyed up like an overstrung guitar, and I'm fed up with all this delay.

Soooo . . . what is the truth and the whole truth and nothing but the truth?" She shook her head. Time had skipped and stretched for her.

Damon said, "In a way, we're in a tiny snow globe I made for myself. It just means they won't see or hear us for a few minutes. Now is the time to get the real talking done."

"So we'd better talk fast." She smiled at him, encouragingly.

She was trying to help him. She knew he needed help. He wanted to tell her the truth, but it was so far against his nature that it was like asking one *hell* of a wild horse to let you ride it, master it.

"There are more problems," Damon got out huskily, and she knew he'd read her thoughts. "They—they tried to make it impossible for me to speak to you about this. They did it in grand old fairy tale style: by making up lots of conditions. I couldn't tell you inside a house, nor could I tell you outside. Well, a widow's walk isn't inside, but you can't say it's outside, either. I couldn't tell you by sunlight or by moonlight. Well, the sun's gone down, and it's another thirty minutes before the moon rises, and I say that that condition is met. And I couldn't tell you while you were clothed or naked." Elena automatically glanced down at herself in alarm, but nothing had changed as far as she could tell.

"And I figure that that condition is met, too, because even though he swore to me he was letting me out of one of his little snow globes, he didn't do it. We're in a house that's not a house—it's a thought in somebody's mind. You're wearing clothes that aren't real clothes—they're figments of imagination."

Elena opened her mouth again, but he put two fingers to her lips and said, "Wait. Just let me go on while I still can. I seriously thought that he might never stop with the conditions, which he had picked up out of fairy tale literature. He's obsessed with that, and with old English poetry. I don't know why, because he's from the other side of the world, from Japan. That's who Shinichi is. And he has a twin sister . . . Misao."

Damon stopped breathing hard after that, and Elena figured that there must have been some internal conditions against him telling her.

"He likes it if you translate his name as *death-first*, or *number one in the matters of death*. They're both like teenagers, really, with their codes and their games, and yet they're thousands of years old."

"Thousands?" Elena prodded gently as Damon coasted to a stop, looking exhausted but determined.

"I hate to think of how *many* thousands of years the two of them have been doing mischief. Misao's the one who's been doing all the things to the girls in town. She possesses them with her malach and then she makes the malach make them do things. You remember your American history? The Salem witches? That was Misao, or someone like her. And it's happened hundreds of times before that. You might look up the Ursuline nuns when you're out of this. They were a quiet convent who became exhibitionists and worse—some went mad, and some who tried to help them became possessed."

"Exhibitionists? Like Tamra? But she's only a child—"

"Misao's only a child, in her head."

"And where does Caroline come in?"

"In any case like this, there's got to be an instigator—someone who's willing to bargain with the devil—or a demon, really—for their own ends. That's where Caroline comes in. But for an entire town, they must be giving her something really big."

"An entire town? They're going to take over Fell's Church . . . ?"

Damon looked away. The truth was that they were going to *destroy* Fell's Church, but there was no point in saying that. His hands were loosely fastened around his knees as he sat on a rickety old wooden chair on the widow's walk.

"Before we can do anything to help anyone, we have to get out of here. Out of Shinichi's world. This is important. I can—block him for short periods of time from watching us—but then I get tired and need blood. I need more than you can regenerate, Elena." He looked up at her. "He's put Beauty in with the Beast here and he'll leave us to see which one will triumph."

"If you mean kill the other, he's in for a long wait on my end."

"That's what you think now. But this is a specially made trap. There's *nothing* in here except the Old Wood as it was when we started driving around it. It's also minus any other human habitations. The *only* house is this house, the only real living creatures are the two of us. You'll want me dead soon enough."

"Damon, I don't understand. What do they *want* here? Even with what Stefan said about all the ley lines crossing under Fell's Church and making a beacon . . ."

"It was *your* beacon that drew them, Elena. They're curious, like kids, and I have a feeling that they may already have been in trouble wherever it is they really live. It's possible they were here watching the end of the battle, watching you be reborn."

"And so they want . . .to destroy us? To have fun? To take over the town and make us puppets?"

"All three, for a while. They could be having fun while someone else pleads their case in a high court in another dimension. And yes, fun, to them, means taking apart a town. Although I believe that Shinichi means to go back on his bargain with me for something he wants more than the town, so they may end up fighting each other."

"What bargain with *you*, Damon?"

"For you. Stefan had you. I wanted you. He wants you."

Despite herself, Elena felt cold pooling in her midriff, felt the distant shaking that began there and worked its way outward. "And the original bargain was?"

He looked away from her. "This is the bad part."

"Damon, what have you done?" she cried, almost screaming it. *"What was the bargain?"* Her whole body was shaking.

"I made a bargain with a demon and, yes, I knew what he was when I did it. It was the night after your friends were attacked by the trees—after Stefan banished me from his room. That and—well, I was angry, but he took my anger and boosted it. He was using me, controlling me; I see that now. That's when he started with the deals and conditions."

"Damon—" Elena began shakily, but he went on, speaking rapidly as if he had to get through this, to see it to its conclusion, before he lost his nerve. "The final deal was that he would help me get Stefan out of the way so I could have you, while he got Caroline and the rest of the town to share with his sister. Thus trumping Caroline's bargain for whatever she was getting from Misao."

Elena slapped him. She wasn't sure how she managed, wrapped up as she was, to get a hand free and to make the lightning-fast movement, but she did. And then she waited, watching a bead of blood hanging on his lip, for him to retaliate or for the strength to try to kill him.

amon just sat there. Then he licked his mouth and said nothing, did nothing.

"You bastard!"

"Yes."

"You're saying that Stefan didn't really walk out on me?"

"Yes. I mean—correct."

"Who wrote the letter in my diary, then?"

Damon said nothing, but looked away.

"Oh, Damon!" She didn't know whether to kiss him or shake him. "How could you—do you *know*," she said in a choked and threatening voice, "what I've gone through since he disappeared? Thinking every minute that he just suddenly decided to up and *leave me*? Even if he intended to come back—"

"I—"

"Don't try to tell me you're *sorry*! Don't try to tell me you know what it feels like feeling that, because you don't. *How could you? You don't have feelings like that!*"

"I think—I've had some similar experience. But I wasn't going to try to defend myself. Only to say that we have a limited time while I can block Shinichi from seeing us."

Elena heart was shattering into a thousand pieces; she could feel each one pierce her. Nothing mattered anymore. "You lied, you broke your promise about never harming each other—"

"I know—and that should have been impossible. But it started that night when the trees closed in on Bonnie and Meredith and . . . Mark. . . ."

"Matt!"

"That night, when Stefan knocked me around and showed me his true Power—it was because of you. He did it so I would stay away from you. Before that he'd just hoped to keep you hidden. And that night I felt . . . betrayed somehow. Don't ask me why that should make sense, when for years before I've knocked him down and made him eat dirt any time I wanted."

Elena tried to make sense of what he was saying in her shattered condition. And she couldn't. But neither could she ignore a feeling that had just dropped down like an angel in chains grabbing hold of her.

Try to look with your other eyes. Look inside, not outside for the answer. You know Damon. You've already seen what is inside him. How long has it been there?

"Oh, Damon, I'm sorry! I know the answer. Damon—Damon. Oh, God! I can *see* what's wrong with you. You're more possessed than any of those girls."

"*I*—have one of those things in me?"

Elena kept her eyes shut while she nodded. Tears were streaming down her cheeks, and she felt sick even as she made herself do it: gather enough human power to see with her other eyes, see as she had somehow learned to see *inside* people.

The malach that she had seen before inside Damon, and the one Matt had described had been huge for insects—as long as an arm, maybe. But now in Damon she sensed something . . . huge. Monstrous. Something that inhabited him completely, its transparent head inside his beautiful features, its chitinous body as long as his torso; its backward-twisted legs inside his legs. For a moment she thought she would faint; but then she controlled herself. Staring at the ghostly image, she thought, What Would Meredith Do?

Meredith would stay calm. She wouldn't lie, but she would find some way to help.

"Damon, it's bad. But there has to be some way to

get it out of you—soon. I'm going to find that way. Because as long as it's in you, Shinichi can make you do anything."

"Will you listen to why I think it's grown so large? That night, when Stefan dismissed me from his room, everyone else went home like good little girls and boys, but you and Stefan took a walk. A fly. A glide."

For a long time it meant nothing to her, even though it had been the last time she'd seen Stefan. In fact, that was its only significance to her: it was the last time she and Stefan had . . .

She felt herself freeze over inside.

"You went into the Old Wood. You were still the little spirit child who didn't really know what was right and what was wrong. But Stefan should have known better than to do that—on my own territory. Vampires take territory seriously. And in my own resting place—right in front of my eyes."

"Oh, Damon! No!"

"Oh, Damon, yes! There you were, sharing blood, too absorbed to have noticed me even if I had leaped out and tried to pry you apart. You were wearing a high-necked white nightgown and you looked like an angel. I wanted to kill Stefan *right then*."

"Damon—"

"And it was *right then* that Shinichi appeared. He didn't

need to be told what I was feeling. And he had a plan, an offer . . . a proposition."

Elena shut her eyes again and shook her head. "He'd prepared you beforehand. You were already possessed and ready to be full of anger."

"I don't know why," Damon went on as if he hadn't heard her, "but I scarcely thought about what it would mean to Bonnie and Meredith and the rest of the town. All I could think of was you. All I wanted was you, and revenge on Stefan."

"Damon, will you listen? By then, you had already been deliberately possessed. I could *see* the malach in you. You admit"—as she felt him swelling up to speak out— "that something was influencing you before that, forcing you to watch Bonnie and the others die at your feet that night. Damon, I think these things are even harder to get rid of than we imagine. For one thing, you wouldn't normally stay and watch people do—private things, would you? Doesn't the fact that you did in itself prove that something was wrong?"

"It's . . . a theory," Damon granted, not sounding happy.

"But don't you see? That was what made you tell Stefan you only saved Bonnie out of whim, and that was what made you refuse to tell everyone that the malach were *making* you watch the trees' attack, hypnotizing you.

That and your stupid, stubborn pride."

"Watch it on the compliments. I may dry up and blow away."

"Don't worry," Elena said flatly, "whatever happens to the rest of us, I have a feeling your ego will survive. What happened next?"

"I made my deal with Shinichi. He would lure Stefan somewhere out of the way where I could see him alone, then smuggle him out of this place to somewhere Stefan couldn't find you—"

Something bubbled up explosively again inside Elena. It was a tight hard ball of compressed elation. "Not kill him?" she managed to get out.

"What?"

"Stefan's alive? He's alive? He . . . he's really alive?"

"Steady," Damon replied coldly. "Steady on, Elena. We can't have you fainting." He held her by the shoulders. "You thought I meant to kill him?"

Elena was trembling almost too hard to answer. "Why didn't you tell me before?"

"I apologize for the omission."

"He's alive—for sure, Damon? You're absolutely sure?"

"Positive."

Without a thought of herself, without a thought of any kind, Elena did what she did best—gave in to impulse. She threw her arms around Damon's neck and kissed him.

For a moment Damon just stood rigid with shock. He had contracted with killers to hijack her lover and decimate her town. But Elena's mind would never see it that way.

"If he were dead—" He stopped and had to try again. "Shinichi's whole bargain depends on keeping him alive—alive and away from you. I couldn't risk you killing yourself or *really* hating me"—again the note of distant coldness. "With Stefan dead, what hold would I have over you, princess?"

Elena ignored all this. "If he's alive, I can find him."

"If he remembers you. But what if every memory he had of you were taken away?"

"What?" Elena wanted to explode. "If every memory of Stefan were taken away from *me*," she said icily, "I would still fall in love with him the very moment I saw him. And if every memory of me were taken away from Stefan, he would wander all over the world looking for something without knowing what he was looking for."

"Very poetic."

"*But, oh, Damon, thank you* for not letting Shinichi kill him!"

He shook his head at her, looking bewildered at himself. "I couldn't—seem to—do that. Something about giving my word. I figured that if he were free and happy and didn't remember, that would satisfy enough . . ."

"Of your promise to me? You figured wrong. But it doesn't matter now."

"It does matter. You've suffered for it."

"No, Damon. All that *really* matters is that he's not dead—and he didn't leave me. There's still hope."

"But Elena," Damon's voice had life now; it was both excited and inflexible: "Can't you see? Past history aside, you have to admit that *we're* the ones that belong together. You and I are simply better suited to each other by nature. Deep down you know that, because we understand each other. We're on the same intellectual level—"

"So is Stefan!"

"Well, all I can say is that he does a remarkable job of hiding it, then. But can't you feel it? Don't you feel"—his grip was becoming uncomfortable now—"that you could be my princess of darkness—that something deep inside you wants to? I can see it, if you can't."

"I can't be *anything* to you, Damon. Except a decent sister-in-law."

He shook his head, laughing harshly. "No, you're only suited for the main role. Well, all I can say is that if we live through the fight with the twins, you'll see things in yourself that you've never seen before. And you'll *know* that we're more suited together."

"And all *I* can say is that if we live through this fight

with the Bobbsey twins from Hell, it sounds as if we're going to need all the spiritual power that we can get afterward. And *that* means getting Stefan back."

"We may not be able to get him back. Oh, I agree—even if we drive Shinichi and Misao away from Fell's Church, the likelihood that we're going to be able to do away with them completely is about zero. You're no fighter. We're probably not even going to be able to hurt them very much. But even I don't know exactly where Stefan is."

"Then the twins are the only ones who can help us."

"If they still *can* help us—oh, all right, I'll admit it. The *Shi no Shi* are probably complete frauds. They probably take a few memories from vampire chumps—memories are the coin of choice in the realm of the Other Side—and then send them away while the cash register is still jingling. They're frauds. The whole place is a giant slum and freakshow—sort of like a rundown Vegas."

"But they're not afraid that the vampires they cheat will want revenge?"

Damon laughed, this time musically. "A vampire who doesn't want to be a vampire is about the lowest object on the totem pole on the Other Side. Oh, except for humans. Along with lovers who've fulfilled suicide pacts, kids who jump off the roof because they think their Superman cape can make them fly—"

Elena tried to pull away from him, to reprove him, but he was surprisingly strong. "It doesn't sound like a very nice place."

"It isn't."

"And that's where Stefan is?"

"If we're lucky."

"So basically," she said, seeing things, as she always did, in terms of Plans A, B, C, and D, "first we have to find out where Stefan is from these twins. Second, we have to get the twins to heal the little girls they've possessed. Third, we have to get them to leave Fell's Church alone— for good. But before any of that, we have to find Stefan. He'll be able to help us; I know he will. And then we just hope we're strong enough for the rest."

"We could use Stefan's help, all right. But you missed the real point—for now, what we have to do is keep the twins from killing us."

"They still think you're their friend, yes?" Elena's mind was flickering through options. "Make them *sure* you are. Wait until a strategic moment comes, and then take the chance. Do we have any weapons against them?"

"Iron. They do badly against iron—they're demons. And dear Shinichi is obsessed with you, although I can't say his sister will approve when she realizes it."

"Obsessed?"

"Yes. With you and with English folk songs, remember?

Although I can't fathom why. The songs, I mean."

"Well, I don't know what we can make of that—"

"But I'll bet that his obsession with you will make Misao angry. It's just a hunch, but she's had him to herself for thousands of years."

"Then we set them against each other, pretend that he's going to get me. Damon—what?" Elena added in tones of alarm as he tightened his grip on her as if concerned.

"He's not going to get you," Damon said.

"I know that."

"I don't quite like the idea of anyone else getting you. You were meant to be mine, you know."

"Damon, don't. I've told you. Please—"

"Meaning 'please don't make me hurt you'? The truth is that you can't hurt me unless I let you. You can only hurt yourself against me."

Elena could at least pull their upper bodies farther apart. "Damon, we just made an agreement, made plans. Now, what are we doing, throwing them all away?"

"No, but I thought of another way to get you a grade-A superhero, right now. You've been saying I should take more of your blood for ages."

"Oh . . . yes." It was true, even if that had been before he had admitted to her the terrible things he'd done. And . . .

"Damon, what happened with Matt in the clearing?

We went looking all over for him, but we didn't find him. And you were *glad*."

He didn't bother to deny it. "In the real world I was angry at him, Elena. He seemed to be just another rival. Part of the reason we're here is so I can remember exactly what happened."

"Did you hurt Matt, Damon? Because now you're hurting me."

"Yes." Damon's voice was light and indifferent suddenly, as if he found it amusing. "I suppose I did hurt him. I used psychic pain on him, and that's stopped a lot of hearts from beating. But your Mutt's tough. I like that. I made him suffer more and more, and yet he still went on living because he was afraid to leave you alone."

"Damon!" Elena wrenched herself back, only to find that it did no good. He was far, far stronger than she was. "How could you do that to him?"

"I told you; he was a rival." Damon laughed suddenly. "You really don't remember, do you? I made him abase himself for you. I made him eat dirt, literally, for you."

"Damon—are you crazy?"

"No. I'm just now finding my sanity. I don't need to convince you that you belong to me. I can take you."

"*No*, Damon. I won't be your princess of darkness or—or anything else of yours without asking. At the most you'll have a dead body to play with."

"Maybe I'd like that. But you forget; I can enter your mind. And you still have friends—at home, getting ready for supper or bed, you hope. Don't you? Friends with all their limbs; who've never known real pain."

It took Elena a long time to speak. Then she said quietly, "I take back every decent thing I ever said about you. You're a monster, do you hear that? You're an abomin—" Her voice wound slowly down. "They're making you do this, aren't they?" she said finally, flatly. "Shinichi and Misao. A nice little show for them. Just like they made you hurt Matt and me before."

"No, I do only what I want to." Was that a flash of red Elena saw in his eyes? The briefest flaring of a flame . . . "Do you know how beautiful you are when you're crying? You're more beautiful than ever. The gold in your eyes seems to rise to the surface and spill down in tears of diamond. I would love to have a sculptor carve a bust of you weeping."

"Damon, I know you're not really saying this. I know that the thing they put inside you is the one saying it."

"Elena, I assure you, it's all me. I quite enjoyed it when I made him hurt you. I liked to hear the way you cried out. I made him tear your clothes—I had to hurt him a lot to get him to do it. But didn't you notice that your camisole had been torn, and that you were barefooted? That was all Mutt."

Elena forced her mind back to the moment she had come to herself leaping out of the Ferrari. Yes, then, and in the time afterward she had been barefooted and bare-armed, wearing only a camisole. Quite a bit of the fabric of her jeans had been left on the roadside after that, and in the surrounding vegetation. But it had never occurred to her to wonder what had happened to her boots and socks, or how her camisole had been torn in strips at the bottom. She'd simply been so grateful for help . . . to the one who had hurt her in her first place.

Oh, Damon must have thought that ironic. She suddenly realized she herself was thinking of *Damon* and not of *the possessor.* Not of Shinichi and Misao. But they weren't the same, she told herself. I've got to remember that!

"Yes, I enjoyed making him hurt you, and I enjoyed hurting you. I made him bring me a willow rod, just the right thickness, and then whipped you with it. You enjoyed that, too, I promise you. Don't bother to look for marks because they've all gone like the others. But all three of us enjoyed hearing your cries. You . . . and me . . . and Mutt, too. In fact, of all of us, he may have enjoyed it most."

"Damon, shut up! I won't listen to you talk about Matt that way!"

"I wouldn't let him see you without your clothes on,

though," Damon confided, as if he hadn't heard a word. "That was when I had him—dismissed. Put into another snow globe. I wanted to hunt you as you tried to get away from me, in an empty globe that you could never get out of. I wanted to see that special look in your eyes that you get when you fight with everything you have— and I wanted to see it defeated. You're no fighter, Elena." Damon laughed suddenly, an ugly sound, and to Elena's shock his arm shot out and he punched through the wall of the widow's walk.

"Damon . . ." She was sobbing by now.

"And then I wanted to do *this*." With no warning, Damon's fist forced her chin up, jerking her head back. His other hand tangled in her hair, bringing her neck back to the exact position he wanted her to be in. And then Elena felt him strike, quick as a cobra, and felt the two tearing wounds in the side of her neck, and her own blood spurting out of them.

Ages later, Elena woke up sluggishly. Damon was still enjoying himself, clearly lost in the experience of having Elena Gilbert. And there was no time to make different plans.

Her body simply took over by itself, startling her almost as much as it startled Damon. Even as he lifted his head, her hand plucked the magical house key off his finger. Then she gripped, twisted, lifted her knees as high as she could, and kicked outward, sending Damon smashing through the splintered, rotted wood that formed the outside railing of the widow's walk.

lena had once fallen off that balcony and Stefan had jumped and caught her before she could hit the ground. A human falling from that height would be dead on impact. A vampire in full possession of his or her reflexes would simply twist in the air like a cat and land lightly on their feet. But one in Damon's particular circumstances tonight . . .

From the sound of it, he had tried to twist, but had only ended up landing on his side and breaking bones. Elena deduced the latter from his cursing. She didn't wait to listen for more specifics. She was off like a rabbit, down to the level of Stefan's room—where instantaneously and almost unconsciously, she sent out a wordless plea—and then down the stairs. The cabin had turned completely into a perfect duplicate of the boardinghouse. Elena didn't know why, but instinctively she ran to the side of the house that Damon would know the least: the old servant's quarters. She got that far before she dared whispering things to the house, asking for them rather than demanding them, and praying that the house would obey her as it had obeyed Damon.

"Aunt Judith's house," she whispered, thrusting the key into a door—it went in like a hot knife into butter and turned almost of its own volition, and then suddenly she was there again, in what had been her home for sixteen years, up until her first death.

She was in the hallway, with her little sister Margaret's open door showing her lying on the floor of her bedroom, staring with wide-open eyes over a coloring book.

"It's tag, sweetie!" she announced as if ghosts appeared every day in the Gilbert household and Margaret was supposed to know how to deal with it. "You go running to your friend Barbara's and then she has to be It. Don't stop running until you get there, and then go see Barbara's mom. But first you give me three kisses." And she lifted Margaret and hugged her tightly and then almost threw her at the door.

"But Elena—you're back—"

"I know, darling, and I promise to see you again another day. But now—*run, baby*—"

"I told them you would come back. You did before."

"*Margaret!* Run!"

Choking on tears, but maybe recognizing in her child-like way the seriousness of the situation, Margaret ran. And Elena followed, but zagging toward a different staircase when Margaret zigged.

And then she found herself confronted by a smirking Damon.

"You take too long to talk to people," he said as Elena frantically counted her options. Go over the balcony into the entry way? No. Damon's bones might still hurt a little but if Elena jumped even one story, she would probably break her neck. What else? Think!

And then she was opening the door into the china closet, at the same time shouting out, "Great-aunt Tilda's house," unsure if the magic would still work. And then she was slamming the door in Damon's face.

And she was in her Aunt Tilda's house, but the Aunt Tilda's house of the past. No wonder they accused poor Auntie Tilda of seeing strange things, Elena thought, as she saw the woman turning while holding a large glass casserole dish full of something that smelled mushroomy, and screaming, and dropping the dish.

"Elena!" she cried. "What—it can't be you—you're all grown up!"

"What's the trouble?" demanded Aunt Maggie, who was Aunt Tilda's friend, coming in from the other room.

She was taller and fiercer than Aunt Tilda.

"I'm being chased," cried Elena. "I need to find a door, and if you see a boy after me—"

And just then Damon stepped out of the coat closet, and at the same time Aunt Maggie tripped him neatly and said, "Bathroom door beside you," and picked up a vase and hit the rising Damon over the head with it. Hard.

And Elena dashed through the bathroom door, crying, "Robert E. Lee High School last fall—just as the bell's rung!"

And then she was swimming against the flow, with dozens of students trying to get to their classes on time—but then one of them recognized her, and then another, and while apparently she'd successfully traveled to a time when she wasn't dead—no one was screaming "ghost"—neither had anyone at Robert E. Lee ever seen Elena Gilbert wearing a boy's shirt over a camisole, with her hair falling wildly over her shoulders.

"It's a costume for a play!" she shouted, and created one of the immortal legends about herself before she had even died by adding, "Caroline's house!" and stepping into a janitor's closet. An instant later, the most gorgeous boy that anyone had ever seen appeared behind her, and rocketed through the same doors saying words in a foreign language. And when the janitor's closet opened, neither boy nor girl was there.

Elena landed running down a hallway and almost crashed into Mr. Forbes, who looked rather wobbly. He was drinking what seemed to be a large glass of tomato juice that smelled like alcohol.

"We don't know where she's gone, all right?" he shouted before Elena could say a word. "She's gone right out of her mind, as far as I can tell. She was talking about the ceremony at the widow's walk—and the way she was dressed! Parents don't have any control over children anymore!" He slumped against the wall.

"I'm so sorry," murmured Elena. *The ceremony.* Well, Black Magic ceremonies were usually held at moonrise or midnight. And it was just a few minutes before midnight. But in those minutes, Elena had just come up with scheme B.

"Excuse me," she said, taking the drink out of Mr. Forbes's hand and dashing it directly into the face of Damon, who had appeared out of a closet. Then she shouted, "Some place *their* kind can't see!" and stepped into . . .

Limbo?

Heaven?

Some place their kind couldn't see. At first Elena wondered about herself, because she couldn't see much of anything at all.

But then she realized where she was, deep in the earth,

beneath Honoria Fell's empty tomb. Once, she had fought down here to save the lives of Stefan and Damon.

And now, where there should have been nothing but darkness and rats and mildew, was a tiny, shining, light. Like a miniature Tinkerbell—just a speck, it hovered in the air, not leading her, not communicating, but . . . protecting, Elena realized. She took the light, which felt bright and cool in her fingers, and around her she traced a circle, big enough for a full-grown person to lie down in.

When she turned back, Damon was sitting in the middle.

He looked strangely pale for someone who had just fed. But he said nothing, not a word, just gazed at her. Elena went to him and touched him on the neck.

And a moment later, Damon was again drinking deep, deep, of the most extraordinary blood in the world.

Usually, he would be analyzing by now: taste of berry, taste of tropical fruit, smooth, smoky, woody, rounded with a silken aftertaste . . . But not now. Not *this* blood, which far surpassed anything for which he had words. This blood that was filling him with power such as he had never known before. . . .

Damon . . .

Why was he not listening? How had he come to be drinking this extraordinary blood that tasted somehow of the afterlife, and why was he not listening to the donor?

Please, Damon. Please fight it . . .

He ought to recognize that voice. He'd heard it enough times.

I know they're controlling you. But they can't control all *of you. You're stronger than they are. You're the strongest . . . .*

Well, that was certainly true. But he was getting more and more confused. The donor seemed to be unhappy and he was a past-master at making donors happy. And he didn't quite remember . . . he really should remember how this had started.

Damon, it's me. It's Elena. And you're hurting me.

So much pain and bewilderment. From the beginning, Elena had known better than to outright fight the tapping of her veins. That would only cause agony, and it wouldn't do her the slightest bit of good except to stop her brain from working.

So she was trying to make him fight off the horrible beast inside him. Well, yes, but the change had to come from inside. If she forced him, Shinichi would notice and just possess him again. Besides, the simple *Damon, be strong* gig wasn't working.

Was there nothing to do but die, then? She could at least fight that, although she knew that Damon's strength would make it pointless. With every swallow he took of her new blood, he got stronger; he changed more and more into . . .

Into what? It was *her* blood. Maybe he would answer

its call, which was also her call. Maybe, somehow inside, he could beat the monster without Shinichi noticing.

But she needed some new power, some new trick . . .

And even as she thought it, Elena *felt* the new Power moving in her, and she knew that it had always been there, just waiting for the right occasion to use it. It was a very specific power, not to be used for fighting or even for saving herself. Still, it was hers to tap. Vampires who preyed on her got only a few mouthfuls, but she had an entire blood supply filled with its enormous vigor. And calling upon it was as easy as reaching toward it with an open mind and open hands.

As soon as she did, she found new words coming to her lips, and most strangely of all, new wings springing from her body, which Damon was holding bent sharply back from the hips. These ethereal wings were not for flying, but for something else, and when they fully unfurled they made a huge, rainbow-colored arch whose very tip circled back again, surrounding and enfolding Damon and Elena both.

And then she said it telepathically. *Wings of Redemption*.

And inside, soundlessly, Damon screamed.

Then the wings opened slightly. Only one who had learned a great deal about magic would have seen what was happening inside them. Damon's anguish was becoming Elena's anguish as she took from him every painful inci-dent, every tragedy, every cruelty that had ever gone into making up the stony layers of indifference and unkindness that encased his heart.

Layers—as hard as the stone at the heart of a black dwarf star—were breaking up and flying away. There was no stopping it. Great chunks and boulders fractured, fine pieces shattered. Some dissolved into nothing more than a puff of acrid smelling smoke.

There was something at the center, though—some nucleus that was blacker than hell and harder than the horns of the devil. She couldn't quite see what happened to it. She thought—she hoped—that at the very end even it blasted open.

Now, and only now, could she call for the next set of wings. She hadn't been sure that she would live through the first attack; she certainly didn't feel as if she could live through this one. But Damon had to know.

Damon was kneeling on one knee on the floor, with his arms clasped tightly around him. That should be all right. He was still Damon, and he'd be a lot happier without the weight of all that hatred and prejudice and cruelty. He wouldn't keep remembering his youth and the other young blades who'd mocked his father for being an old fool, with his disastrous investments and his mistresses younger than his own sons. Neither would he endlessly dwell on his own childhood, when that same father had beaten him in drunken rages when he neglected his studies or took up with objectionable companions.

And, finally, he would not go on savoring and contemplating the many terrible things he'd done himself. He
had been redeemed, in heaven's name and in heaven's
time, by words put into Elena's mouth.

But now . . . there was something that he needed to
remember. If Elena was right.

If only she were right.

"Where is this place? Are you hurt, girl?"

In his confusion, he couldn't recognize her. He had
knelt; now she knelt beside him.

He gave her a keen glance. "Are we at prayer or were
we making love? Was it the Watch or the Gonzalgos?"

"Damon," she said, "it's me, Elena. It's the twenty-first
century, now, and you are a vampire." Then, gently embracing him, with her cheek against his, she whispered, *Wings
of Remembrance.*"

And a pair of translucent butterfly wings, violet, cerulean, and midnight blue in color, sprouted from her backbone, just above her hips. The wings were decorated with
tiny sapphires and translucent amethysts in intricate patterns. Using muscles she had never used before, she easily
drew them up and forward until they curled inside out,
and Damon was shielded within them. It was like being
enclosed in a dim, jewel-studded cave.

She could see in Damon's fine-bred features that he
didn't want to remember anything more than he did right
now. But new memories, memories connected with her,

were already welling up inside him. He looked at his lapis lazuli ring and Elena could see tears come to his eyes. Then, slowly, his gaze turned on her.

"Elena?"

"Yes."

"Someone possessed me, and took the memories of the times I was possessed," he whispered.

"Yes—at least, I think so."

"And someone hurt you."

"Yes."

"I swore to kill him or make him your slave a hundred times over. He *struck* you. He took your blood by force. He made up ludicrous stories about hurting you in other ways."

"Damon. Yes, that's true. But, please—"

"I was on his track. If I'd met him I might have run him through; might have ripped his beating heart out of his chest. Or I might have taught him the most painful lessons I've heard tales of—and I've heard a lot of tales—and at the end, through the blood in his mouth, he would have kissed your heel, your slave until he died."

This wasn't good for him. She could see it. His eyes were white all around, like a terrified colt's.

"Damon, I *beg* you . . ."

"And the one who hurt you . . . was me."

"Not you by yourself. You said it yourself. You were *possessed*."

"You feared me so much you stripped yourself for me."

Elena remembered the original Pendleton shirt.

"I didn't want you and Matt fighting."

"You let me bleed you when it was against your true will."

This time she could find nothing to say but, "Yes."

"I—*dear God!*—I used my powers to afflict you with terrible grief!"

"If you mean an attack that causes hideous pain and seizures, then yes. And you were worse to Matt."

Matt wasn't on Damon's radarscope. "And then I kidnapped you."

"You *tried*."

"And you jumped out of a speeding car rather than take your chances with me."

"You were playing rough, Damon. They had told you to go out and play rough, maybe even to break your toys."

"I've been looking for the one who made you jump from the car—I couldn't remember anything before that. And I swore to take out his eyes and his tongue before he died in agony. You couldn't walk. You had to use a crutch to get through the forest, and just when help should have come, Shinichi drew you into a trap. Oh, yes, I know him. You wandered into his snow globe . . . and would be wandering still if I hadn't broken it."

"No," Elena said quietly. "I would have been dead a long time ago. You found me at the point of suffocation, remember?"

"Yes." A moment of fierce joy on his face. But then the trapped, horrified look returned. "I was the tormenter, the persecutor, the one you were so terrified of. I made you do things with—with—"

"Matt."

"O God," he said, and it was clearly an invocation to the deity, not just an exclamation, because he looked up, holding his clenched hands to heaven. "I thought I was being a hero for you. Instead *I'm* the abomination. What now? By rights, I should be dead at your feet already." He looked at her with wide, feral, black eyes. There was no humor in them, no sarcasm, no holding back. He looked very young and very wild and desperate. If he'd been a black leopard he'd have been pacing his cage frantically, biting at the bars.

Then he bowed his head to kiss her bare foot.

Elena was shocked.

"I'm yours to do what you please with," he said in that same stunned voice. "You can order me to die right now. After all my clever talk, it turns out that I'm the monster."

And then he wept. Probably no other set of circumstances could have brought tears to Damon Salvatore's eyes. But he had boxed himself in. He never broke his word, and he'd given his word to break the monster, the one who had done all this to Elena. The fact that he had been possessed—at first a little, and then more and more, until his entire mind was simply another of Shinichi's toys, to be picked up and put down at leisure— didn't make up for his crimes.

"You know that I—I'm damned," he told her, as if perhaps that might go a small way toward restitution.

"No, I *don't*," Elena said. "Because I don't believe that's true. And Damon, think of how many times you fought them. I'm sure they wanted you to kill Caroline that first night you said you felt something in her mirror. You said you almost did it. I'm sure they want you to kill me. Are you going to do it?"

He bent toward her foot again, and she hastily grabbed him by the shoulders. She couldn't stand to see him in such pain.

But now Damon was looking this way and that, as if he had a definite purpose. He was also twisting the lapis lazuli ring.

"Damon—what are you thinking? Tell me what you're thinking!"

"That he may pick me up as a puppet again—and that this time there may be a *real* birch rod. Shinichi—he's monstrous beyond your innocent belief. And he can take me over at a moment's notice. We've seen that."

"He can't if you'll let me kiss you."

"What?" He looked at her as if she hadn't been following the conversation properly.

"Let me kiss you—and strip out that dying malach inside you."

"Dying?"

"It dies a little more each time you gain enough strength to turn your back on it."

"Is—it very big?"

"As big as you are by now."

"Good," he whispered. "I only wish I could fight it myself."

"*Pour le sport?*" Elena answered, showing that her summer in France last year hadn't been entirely wasted.

"No. Because I hate the bastard's guts and I'd happily suffer a hundred times its pain as long as I knew I was hurting *it*."

Elena decided this was no time for delay. He was ready. "Will you let me do this one last thing?"

"I told you before—the monster who hurt you is your slave now."

All right. They could argue about that point later. Elena leaned forward and tilted her head up, lips pursed slightly.

After a few moments, Damon, the Don Juan of darkness, got the point.

He kissed her very gently, as if afraid to make too much contact.

"Wings of Purification," Elena whispered against his

lips. These wings were as white as untrammeled snow, and lacelike, barely existing in some places at all. They arched high above Elena, shimmering with an iridescence that reminded her of moonlight on frosted cobwebs. They encased mortal and vampire in a web made of diamond and pearl.

"This is going to hurt you," Elena said, not knowing how she knew. The knowledge seemed to come moment by moment as she needed it. It was almost like being in a dream where great truths are understood without needing to be learned, and accepted without astonishment.

And that was how she knew that *Wings of Purification* would seek out and destroy anything foreign inside Damon and that the feeling could be very unpleasant for him. When the malach didn't seem to be coming out of its own accord, she said, prompted by her inner voice, "Take off your shirt. The malach is attached to your spine and it's closest to the skin at the back of your neck where it entered. I'm going to have to strip it out by hand."

"Attached to my spine?"

"Yes. Did you ever feel it? I think it would have felt like a bee sting at first, as it entered you, just a sharp little drill and a blob of jelly that attached to your spine."

"Oh. The mosquito bite. Yes, I felt that. And then later, my neck began to ache, and at last my whole body. Was it . . . growing inside me?"

"Yes, and taking over more and more of your nervous system. Shinichi was controlling you like a marionette."

"Dear God, I'm *sorry*."

"Let's make him be sorry instead. Will you take off your shirt?"

Silently, like a trusting child, Damon took off his black jacket and shirt. Then, as Elena motioned him into position, he lay across her lap, his back hard with muscle and pale against the dark ground on either side.

"I'm sorry," she said. "Getting rid of it this way—pulling it out through the hole where it entered—will *really* hurt."

"Good," grunted Damon. And then he buried his face in his lithe, flat-muscled arms.

Elena used the pads of her fingers, feeling at the top of his spine for what she was looking for. A squishy point. A blister. When she found it, she pinched it with her fingernails until blood suddenly spurted.

She almost lost it then as it tried to go flat, but she was pursuing it with sharp nails—and it was too slow. At last she had it held firmly between thumbnail and two fingernails.

The malach was still alive and aware enough to feebly resist her. But it was like a jellyfish trying to resist—only jellyfish broke apart when you pulled. This slick, slimy, man-shaped thing retained its shape as she slowly pulled it through the breach in Damon's skin.

And it was hurting him. She could tell. She started to take some of the pain into herself, but he gasped, *"No!"* with such vehemence that she decided to let him have his way.

The malach was much larger and more substantial than she had realized. It must have been growing a long time, she thought—the little blob of jelly that had expanded until it controlled him to the fingertips. She had to sit up, then scoot away from Damon and back again before it lay on the ground, a sickly, stringy, white caricature of a human body.

"Is it done?" Damon was breathless—it really had hurt, then.

"Yes."

Damon stood and looked down at the flabby white thing—barely twitching—that had made him persecute the person he cared most about in the world. Then, deliberately, he trampled on it, crushing it under the heels of his boots until it lay torn in pieces, and then trampling the pieces. Elena guessed that he didn't dare blast it with Power for fear of alerting Shinichi.

At last, all that was left was a stain and a smell.

Elena didn't know why she felt so dizzy then. But she reached for Damon and he reached for her and they went to their knees holding each other.

"I release you from every promise you made—while

in the possession of that malach," Elena said. This was strategy. She didn't want to release him from the promise of caring for his brother.

"Thank you," Damon whispered, the weight of his head on her shoulder.

"And now," said Elena, like a kindergarten teacher who wants to move quickly on to another activity, "We need to make plans. But to make plans in utter secrecy . . ."

"We have to share blood. But Elena, how much have you donated today? You look white."

"You said you'd be my slave—now you won't take a little of my blood."

"You said you released me—instead you're going to hold that over me forever, aren't you? But there's a simpler solution. You take some of *my* blood."

And in the end that was what they did, although it made Elena feel slightly guilty, as if she were betraying Stefan. Damon cut himself with the minimum of fuss, and then it began to happen—they were *sharing* minds, melting seamlessly together. In much shorter a time than it would take to speak the sentences aloud, it was done: Elena had told Damon of what her friends had found about the epidemic among the girls of Fell's Church— and Damon had told Elena everything he knew about Shinichi and Misao. Elena concocted a plan for scaring out any other possessed youngsters like Tami, and

Damon promised to try to find out where Stefan was from the kitsune twins.

And, finally, when there was nothing more to say, and Damon's blood had restored faint color to Elena's cheeks they made plans as to how to meet again.

At the ceremony.

And then there was only Elena in the room, and a large raven winging its way toward the Old Wood.

Sitting on the cold stone floor, Elena took a moment to put all she now knew together. No wonder Damon had seemed so schizophrenic. No wonder he had remembered, and then forgotten, and then remembered that he was the one she was running from.

He remembered, she reasoned, when Shinichi was not controlling him, or at least was keeping him on a very loose rein. But his memory was spotty because some of the things he'd done were so terrible that his own mind had rejected them. They had seamlessly become part of the possessed Damon's memory, for when possessed Shinichi was controlling every word, every deed. And in between episodes, Shinichi was telling him that he had to find Elena's tormentor and kill him.

All very amusing, she supposed, for this kitsune, Shinichi. But for both her and Damon it had been hell.

Her mind refused to admit that there had been

moments of heaven mixed in with the hell. She was Stefan's, alone. That would never change.

Now Elena needed one more magical door, and she didn't know how to find one. But there was the twinkling fairy light again. She guessed it was the last of the magic that Honoria Fell had left to protect the town she had founded. Elena felt a little guilty, using it up—but if it wasn't meant for her, why had she been brought here?

To try for the most important destination she could imagine.

Reaching for the speck with one hand and clenching the key in the other she whispered with all the force at her command:

"Somewhere I can see and hear and touch Stefan."

prison, with filthy rushes on the floor and bars between her and the sleeping Stefan.

Between her and *Stefan*!

It was really him. Elena didn't know how she could know. Undoubtedly they could twist and change your perceptions here. But just now, perhaps because nobody had been expecting her to drop into a dungeon, no one was prepared with anything to make her doubt her senses.

It *was* Stefan. He was thinner than before, and his cheekbones stuck out. He was beautiful. And his mind *felt* just right, just the right mixture of honor and love and darkness and light and hope and grim understanding of the world he lived in.

"Stefan! Oh, *hold me*!"

He woke and half sat up. "At least leave me my sleep.

And meanwhile go away and put on another face, bitch!"

"Stefan! Language!"

She saw muscles in Stefan's shoulders freeze.

"What . . . did you . . . say?"

"Stefan . . . *it's really me.* I don't blame you for cursing. I curse this whole place and the two who put you here. . . ."

"Three," he said wearily, and bent his head. "You'd know that if you were real. Go and let them teach you about my traitor brother and his friends who sneak up on people with kekkai crowns . . ."

Elena couldn't wait to debate about Damon now. "Won't you *look* at me, at least?"

She saw him turn slowly, look slowly, then saw him leap up from a pallet made of sickly-looking hay, and saw him stare at her as if she were an angel dropped down from the sky.

Then he turned his back on her and put his hands over his ears.

"No bargains," he said flatly. "Don't even mention them to me. Go away. You've gotten better but you're still a dream."

"Stefan!"

"I said, go away!"

Time was wasting. And this was too cruel, after what she had been through just to speak to him.

"You first saw me just outside the principal's office the day you brought your papers into school and influenced the secretary. You didn't need to look at me to know what I looked like. Once I told you that I felt like a murderer because I said, 'Daddy, look' and pointed to—something outside—just before the car accident that killed my parents. I've never been able to remember what the something was. The first word I learned when I came back from the afterlife was *Stefan*. Once, you looked at me in the rearview mirror of the car and said that I was your soul. . . ."

"Can't you stop torturing me for one hour? Elena—the real Elena—would be too smart to risk her life by coming here."

"Where's 'here'?" Elena said sharply, frightened. "I need to know if I'm supposed to get you out."

Slowly Stefan uncovered his ears. Even more slowly he turned around again.

"Elena?" he said, like a dying boy who has seen a gentle ghost in his bed. "You're not real. You can't be here."

"I don't think I am. Shinichi made a magic house and it takes you wherever you want if you name it and open the door with this key. I said, 'Somewhere I can hear and see and touch Stefan.' But"—she looked down—"you say I *can't* be here. Maybe it's all an illusion anyway."

"Hush." Now Stefan was clenching the bars on his

side of the cell.

"Is this where you've been? Is this the *Shi no Shi*?"

He gave a little laugh—not a real one. "Not exactly what either of us expected, is it? And yet, they didn't lie in anything they said, Elena. Elena! I said 'Elena.' Elena, you're really here!"

Elena couldn't bear to waste any time. She took the few steps through damp, crackly straw and scampering creatures to the bars that separated her from Stefan.

Then she tilted up her face, clutching bars in either hand, and shut her eyes.

I will touch him. I will, I will. I'm real, he's real—I'll touch him!

Stefan leaned down—to humor her, she thought—and then warm lips touched hers.

She put her arms through the bars because they were both weak at the knees: Stefan in astonishment that she could touch him, and Elena in relief and sobbing joy.

But—there was no time.

"Stefan, take my blood *now*—take it!"

She looked desperately for something to cut herself with. Stefan might need her strength, and no matter what Damon had taken from her, she would always have enough for Stefan. If it killed her, she would have enough. She was glad, now, that in the tomb, Damon had persuaded her to take his.

"Easy. Easy, little love. If you mean it, I can bite your wrist, but . . ."

"Do it *now*!" Elena Gilbert, the princess of Fell's Church, ordered. She had even gotten the strength to pull herself off her knees. Stefan gave her half a guilty glance.

"*NOW!*" Elena insisted.

Stefan bit her wrist.

It was an odd sensation. It hurt a little more than when he pierced the side of her neck as usual. But there were good veins down there, she knew; she trusted Stefan to find the largest so that this would take the least amount of time. Her urgency had become his.

But when he tried to pull back, she clutched a handful of his wavy dark hair and said, "More, Stefan. You need it—oh, I can tell, a*nd we don't have time to argue.*"

The voice of command. Meredith had told her once that she had it, that she could lead armies. Well, she might need to lead armies to get into this place to save him.

I'll get an army somewhere, she thought fuzzily.

The starving bloodfever that Stefan had been in— they obviously hadn't fed him since she had last seen him—was dying into the more normal blood-taking that she knew. His mind melted into hers. *When you say you'll get an army, I believe you. But it's impossible. No one's ever come back.*

Well, you will. I'm bringing you back.

Elena, Elena . . .

Drink, she said, feeling like an Italian mother. *As much as you can without being sick.*

But how did—no, you told me how you got here. That was the truth?

The truth. I always tell you the truth. But Stefan, how do I get you out?

Shinichi and Misao—you know them?

Enough.

They each have half a ring. Together it makes a key. Each half is shaped like a running fox. But who knows where they may have hidden the pieces? And as I said, just to get into this place, it takes an army. . . .

I'll find the pieces of the fox ring. I'll put them together. I'll get an army. I'll get you out.

Elena, I can't keep drinking. You'll collapse.

I'm good at not collapsing. Please go on.

I can hardly believe it's you—

"No kissing! Take my blood!"

Ma'am! But Elena, truly, I'm full now. Overfull.

And tomorrow?

"I'll still be overfull." Stefan pulled away, a thumb on the places where he had pierced veins. "Truly, I *can't*, love."

"And the next day?"

"I'll manage."

"You will—because I brought *this*. Hold me, Stefan," she said, several decibels softer. "Hold me through the bars."

He did, looking bewildered, and she hissed in his ear, "Act like you love me. Stroke my hair. Say nice things."

"Elena, lovely little love . . ." He was still close enough mentally to say telepathically: Act *like I love you?* But while his hands were stroking and squeezing and tangling in her hair, Elena's own hands were busy. She was transferring from under her clothes to under his a flask full of Black Magic wine.

"But where did you get it?" Stefan whispered, seeming thunderstruck.

"The magic house has everything. I've been waiting for my chance to give it to you if you needed it."

"Elena—"

"What?"

Stefan seemed to be struggling with something. At last, eyes on the ground, he whispered, "It's no good. I can't risk you getting killed for the sake of an impossibility. Forget me."

"Put your face to the bars."

He looked at her but didn't ask any questions, obeying.

She slapped him across the face.

It wasn't a very hard slap . . . although Elena's hand hurt from colliding with the iron on either side.

"Now, *be ashamed*!" she said. And before he could say anything else, *"Listen!"*

It was the baying of hounds—far away, but getting closer.

"It's *you* they're after," Stefan said, suddenly frantic. "You have to go!"

She just looked at him steadily. "I love you, Stefan."

"I love you, Elena. Forever."

"I—oh, I'm *sorry*." She *couldn't* go; that was the thing. Like Caroline talking and talking and never leaving Stefan's apartment, she could stand here and speak about it, but she couldn't do it.

"Elena! You *have* to. I don't want you to see what they do—"

"I'll kill them!"

"You're no killer. You're not a fighter, Elena—and you shouldn't see this. Please? Remember once you asked me if I'd like to see how many times you could make me say 'please?' Well, each counts for a thousand now. Please? For me? Will you go?"

"One more kiss . . ." Her heart was beating like a frantic bird inside her.

"*Please!*"

Blind with tears, Elena turned around and grasped hold of the cell door.

"Anywhere outside the ceremony where no one will see me!" she gasped and wrenched the door to the corridor open and stepped through.

At least she'd seen Stefan, but for how long that would last to keep her heart from shattering again—

—oh, my God, I'm *falling*—

—she didn't know.

* * *

Elena realized that she *was* outside the boardinghouse somewhere—at least some eighty feet high—and plummeting rapidly. Her first, panicked conclusion was that she was going to die, and then instinct kicked in and she reached out with arms and hands and kicked in with legs and feet and managed to arrest her fall after twenty agonizing feet.

I've lost my flying wings forever, haven't I? she thought, concentrating on a single spot between her shoulder blades. She knew just where they should be—and nothing happened.

Then, carefully, she inched her way closer to the trunk, pausing only to move to a higher twig a caterpillar that was sharing the branch with her. And she managed to find a sort of place where she could sit by sidling and then pushing backward. It was far too high a branch for her personal taste.

As it was, she found that she could look down and see the widow's walk quite clearly, and that the longer she looked at any particular thing the clearer her vision got. Vampire vision plus, she thought. It showed her that she was Changing. Or else—yes, somehow here the sky was getting lighter.

What it showed her was a dark and empty boardinghouse, which was disturbing because of what Caroline's father had said about "the meeting" and what she had learned telepathically from Damon about Shinichi's plans for this Moonspire night. Could this be not the real boardinghouse at all, but another trap?

"We made it!" Bonnie cried as they approached the house. She knew her voice was shrill, was over-shrill, but somehow the sight of that brightly lit boardinghouse, like a Christmas tree with a star on top, comforted her, even if she knew that it was all wrong. She felt she could cry in relief.

"Yes, we did," Dr. Alpert's deep voice said. "All of us. Isobel's the one who needs the most treatment, the fastest. Theophilia, get your nostrums ready, and somebody else take Isobel and run her a bath."

"I'll do it," Bonnie quavered, after a brief hesitation. "She's going to stay tranquilized like she is now, right? Right?"

"*I'll* go with Isobel," Matt said. "Bonnie, you go with Mrs. Flowers and help her. And before we go inside, I want to make one thing clear: nobody goes anywhere alone. We all travel in twos or threes." There was the ring of authority in his voice.

"Makes sense," Meredith said crisply and took up a place by the doctor. "You'd better be careful, Matt; Isobel is the most dangerous."

That was when the high, thin voices began outside the house. It sounded like two or three little girls singing.

"Isa-chan, Isa-chan,
Drank her tea and ate her gran."

"Tami? Tami Bryce?" Meredith demanded, opening the door as the tune began again. She darted forward, then she grabbed the doctor by the hand, and dragged her along beside her as she darted forward again.

And, yes, Bonnie saw, there were three little figures, one in pajamas and two in nightgowns, and they were Tami Bryce and Kristin Dunstan and Ava Zarinski. Ava was only about eleven, Bonnie thought, and she didn't live near either Tami or Kristin. The three of them all giggled shrilly. Then they started singing again and Matt went after Kristin.

"Help me!" Bonnie cried. She was suddenly hanging on to a bucking, kicking bronco that lashed out in every direction. Isobel seemed to have gone crazy, and she went crazier every time that tune was repeated.

"I've got her," Matt said, closing in on her with a bear hug, but even the two of them couldn't hold Isobel still.

"I'm getting her another sedative," Dr. Alpert said, and Bonnie saw the glances between Matt and Meredith—glances of suspicion.

"No—no, let Mrs. Flowers make her something," Bonnie said desperately, but the hypodermic needle was already almost at Isobel's arm.

"You're not giving her anything," Meredith said flatly, dropping the charade, and with one chorus-girl kick, she sent the hypodermic flying.

"Meredith! What's wrong with you?" the doctor cried, wringing her wrist.

"It's what's wrong with *you* that's the matter. Who are you? Where are we? This can't be the real boarding-house."

"Obaasan! Mrs. Flowers! Can't you help us?" Bonnie gasped, still trying to hold on to Isobel.

"I'll try," Mrs. Flowers said determinedly, heading toward her.

"No, I meant with Dr. Alpert—and maybe Jim. Don't you—know any spells—to make people take on their true forms?"

"Oh!" Obaasan said. "I can help with that. Just let me down, Jim dear. We'll have everyone in their true forms in no time."

Jayneela was a sophomore with large, dreamy, dark eyes that were generally lost in a book. But now, as it neared midnight and Gramma still hadn't called, she shut her book and looked at Ty. Tyrone seemed big and fierce and mean on the playing field, but off it he was the nicest, kindest, gentlest big brother a girl could want.

"You think Gramma's okay?"

"Hm?" Tyrone had his nose in a book, too, but it was one of those help-you-get-into-the-college-of-your-dreams books. As a senior-to-be, he was having to make some serious decisions. "Of course she is."

"Well, I'm going to check on the little girl, at least."

"You know what, Jay?" He poked her teasingly with one toe. "You worry too much."

In moments he was lost again in Chapter Six, "How to Make the Most of Your Community Service." But then the screams started coming from above him. Long, loud, high screams—his sister's voice. He dropped the book and ran.

"Obaasan?" Bonnie said.

"Just a moment, dear," Grandma Saitou said. Jim had put her down and now she was facing him squarely: she looking up, and he looking down. And there was something . . . very wrong about it.

Bonnie felt a wave of pure terror. Could Jim have done something evil to Obaasan as he carried her? Of course he could. Why hadn't she thought of that? And there was the doctor with her syringe, ready to tranquilize anyone who got too "hysterical." Bonnie looked at Meredith, but Meredith was trying to deal with two squirming little girls, and could only glance helplessly back.

All right, then, Bonnie thought. I'll kick him where it

hurts most and get the old lady away from him. She turned back to Obaasan and felt herself freeze.

"Just one thing I have to do . . . ," Obaasan had said. And she was doing it. Jim was bent at the waist, folded in half toward Obaasan, who was on her tiptoes. They were locked in a deep, intimate kiss.

Oh, God!

They had met four people in a wood—and assumed that two were sane and two insane. How could they tell which were the insane ones? Well, if two of them see things that aren't there . . .

But the house *was* there; Bonnie could see it, too. Was *she* insane?

"Meredith, come on!" she screamed. Her nerve breaking completely, she began to run away from the house toward the forest.

Something from the skies plucked her up as easily as an owl picks up a mouse and held her in an unrelenting iron grip.

"Going somewhere?" Damon's voice asked from above her as he glided in the last few yards to a stop, with her neatly tucked under one steely arm.

"Damon!"

Damon's eyes were slightly narrowed, as though at a joke only he could see. "Yes, the evil one himself. Tell me something, my fiery little fury."

Bonnie had already exhausted herself trying to make

him let go. She hadn't even succeeded in tearing his clothes.

"What?" she snapped. Possessed or not, Damon had last seen her when she had Called him to save her from Caroline's insanity. But according to Matt's reports, he had done something awful to Elena.

"Why do girls love to convert a sinner? Why can you feed them almost any line if they feel that they've reformed you?"

Bonnie didn't know what he was talking about, but she could guess. "What did you do with Elena?" she said ferociously.

"Gave her what she wanted, that's all," Damon said, his black eyes twinkling. "Is there anything so awful about that?"

Bonnie, frightened by that twinkle, didn't even try to run again. She knew it was no use. He was faster and stronger, and he could fly. Anyway, she had seen it in his face: a sort of distant remorselessness. They were not just Damon and Bonnie here together. They were natural predator and natural prey.

And now here she was back with Jim and Obaasan—no, with a boy and girl she'd never seen before. Bonnie was in time to watch the transformation. She saw Jim's body shrink and his hair turn black, but that wasn't the striking thing about it. The striking thing was that all around the edges, his hair was not black but crimson. It was as if flames were licking up from the tips into darkness. His eyes were golden and smiling.

She saw Obaasan's doll-like old body grow younger and stronger and taller. This girl was a beauty; Bonnie had to admit it. She had gorgeous sloe-black eyes and silky hair that fell almost to her waist. And her hair was just like her brother's—only the red was even brighter, scarlet instead of crimson. She was wearing a barely-there laced black halter that showed how delicately built she was on top. And, of course, low-rise black leather pants to show the same thing on the bottom. She was wearing expensive-looking black high-heeled sandals, and her toenails were enameled the same brilliant red as the tips of her hair. At her belt, in a sinuous circle, was a curled-up whip with a scaly black handle.

Dr. Alpert said slowly, "My grandchildren . . . ?"

"They don't have anything to do with this," the boy with the strange hair said charmingly, smiling. "As long as they mind their own business, you don't have to worry about them a bit."

"It's suicide or an attempted suicide—or something," Tyrone told the police dispatcher, almost weeping. "I think it was a guy named Jim who went to my high school last year. No, this is nothing to do with any drugs—I came here to watch my little sister Jayneela. She was baby-sitting—look, just come over, will you? This guy's chewed off most of his fingers, and as I came in, he said, 'I'll always love you, Elena,' and he took a pencil and—no, I can't tell if he's alive or dead. But there's an old lady upstairs and I'm sure *she's* dead. Because she's not breathing."

"Who the hell are you?" Matt was saying, eyeing the strange boy belligerently.

"I'm the—"

"—and what the hell are you doing here?"

"I'm the hell Shinichi," the boy said in a much louder voice, looking annoyed to be interrupted. When Matt just stared at him, he added in an annoyed voice, "I'm the kitsune—the were-fox, you could say—who's been messing with your town, idiot. I came halfway around the world to do it, and I'd think you'd at least have heard of me by now. And this is my lovely sister, Misao. We're twins."

"I don't care if you're triplets. Elena said somebody besides Damon was behind this. And so did Stefan before he—hey, what did you do to Stefan? *What did you do to Elena?*"

While the two strange males were bristling at each other—quite literally in Shinichi's case, since his hair was almost standing on end—Meredith was picking out Bonnie, Dr. Alpert, and Mrs. Flowers by eye. Then she glanced at Matt and touched herself lightly on the chest. She was the only one strong enough to womanhandle him, although Dr. Alpert gave a quick nod that said she would be helping.

And then, while the boys were working up to shouting volume, Misao was giggling at the ground, and Damon was leaning against a door with his eyes shut, they moved. With no signal at all to unite them, they were running, instinctively, as one group. Meredith and Dr. Alpert grabbed Matt from either side and simply lifted him off his feet, just as Isobel quite unexpectedly jumped on Shinichi with a guttural scream. They hadn't expected anything from her, but it was certainly convenient, Bonnie thought as she hurtled over obstacles without even seeing them. Matt was still shouting and trying to run the other way and take out some primitive frustration on Shinichi, but he couldn't quite manage to get free to do it.

Bonnie could scarcely believe it when they made it into the Wood again. Even Mrs. Flowers had kept up and most of them still had their flashlights.

It was a miracle. They had even escaped Damon. The thing now was to be very quiet and to try to get through the Old Wood without disturbing anything. Maybe they could find their way back to the real boardinghouse, they decided. Then they could figure out how to save Elena from Damon and his two friends. Even Matt finally had to admit that it was unlikely that they would be able to overcome the three supernatural creatures by force.

Bonnie just wished they'd been able to take Isobel with them.

* * *

"Well, we have to go to the real boardinghouse anyway," Damon said, as Misao finally got Isobel subdued and semi-conscious. "That's where Caroline will be."

Misao stopped glaring at Isobel and seemed to start slightly. "Caroline? Why do we want Caroline?"

"It's all part of the fun, isn't it?" Damon said in his most charming, flirtatious voice. Shinichi immediately stopped looking martyred and smiled.

"That girl—she's the one you've been using as a carrier, right?" He looked mischievously at his sister, whose smile seemed slightly strained.

"Yes, but—"

"The more the merrier," Damon said, more cheerful with every minute. He didn't seem to notice Shinichi smirking at Misao behind his back.

"Don't sulk, darling," he said to her, tickling her under the chin while his golden eyes gleamed. "I've never set eyes on the girl. But of course, if Damon says it'll be fun, it *will* be." The smirk became a full-fledged gloating smile.

"And there's no chance of any of them actually getting away at all?" Damon said, almost absently, staring into the darkness of the Old Wood.

"Give me a little credit, please," the kitsune snapped. "You're a damned—a vampire, aren't you? *You're* not supposed to hang out in the woods at all."

"It's my territory, along with the cemetery—" Damon was beginning mildly, but Shinichi was determined to finish first this time. "I *live* in the woods," he said. "I control the bushes, the trees—and I've brought a few of my own little experiments along with me. You'll all see them soon enough. So, to answer your question, no, not one of them is going to escape."

"That was all I asked," Damon said, still mildly, but locking gazes with the golden eyes for another long moment. Then he shrugged and turned away, eyeing the moon that could be seen between swirling clouds on the horizon.

"We've got hours before the ceremony yet," Shinichi said, behind him. "We're hardly going to be late."

"We'd better not," Damon murmured. "Caroline can do an awfully good impression of that pierced girl in hysterics when people are late."

As a matter of fact, the moon was riding high in the sky as Caroline drove her mother's car to the porch of the boardinghouse. She was wearing an evening dress that looked as if it had been painted on her, in her favorite colors of bronze and green. Shinichi looked at Misao, who giggled with one hand covering her mouth and looked down.

Damon walked Caroline up the porch steps to the front door and said, "This way to the good seats."

There was some bewilderment as people got themselves sorted out. Damon spoke cheerfully to Kristin and

Tami and Ava: "The peanut gallery for you three, I'm afraid. That means you sit on the ground. But if you're good, I'll let you come sit up with us the next time."

The others followed him with more or less exclamation, but it was Caroline who looked annoyed, saying, "Why do we want to go *inside*? I thought they were supposed to be *outside*."

"Closest seats not in danger," Damon said briefly. "We can get the best view from up there. Royal box seats, come on, now."

The fox twins and the human girl followed him, switching on lights in the darkened house all the way up to the widow's walk on the roof.

"And now where are they?" Caroline said, peering down.

"They'll be here any minute," Shinichi said, with a glance that was both puzzled and reproving. It said: Who does this girl think she is? He didn't spout any poetry.

"And Elena? She'll be here, too?"

Shinichi didn't answer that at all, and Misao just giggled. But Damon put his lips close to Caroline's ear and whispered.

After that, Caroline's eyes shone green as a cat's. And the smile on her lips was the one of a cat who has just put its paw on the canary.

36

Elena had been waiting in her tree.

It wasn't, as a matter of fact, all that different from her six months in the spirit world, where she had spent most of her time watching other people, and waiting, and watching them some more. Those months had taught her a patient alertness that would have astounded anyone who knew the old, wildfire Elena.

Of course, the old, wildfire Elena was still inside her, too, and occasionally it rebelled. As far as she could see, nothing was happening in the dark boardinghouse. Only the moon seemed to move, creeping slowly higher into the sky.

Damon said this Shinichi had a thing about 4:44 in the morning or evening, she thought. Maybe this Black Magic was working to a different schedule than any she'd heard of.

In any case, it was for Stefan. And as soon as she thought that she knew that she would wait here for days, if that's what it took. She could certainly wait until daybreak, when no self-respecting Black Magic-worker would ever thing of beginning a ceremony.

And, in the end, what she was waiting for came to rest right below her feet.

First came the figures, walking sedately out of the Old Wood and toward the gravel pathways of the boarding-house. They weren't hard to identify, even at long range. One was Damon, who had a *je ne sais quois* about him that Elena couldn't miss at a quarter of a mile—and then again there was his aura, which was a very good facsimile of his old aura: that unreadable, un-breachable ball of black stone. A *very* good imitation, in fact. Actually, it was almost exactly like the one . . .

It was then, Elena later realized, that she felt her very first qualm.

But right now she was so caught up in the moment that she brushed the uneasy thought away. The one with the deep gray aura with crimson flashes would be Shinichi, she guessed. And the one with the same aura as the possessed girls: a sort of muddy color slashed with orange must be the twin sister Misao.

Only those two, Shinichi and Misao, were holding hands, even occasionally nuzzling each other—as Elena could see as they came up close to the boardinghouse. They certainly weren't acting like any brother and sister that Elena had seen.

Moreover, Damon was carrying a mostly-naked girl over his shoulder, and Elena couldn't imagine who that might be.

Patience, she thought to herself. *Patience*. The major players are here at last, just as Damon promised they would be. And the minor players . . .

Well, first, following Damon and his group were three little girls. She recognized Tami Bryce instantly from her aura, but the other two were strangers. They hopped, skipped, and *frisked* out of the Wood and to the boarding-house, where Damon said something to them and they came around to sit in Mrs. Flowers' kitchen garden, almost directly below Elena. One look at the auras of the strange girls was enough to identify them as more of Misao's pets.

Then, up the driveway came a very familiar car—it belonged to Caroline's mother. Caroline stepped out of it and was helped into the boardinghouse by Damon, who had done something—Elena had missed what—with his burden.

Elena rejoiced as she saw lights coming on as Damon and his three guests traveled up the boardinghouse, light-ing their way as they went. They came out on the very top, standing in a row on the widow's walk, looking down.

Damon snapped his fingers, and the backyard lights went on as if it were a cue for a show.

But Elena didn't see the actors—the victims of the ceremony that was about to begin, until just then. They were being herded around the far corner of the boardinghouse. She could see them all: Matt and Meredith and Bonnie, and Mrs. Flowers and, strangely, old Dr. Alpert. What Elena didn't understand was why they weren't fighting harder—Bonnie was certainly making enough noise for all of them, but they acted as if they were being pushed forward against their will.

That was when she saw the looming darkness behind them. Huge dark shadows, with no features that she could identify.

It was at that point that Elena realized, even over Bonnie's yelling, if she held herself still inside and focused hard enough, she could hear what everyone on the widow's walk was saying. And Misao's shrill voice cut through the rest.

"Oh lucky! We got all of them back," she squealed, and kissed her brother's cheek, despite his brief look of annoyance.

"Of course we did. I said so," he was beginning, when Misao squealed once more.

"But which of them do we start with?" She kissed her brother and he stroked her hair, relenting.

"You pick the first one," he said.

"You darling," Misao cooed shamelessly.

These two, Elena thought, are real charmers. Twins, huh?

"The little noisy one," Shinichi said firmly, pointing to Bonnie. "*Urusei*, brat! Shut up!" he added as Bonnie was pushed or carried forward by the shadows. Now Elena could see her more clearly.

And she could hear Bonnie's heartrending pleas to Damon not to do this to . . . *the others*. "I'm not begging for myself," she cried, as she was dragged into the light. "But Dr. Alpert is a good woman; she has nothing to do with this. Neither does Mrs. Flowers. And Meredith and Matt have already suffered enough. *Please!*"

There was a ragged chorus of sound as the others apparently tried to fight and were subdued. But Matt's voice rose above it all. "You touch her, Salvatore, and you'd better make damn sure you kill me, too!"

Elena's heart jerked as she heard Matt's voice sounding so strong and well. She'd found him at last, but she couldn't think of a way to save him.

"And then we have to decide what to do with them to start with," Misao said, clapping like a happy child at her birthday party.

"Take your pick." Shinichi caressed his sister's hair and whispered into her ear. She turned and kissed him on the mouth. Not hastily, either.

"What the—what's going on?" Caroline said. She had never been shy, that one, Elena thought. Now she had moved forward to cling to Shinichi's unoccupied hand.

For just an instant, Elena thought he would throw her off the widow's walk and watch her plunge to the ground. Then he turned, and he and Misao stared at each other.

Then he laughed.

"Sorry, sorry, it's so hard when you're the life of the party," he said. "Well, what do you think, Carolyn—Caroline?"

Caroline was staring at him. "Why's she holding you that way?"

"In the *Shi no Shi*, sisters are precious," Shinichi said. "And . . . well, I haven't seen her in a long time. We're getting reacquainted." But the kiss he planted on Misao's palm was hardly brotherly. "Go on," he added quickly, to Caroline. "You choose the first act in the Moonspire Festival! What shall we do with her?"

Caroline began to imitate Misao, kissing Shinichi's cheek and ear. "I'm new here," she said flirtatiously. "I don't really know what you want me to pick."

"Silly Caroline. Naturally, how she di—" Shinichi was suddenly smothered by a great hug and kiss from his sister.

Caroline, who had obviously wanted the attention of

choice put to her, even if she didn't understand the subject, said huffily, "Well, if you don't tell me, I can't choose. And anyway, where's Elena? I don't see her anywhere!" She seemed about to say more when Damon glided over and whispered in her ear. Then she smiled again, and they both looked at the pine trees surrounding the boarding-house.

That was when Elena had her second qualm. But Misao was already speaking and that required Elena's full attention.

"Lucky! Then I'll pick." Misao leaned forward, peeking over the edge of the roof at the humans below, her dark eyes wide, summing up the possibilities in what looked like a barren clearing. She was so delicate, so graceful as she got up to pace and think; her skin was so fair, and her hair so glossy and dark that even Elena couldn't take her eyes off her.

Then Misao's face lit up and she spoke. "Spread her on the altar. You brought some of your half-breeds?"

The last was not so much a question as an excited exclamation.

"My experiments? Of course, darling. I told you so," Shinichi replied and added, staring into the forest, "Two of you—er, men—and Old Faithful!" And he snapped his fingers. There were several minutes of confusion during which the humans around Bonnie were struck, kicked, thrown to the ground, trampled on, and crushed as they fought with the shadows. And then the things that had shambled forward before, shambled farther forward with Bonnie held in between them, dangling limply from each by a slim arm.

The half-breeds were something like men and something like trees with all the leaves stripped off them. If they had been *made*, it looked as if they had been made specifically to be grotesque and asymmetrical. One had a crooked, knobby left arm that reached almost to its feet, and a right arm that was thick, lumpy, and only waist-high.

They were hideous. Their skin was similar to the chitin-like skin of the insects, but much bumpier, with knotholes and burls and all the outward aspects of bark on their branches. They had a shaggy, unfinished look in places.

They were terrifying. The way their limbs were twisted; the way they walked, shambling forward like apes, the way their bodies ended on top with treelike caricatures of human faces, surmounted by a tangle of thinner branches sticking out at odd angles—they were calculated to look like creatures of nightmare.

And they were naked. They had nothing in place of clothes to disguise the ghastly deformities of their bodies.

And then Elena really knew what terror meant, as the two shambling malach carried the limp Bonnie to a sort of roughly hewn stump of tree like an altar, laid her on it and began to pluck at the many layers of her clothing, clumsily, pulling at them with sticklike fingers that broke off with little crackling sounds even as cloth tore. They didn't seem to care that they broke their fingers off—as long as they accomplished their task.

And then they were using bits of torn cloth, even more clumsily, to tie Bonnie, spread-eagled, to four knobby posts snapped off their own bodies and hammered into the ground around the trunk with four powerful blows by the thick-armed one.

Meanwhile, from somewhere even farther away in the shadows, a third man-tree shuffled forward. And Elena saw that this one was, undeniably, unmistakably male.

For a moment Elena worried that Damon might lose it, go mad, turn around and attack both the were-foxes, revealing his true allegiance now. But his feelings about Bonnie had obviously changed since he had saved her at Caroline's. He appeared perfectly relaxed beside Shinichi and Misao, sitting back and smiling, even saying something that made them laugh.

Suddenly something inside Elena seemed to plummet. This wasn't a qualm. It was full-blown terror. Damon had never looked so natural, so in tune, so *happy* with anyone as he did here with Shinichi and Misao. They couldn't possibly have changed him, she tried to convince herself. They *couldn't* have possessed him again so quickly, not without her, Elena, knowing it. . . .

But when you showed him the truth, he was miserable, her heart whispered. Desperately miserable—miserably desperate. He might have reached for possession as a defiant alcoholic reaches for a bottle, wanting only forgetfulness. If she knew Damon, he had willingly invited the darkness back in.

He couldn't stand to stand in the light, she thought. And so now, he's able to laugh even at Bonnie's suffering.

And where did that leave her? With Damon defected to the other side, no longer ally, but enemy? Elena began to tremble with anger and hatred—yes, and fear, too, as she contemplated her position.

All alone to struggle against three of the strongest enemies she could imagine, and their army of deformed, conscienceless killers? Not to mention Caroline, the cheerleader of spite?

As if to corroborate her fears, as if to show her how slim her chances really were, the tree she was clinging to seemed suddenly to let go of her, and for a moment Elena thought she would fall, spinning and screaming, all the way to the ground. Her handholds and footholds seemed to disappear all at once, and she only saved herself by a frantic—and painful—scrambling through serrated pine needles up to the grooved, dark bark.

You are a human girl now, my dear, the strong, resinous smell seemed to be telling her. *And you are up to your neck in the Powers of the undead and of sorcery. Why fight it? You've lost before you've begun. Give in now and it won't hurt so much.*

If a *person* had been telling her this, trying to hammer it in, the words might have sparked some kind of defiance from the flint of Elena's character. But instead this was just a feeling that came over her, an aura of doom, a knowledge of the hopelessness of her cause, and the inadequacy of her weapons, that seemed to settle over her as gently and as inescapably as a fog.

She leaned her throbbing head against the trunk of the tree. She had never felt so weak, so helpless—or so alone, not since she had been a newly wakened vampire. She wanted Stefan. But Stefan hadn't been able to beat these three, and because of that she might never see him again.

Something new was happening on the roof, she realized wearily. Damon was looking down at Bonnie on the altar, and his expression was petulant. Bonnie's white face was staring up at the evening sky in determination, as if refusing any longer to weep or beg again.

"But . . . are all the *hors d'oeuvres* so predictable?"

Damon asked, seeming genuinely bored.

You bastard, you'd turn on your best friend for amuse-ment, Elena thought. Well, just you wait. But she knew the truth was that without him, she couldn't even put together Plan A, much less fight against these kitsune, these were-foxes.

"You told me that in the *Shi no Shi*, I would see acts of genuine originality," Damon was going on. "Maidens hypnotized to cut themselves . . ."

Elena ignored his words. She concentrated all her energy on the thudding pain in the center of her chest. She felt as if she were drawing blood from her tiniest cap-illaries, from the far reaches of her body, and collecting it here at her center.

The human mind is infinite, she thought. It is as strange and as infinite as the universe. And the human soul . . .

The three youngest of the possessed began dancing around the spread-eagled Bonnie, singing in falsely sweet little-girl voices:

"You are going to *die* in here,
When you die in *here*, out *there*
They throw *dirt* right on your face!"

How delightful, Elena thought. Then she tuned back in to the drama unfolding on the roof. What she saw startled her. Meredith was now up on the widow's walk, moving as if she were underwater—entranced. Elena had missed how she'd gotten there—was it by some sort of magic? Misao was facing Meredith, giggling. Damon was laughing, too, but in mocking disbelief.

"And you expect me to believe that if I give *this* girl a pair of scissors . . ." he said, "she would actually cut her own—"

"Try and see for yourself," Shinichi interrupted, with one of his languid gestures. He was leaning against the cupola in the middle of the widow's walk, still trying to out-lounge Damon. "Didn't you see our prizewinner, Isobel? *You* carried her all the way here—didn't she ever try to speak?"

Damon held out a hand. "Scissors," he said, and a dainty pair of nail scissors rested in his palm. It seemed that, as long as Damon had Shinichi's magic key, the magic field around them would continue to obey him even in the real world. He laughed. "No, adult-size scissors, for gardening. The tongue's made of strong muscles, not paper."

What he held in his hand then were large pruning shears—definitely not toys for children. He hefted them, feeling their weight. And then, to Elena's utter shock, he looked straight up at her in her treetop refuge, not needing to search for her there at all—and winked.

Elena could only stare back in horror.

He knew, she thought. He knew where I was all the time.

That was what he had been whispering to Caroline about.

It hadn't worked—the *Wings of Redemption* hadn't worked, Elena thought, and it felt as if she were falling and would fall forever. I should have realized it would be no good. No matter what's done to him, Damon will always be Damon. And now he's offering me a choice: see my two best friends tortured and killed, or step forward and stop this horror by agreeing to his terms.

What could she do?

He had arranged the chess pieces brilliantly, she thought. The pawns on two different levels, so that even if Elena could somehow climb down to try to save Bonnie, Meredith would be lost. Bonnie was tied to four strong posts and guarded by Tree-Men. Meredith was closer, up on the roof, but to get her off Elena would have to *get* to her and then through Misao, Shinichi, Caroline, and Damon himself.

And Elena had to choose. Whether to step forward now, or be pushed forward by the anguish of one of the two who were almost a part of her.

She seemed to catch a faint strain of telepathy as Damon stood beaming there, and it said, *This is the best night of my life.*

You could always just jump, came the fog-like hypnotic

whisper of annihilation once again. *End the dead-end road you're on. End your suffering. End all the pain . . . just like that.*

"Now it's my turn," Caroline was saying, brushing past the twins to face Meredith herself. "It was supposed to be my choice in the first place. So it's my turn now."

Misao was laughing hysterically, but Meredith was already stepping forward, still in a trance.

"Oh, have it your own way," Damon said. But he didn't move, still staring curiously, as Caroline said to Meredith, "You've always had a tongue like an adder's. Why don't you make it forked for us—right here, right now? Before you cut it into pieces."

Meredith held out her hand without a word, like an automaton.

Still with her eyes on Damon, Elena breathed in slowly. Her chest seemed to be going into spasms as it had when the sucker plants had wound their way around her and cut off her breath. But not even sensations in her own body could stop her.

How could I choose? she thought. Bonnie and Meredith—I love both of them.

And there's nothing else to do, she realized numbly, the feeling draining from her hands and her lips. I'm not even sure if Damon can save both of them, even if I agree to . . . submit to him. These others—Shinichi, Misao, even Caroline—they want to see blood. And Shinichi not only controls trees, but just about everything in the Old Wood, including those monstrous Tree-Men. Maybe this time Damon has over-reached himself, taken on more than he could handle. He wanted me—but he went too far to get me. I can't see any way out.

And then she did see. Suddenly everything fell into place and was brilliantly clear.

She *knew*.

Elena stared down at Bonnie, almost in a state of shock. Bonnie was looking at her, too. But there was no expectation of rescue in that small, triangular face. Bonnie had already accepted her fate: agony and death.

No, Elena thought, not knowing whether Bonnie could hear her.

Believe, she thought to Bonnie.

Not blindly, never blindly. But believe in what your mind tells you is the truth, and what your heart tells you is the right path. I would never let you go—or Meredith either.

I believe, Elena thought, and her soul was rocked by the force of it. She felt a sudden surge within herself, and she knew that it was time to go. One word was ringing in her mind as she stood and let go of her handholds on the tree trunk. And that one word echoed in her mind as she dove headfirst from her sixty-foot perch in the tree.

Believe.

37

As she fell, it all rushed through her mind.

The first time she had seen Stefan . . . she had been a different person then. Ice-cold outside, manic inside—or was it the other way around? Still numb from the death of her parents so long ago. Jaded by the world and by anything to do with boys . . . A princess in an icy tower . . . with a lust only for conquest, for power . . . until she'd seen *him.*

Believe.

Then the world of the vampires . . . and Damon. And all the wicked wildness she'd found inside herself, all the passion. Stefan was her lynchpin, but Damon was the fiery breath beneath her wings. However far she went, Damon seemed to lure her on just a little farther. And she knew that one day it would be too far . . . for both of them.

But for now, all she had to do was simple.

Believe.

And Meredith, and Bonnie, and Matt. She had changed relations with them, oh, most definitely. At first, not knowing what she had done to deserve friends like these three, she hadn't even bothered to treat them as they deserved. Yet they had all stuck by her. And now she *did* know how to appreciate them—knew that if it came to that, she would die for them.

Below, Bonnie's eyes had followed her dive. The audience on the widow's walk looked, too, but it was Bonnie's face that she stared into: Bonnie startled and terrified and disbelieving and about to scream and realizing at the same time that no screaming would save Elena from a headlong dive to her death.

Bonnie, believe in me. I'll save you.

I remember how to fly.

onnie knew that she was going to die.

She had had a clear premonition of it just before those *things*—the trees that moved like humans, with their hideous faces and their thick, knotted arms—had surrounded the little band of humans in the Old Wood. She had heard the howl of the black weir dog, turned, and just caught a glimpse of one vanishing in the glare of her flashlight. The dogs had a long history in Bonnie's family: when one of them howled, a death was soon to come.

She'd guessed then that it would be hers.

But she hadn't said anything, even when Dr. Alpert had said, "What in the name of *heaven* was *that*?" Bonnie was practicing being brave. Meredith and Matt were brave. It was something built into them, an ability to keep going when any sane person would run away and hide. They both put *the group's* good ahead of their own. And of course Dr. Alpert was brave, not to mention strong, and Mrs. Flowers seemed to have decided that the teenagers were her own special charges to take care of.

Bonnie had wanted to show that she could be brave, too. She was practicing holding her head up and listening for things in the bushes, while simultaneously listening with her psychic senses for any sign of Elena. It was hard to juggle the two kinds of hearing. There was a lot to hear with her real ears; all kinds of quiet chucklings and whisperings from the bushes that didn't belong there. But from Elena there wasn't a sound, not even when Bonnie called her name over and over: *Elena, Elena, Elena!*

She's human again, Bonnie had realized sadly, at last. *She can't hear me or make contact. Out of all of us, she's the only one who didn't miraculously escape.*

And it was then that the first of the Tree-Men loomed up in front of the group of searchers. Like something out of a nursery-tale nightmare, it was a tree and then— suddenly—it was a *thing*, a treelike giant that suddenly moved swiftly toward them, its upper branches bunching together to become long arms, and then everyone was screaming and trying to get away from it.

Bonnie would never forget how Matt and Meredith

had tried to help her run then.

The Tree-Man wasn't fast. But when they turned and ran from it they found that there was another one behind them. And more to the right and the left. They were surrounded.

And then, like cattle, like slaves, they were herded. Any of them that tried to resist the trees were slapped and cuffed by hard and sharp-thorned branches, and then, with a lithe branch wound around the neck, were *dragged*.

They'd been caught—but they hadn't been killed. Instead they were being taken somewhere. It wasn't hard to imagine why: in fact Bonnie could imagine a whole lot of different whys. It was just a matter of picking which was the scariest.

In the end, after what seemed like hours of forced walking, Bonnie began to recognize things. They were going back to the boardinghouse again. Or rather, they were going back to the *real* boardinghouse for the first time. Caroline's car was outside. The house was again lit from top to bottom, but there were dark windows here and there.

And their captors were waiting for them.

And now, after her outburst of weeping and pleading, she was trying to be brave once more.

When that boy with the strange hair had said that she

would be the first, she'd understood exactly what he meant, and how she was going to die—and suddenly she wasn't brave at all—inside. But she wouldn't scream again.

She could just see the widow's walk, and the sinister figures on it, but Damon had *laughed* when the Tree-Men had begun to pluck her clothes off. Now he was *laughing* as Meredith held the garden shears. She wouldn't beg him again, not when it wouldn't make any difference anyway.

And now she was on her back, with her arms and legs tied so she was helpless, clothed in strips and rags. She wanted them to kill her first, so she wouldn't have to watch Meredith cut her own tongue to pieces.

Just as she felt a last scream of fury welling up inside her like a snake climbing a pole, she had seen Elena high above her in a white pine tree.

"*Wings of the Wind,*" Elena whispered as the ground rushed up toward her, very fast.

The wings unfolded instantly from somewhere inside Elena. They weren't real, they spanned some forty feet and were made of golden gossamer, the color ranging from deepest Baltic amber at her back to ethereal pale citrine at the tips. They were almost still, barely rising and falling, but they held her up, the wind rushing under them, and they got her to exactly where she needed to go.

Not to Bonnie. That was what they would all be expecting. From her height, she just might be able to snatch Bonnie free, but she had no idea how to cut Bonnie's bonds or whether she could lift off again.

Instead Elena swerved toward the widow's walk at the last moment, snatched the pruning shears out of Meredith's upraised hand, and then caught a handful of long, silky black-and-scarlet hair. Misao shrieked. *And then* . . .

That was when Elena really needed some belief. So far she had really just been gliding, not flying. But now she needed uplift; she needed the wings to *work* . . . and once again, although there was no time, she was with Stefan, and feeling . . .

. . . the first time she had kissed him. Other girls might have waited until it was the other way around, letting the boy take the lead, but not Elena. Besides, at first Stefan had thought that all kissing meant was seducing prey. . . .

. . . the first time *he* had kissed her, understanding that it wasn't a predatory relationship . . .

And now she needed to *really fly*. . . .

I know I can. . . .

But Misao was just so heavy—and Elena's memory was faltering. The great golden wings trembled and became still. Shinichi was trying to climb a creeper to get to her, and Damon was holding Meredith motionless.

And, too late, Elena realized that it wasn't going to work.

She was alone, and she couldn't fight this way. Not against so many.

She was alone, and pain that made her want to shriek was lancing through her back. Misao was somehow making herself heavier, and in another minute she would be too heavy for Elena's trembling wings to hold up.

She was alone, and like the rest of the humans, she was going to die—

And then, through the agony that was causing fine sweat to break out all over her body, she heard Stefan's voice.

"Elena! Let go! Fall and I'll catch you!"

How strange, Elena thought, as if in a dream. His love and panic had distorted his voice somehow—making him sound different. Making him sound almost like—

"Elena! I'm *with* you!"

—like Damon.

Shaken out of her dream, Elena looked below her. And there was Damon, standing protectively in front of Meredith, looking up at her, with his arms held out.

He was with her.

"Meredith," he went on, "girl, this is no time to

be sleepwalking! Your friend needs you! *Elena* needs you!"

Slowly, dully, Meredith turned her face up. And Elena saw life and animation restored to it as her eyes focused on the trembling of the great golden wings.

"Elena!" she shouted, "I'm with you! Elena!"

How did she know to say that? The answer was— that she was Meredith—and Meredith always knew what to say.

And now the cry was being taken up by another voice: Matt's.

"Elena!" he shouted, in a sort of acclamation. "I'm with you, Elena!"

And Dr. Alpert's deep voice: "Elena! I'm with you, Elena!"

And Mrs. Flowers, surprisingly strong: "Elena! I'm with you, Elena!"

And even poor Bonnie: "Elena! *We're with you, Elena!*"

While deep in her heart, the real Stefan whispered, "I'm with you, my angel."

"We're all with you, Elena!"

She didn't drop Misao. It was as if the great golden wings had caught an updraft; in fact, they almost lifted her straight up, out of control—but somehow she managed to keep herself steady. She was still looking down and she saw the tears spill from her eyes and fall toward

Damon's outstretched arms. Elena didn't know why she was crying, but part of it was sorrow for ever having doubted him.

Because Damon wasn't just on her side. Unless she was wrong, he was willing to die for her—was courting death for her. He threw himself into the entangling creepers and vines, all reaching for Meredith or for Elena.

It had only taken an instant to get hold of Misao, but Shinichi was already leaping toward Elena, in fox form, lips drawn back, aiming to tear her throat out. These were no ordinary foxes. Shinichi was almost as big as a wolf—certainly the size of a large dog—and as vicious as a wolverine.

Meanwhile the entire widow's walk burst into a maze of vines, creepers, and fibrous tendrils, and Shinichi was being *lifted* by them. Elena didn't know which way to dodge. She needed time, and she needed a clear shot out of here.

All Caroline was doing was screaming.

And then Elena saw her opening. A gap in the creepers that she threw herself at, knowing in her subconscious that she was throwing herself over the railing as well, and some-how keeping her hold on Misao's hair. In fact, it must have been an extremely painful experience for the female kit-sune as she swung back and forth like a pendulum below Elena.

The one glance Elena was able to give over her shoulder showed Damon, still moving faster than anything Elena had ever seen. He had Meredith in his arms now and was hurrying her through a gap that led to the cupula door. As soon as she stepped in, she appeared down on the ground and ran toward the altar where Bonnie was lying, only to slam into one of the Tree-Men. For a moment, as Damon glanced toward Elena, their gazes met and something electric passed between them. It made Elena tingle all over, that look did.

Then she refocused: Caroline was screaming again; Misao was using her whip to get a grip on Elena's leg and was calling on Tree-Men to give her a lift. Elena needed to fly higher. She had no idea how she was controlling her golden gossamer wings, but nothing seemed to snarl them; and they obeyed her slightest whim as though she had always had them. The great trick was to not think of *how* to get somewhere, but just to imagine being there.

On the other hand, the Tree-Men were growing. It was like some childhood nightmare of giants, and at first it made Elena feel that it was she who was shrinking. But the hideous creatures were actually overtopping the house now, and their upper, snake-like branches slashed into her legs while Misao lashed out with her whip. Elena's jeans were in shreds now. She swallowed a cry of pain.

I have to fly higher.

I can do it.

I'm going to save you all.

I believe.

Faster than the swoop of a hummingbird, she was darting up in the clear air again, still holding Misao by her long black-and-red hair. And Misao was screaming, screams that Shinichi echoed even as he fought with Damon.

And then, just as she and Damon had planned, just as she and Damon had *hoped*, Misao turned into her true form and Elena was holding a large and heavy, writhing vixen by the scruff of its neck.

There was a difficult moment while Elena got the balance right. She had to remember that there was more weight in back because Misao had six tails and was heaviest where a real fox would be lightest.

By then she had swooped back to her perch in the tree, and she stood there, able to look down on the scene below, the Tree-Men too slow to keep up. The plan had gone perfectly, except that Damon, of all people, had forgotten what he was supposed to be doing. Far from retreating into possession, he had fooled Shinichi and Misao beautifully—and Elena, too. Now, according to their plan he was supposed to be taking care of any innocent bystanders, letting Elena lure Shinichi on.

Instead something inside him seemed to have snapped; and he was methodically beating the human-shaped

Shinichi's head against the house, shouting: "Damn . . . you! Where . . . is . . . my . . . *brother*?"

"I—could kill you—right now—" Shinichi shouted back, but he was short of breath. He wasn't finding Damon an easy opponent.

"Do it!" Damon returned immediately. "And then she"—pointing to the perching Elena—"will cut your sister's throat!"

Shinichi's contempt was scathing.

"You expect me to believe that a girl with an aura like *that* will *kill*—"

There comes a time when you have to make a stand. And for Elena, blazing with defiance and glory, this was that time. She took a deep breath, begged the Universe's forgiveness, and leaned down, positioning the pruning shears. Then she squeezed as hard as she could.

And a red-tipped black vixen's tail fell twisting to the ground, while Misao shrieked in pain and rage. As the tail fell it writhed, and it lay in the middle of the clearing, squirming like a snake that wasn't quite defeated yet. Then it became transparent and faded away.

That was when Shinichi really screamed, "Do you know what you've done, you ignorant bitch? I'll bring this place down on top of you! I'll tear you apart!"

"Oh, yes, of course you will. But first," Damon spoke each word deliberately, "you have to get past me."

Elena barely registered their words. It hadn't been easy for her to squeeze those shears. It had meant thinking about Meredith with the shears in her own hands, and Bonnie lying on the altar, and Matt, earlier, writhing on the ground. And Mrs. Flowers, and the three lost little girls, and Isobel and—a great deal—about Stefan.

But as for the first time in her life she drew another's blood with her own hands, she had a sudden strange sense of responsibility—of new *accountability*. As if an icy wind had blown her hair back sharply and said into her frozen, gasping face: *Never without reason. Never without necessity. Never unless there's no other solution available.*

Elena felt something inside her grow up, all at once. Too fast to say good-bye to childhood, she had become a warrior.

"You all thought I couldn't fight," she called to the assembled group. "You were wrong. You thought I was powerless. You were wrong there, too. And I'll use the last drop of my Power in this fight, because you twins are real monsters. No, you're—abominations. And if I die I'll rest with Honoria Fell, and I'll watch over Fell's Church again."

Fell's Church will rot and die writhing with maggots, a voice near her ear said, and it was a deep bass voice, nothing like Misao's shrill screaming. Elena knew even as she turned that it was the white pine tree. A hard scaly bough, laden with those serrated, resin-sticky needles, slammed into her midriff, throwing her off balance— and making her involuntarily open her hands. Misao promptly escaped, and burrowed into the Christmas-tree-like branches.

"Bad . . . trees . . . go . . . to . . . *Hell*," Elena cried, throwing her entire body weight into digging the shears she held into the base of the branch that had tried to crush her. It tried to pull away, and she twisted the shears in the wounded dark bark, relieved when a large piece fell off, with only a long string of resin left to show where it had been.

Then she looked for Misao. The fox wasn't finding it as easy as she might have thought, navigating a tree. Elena looked at the cluster of tails. Strangely, there was no stump, no blood, no sign that the fox had been injured.

Was that why she wasn't turning human? The loss of a tail? Even if she were naked when she changed back to her human self—as some stories of werewolves had it— she'd be in better condition to climb down.

Because Misao seemed finally to have chosen the slow but sure method of descent—to have branch after branch take hold of her fox body and pass it down to the next. Which meant she was only about ten feet below Elena.

And all Elena had to do was to coast over the needles

down to her and then—by wings or other means—stop. If she believed in her wings. If the tree didn't throw her off.

"You're too slow," Elena shouted. Then she began the coast to overcome the distance—not far in human body-lengths—to her goal.

Until she saw Bonnie.

Bonnie's slight body was still lying on the altar, pale and cold-looking. But now *four* of the hideous Tree-Men had hold of her, one at each hand and one at each foot. They were already pulling so hard that she was lifted up into the air.

And Bonnie was awake. But not screaming. Not making a noise to attract attention to herself; and Elena realized with a rush of love and horror and desperation that *that* was why she hadn't been making a fuss before. She wanted the major players here to fight their fight without the bother of rescuing her.

The Tree-Men leaned back.

Bonnie's face contorted in agony.

Elena *had* to get to Misao. She *needed* the double fox key to free Stefan, and the only people who could tell her where it was were Misao and Shinichi. She looked up at the darkness above and noticed that it seemed a little less dark than when she had last seen it, the sky a dark swirling gray instead of dead black—but there was no help there. She looked down. Misao, making a little better time with her escape. If Elena let her get away . . . Stefan was her love. But Bonnie—Bonnie was her friend—ever since childhood. . . .

And then she saw Plan B.

Damon was fighting Shinichi—or trying.

But Shinichi was always an easy centimeter away from where Damon's fist was. Shinichi's fists, on the other hand, always connected solidly with their targets, and right now Damon's face was a bloody mask.

"*Use wood!*" Misao was coaching in a shriek, her child-like manner having suddenly vanished. "You men, you *idiots*, all you think of is your *fists*!"

Shinichi broke a pillar support from the widow's walk one-handed, showing his true strength. Damon smiled beatifically. He was, Elena knew, going to enjoy this, even though it meant all the many little wounds those wooden splinters would entail.

It was in the middle of this that Elena shouted, "Damon, look down!" Her voice seemed weak over the cacophony of shrieks and sobs and screams of fury all around. "Damon! Look down—at *Bonnie*!"

Nothing so far had been able to break Damon's concentration—he seemed determined to find out where Stefan was being kept—or to kill Shinichi trying.

Now, to Elena's slight surprise, Damon's head jerked around immediately. He looked down.

"A cage," shouted Shinichi. "Build me a cage."

And tree branches leaned in from all sides to pin him and Damon into their own little world, a lattice to keep them contained.

The Tree-Men leaned back farther. And despite herself, Bonnie screamed.

"You see?" laughed Shinichi. "Each of your friends will die in that agony or worse. One by one, we will take you!"

That was when Damon really seemed to go crazy. He began moving like quicksilver, like a leaping flame, like some animal with reflexes far faster than Shinichi's. Now there was a sword in his hand, undoubtedly conjured up by the magical housekey, and the sword slashed through the branches even as the branches reached out to trap him. And then he was airborne, leaping over the railing for the second time that night.

This time Damon's balance was perfect, and far from breaking bones, he made a graceful, catlike landing just beside Bonnie. And then his sword was flashing in an arc, sweeping all around Bonnie, and the tough, fingerlike tips of the branches that held her were cut cleanly away.

A moment later, Bonnie was being lifted, being held by Damon as he leaped easily off the rough-hewn altar and was lost in the shadows near the house.

Elena let out the breath she'd been holding and turned

back to her own affairs. But her heart was beating more strongly and faster, with joy and with pride and with gratitude, as she slid down the painful, cutting-edged needles, and almost flashed past Misao, who was being whisked out of her way—not quite in time.

She got a good grip on the nape of the fox's neck. Misao keened a strange animal lament and sank her teeth into Elena's hand so hard that it felt as if they were going to meet. Elena bit her lip until she felt blood come, trying not to scream.

Be crushed, and die, and turn to loam, the tree said in Elena's ear. *Your kind can feed my kin for once.* The voice was ancient, malevolent and very, very frightening.

Elena's legs reacted without pausing to consult her mind. They pushed off hard and then the golden butterfly wings unfurled again, not beating but undulating, holding Elena steady above the altar.

She pulled the snarling vixen's muzzle up—not too close—to her own face. "Where are the two pieces of the fox key?" she demanded. "Tell me or I'll take off another tail. I *swear* I will. Don't fool yourself—it's not just your pride that you're losing, is it? Your tails are your Power. What would it feel like to have none at all?"

"Like being a human—except *you*, you freak." Now Misao was laughing again in her panting-dog way, her fox ears flat to her head.

"Just answer the question!"

"As if you would understand the answers I could give. If I told you that one was inside the silver nightingale's instrument, would that give you any kind of idea?"

"It might if you explained it a little more clearly!"

"If I told you that one was buried in Blodwedd's ballroom, would you be able to find it?" Again the panting grin as the fox gave clues that led nowhere—or everywhere.

"Are those your answers?"

"*No!*" Misao shrieked suddenly and kicked with her feet, as if they were dog's legs scrabbling in the dirt. Except that the dirt was Elena's midriff, and the scrabbling legs felt as if they might well puncture her entrails. She felt her camisole tear.

"I told you; I'm not playing around here!" Elena cried. She lifted the vixen with her left arm, even though it ached with tiredness. With her right hand, she positioned the shears.

"Where is the first part of the key?" Elena demanded.

"Search for yourself! You only have the whole world to look through, and every thicket besides." The fox went for her throat again, white teeth actually scoring Elena's flesh.

Elena forced that arm to hold Misao higher. "I warned you, so don't say that I didn't or that you have any reason to complain!"

She squeezed the shears.

Misao gave a squeal that was almost lost in the general commotion. Elena, feeling more and more tired, said, "You're a complete liar, aren't you? Look down if you want. I didn't cut anywhere close to you. You just heard the shears click and screamed."

Misao very nearly got a claw into Elena's eye. Oh, well. Now, for Elena, there were no more moral or ethical issues. She wasn't causing pain, she was simply draining Power. The shears went *snap, snap, snap*, and Misao screamed and cursed her, but below them the Tree-Men were shrinking.

"Where is the first part of the key?"

"Let me go and I'll tell." Suddenly Misao's voice was less shrill.

"On your honor—if you can say that without laughing?"

"On my honor and my word as a kitsune. Please! You can't leave a fox without a real tail! That's why the ones you cut didn't hurt. They're badges of honor. But my real tail is in the middle, it's tipped with white, and if you cut me there; you'll see blood and it will leave a stump." Misao seemed thoroughly cowed, thoroughly ready to cooperate.

Elena knew about judging people and intuition, and both her mind and her heart were telling her not to trust this creature. But she wanted so much to believe, to hope. . . .

Making a slow curving descent so that the vixen was close to the ground—she would not give in to the temptation to drop her from sixty feet up—Elena said, "Well? On you honor, what are the answers?"

Six Tree-Men came to life around her and plunged at her, with greedy, grasping finger branches.

But Elena wasn't taken completely off guard. She hadn't let go of her grip on Misao; only slackened it. Now she tightened the grip again.

A wave of strength buoyed her so that she lifted fast and swept by the widow's walk and a furious Shinichi and weeping Caroline. Then Elena met Damon's eyes. They were filled with hot, fierce pride in her. She was filled with hot, fierce passion.

"I am not an angel," she announced to any of the group who hadn't quite managed to grasp this yet. "I am not an angel and I am not a spirit. I'm Elena Gilbert and I've been to the Other Side. And right now I'm ready to do whatever needs to be done, which seems to include kicking some ass!"

There was a clamor below that at first she couldn't identify. Then she realized it was the others—it was her friends. Mrs. Flowers and Dr. Alpert, Matt and even wild Isobel. They were cheering—and they were visible because suddenly the backyard was in daylight.

Am I doing that? Elena wondered, and realized that somehow she was. She was lighting up the clearing in which Mrs. Flowers' house stood, while leaving the woods around dark.

Maybe I can extend it, she thought. Make the Old Wood into something younger and less evil.

If she had been more experienced, she would never have attempted it. But right here and right now she felt that she could take anything on. She looked at the four directions of the Old Wood around her quickly, and she cried, "*Wings of Purification!*" and watched the huge, frosty, iridescent butterfly wings spread high and wide, and then wider, and then spread some more.

She was aware of a silence, of being so enrapt in something she was doing that even Misao's struggles didn't matter. It was a silence that reminded her of something: of all the most beautiful strains of music coming together into one, single, powerful chord.

And then the Power blasted out from her—not destructive Power like that Damon had sent many times, but a Power of renewal, of springtime, of love, youth, and purification. And she watched as the light spread farther and farther, and the trees grew smaller and more familiar, with more clearings in between thickets. Thorns and hanging creepers disappeared. On the ground, spreading out like a circle expanding, flowers of all colors bloomed, sweet violets in clumps here and banks of Queen Anne's lace there, and wild roses climbing everywhere. It was so beautiful that it made her chest ache.

Misao hissed. Elena's trance was finally broken, and she looked around to see that the shambling, hideous Tree-Men had disappeared in the full sunlight and in their place was a wide patch of sorrel dotted with fossilized trees in odd shapes. Some looked almost human. For a moment Elena regarded the scene, puzzled, and then she realized what else was different. All the real humans were gone.

"I never should have brought you here!" And that, to Elena's surprise, was Misao's voice. She was speaking to her brother. "You spoiled everything because of that girl. *Shinichi no baka!*"

"Idiot, yourself!" Shinichi shouted at Misao. "*Onore!* You're reacting just the way they want—"

"What else am I supposed to do?"

"I heard you giving the girl clues," Shinichi snarled. "You'd do anything for the sake of your looks, you selfish—"

"You can say that to me? While you haven't lost even one tail yourself?"

"Just because I'm faster—"

Misao cut him off. "That's a lie and you know it! Take it back!"

"You're too weak to fight! You should have run long ago! Don't come crying to me about it."

"Don't you *dare* speak to me like that!" And Misao leaped from Elena's grasp and attacked Shinichi. He had been wrong. She was a good fighter. In a second they were a destruction zone, rolling over and over as they fought changing forms all the while. Black and scarlet fur flew. Out of the ball of turning bodies came scraps of speech—

"—still won't find the keys—"

"—not both of them, anyway—"

"—even if they did—"

"—what would it matter?"

"—still have to find the boy—"

"—I say it's only sporting to let them try—"

Misao's horrible shrill giggle. "And see what they find—"

"—in the *Shi no Shi*!"

Abruptly the fight ended and they both became human. They were battered, but Elena felt that there was nothing more that she could do if they chose to fight again.

Instead Shinichi said, "I'm breaking the globe. *Here,*" he turned to Damon and shut his eyes, "is where your precious brother is. I'm putting it into your mind—if you can decode the map. And once you get there, you'll die. Don't say I didn't warn you."

To Elena he bowed and said, "I regret that you'll be dying, too. But I've memorialized you in an ode.

Wild rose and lilac,
Bee's balm and daisy,
Elena's smile chases
The winter away.

Bluebell and violet,
Foxglove and iris,
Watch where she treads
And then watch the grass sway.

Wherever her feet pass,
White flowers part the grass—"

"I'd rather hear a straight explanation of where the keys are," Elena said to Shinichi, knowing that after that song she wouldn't get any more from Misao. "Frankly, I'm sick and tired of all your *bullshit.*"

She noticed that once again everyone was staring at her and she could feel why. She could feel a difference in her voice, in her stance, in her patterns of speech. But mostly, *inside*, what she felt was freedom.

"We'll give you this much," Shinichi said. "We won't move them. Find them from the clues—or by other means, if you can." He winked at Elena and turned away—to meet a pale and trembling Nemesis.

Caroline. Whatever else she'd been doing for the last few minutes, she had been crying, and rubbing her eyes, and wringing her hands—or so Elena guessed from the distribution of her makeup.

"You, too?" she said to Shinichi. *"You, too?"*

Shinichi smiled his lazy smile. "And what two am I?" He held up two fingers in the V symbol to differentiate his two from Caroline's.

"You've fallen for her, too? Making up songs—giving her clues to find Stefan—"

"They're not very good clues," Shinichi said comfortingly and smiled again.

Caroline tried to hit him, but he caught her fist. "And you think you're leaving now?" Her voice was pitched at a scream—not as high as Misao's glass-splintering shriek, but with its own fearsome vibrato.

"I *know* we're leaving." He glanced at the sullen Misao. "After one more item of business. But not with you."

Elena tensed up, but Caroline was trying to attack Shinichi again. "After what you said to me? After all that you *said*?"

Shinichi looked her up and down, seeming to actually see her for the first time. He also looked genuinely bewildered. *"Said* to you?" he asked. "Have we spoken before tonight?"

There was a high-pitched giggle. Everyone turned. Misao was standing, giggling, her hands over her mouth.

"I used your image," she said to her brother, her eyes on the floor as if confessing to a minor fault. "And your voice. In the mirror, when I would give her orders. She was on the rebound from some guy who'd dumped her. I told her I'd fallen in love with her and that I wanted to get revenge on her enemies—if she'd just do a few little things for me."

"Like spreading malach through little girls," Damon said grimly.

Misao giggled again. "And a boy or two. I know what it feels like to have those malach inside you. It doesn't hurt at all. They're just—there."

"Have you ever had one force you to do something you didn't want to?" Elena demanded. She could feel her blue eyes blazing. "Do you think *that* would hurt, Misao?"

"It wasn't you?" Caroline was still looking at Shinichi; she obviously couldn't keep up with the script. "It wasn't *you*?"

He sighed, smiling slightly. "Not me. Golden hair is my undoing, I'm afraid. Golden . . . or fiery red against black," he added hastily, glancing at his sister.

"So it was all a lie," Caroline said, and for a moment, desperation was written on her face larger than anger, with sadness larger than both. "You're just another Elena fan."

"Look," Elena said bluntly, "I don't want him. I hate him. The only guy I care about is Stefan!"

"Oh, he's the only guy, is he?" Damon asked, with a glance toward Matt, who had carried Bonnie up close to them while the fox-fight was going on. Mrs. Flowers and Dr. Alpert had followed.

"You know what I mean," Elena told Damon.

Damon shrugged. "Many a golden-haired lassie ends as the rough yeoman's bride." Then he shook his head. "Why am I spouting drek like this?" His compact body seemed to tower over Shinichi.

"It's just a residual effect . . . from being possessed . . . you know." Shinichi fluttered his hands, his eyes still on Elena. "My thought patterns . . ."

It looked as if another fight was brewing, but then Damon just smiled and said, narrow-eyed, "So you let Misao have her way with the town while you went after Elena and me."

"And—"

"Mutt," Damon said hastily and automatically.

"I was going to say Stefan," Elena said. "No, I would guess that Matt was the victim of one of Misao and Caroline's little schemes before he and I ran into you when you were completely possessed."

"And now you think you can just walk away," Caroline said, in a shaking, menacing voice.

"We *are* walking away," Shinichi said stiffly.

"Caroline, wait," Elena said. "I can help you—with *Wings of Purification*. You're being controlled by a malach."

"I don't need your help! I need a *husband*!"

There was utter silence on the roof. Not even Matt stepped up to the plate on this one.

"Or at least a fiancé," Caroline muttered, one hand on her abdomen. "My family would accept *that.*"

"We'll work it out," Elena said softly—then, firmly, "Caroline, believe it."

"I wouldn't believe in you if . . ." Caroline's answer was obscene. Then she spat in Elena's direction. And then she was silent, by her own choice or because the malach inside her wanted it.

"Back to business," Shinichi said. "Let's see, our price for the service of the clues and the location is a little block of memory. Let's say . . . from the time I first met Damon until now. Taken from Damon's mind." He smiled nastily.

"You can't do that!" Elena felt panic shoot through her, starting in her heart and flying out to the farthest reaches of every limb. "He's different now: he's remembered things—he's changed. If you take that memory away—"

"So will all the sweet changes go," Shinichi told her. "Would you rather I took your memory?"

"Yes!"

"But you were the only one who heard the clues about the key. And in any case I don't want to see things from your eyes. I want to see you . . . through *his* eyes."

By now, Elena was ready to start another fight on her own. But Damon said, distancing himself already, "Go ahead and take what you like. But if you don't get out of this town right after, I take off your *head* with these shears."

"Agreed."

"*No*, Damon—"

"Do you want Stefan back?"

"Not at that price!"

"Too bad," Shinichi put in. "There *is* no other bargain."

"Damon! Please—think about it!"

"I have thought. It's my fault that the malach spread so far in the first place. It's my fault for not investigating what was going on with Caroline. I didn't care what happened to humans as long as the new arrivals kept away from *me*. But I can fix some of the things I did to you by finding Stefan." He half turned to her, the old devil-may-care smile on his lips. "After all, taking care of my brother is my job."

"Damon—*listen* to me."

But Damon was looking at Shinichi. "Agreed," he said. "You have yourself a deal."

"We won the battle, but not the war," Elena said sadly. She thought it was the day after their fight with the kitsune twins. She couldn't be sure of anything except that she was alive, that Stefan was gone, and that Damon was back to his old self again.

"Maybe because we didn't have my precious brother," he said, as if to prove it. They were driving in the Ferrari, trying to find Elena's Jaguar—in the real world.

Elena ignored him. She also ignored the soft but vaguely annoying hiss that came from some device he'd installed that was not a radio, that just seemed to play voices and static.

A new kind of Ouija board? Audio instead of all that tedious spelling?

Elena felt herself shiver inside.

"You did give your word to go with me and find him. I swear it by—by the Other World."

"You tell me that I did, and you're not a liar—no, not to me. I can read your facial expressions now that you're a human. If I gave my word, I gave my word."

Human? Elena thought. Am I? *What* am I?—with the kind of Powers I have? Even Damon can see that the Old Wood has changed in the real world. It's not an ancient, half-dead forest anymore. There are spring flowers in mid-summer. There's life everywhere.

"And in any case, it will give me plenty of time to be alone with you—my princess of darkness."

And we're back to that again, Elena thought wearily. But he'd leave me here stranded if I once suggested that we had laughed and walked in a clearing together—with him on his knees to adjust my footstool. Even I'm beginning to wonder if it was real.

There was a slight bump—as nearly as one could tell from Damon's style of driving.

"Got it!" he cheered himself—and then, when Elena turned, ready to wrench the wheel to make him stop—he added coolly, "It was a piece of *tire*, for your information. Not many animals are black, arched, and a few tenths of an inch thick."

Elena said nothing. What was there to say to Damon's quips? But deep down she felt relieved that Damon wasn't given to running over furry little animals as an amusement.

We're going to be alone together for quite some time, she thought—and then realized that there was another reason she couldn't just tell Damon to dry up and die. Shinichi had put the location of Stefan's cell into Damon's mind, not hers. She needed him desperately, to take her to the location, and to fight whoever was keeping Stefan captive.

But it was fine if he had forgotten that she had any Powers. Something to save for a rainy day.

At just that moment, Damon exclaimed "What the—" and leaned forward to adjust dials on the not-radio.

"—peating; all units be on the lookout for one Matthew Honeycutt, male Caucasian, five foot eleven inches, blond hair, blue eyes—"

"*What is that?*" Elena demanded.

"A police scanner. If you want to be able to really live in this great land of freedom, it's best to know when to run—"

"Damon, don't get me started on your lifestyle. I meant what was that about Matt?"

"It looks as if they've decided to bring him in at last. Caroline didn't get much revenge yesterday night. I guess she's taking a shot at it now."

"Then we've got to get to him first—*anything* could happen if he stays in Fell's Church. But he can't take his car, and he won't fit in this one. What are we going to do?"

"Leave him to the police?"

"Don't, please. We have to—" Elena was beginning, when in a clearing to the left, like some vision sent to approve her scheme, the Jaguar appeared.

"*That's* the car we're taking," she told Damon flatly. "At least it's roomy. If you want your police scanner doo-hickey in it, then you'd better start uninstalling it from this one."

"But—"

"I'll go get Matt. I'm the only one he'll listen to. Then we'll leave the Ferrari in the Wood—or dump it in the creek if you want."

"Oh, the creek, by *all* means."

"Actually, we may not have time for that. We'll just leave it in the Wood."

Matt stared at Elena. "No. I won't run."

Elena turned the full intensity of her blue eyes on him. "Matt, get in the car. *Now*. You have to. Caroline's dad is related to the judge who signed the order to get you. It's a lynching, Meredith says. Even Meredith is telling you to run. No, you don't need clothes; we'll get clothes."

"But—but—it's not true—"

"They'll make it true. Caroline will weep and sob. I never thought a girl would do this to get revenge, but

Caroline is in a class of her own. She's gone nuts."

"But—"

"*I said, get in!* They'll be here any minute. They've already been to your house and Meredith's house. What are you doing at Bonnie's, anyway?"

Bonnie and Matt glanced at each other. "Uh, just having a look at Bonnie's mom's car," Matt said. "It's on the fritz again, and—"

"Never mind! Come with me! Bonnie, what are you doing? Calling Meredith back?"

Bonnie jumped slightly. "Yes."

"Tell her good-bye and we love her and good-bye. Take care of the town—we'll be in touch—"

As the red Jaguar pulled away, Bonnie said into the phone, "You were right. She's pulling a Straight A away. I don't know whether Damon's going—he wasn't in the car."

She listened for a moment and then said, "Okay, I will. I'll see you."

She hung up and got into action.

> *Dear Diary,*
>
> *Today I ran away from home.*
>
> *I guess you can't really call it running away when you're almost 18 and you take your own car—and when nobody knew you were home in the first place.*

So I'll just say, tonight I'm on the run.

The other slightly shocking thing is that I ran away with two different guys. And neither of them is __my__ guy.

I say that, but . . . I can't help remembering things. The look in Matt's eyes in the clearing—I honestly think he was prepared to die to protect me. I can't help but think about what we once were to each other. Those blue eyes . . . oh, I don't know what's wrong with me!

And Damon. I know now that there's living flesh under the layers and layers of stone he's wrapped around his soul. It's deeply hidden, but it's there. If I'm being honest with myself, I have to admit that he touches something deep inside me that makes me shiver—a part of myself even I don't understand.

Oh, Elena! Stop right now! You can't go near that dark part of yourself, especially now that you have Power. You don't __dare__ go near it. Everything is different now. You have to be more responsible (something you're not at all good at!).

And Meredith won't be here to help me be responsible, either. How is this ever going to work out? Damon and Matt in the same car? On a road trip together? Can you imagine? Tonight, it was so late and Matt was so stunned by the situation that he couldn't really take anything in. And Damon only smirked. But he'll be in demonic form tomorrow, I know he will.

I still think it was a great pity that Shinichi had to take <u>Wings of Redemption</u> from Damon along with his memories. But I firmly believe that, deep down, there's a tiny part of Damon that remembers how he was when we were together. And now he has to be worse than ever to prove that what he remembers was all a lie.

So while you're reading this, <u>Damon</u>—I know you'll get hold of it somehow and snoop—let me tell you that you were nice for a while, actually <u>NICE</u>, and it was fun. We talked together. We even laughed—at the same jokes. And you . . . you were gentle.

And now you're going, "Nah, it's just another Elena-plot to get me to think I can turn around— but <u>I know where I'm going, and I don't care.</u>" Does that ring a bell, Damon? Have you <u>said</u> those words to someone recently? And if not, how do I know them? Could it be that for once I'm telling the truth?

Now I'm going to forget that you're totally besmirching your honor by reading secret things that don't belong to you.

What else?

First: I miss Stefan.

Second: I didn't really pack for this. Matt and I swung by the boardinghouse, and he grabbed the money Stefan left for me while I grabbed an armful of clothes out of the closet—heaven knows what I've got: Bonnie's tops and Meredith's pants, and not a decent nightgown to my name.

But at least I also got you, precious friend, a present Stefan was saving for me. I never really liked typing in a file marked "Diary" anyway. Blank books like you are my style.

Third: I miss Stefan. I miss him so badly that I'm crying while I'm writing about clothes. It looks as if that's what I'm crying about, which makes me seem insanely shallow. Oh, sometimes I just want to scream.

Fourth: I want to scream <u>now</u>. It was only when we got back to Fell's Church that we found what horrors the malach had left for us. There is a fourth little girl I think may be possessed like Tami, Kristin, and Ava—I couldn't really tell, so I couldn't do anything. I have the feeling that we definitely haven't heard the last of this possession thing.

Fifth: But worst is what happened in the Saitou

*house. Isobel is in the hospital with raging infec-
tions in all her piercings. Obaasan, as everyone
calls Isobel's grandmother, was not dead as the
first paramedics who got there thought. She was in
a deep trance—reaching out to <u>us</u>. Whether some of
the courage I got, some of the belief in myself, was
really due to her, is something I'll never know.*

*But in the den was Jim Bryce. He had . . . oh,
I can't write it. He was the captain of the <u>basket-
ball</u> team! But he had <u>eaten</u> away at himself: his
whole left hand, most of his right-hand fingers, his
lips. And he had put a pencil through his ear into
his brain. They say (I heard this through Tyrone
Alpert, the doctor's grandson) that it's called
Lesch-Nyhan Syndrome (sp? I only heard it said)
and that it's rare, but there are others just like him.
That's what the doctors say. I say it was a malach
making him do it. But they wouldn't let me in to
try to take it out of him.*

*I can't even say he's alive. I can't say if he's
dead. He's going to a sort of institution where they
keep long-term cases.*

*We failed there. <u>I</u> failed. It wasn't really Jim
Bryce's fault. So he was with Caroline just one
night, and from there he passed the malach to his
girlfriend Isobel and to his little sister Tami. Then*

both Caroline and little Tami passed it along to others. They tried to give it to Matt, but he wasn't about to let them.

Sixth, the three little girls that most definitely did get it were all under the orders of Misao, from what Shinichi said. They say that they don't remember anything about decorating themselves or propositioning strangers. They don't seem to remember anything about the time of their possession, and they act like very different little girls now. Nice. Calm. If I thought Misao gave up easily then I would be sure they'll be all right.

Worse is the thought of Caroline. She was a friend once and now—well, now I think she needs help more than ever. Damon got to her diaries— she kept her own diary by recording herself on video, and we watched her talk to the mirror . . . and watched the mirror talk back. Mostly it was her own image that showed, but sometimes, at the beginning or end of a session, it was Shinichi's face. He's good-looking, if a little wild. I can see how Caroline might fall for him and agree to be his carrier of malach in the town.

That's all over. I used the last of whatever Power I know I have taking the malach out of those girls.

Caroline, of course, wouldn't let me near her.

And then there were those fateful words of Caroline's: "I need a husband!" Any girl knows what that means. Any girl feels sorry for another who says it, even if they're unfriends.

Caroline and Tyler Smallwood were going together until about two weeks ago. Meredith says Caroline dropped him, and that kidnapping her for Klaus was Tyler's revenge. But if before that they'd been sleeping together with no protection (and Caroline is dumb enough to do it), she could certainly have known she was pregnant and been looking for another guy by the time Shinichi turned up. (Which was just before I—returned to life.) Now she's trying to pin it on Matt. It was pure bad luck that she said it happened on the same night the malach attacked Matt and that that old man from the Neighborhood Watch saw Matt drive home and pass out at the steering wheel as if he were drunk or on drugs.

Or maybe it wasn't just luck. Maybe that was all part of Misao's game, too.

I'm going to sleep now. Too much thinking. Too much worry. And, oh, I miss Stefan! He would help me deal with the worry in his own gentle but keen-sighted way.

I'm sleeping inside the car with the doors locked.

The guys are sleeping outside it. At least, that's how we're starting—at their insistence. At least they agreed on that.

I don't think Shinichi and Misao will stay away from Fell's Church for long. I don't know if they'll leave it alone for a few days, or weeks, or a few months, but Misao will heal and they'll come back for us eventually.

That means that Damon, Matt, and I—we're fugitives in two worlds.

And I have no idea what's going to happen tomorrow.

Elena

Turn the page for a sneak peek of

THE RETURN:
VOL. 2 SHADOW SOULS

lena appeared, coming up the bank of a stream, looking clean and refreshed. Damon was stricken speechless by the very sight of her. By her grace, by her beauty, by the unbearable closeness of her. He could smell her freshly washed skin, and couldn't help deliberately breathing in more and more of her unique fragrance.

He didn't see how he could put up with another day of this.

And then Damon suddenly had an Idea.

"Would you like to learn something that would help you to control that aura of yours?" he asked as she passed him, heading for the car.

Elena threw him a sidelong glance. "So you've decided

to talk to me again. Am I supposed to faint with joy?"

"Well—that would always be appreciated—"

"Would it?" she said sharply, and Damon realized that he had underestimated the storm he had brewed inside this formidable girl.

"I'm being serious," he said, fixing his dark gaze on her.

"What is it, then?"

"It's learning how to circulate your Power. Blood circulates, yes? And Power can be circulated, too. Even humans have known that for centuries, whether they call it life force or *chi* or *ki*. As it is, you're simply dissipating your Power into the air. That's an aura. But if you learn to circulate it, you can build it up for some really big release, and you can be more inconspicuous as well."

Elena was clearly fascinated. "Why didn't you tell me before?"

Because I'm stupid, Damon thought. Because to vampires it's as instinctive as breathing is to you. He lied unblushingly. "It takes a certain level of competence to accomplish."

"And I can do it now?"

"I think so." Damon put slight uncertainty in his voice.

Naturally, this made Elena even more determined. "Show me!" she said.

"You mean right now?" He glanced around.

"Oh, please, Damon? Please?" Elena looked at Damon with her huge blue eyes. She touched his arm.

Damon glanced down at his arm, felt his good sense and his will wavering. *How does she do that?*

He sighed. There were at least three or four billion people on this dust mote of a planet who would give anything to be with Elena Gilbert. The problem was that he happened to be one of them—and that she clearly didn't give a damn for him.

Of course not. She had dear Stefan, Damon thought abruptly, bitterly. That surprised him a little, the bitterness.

But he found that he *was* bitter, bitter and angry enough that he answered without warmth, "All right. But after today, just practice doing it alone."

Don't miss L. J. Smith's spellbinding series

Here's a sneak peek from *The Secret Circle: The Initiation*!

The gray cashmere sweater or the blue-and-white Fair Isle cardigan, that was the question.

Now that the first day of school had actually come, Cassie found that she was excited. Of course, she was nervous too, but it wasn't the stark and hopeless dread she'd expected to feel. There was something interesting about beginning school in a new place. It was like starting her life over. Maybe this year she'd be Cassie the Extrovert or even Cassie the Party Girl.

The school was an impressive three-story red brick building.

God, it looked like a *college* or something. Like a historical landmark. The bold stone facing on the front read NEW SALEM HIGH SCHOOL, and below was a sort of crest with the words *Town of New Salem, Incorporated 1693.*

An incredibly loud roar made her head jerk around, and sheer instinct sent her jumping to the side just in time to avoid being run over. Heart pounding, she stood and gawked at what had almost hit her. It was a motorcycle on the bike path. But even more astonishing was its rider—a girl. Cassie saw that her face was ravishingly pretty, marred only by a belligerent expression.

"What are you staring at?" the girl demanded.

"I'm sorry—I didn't mean to—" Cassie tried to tear her eyes away, but it was hard. The girl was wearing a skimpy black midriff top, and Cassie glimpsed what looked like a small tattoo of a crescent moon just above the material. "I'm sorry," Cassie said again, helplessly.

"You better be."

God, what a horrible way to start the first day of school, Cassie thought, hurrying toward the entrance.

Her first class was writing for publication, an English elective, and Cassie was glad she had it. She liked creative writing, and the course would offer opportunities for publication in the school literary magazine and newspaper.

She found the class without much trouble and took an inconspicuous desk near the back. She began doodling ferociously on the front of her notebook, trying to look as if she weren't the only one in class sitting alone.

"You're new, aren't you?"

The boy in front of her had turned around. His smile was genuinely friendly, but it was also dazzling.

"Yes," said Cassie, and was furious to hear her voice shake. But this guy was so good-looking. . . . "I'm Cassie Blake. I just moved here from California."

"I'm Jeffrey Lovejoy," he said.

"Oh," Cassie said, trying to make it sound as if she'd heard of him before, since this seemed to be what he expected.

"Center on the basketball team," he said. "Also captain."

"Oh, how great." Oh, how *stupid*. She had to do better than this. "I mean—that must be really interesting."

"Are you interested in basketball? Maybe we could talk about it sometime." Suddenly Cassie felt very grateful to him. He was ignoring her blundering, her lameness. Okay, so maybe he liked to be admired, but what difference did that make?

"That would be great," she said, wishing she could think of another adjective. "Maybe—maybe at lunch . . ."

A shadow fell over her. Or at least that was how it felt.

A girl was standing there, the most striking girl Cassie had ever seen. She had a mane of pitch-black hair and her pale skin was touched with the glow of confidence and power.

"Hello, Jeffrey," she said. Her voice was low for a girl's;

vibrant and almost husky.

"Faye." Jeffrey's voice, by contrast, was noticeably unenthusiastic. He looked tense. "Hi."

The girl leaned over him, one hand on the back of his chair, and Cassie caught the scent of some heady perfume. "I didn't see much of you over summer vacation," she said. "You shouldn't keep yourself hidden away. Naughty boy." Faye was wearing an off-the-shoulder top. It left a great deal of skin exposed just at Jeffrey's eye level. But it was her face Cassie couldn't help staring at. "You know, there's a new horror movie at the Capri this week," she said. "I like horror movies, Jeffrey."

"I can take them or leave them myself," Jeffrey said.

Faye chuckled, a rich, disturbing sound. "Maybe you just haven't seen them with the right girl."

Jeffrey wet his lips, looking fascinated in spite of himself, but also scared.

"I was going to take Sally down to Gloucester this weekend—" he began, voice strained.

"Well, you'll just have to tell Sally that . . . something came up," Faye said, raking him with her eyes. "You can come get me Saturday night at seven."

"Faye, I—"

"Oh, and *don't* be late, all right?"

All this time, the black-haired girl had not even glanced at Cassie. But now, as she straightened up to leave, she did. The look she turned on Cassie was sly and secretive, as if she were perfectly aware that Cassie had been listening, and she liked it. Then she turned back to Jeffrey.

"Oh, and by the way," she said, lifting one hand in a languid gesture, "*she's* from Crowhaven Road too."

Jeffrey's jaw dropped. He stared at Cassie a moment with an expression of shock and distaste, and then he quickly turned around to face the front of the room.

What is going *on*? Cassie thought wildly. What difference did it make where she lived? The only thing she could see now of Jeffrey-of-the-dazzling-smile was his rigid back.

She had no time to think anything more, because the teacher was talking. He was a mild-looking man with a graying beard and glasses. He introduced himself as Mr. Humphries.

"Since you've all had a chance to talk during your summer vacation, now I'll give you a chance to write," he said. "I want you to write a poem, right now, spontaneously. We'll read some of them aloud afterward."

There were groans from the class, which gradually died into silence and pen chewing.

When Mr. Humphries announced that the time was up, Cassie had a poem, and reading it over she felt a thin chill of excitement. It was good—or at least *she* thought so.

Mr. Humphries was calling for volunteers. Predictably,

no hands were raised . . . until one went up in the back.

"Faye Chamberlain," Mr. Humphries said at last.

He sat on the edge of his desk as the tall, striking girl came to stand beside him, but Cassie had the oddest feeling that he would have moved away if he could. An almost palpable air of tension had filled the room.

"This is my poem," she said in her lazy, husky voice. "It's about fire."

Shocked, Cassie looked down at the poem on her own desk. Then Faye's voice caught her attention.

I dream about fire—
Tongues of flame licking me.
My hair burns like a torch;
My body burns for you.
Touch my skin and your fingers will stick—
You'll blacken like a cinder.
But you'll die smiling;
Then you'll be part of the fire too.

As the entire class watched, riveted, Faye produced a match and somehow—Cassie didn't quite see how—managed to light it. She touched it to the paper. Then, walking slowly, she moved to stand directly in front of Jeffrey Lovejoy, waving the burning paper gently before his eyes.

Howls, whistles, and desk banging from the audience. Many of them looked scared, but most of the guys looked excited, too.

Jeffrey just sat there, the back of his neck flushing dull red.

As the paper was about to burn her fingers, Faye sashayed away from Jeffrey and dropped it in the metal wastebasket. Mr. Humphries didn't flinch when something in the wastebasket flared up.

"Thank you, Faye," he said evenly. "Class, I think we can call what we've just seen an example of . . . concrete poetry. Tomorrow we'll study some more traditional methods. Class dismissed."

Cassie looked at her own poem. Fire. She and Faye had both written about the same thing. . . .

With a girl like *that* around, who was ever going to notice Cassie?

And yet they all seemed almost afraid of her, she thought. Even the teacher. Why didn't he give her a detention or something?

And why did Jeffrey let her hit on him that way? And why did he care where I *live*, for God's sake?

In the hall, she nerved herself to stop someone and ask where room C310 was.

"It's on the third floor," the girl said. "Go up that stairway—"

"Yo! Look out! Heads up, everybody!" a shouting voice interrupted. Dumbfounded, Cassie saw that it was two guys on roller blades, laughing and bellowing as they tore through the crowd. The boys were identical, except that one was wearing a Megadeth T-shirt and the other's said Mötley Crüe.

They were creating chaos as they went, knocking books out of people's arms and grabbing at girls' clothes.

"Why doesn't somebody stop them—or report them—or *something*. . . ." Cassie blurted out. Was everybody in this school crazy?

"Are you kidding? Those are the Henderson brothers," the girl said, and she walked away, joining another girl. Cassie heard a fragment of a sentence float back: ". . . doesn't even know about the Club . . ."

What Club? That girl had said it as if it had capital letters. What did a club have to do with breaking school rules? What kind of place *was* this?

Another bell rang, and Cassie realized that she was now late for class. She slung her backpack over her shoulder and ran for the stairs.

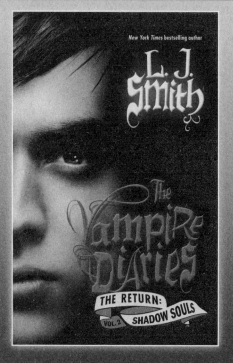

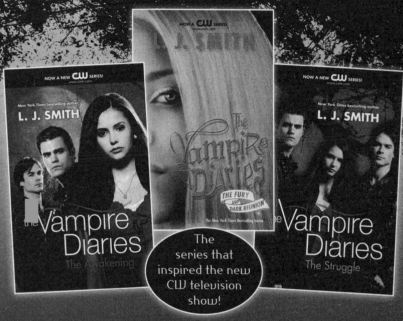